TOMLINSON'S WAKE

ALSO BY RANDY WAYNE WHITE

DOC FORD SERIES

Sanibel Flats

The Heat Islands

The Man Who Invented Florida

Captiva

North of Havana

The Mangrove Coast

Ten Thousand Islands

Shark River

Twelve Mile Limit

Everglades

Tampa Burn

Dead of Night

Dark Light

Hunter's Moon

Black Widow

Dead Silence

Deep Shadow

Night Vision

Chasing Midnight

Night Moves

Bone Deep

Cuba Straits

Deep Blue

Mangrove Lightning

Caribbean Rim

Salt River

One Deadly Eye

HANNAH SMITH SERIES

Gone

Deceived

Haunted

Seduced

SHARKS, INC. SERIES

Fins

Stingers

Crocs

Megalops

NONFICTION

Randy Wayne White's Ultimate Tarpon Book (with Carlene Brennen)

Batfishing in the Rainforest

The Sharks of Lake Nicaragua

Last Flight Out

An American Traveler

Gulf Coast Cookery (with Carlene Brennen)

Introduction to Tarpon Fishing in Mexico and Florida

Doc Ford Country (available exclusively as an ebook)

FICTION AS RANDY STRIKER

Key West Connection

The Deep Six

Cuban Death-Lift

The Deadlier Sex

Assassin's Shadow

Grand Cayman Slam

Everglades Assault

FICTION AS CARL RAMM

Florida Firefight

L.A. Wars

Chicago Assault

Deadly in New York

Houston Attack

Vegas Vengeance

Detroit Combat

Terror in D.C.

Atlanta Extreme

Denver Strike

Operation Norfolk

TOMLINSON'S WAKE

A DOC FORD NOVEL

RANDY WAYNE WHITE

HANOVER
SQUARE
PRESS

ISBN-13: 978-1-335-01429-0

Tomlinson's Wake

Hanover Square Press
22 Adelaide St. West, 41st Floor
Toronto, Ontario M5H 4E3, Canada
HanoverSqPress.com

HarperCollins Publishers
Macken House,
39/40 Mayor Street Upper,
Dublin 1, D01 C9W8, Ireland
www.HarperCollins.com

Printed in U.S.A.

For the tight-knit little fishing guide community at Tarpon Bay, Sanibel Island, Florida, who continue to be the inspiration for Doc Ford's Dinkin's Bay Marina: Mack and Eleanor Hamby, Graeme Mellor, Nick Clements, Alex Payne, Neville Robeson, Dave Case, Ted Cole, Duke Sells, Doug Fisher, Jerry Way, and Ralph Woodring. Fine, fine people and Captains all.

"In the jungle, during one night in each month, the moths did not come to the lanterns; through the black reaches of the outer night, so it was said, they flew toward the full moon."

—Peter Matthiessen, *At Play in the Fields of the Lord*

"In the jail yard, the captured Indians were whipped. The soldiers guarding [King] Canek were left speechless: the stripes of his friend's lashes appeared on Canek's back."

—Ermilio Abreu Gómez, *Canek: History and Legend of a Maya Hero*

TOMLINSON'S
WAKE

ONE

My Zen Buddhist hipster pal, Tomlinson, after I'd tracked him to a village in Honduras, said without looking up, "Can't leave, man. Not yet. I've got human traffickers, gangbangers, a shaman, and a pickleball-playing shrink hot on my ass."

"A what? A psychiatrist?"

"A neurologist. But she has the instincts of a Mississippi bloodhound—like most amateur bird-watchers. The pickleball thing, I think it mostly has to do with the name. Pickle? Ball? The woman's got some kinks."

"Are you making this up?" I said. "You sound drunk. Or delirious."

"Hah. If you knew me, you wouldn't be surprised."

I did know him. I wasn't.

"They're after you why?" I said.

"Metaphorically," he replied. "They want something I can't give them. I already died once this month and my secret life is nearing its expiration date. That only gives me about a week to find out who's kidnapping kids from the jungle and square my sinful-ass ways with Universal Consciousness. After that, it's time to call in the fire and piss on the dogs. I'm outta here, man."

"Back to Florida, you mean."

"No, dead. Dead as six loons. You hungry?"

He sat on a three-legged metate—a grinding stone from pre-Colombian times—peeling a mango. He wore peasant clothes, baggy gaucho pants, a tank top, and a straw hat favored by *paisanos* who work on mountain palm oil plantations. Blood had seeped through the hat—perhaps a serious head injury suffered during a recent hurricane or when his sailboat had gutted itself on a nearby reef.

"Maybe later," I said.

We were in a rainforest clearing. Goats, chickens, a skinny Brahma cow with horns dozed among thatch-roofed huts. It was an indigenous settlement not found on maps at tourist hotels on the island of Roatán thirty miles north as the crow flies. But a long trip upriver in a dory-shaped boat known locally as a *panga*. Rather than rent the thing, I'd paid cash and equipped it with enough food, fuel, and survival supplies for a week.

Old habit. Venture alone into a rainforest, expect the expected. Lessons I'd learned years ago, at the ass-busting Jungle Survival School, Fort Sherman, Panama, were still hardwired in the lizard brain.

Unknown to Tomlinson, he wasn't the only reason I was here. Honduras is a key player in a trafficking pipeline that includes women, children, drugs, sometimes weaponry. The pipeline flows north from Colombia, across the Darién Trail, then skips seaward past Panama and Costa Rica, before going aground where Tomlinson's *No Más* had foundered like so many other vessels on the Horn of Nicaragua and the Mískito Coast. Called that not just because of the biting hordes but because of the indigenous Mískito people who populate the mountain coastline.

A gifted demographic. People are a mix of ancient Olmec, Maya, and first contact invaders. Conquistadors, shipwrecked Cimarrons, pirates, and a few descendants from leper colony swamps. Dominant language is indigenous Miskito enriched by a patois of English and African. Spanish, though, was workable.

My hipster pal, tall, left-handed, all bone and tendons, his hair knotted samurai style, finally glanced my way. He squinted. Disoriented eyes met mine then rotated upward to search the memory banks. "I admit my vison is totally F-ed up at close range, but we apparently know each other, right? Don't tell me. I never forget the voice of a pissed-off husband or a guy who's been hired to kill me." He grimaced. "Oh, crapola. Please tell me you're not both."

Yep. A concussion, serious, or he wouldn't have tried to diminish it with humor. Unless this was an act.

I said, "Are you kidding?"

"Back off, man, give me a sec. It's not like I'm asking for a photo I.D."

"Come on . . . it's *me*. Marion. Marion Ford from Sanibel Island. Our marina, Dinkin's Bay. Mack, Jeth, the fishing guides. Remember? It's where you . . . it's where we lived until the place got wiped out by a storm. That was more than a month ago. We've got to get you to a hospital."

It was the second time I'd said this.

Glazed eyes sparked. He stood, distanced us with several backward steps and wiped mango hands on his pantaloons. "Well, I'll be go to hell. Doc! What took you so long, *hermano*?"

I said, "Geezus, the least you could do is say hello. Do you have any idea how hard it was to find you? I thought you were dead."

"I was dead. Didn't I just say that? You alone?" He did a slow pan. "Awhile back, can't remember when, I was drunk, some thugs—two Bolshevik types—kicked me silly. They were convinced I knew something about some asshole American spy."

"*Huh?* Say that again?"

He did.

"Where was this?"

"The beach. One of those gunkhole bars you think you'll never forget but can't find your way back the next morning."

He paused as if assembling a schematic of my flaws.

"Oh, shit-the-bed. It's all coming back. Yep, those wire-rimmed glasses, your tight sphincter aura and those sniper eyes—it is you, dude. Get, get away." He used his fingers to shoo me. "You and the Shaman—my *Ahk'inob*—ain't going to hit it off, and we've got a religious ceremony to perform tonight."

"Ahk-inob? What's that?"

"A teacher, kind of a guru deal. It's Mayan."

"An actual indigenous . . . a real shaman?"

"You heard me. An enlightened dude who knows ancient psychotropic recipes."

"As in psychedelics," I said. No need to add a question mark. "Just what you need after a head injury. That makes as much sense as strangers kicking you in a bar."

I was concerned by more than his disjointed rambling. The bar incident was a bright yellow caution light. Days prior to my arrival, a billionaire oligarch had gone missing during a night swim off the Yucatan Peninsula. It was no coincidence that I'd been traveling incognito ever since with a diplomatic passport compliments of one of the British Overseas Protectorate Territories—the Cayman Islands in this case. A new employer. British. Maybe. I wasn't sure.

"What do you mean Bolshevik types? Russians?"

Tomlinson said, "My fling with Marxism blessed me with an ear for accents." He studied me again, his expression clinical, a look of mathematical dissection. This was not like the man

I'd known for decades. He seemed to be in a fugue state—a complicated pathology I wasn't qualified to diagnose.

But the loss of memory fit. So did his childlike manner when he asked, "Who'd you kill this time, Doc? If you've got Commies after you, I truly don't need the hassle. I've washed my hands of all politics and evil."

"Are you already high on something? 'Shrooms? Peyote? You can tell me."

"Stronger shit than that is what I'm hoping. Who knows, tonight might be the night."

"Then why all this . . . ? You're no saint but you're not—"

"Am too. I'm a narcissistic evil dog—reverse the spellings. Sort of like checking your math. A lifetime of dyslexia went out the window when I cracked my head open. Probably more than once. I don't know how many days exactly I got pistol-whipped by that goddamn hurricane. And then *No Más* harikaried herself on a reef."

No Más, his sailboat, had been the man's floating home, his vagabond universe, for decades. At least that detail hadn't been blotted out.

"What I remember best is, seas were running thirty, thirty-five, and being launched headfirst into a bulkhead. A white tunnel, bright, into a distant reality. Then blackness. I was dead—but turned out God added a few weeks to the meter thanks to this kid who brought me back to life."

"Resuscitated you?"

"Resusci—no, that's for lifeguards. The kid—I can't reveal his identity until you're willing to believe. He prayed over me. Put his hand over my nose and mouth until I blacked out again."

"Put his . . . ? Sounds more like he was trying to kill you. I supposed he robbed you, too."

"No, the guru I mentioned, he's the guy who robbed me. The kid might have tried but he only has one arm. Well, only one good arm—kind of birth defect thing. But you're not listening, man. I was already dead, remember? So it was like a total reboot."

"What did he take? The shaman."

"Money, what do you expect? The typical suff. Look, man, he was unburdening me of all my greed and earthly baggage."

"He told you that I suppose. How much cash did he unburden you from?"

"Just folding money. A grand or two. He knows I inherited a bundle. Doesn't care, man."

"You *told* him you're wealthy?"

"Maybe. Why wouldn't I? In Mayan culture, a divine teacher isn't hung up on the whole capitalistic monetary trap thing."

"Oh, I bet," I said. "What about worldly stuff like your passport? Your phone? Was it in a waterproof case?"

"Could be. Can't remember, man. It's all foggy. My passport, though, I probably stuck that in my secret hidey-hole aboard *No Más* before she hit the reef. Damn, now that I think of it, we should probably go back there. Dive it and see if the local thieves missed anything. I hid another hundred grand in cash and coins in the same compartment. I might have mentioned that to the guru, too."

In my friend's mind, shaman and guru apparently meant the same thing.

I checked my burner phone for a signal—a pointless habit in the jungle—and played along. "You've had yourself quite an adventure."

"No shit, Watson. This kid, I tell you, a truly divine *Curandero*. A healer, that's what they call them down here. The ones with a divine gift. He split before I could . . . well, I was bat-blind at the time so I couldn't follow him. Blind for days. Then the guru arrived as my spirit guide."

"You're talking about the guy who robbed you."

"No . . . yes, the Shaman. But it was a blessing. Now I've got the left eye of a praying mantis and the right eye of a carrion bird—a raven I prefer to believe."

He squinted.

"Everything I see is through a prism but fractal, linear. I'm not the same man you knew, Doc. And sand is pouring through the hourglass. I need to find that kid if this village and the Miskito people are to survive the modern shitstorm heading this way." His head pivoted. "Gangbangers and foreign profiteers, man. Chaos and haters. They're the next great extinction meteor."

Meteor?

Tomlinson interpreted my expression. "As in a giant damn asteroid. Read your history, Marion. Life on Earth ended not far from where we're standing right now. Killed all the dinosaurs. And it could happen again. Better, I think, to skip ahead sixty million years."

"Interesting concept," I replied. "We might be better off without dinosaurs. Probably the only time in history—well, prehistory, anyway—when the land was more dangerous than being on the water."

My pal, on an apocalyptic roll, added, "And in Honduras, of course, you've got your earthquakes. They average about eight hundred quakes a year down here."

"You're not making that up," I agreed because it was true. He took the remark as sarcasm.

"Straight gospel, man. Read it on the bar napkin which, these days, kicks the Internet's ass when it comes to accuracy. Mostly low-Richter blips that I felt two or three times this month alone. Trick is go barefoot. Or pull up a chair and stare into the toilet for a couple of hours—like your own personal seismograph. But the real killer quakes—Mag Sevens or Eights? Statistically, the true widow-makers happen every twelve-point-six years. The mudslides and the tsunamis kill thousands."

He savored what came next. "Know how long it's been since the last bad one?"

"Twelve years," I said. It wasn't much of a guess.

"Twelve years, nine months to the week. Exactly. So we've got that going for us, huh?"

In my pocket was a mini key chain light. Fugue confusion, in my layperson mind, suggested a severe concussion. Retrograde amnesia, maybe a cranial leak. I got up. "Let me check your pupils. Forget about asteroids and that one-armed kid. If you're right about Russians, we've got to get the hell out of here fast. I've got a boat hidden about a quarter mile from here. On the river."

"You stole a powerboat?" He was interested but in a sly, sneaky way. It was in his tone.

"I bought it, so don't get any crazy ideas. Grab your stuff. We've still got some daylight left. It took two hours to get here, but that was fighting the current. We can make the coast while the moon's still high. There's a beach hotel not far from the mouth of the river. I've got a room there."

Tomlinson refused by switching topics. "The hurricane, how bad was it?"

"On Sanibel?"

"Where else? Weren't we just talking about hurricanes?"

I said, "It was an end-of-the-world human screwup, according to the media. Which is typical. But it *was* the worst in a century. We can discuss it on the way. You should be in a hospital."

"Dinkin's Bay. The marina's gone? You . . . you lived in a house with fish . . . a lot of aquariums. Doc Ford, the marine biologist. Yeah, yeah, it's coming back. Now you're homeless. Are we all homeless? Mack. What about Mack? The whole marina family?"

Mack had owned the marina prior to the storm. The marina family consisted of a quirky bunch of liveaboards, male and female, plus fishing guides and staff.

"They're rebuilding, but . . ."

"Don't crawfish, man. The place will never be the same again. Admit it. I had a vision weeks before I left Dinkin's Bay. Homes, the marina all gone. Freakin' predestination is a redundant bitch."

I looked around seeing no power lines, no cable, no antennas, but an emaciated horse, saddled, no rider, had sleepwalked its way into the clearing.

"Have you been in touch with someone on shortwave radio?" Tomlinson was a Morse code aficionado with an advanced FCC license.

"I wish, man. My last Q-S-0 was with a Ham in Pinar Del Rio, Cuba. That was just before *No Más* pitchpoled—did a full damn gainer. My comrades there are probably still looking for my ass."

I said, "Then how could you possibly know what happened at Dinkin's Bay?"

"A vision. I just told you. Being homeless hasn't dented my paranormal powers."

"Okay, whatever you say. Homeless. Yeah. For now, I guess. Let's go."

My concussed friend grinned. He beckoned me to follow. "That's number three on my to-do list. Find us a new expat home—Dinkin's Bay in exile. I've already made progress. Built me a tree house, all bamboo. Totally sustainable—if you don't get sucked down the waterfall, of course. Not falling to one's death, I've come to believe, is key to much of living a happy life."

I said, "Nope, we're leaving. You have a bag or something?"

Laughing, a contemptuous snort, Tomlinson shook his head, then changed his mind. "Bag, uh, yeah, sure. Come with me, I'll get it."

Again, a veiled inflection.

"A quick stop, that's all. No more bullshit, right?"

He had walked to the sleepy horse to neaten its forelock. "Have you ever seen a more beautiful animal in your life? Magnificent stallion—all muscle, a true thoroughbred. See, my sense of direction has been diddly-squat since the storm. So destiny hooked the two of us up. Drunk, sober, late at night, Roy's better than a GPS." He patted the horse on the withers. "Aren't you, big fella. Play your cards right, I'll put you out to stud and split the fees."

"You can't be . . . ? Who's Roy?"

"Him, Roy, who do you think? Horse needs a name. Wasn't gonna call him Trigger. Even dead, I hate cliches. Good boy, Roy, yes you are . . . here, eat the rest of my mango."

The aged gelding, swaybacked, ribs showing, chomped the fruit while Tomlinson wove his fingers into the animal's tail and made a *nick-nick* sound. The horse plodded uphill toward the cloud forest, my pal in tow as if hitching a ride on a ski lift.

I shouldered my tactical bag and followed. "Hold it. How far is your . . ."

Tomlinson misheard. He looked back. "How far's the Guru? Not even sure he's there yet. Don't try to talk to him. I'll translate if he thinks you're worthy—which he won't. And Doc? Try to act harmless. Not like some assassin asshole. I don't want you to scare him off."

I was thinking, *the Guru sounds like the asshole*, but said, "How'd you meet this guy? A shaman who makes house calls? The man robs you and you consider it a blessing."

"Hell, yes. All I remembers is, when the Guru showed up, the Bolsheviks stopped kicking me. Heaven sent, man."

Right away, I thought of my friend's cell phone and all the contact information it contained.

I said, "Let me get this straight. A native shaman robs you and just happens to be in the same bar with a couple of Russians who kicked you senseless—and they were asking about me? Why you wouldn't want me to scare him off?"

My pal replied, "I didn't say 'native' shaman. Not that it matters. The Guru was spiritually called to the jungle and studied with elder wisemen. For years, traveled the mountains, village to village. Now he's accepted."

"By who? Where's the guy come from? I'm guessing Eastern Europe."

Tomlinson was getting frustrated. "Where's he—he's from Minnesota, for God's sake, via some New York shithole. But you're missing the—"

"Minnesota?" I cut in. "What's his name?"

"I already said—the Guru, I call him. Or sometimes 'Honored Sensei.' That means—"

"Teacher. I know what Sensei means," I said. "What's his real name?"

"Wing . . . Wingo Bogdan. Or Bogman. Something totally unimportant because he's abandoned his previous incarnation and—"

"Wingo Bogdan from Minnesota," I clarified, heavy on the sarcasm.

"Yes! Even has the Gopher accent. Pronounces the letter 'O' likes he's been goosed in the ass. Come on, Doc. Try to stay on topic. What matters is, the Guru was reborn in the jungle and saved my *cojones*. We have a spiritual connection, the two of us."

I wondered how much of the man's addled behavior was an act. How much was intentional—and to what purpose? I didn't doubt he'd suffered a severe concussion. The story about the woman neurologist and his savant eyesight rang as honest, if not true. However, to trust a thieving "shaman" seemed dumb even by my pal's intuitive, let-God-decide standards.

Concussed or not, Tomlinson possesses the heart of an errant knight regarding whatever cause he happens to embrace at the moment. Children in need, ladies in distress—young, middle-aged, or old—it makes no difference, although a beautiful woman in fear of an abusive male seems to add to the allure.

My pal was a sap when it came to lost causes. As a supposed pacifist, violence was not a deterrent. This was true during his years as a counterculture revolutionary. By rights, the man should have been jailed long ago in connection with the bombing of a military base.

Jailed or worse if a certain U.S. operative—or a long list of pissed-off husbands—had squeezed the trigger.

Yes, the sailor and I had a complicated bipolar connection.

I said, "Let me get this straight. A jungle shaman from Minnesota robs you and just happens to be in the same bar with a couple of Russians."

"*Precisely,*" Tomlinson said. "Like a gift from Heaven, my brother. I mean, what are the odds?"

TWO

I didn't get a chance to meet the Minnesota Guru until long after Tomlinson had lured me to the tree house he was building. As a setting, he'd selected the precipice of a waterfall, a torrent of gray that dropped into the silence of a turquoise lagoon a hundred feet below. Nearby, a feeder stream flowed clear and clean into a series of terraced downhill pools.

It was ten, fifteen degrees cooler up here. Air dense. Elephant-eared leaves dripped with condensation.

"You paid the villagers to do the carpentry work?" I asked. My pal was a maritime master when it came to boat repairs, but he couldn't hammer a straight nail.

"Bro, the Miskito locals treat me like I'm the long-lost village idiot. Polite enough, you know but . . . They're sick of rich gringos—*chéy-lees,* they call us—trying to teach them what they've been experts at for umpteen generations. The do-gooder volunteers—medical, archaeology, evangelist types, mostly. They drop in and act like they're dealing with butt-dumb kids. Make all kinds of modern suggestions then skedaddle back to the nearest five-star."

The horse stopped, raised its tail and dropped a steaming

pile at Tomlinson's feet. Ants, flies swarmed and began the instant recycling process.

My friend continued to beam at his bamboo hut.

"Hermano, I've worked nonstop day and night. For the last month, survived on nothing but goat cheese and tortillas. Classic design, huh? Neo-primitive with an obvious nod to Tarzan and Frank Lloyd Wright."

"All the elements are there," I said agreeably.

"I'm tellin' you, dude, since that bump on the head, my brain processes shit differently. Three weeks ago I found this waterfall and, right away, fixated on that mahogany tree. Thing lit up like the Sanibel Lighthouse. Same with the coconut palms and that stand of bamboo. In a flash, there it was in my head, a detailed blueprint of the future. An architectural vision, all precisely metric, of course. Exactly what you see now."

He sniffed and smiled, hands on his hips. "Well, almost. The shitter's not done, and I still need a mill wheel to shlep water up from the creek. There will be pulley systems and fans. A generator—wind powered, of course. What do you think? Swiss Family Robinson, right out of the old Disney flick. My left-brain masterpiece."

It had been a two-mile hike uphill. All mist and moss, centuries of rot amid the siren howl of insects. Now we stood in a biosphere of bromeliads, orchids, gnats, jellybean-colored frogs beneath a towering canopy frosted with clouds. Sunlight, dusty columns, painted Tomlinson's thatch-roofed hut. It was built high in the limbs of the load-bearing mahogany. Bamboo stairs, wraparound porch, bamboo deck and slatted railing. It had a cross-tied symmetry of verticals and horizontals that reminded me of native longhouses in Cambodia. Vines served as ropes, quick egress if needed or to haul up supplies. The man had, indeed, worked obsessively for weeks.

Impressive, but there was nothing precise, metrically or

otherwise, about the place. Walls were out-of-square. Double-decker platforms tilted like layers of a drunken wedding cake.

This wasn't the only evidence that Tomlinson's perception of reality had become a gilded fantasy. His scrawny horse, Roy, was a bag of bones, not a thoroughbred and definitely not a stallion. The tree house wasn't a masterpiece. And how could my pal, a noted author and an ordained Buddhist priest, accept a thieving shaman from the Gopher State as his spiritual guide?

"More like 'A Cowboy in the Jungle,'" I said. A useful evasion.

"Wow. I like that. Another Captain James B. classic. Now you're getting into the vibe."

Tomlinson didn't bother tethering the horse. "What you're gonna love is pissing off the upstairs porch. Perfectly mimics the effect of air molecules on a knuckleball. The stream breaks left, floats right. Random certainty—the Achilles' heel of physics. Punish your bladder long enough, if the wind's right, you can piss your initials in the lagoon. Come on. *Watch* me."

He clomped up the stairs. I crossed my arms.

"I'll wait. Grab whatever you need. We're leaving."

"But you haven't seen the tiki bar, man. I've got a bucket of beer in the plunge pool and a bottle of rum just waiting for—"

I said, "Tomlinson. Stop, take a breath. Listen to me. You've got a concussion. Maybe a brain bleed. Look—" I trailed him up to the first deck "—I haven't been tracking you for the last six days to take you home in a coffin. You need x-rays, scans, all the protocols. Do it for your friends. Please? After the hurricane, the last thing the marina needs to suffer through is another wake."

This was a slip of the tongue. I wasn't ready to share which marina stalwart had recently died.

My friend didn't notice.

"Already been to a doctor. Already had most those tests. Bloodwork, the whole shebang. I'm right as rain."

"No, you didn't. And no, you're not."

"Seriously. I'm getting used to seeing the world in stereo. Sort of like a raven with my left eye. And the right eye, everything is geometrical with crosshairs, like a hungry carnivorous bug. Keep climbing, we'll work our way back down during the tour, take our time."

A *tour*, talking about a structure the size of two sheds on stilts.

I said, "You're a grown man. No need to lie if you're determined to stay. I'm asking you as a favor."

"Lie? When have I ever . . . okay, I've told you a pack of lies over the years. But this time, I'm . . ."

I interrupted, "There's not a modern hospital within, what, a hundred miles? Maybe Roatán, but I doubt if even they have the facilities. Your judgment is all ass backwards, ol' buddy. That's an objective observation. You're not yourself."

"Hell, dude, what you expect? I'm no longer among the living. That's what I'm trying to tell you. I'll explain but let's start on the top deck, okay? I gotta bilge ship."

Urinate, he meant.

The bamboo stairs squeaked and swayed beneath our weight. Windows, unscreened, no glass, allowed me a peek inside the lower cabin. Vacant space sparsely furnished. Coffee sacks for curtains, a woven hammock strung wall to wall. A couple of stone pedestals and a five-gallon bucket for guests.

In the upstairs room, same stuff plus a manhole-sized stone in the middle of the floor, ornate with Mayan glyphs. Candles and melted wax suggested it was a type of altar. A woven mat, a fan made of white bird feathers, a hookah, an empty kettle and two wooden cups added to the lava-lamp effect.

I said, "Now you're stealing artifacts? If you're hosting a tea party, cancel it. At least let me get a doctor to examine you."

"Borrowing," Tomlinson replied. "Gifts from the jungle. Hell, artifacts are everywhere up here. The Guru says spirits of the Old Ones have welcomed me. Tonight, if the Honorable *Sensei* shows up, he's going to guide me through an all-night Ayahuasca tea ceremony—a tribal ritual a thousand years old. It damn near guarantees enlightenment in the afterlife."

He pronounced the indigenous word, *Ayahuasca*, as *eye-ya-WAZ-kah*.

"If you live that long," I said, and turned away before he could flop his member over the railing to pee.

The sound he made: *Ahhhh.* "The golden helix, amigo." He paused to do calculations. "The lagoon's a vertical drop of thirty-point-four meters at an angled declination of sixty-two degrees. That's through my bug eye, and damn if I'm not zeroed in. If there were Lilliputians down there, I bet they'd be assembling virgins to appease the—" He stopped after a luxurious sigh. Zipped and turned. "Lying, huh? Come on. I've got proof."

"Of what?" A beat later, I understood he was talking about medical tests.

We went inside. He handed me a glossy pamphlet and explained that, after he'd been dragged from the wreckage of his boat, a nun had been summoned from a local orphanage. The nun knew that a humanitarian group, Doctors with Wings, was partying at a hotel on the nearby Bay Islands. They were celebrating after a week of living rough, physicians, nurses, a dentist, fixing cleft palates, doing surgeries and providing free health care to coastal villages. An annual volunteer project for them.

"A fun bunch, total pros even when they're drunk, as I

recollect. Which isn't much," Tomlinson told me. "They have this tricked-out specialty bus, a hospital bed, all sorts of tubes, surgical lights and anyway . . ."

I tuned him out and skimmed the pamphlet. *"The Infra-Scanner, a handheld brain scanner, is an AMA approved detector of traumatic supratentorial hematomas of greater than 3.5 Ml in volume and . . ."*

I skipped down: *". . . the unit contains a diode laser that's optically coupled to the patient's skull. In real time, the unit provides digitized analysis to a single on-board computer that also measures . . ."*

Tomlinson's voice demanded attention. "Hey . . . you didn't answer my question. Is there some sort of medical side effect that would explain my . . . that painful area I mentioned?"

"Explain what? What are you talking about?"

He murmured, "Geezus frogs," in frustration. "Pay attention. On the surgical table, I was out of it most of the night—they didn't want me to sleep. And when I woke up—well, a few days later, anyway—my butt hurt. Do I gotta paint a picture?"

With emphasis, he repeated, "Dude, my . . . butt . . . *hurt.* Comprendo?"

"Huh? You mean . . . you're not suggesting . . ."

"Hey man, we're all human. I don't want to blame that dentist, although he was very damn friendly the next morning. Replaced some of my old fillings for free so—" my pal shrugged "—what the hell. An oversight on my part. It needs to be in Chapman's guide. All rum-loving sailors should have 'Exit Only' tattooed on their ass."

I shrugged that away and slapped the pamphlet. "I'll be darned, it seems you really did get a brain scan. I owe you an apology. What about other tests? Do you have the results?"

"Dude, can we stick with the dentist for a sec? Or wait, now that I think back—this was during the hurricane—the first time *No Más* turned turtle, I did the cheerleader splits on the tiller. Bruised the hell out of Zamboni and the Hat Trick Twins. But I'm talking about my bunghole, not my goodies. Are we clear on that point? What's your—don't spare my feelings. What's your professional opinion?"

I said, "You've been eating nothing but goat cheese for the last few weeks? No wonder your butt hurts. What about x-rays, blood work? And there had to be a long list of diagnostic questions. How many days did they keep you for observation?"

"In the hospital bus? Four nights before I escaped, but the woman shrink wanted me to stay for a hell of a lot more testing. Said the brain injury had changed my wiring—a rarity. One in a million. Maybe 'acquired savant syndrome,' it's called. Could be that's why I have—in her words—bi-hemisphere ocular anomalies. When I *can* see. Like a rare gift. You've read about that stuff."

We all have. A high school dropout gets kicked in the head by a mule, wakes up and he's suddenly a math genius. Or can sit at a piano and play Mozart first try.

Tomlinson added, "I told you about her. The pickleball-playing neurologist? She was all excited about her diagnosis. Plus, I think she has the hots for . . . well, let's face it. Why should she be any different? Doc, you think it might have been her that made that booty call, not the dentist? Medical doctors, especially from the female shrink phylum, have kinks that would shame monkeys. I bet it has to do with desensitization regarding certain, you know . . . *orifices.*"

I countered, "More tests might not be a bad idea. Come back to Florida, get a full workup. How about it? Grab your stuff and let's go. Forget about the Shaman and your whatever-it-is drug ceremony."

He ignored that. "Dr. Naomi Cruz—is that some name?"
"Who?"

"The neurologist. A native Honduran with money. She's determined to write an article for the medical journals. Personally,

I think the good doctor wants to get in my knickers again, then use my concussion to make her academic bones."

"Or," I said, "it could be she's just a competent physician trying to do her job."

"*Right.* Then why's she offering a reward to anyone who drops a dime on me? That's what the villagers heard, anyway. A month, she wants a full month, just the two of us, me wired to machines. She as good as *told* me that. Well . . . it was mostly in her body language. Dude, it's the white man's way: Kill it and study it. Or put it in a cage."

I said, "Your savantism—is that even a word? Your goofed up eyesight isn't exactly Mozart."

"Oh, *really?*" Tomlinson made binoculars with his hands. "Let's try my raven left-brain orb. Check it out, man. On the other side of the lagoon, see that dead tree and the birds hopping around on the trunk? It's a. . . . a butternut tree, maybe."

I removed my glasses and cleaned them. "The huge tree with buttress roots? Yeah. But birds, hell, that's gotta be half a mile away downhill."

"Damn straight it is. They're quetzal birds. Emerald green. Same color as the lagoon. The sacred bird of the ancient Maya, all related to the God Quetzalcoatl. Their feathers—the shrink bird-watcher told me this—their feathers reflect ultraviolet light. You savvy? *Ultraviolet vision.*"

Tomlinson looked over. "Not Mozart, maybe, but I've gotten a taste of having superpowers. And I *love* it."

He used his make-believe binocs again. "I count four . . . five quetzals way up high. Two males, tail feathers long as my arm. And I can . . . okay, now a whole flock of red macaws just came tumbling in. Lower branches. Yeah, a Cuipo tree."

"What kind?"

"You've seen them. A canoe tree. For thousands of years, they've been a favorite of boat builders. Yeah. The birds are feeding. Or have nests."

He offered me his make-believe binocs. I ignored him and squinted. In the distance, a scattering of amber pepper flakes might have been scarlet macaws. The quetzals—if they were quetzals this close to the sea—remained invisible.

Tomlinson lowered his hands, concerned about something. "Uh-oh. There are some kids under the tree, one with a slingshot, the others messing with ropes. Young kids, half a dozen, who—" He stood straighter and exclaimed, "Oh shit, we've gotta get down there, man. *Now.*"

Down the bamboo steps he ran, two at a time.

I followed, didn't need prodding when he called, "Please tell me you've got a gun in that bag of yours. Don't you always? Some kind of weapon."

That's a question I've been programmed not to answer.

I stopped. "Because of kids with slingshots? You're not . . . They shouldn't be shooting rare birds, yeah, I agree, but we don't need . . ."

Tomlinson hollered, "Come on, come on. Not that. There're three guys in uniforms, camo dudes with rifles. They're sneaking up on the kids through the trees."

"Could be local cops. Don't do anything stupid. Wait up, stop . . . let me do the talking."

Over his shoulder, my pal replied, "Cops, hell. That's what I'm worried about. *Federales,* gangbangers, and narcos, there's not a damn bit of difference in Honduras. On this coast they're all criminals. And one of the kids is my guy."

"What?"

"I recognized him. The kid who saved my life. The *Curandero,* the one-armed healer? I've been looking for him. Get your ass in gear."

I backtracked, grabbed my tactical bag. By the time I got down, Tomlinson was aboard the scrawny horse, still struggling to get his feet in the stirrups as they galloped off downhill.

THREE

A trail on the other side of the stream corkscrewed sharply downhill. It gave the waterfall wide berth until the landscape flattened. I jogged along and got a glimpse of Tomlinson on horseback, several hundred yards ahead. He still hadn't found the stirrups, so he listed from port to starboard, bouncing in the saddle like a drunk.

I hollered, "Slow down before you kill yourself."

The only response was a muted boom that reminded me of Fourth of July fireworks. The sound was benign compared to what I heard next: a single gunshot then a double tap. The piercing reports suggested "assault rifle" ammunition.

My God, the men were shooting at kids?

At a run, I traveled beneath old growth forest, a cavern of green hundreds of feet high. Howler monkeys, tribal, roared while unseen males tried to defecate on me from altitude. A smaller variety—spider monkeys, my guess—screamed chirping warnings and hurled branches.

A telling difference between man and apes, aside from two absent chromosomes, is that humans have learned to mask our simmering territorial rage—the true missing link.

I felt a jolt of anger myself when I heard a sixth rifle report.

Six boys by the lagoon, Tomlinson had said. From the shoulder bag, I transferred a 9 mm pistol to a concealed holster and charged toward a grove of coconut palms. The swaybacked horse was there munching weeds. My pal had taken a spill. He was on one knee trying to get up.

"Turns out Roy's a tad gun-shy," he grunted when I was close enough. "Trigger my ass. This cowboy shit . . . *ouch* . . . it's not as easy as it looks. But I could totally get into it."

"You hurt?"

"Didn't help my butt any. Can you see the boys?"

"We're close, so keep your voice down."

"That noise, was it gunfire or an explosion? I heard a big boom and went flying over Roy's head when the damn nag hit the brakes."

I said, "A rifle. At least six shots and some other ordnance. Didn't sound like a gun. Can you walk?"

Tomlinson retrieved his straw hat. "Bastards. If they killed Aléto, I'll . . . Geezus hell, Doc—"

"Who?"

"The kid. The one-armed kid. What the hell are we gonna do? If those men are cops, they'll probably shoot us, too. The *Maras*—the gangbangers—and the feds, they're all on the same team in this country. Along with the traffickers and petroleum whores. But we can't just—"

"Quiet," I said. "Stay here. If I don't motion for you to follow, get on that horse and go for help."

Ahead, through the palms, the dead tree marked the rim of the lagoon. A tangle of white torch scrub screened the water. I drew the pistol, a Sig Sauer P365, and crept through the brush until I had a view. Three male soldier types in camo fatigues had abandoned their rifles against a massive buttress root, common in the rainforest. One yelled orders at five shirtless, emaciated boys who struggled to untangle a hundred yards of netting that was alive with squawking macaws and other birds I couldn't identify.

The kids obeyed with the sullenness of indentured servants.

I saw no dead bodies, no wounded one-armed boy, so maybe the sixth boy, Tomlinson's *Curandero*, had escaped.

Theirs was not an improvised operation. The camo guys had used a rocket-propelled mist-net commonly used by researchers, not poacher types. The net had been detonated from a distance before gunfire had spooked the birds to flight. The men had large plastic cages open and ready. They wore heavy gloves. The kids did not. I doubt pirate stories about macaws snipping off human fingers, but a two-pound bird that cracks nuts for a living has one hell of a bite.

The boys, gaunt, ribs showing, yipped and howled while battling the macaws, which the men—barely out of their teens—found funny. Lots of profane jeering in Spanish.

I was about to summon Tomlinson when I was struck by an oddity. There had been three military type rifles braced against the back of the tree. Now there were only two.

How was that possible?

I searched the jungled background and waited. Many seconds passed before my attention wandered. When I looked back, only one rifle remained.

What the hell?

Someone or something was out there, watching the men and methodically disarming them.

Several more scarlet macaws had been manhandled into cages when I finally figured it out. On the ground behind the tree was a large yellow bromeliad plant. It was spiked like the crown of a pineapple and appeared to be moving. It sat atop a canoe-sized banana leaf. The yellow crown, with the speed of a worm, crept closer and closer toward the last remaining rifle, pulling the banana leaf with it.

I crabbed backward, gave Tomlinson a wave, and returned with him to my observation cranny.

"Slave labor," he whispered, taking in the scene. "Guess I know now who's been kidnapping kids. Looks like they're starving. Those military scum ought to be dick-savaged by zebras."

I replied, "They're just hired help. Traffickers, the real money guys, would be way up the ladder."

"Hey . . . where's my kid, the one-armed kid? He was part of the group. I'm damn sure he was—"

I shushed him and pointed. "Watch."

The banana leaf stopped. The yellow bromeliad levitated a few inches off the ground. It became a crown on the head of a small, cinnamon-skinned boy. From beneath the banana leaf, a single skinny arm appeared. A small hand snatched the last rifle, and the banana leaf began its slow return to safety, I assumed. But I was wrong.

Tomlinson whispered, "That's him. *Aléto.* I recognize his face."

"You're sure? He told you his name?"

"A nickname. The other kids called him that the night he saved my life. Mayan for some kind of fish. Something with fins. I asked the villagers. You'll understand if we—"

I signaled for silence because, instead of retreating, the boy beneath the banana leaf did something unexpected. He rolled clear, jumped to his feet and, using his good left arm, not only leveled the rifle but marched toward the men, hollering threats in Spanish.

"Run, coward putas. I'll shoot. I'll shoot! Run, leave us alone." Without a look, he gave the other boys orders in Miskito patois, some of it decipherable, most not. All five scattered into the jungle.

The skinny little kid stood his ground.

Tomlinson had to be held back. I had my pistol drawn, a

round chambered. With a look, I told him, *Wait. Let's see what happens.*

What happened was, two of the men treated the boy's threats as thigh-slapping hilarity. They laughed insults and taunted this shirtless child in tattered pants, maybe twelve years old but small for his age, and with only one normal arm—his left arm. What Tomlinson had described as a birth defect was apparent. A dwarf appendage sprouted from the boy's right shoulder, a stub with a few curled fingers. *Aléto.* A cruel nickname that made sense. His crippled hand resembled a tiny fin.

As the father of a toddler son, the deformity squeezed the heart—until the kid proved he was anything but handicapped. Only one of the camo guys didn't find his taunting funny. When he marched toward the boy, the boy braced the rifle under his armpit, shucked the bolt with his crippled append-age and took aim left-handed.

The guy kept coming. No one expected the kid to open fire. But he did. What saved the three men was that the AR's selection switch was set to full automatic—a new experience for a ten-or twelve-year-old who didn't know enough to release the trigger. Rapid fire, deafening, the rifle's recoil launched the barrel upward.

The men, after a moment of shock, ducked and sprinted for a place to hide.

"Geezus hell," Tomlinson exclaimed, covering his ears. "That kid's not only a divine healer, he's batshit crazy, dude."

Once again, I had to restrain my pal back because Aléto was a quick study. And he wasn't done. One-handed, the boy re-shouldered the AR, took a calming breath, and popped off a series of single rounds. One round exploded a slice of flesh from the slowest man's thigh. I saw the blood spray. The guy stumbled, regained his balance, and kept going.

The men didn't look back until they were behind a rocky ledge a football field away.

Tomlinson, with his savant eyes, said, "One of those bastards is taking pictures. Maybe video. He'll use it as evidence to give the *federales*. Oh . . . this is bad. A nationwide search for a one-armed Indio boy. That won't take long. The kid will be screwed."

I said, "Don't step out while he's filming or we're screwed, too. We can't help anyone from jail."

"But Marion, we've got to get to the kid. Got to warn him and the others that they'll soon be on the police shit list."

"We will, we will, just stay put. Those soldiers—whatever they are—they have to get their buddy to a doctor before he bleeds to death. Stiches at the very least."

"But what if one of the dudes sticks around, comes back with another gun?"

I replied, "If that happens . . . people disappear all the time in the rainforest."

Tomlinson and I have been friends for a long time. He chose not to question my meaning. So we watched the boy, Aléto, who still refused to run. He kept an eye on the camo guys while he used a knife to hack holes in the mist net. Macaws and other birds squawked in protest, then tumbled free, one by one. They tested their wings and flew off.

A smaller, more delicate bird, its emerald plumage iridescent, lay motionless when cut free. It was a male quetzal, red-breasted. Its tail feathers were so long they touched the ground when the boy lifted the bird to his waist.

He stared for a moment, faced the men and raised the quetzal bird over his head as if to show them what they'd done. There was an intensity in that simple act that communicated something dire. Defiance. A threat, perhaps. Yet, the boy said nothing and returned to his work. When both plastic cages had been emptied of birds, the kid, in no rush, slung the rifle over his shoulder, and followed his friends into the rainforest. He carried the dead quetzal in the pit of his deformed arm as if keeping it warm.

Tomlinson said, "Finally. Those bastards, the one with the camera, all of them, they're leaving."

"You're sure?" My shirt was sweat-soaked, my glasses fogged.

"It doesn't look like they're heading back to the village. Who cares. Okay . . . they're gone. Come on."

Tomlinson crane-walked off in pursuit of the boy who didn't have much of a head start. Two or three minutes at most. I expected to find him right away.

We didn't.

"Where the hell did he disappear to?"

"Like a ghost," Tomlinson mused. He liked the concept. I could tell.

The forest floor was a resilient sponge. Even my heavy boots didn't leave lasting impressions. I searched for broken twigs. Fresh scars on rotten logs. Nothing. My pal offered to use his savant eyes for guidance. The dead quetzal, he reminded me, had feathers that reflected ultraviolet light.

"You noticed something?"

"Not yet."

"Might as well give it a try."

Several minutes later, my pal sighed. "Ants. Leaf cutters lined up like Cheeseheads at a Packers game. Never seen so many freakin' ants in my life. This forest man, the entire molecular structure, is alive. Lots of scorpions, too. Geezus hell. That neon glow scorpions give off, you know? My bug eye's starting to hurt. Know what I'd love to see? A harpy eagle. Largest eagle in the Americas. Talons the size of bear claws."

I said, "Screw it. Keep it simple. None of those boys were wearing shoes. You notice? So they couldn't have come far on foot. Let's go straight to the river."

I turned west toward an elevated area where a curtain of vines choked out ground foliage.

Tomlinson wasn't so sure. "West? How do we know that's

west? Can't even see the damn sun. Don't worry, if we're lost, we can always go back and get Roy. I never ever go into the jungle without Roy."

He followed me, anyway.

"Your kid came past here," I said. This was only a minute later. At my feet was a scythe-shaped rifle magazine that had been jettisoned or dropped. I picked it up. The mag contained only one round.

"Smart kid like him," I said, "wouldn't have left this behind unless he and his pals took the loaded rifles with them. How old you think they are? Ten, twelve years old at most. With automatic weapons. Those boys are headed for trouble."

"Or running from it," Tomlinson said. "They can't be far. Close enough to hear us I bet." Before I could object, he cupped his hands and called in broken Spanish, "Aléto! It is your friend. The man you saved. Remember me?" Then added something else, a sentence or two in the indigenous Miskito language.

Atop the incline, the curtain of vines parted. The barrel of a rifle appeared, and I got a glimpse of a skinny left arm.

I hollered, "Get down!" and we did, just before two quick shots whistled through branches high overhead.

The curtain of vines stirred. The opening closed.

"A friend of yours, huh?" I said. "The night your boat wrecked, maybe he *was* trying to kill you."

I didn't believe it, though. Wasn't convinced, anyway, because, if the kid was marksman enough to hit a fleeing man at fifty yards, we would've been easy targets. He'd put those rounds into the tree canopy intentionally.

Tomlinson wasn't convinced, either.

"You try calling him, Doc. Your Spanish is better. We've got to make those kids believe we're not cops or deviant scum."

I replied, "You speak local Miskito? What the hell did you say?"

"I'm not sure. That we wanted to help—at least, I hope that's what I said. Goddamn—" Tomlinson had to smile "—that boy is everything I'd hoped for. And more."

I lifted my head to confirm the veil of vines was still closed. "What's that supposed to mean?"

Tomlinson got to his feet. "I'm going after him. He won't shoot me. And, if he does, what the hell? My ticket's already been punched. I've been playing with house money long enough."

I said, "Give them a few minutes to get to the river. We'll pick up their trail there. Come on. What's so special about the kid? And don't give me that he brought-you-back-from-the-dead nonsense."

"Nonsense, huh? It's true, man."

"Right. So you feel like you owe him. That's worth getting shot?"

Tomlinson squatted. "Yeah, for sure. It's bigger than that. Doc, I shouldn't . . . I can't. If I tell you, you'll have a target on your back. You wouldn't believe me anyway, man."

I was trying to buy time but getting impatient. "Ol' buddy, I already have a target on my back. And I don't believe most of what you tell me anyway. So out with it."

"Hey . . . that's a cruel thing to say to anyone."

"Damn it, Tomlinson, just tell me."

"*Okay.* You ever hear of *King Jacinto*?"

"Nope," I said and thought, *Here we go again.*

"Historic fact," my friend said. "Canek was born in seventeen-twenty something, died thirty, forty years later. Tortured and executed by Spanish invaders who raped and robbed this region blind. Well, Aléto—I don't even know the name his family uses these days—Aléto is his direct descendant."

I said, "The boy's a direct descendant of Jacinto . . . the guy you're talking about. So?"

"Jacinto Canek. 'Jacinto the Great,' his followers called him. After that, his whole family had to go underground. Generation after generation, had to change their names. Always on the run."

I was lost. "Who told you all this?"

"Sources, man. Last year, they found Jacinto's grave and did the DNA thing. All on the Q-T, but I would've figured it out. The kid, he's got a special, I don't know, a weird, special light about him. You didn't sense it? There's a lot more to the story."

"I hope so," I replied. "What I've heard so far sounds like . . . well, I'm just gonna say it. I'd like to help those kids, sure. If the bird poachers are somehow involved in human trafficking, damn right. I know people who might help bust them. But you need to be in a hospital, and the sooner the better. *Listen to me*. You're not thinking straight. Your logic, your judgment is totally screwed up. In fact, you sound about half crazy. No offense."

Offended, Tomlinson gave me a strange look. Indulgent but also patronizing. "Crazy huh? Then you're gonna love this. That boy—"

I interrupted. "I don't want to hear the whole story. Not now."

"Let me finish," my pal said. Sounded a tad chilly. "That boy, by rights, is the hereditary king. The first king since Jacinto the Great almost three hundred years ago."

"Uh-huh. King of what?"

"Of the lost Itza tribe." Tomlinson gave it a beat. "In the hierarchy, that makes the boy king of what's left of the great Mayan civilization."

"King of the Maya," I said.

"*Precisely*. There's least a million indigenous people between here and the Yucatan, and they've been waiting for generations for Jacinto to return. The Shaman knows it's true. So do the feds. But no one admits it."

I said, "What's it matter? He's a little boy. And even if you're . . . face it, people don't care about kings anymore."

"Don't they? Revolution, man. Honduras, countries on both sides, they're the most violent in the Americas. Child trafficking—we just witnessed it. The return of a tribal king, villagers whisper about that stuff. Like God and the quetzal bird. The prophecy is part of tribal lore."

It was hot and buggy. I remained patient. "The Second Coming, sure. It's a popular—" I'd almost said "myth" but rephrased. "It's a popular belief. I can appreciate that."

"Then you understand. If I'm stuck in a hospital, the feds, the foreign power whores, will hunt down the one-armed king and kill him. Just like they did Jacinto the Great three centuries ago."

My concussed friend headed for the river, saying, "No biggie, Doc. Think it over. The future of the entire freakin' Maya civilization and the Miskito Coast is all totally up to you."

FOUR

The river flowed toward the sea in gelatinous swirls, jungle on both sides, water tannin stained but clear in depths that ranged from deep green pools to rocks that pierced the surface.

Tomlinson discovered children's footprints in the sand. What might have been a gator slide, I decided, was where someone had beached a dugout canoe. A common form of transportation in this part of the world.

"Six kids arrived here in one dugout?" Tomlinson wondered. "*Pip-an-tes*. That's what the mountain people call dugouts. I don't buy it, man. Too small even for kids. Too much weight to paddle upstream. If they all escaped downstream, though, that's a different story."

Clarity was provided by a rusty mooring post a few hundred yards to the north. Lots of tracks there. Men in boots thatched by the imprints of barefooted youngsters. If I had any doubts, blood spore, a splattered black line in the sand, connected the wounded guy's exit to another path that probably led to the lagoon.

We'd been talking in normal tones. Now I whispered. "Damn, we almost walked right into them—the poachers.

They just left in a rigid hull from the markings. They came by boat. Brought the five boys along to do the dirty work." I motioned behind us. "Your kid, Aléto, must've arrived later in a canoe. Alone. Somehow, the men caught him. Back at the tree house, you spotted the boy, right? He was already captive, you said. One of six."

Tomlinson was distracted by something in the tree canopy. A bird called a flutelike, *kee-ow . . . kee-ow . . . keee-loo* somewhere in the highest limbs. On my pal's face was a knowing look.

He said, "More likely, Aléto wanted to get caught. The kid's got stones of brass, man. He shows up alone—in my head, I can see this happening—he marches in, gets captured on purpose. Already had a plan to rescue his buddies, but decided it was smarter to get to know the enemy first. Puts the camo guys on their heels. Who's afraid of a skinny little one-arm ten- or twelve-year-old? Disappears when the dumbasses lose track of their guns, then pops out and freakin' *shoots them.* You can't teach that shit. Exactly the sort of blood justice you'd expect from a Mayan king."

I said to the hipster pacificist, "That concussion might have done you some good. The place I hid my boat can't be far from here. If we hurry, maybe we can catch your Mayan King before he and the boys get to wherever they're going. Even paddling downstream, they couldn't have gotten far."

"Sarcasm." Tomlinson was still searching the trees. "Hey—" he pointed, saying "—then explain *that.*"

From the highest limbs, an iridescent green bird emerged, paused in flight. Shook its ruffled feathers, disoriented, then disappeared downriver instead of toward the misty cloud forest where mountain birds belong.

Tomlinson gave me a look but was too cool to gloat.

In his mind, the young Mayan King had brought the quetzal bird back to life.

. . .

It was a fifteen-minute bushwhack to where villagers beached their dugouts or tied them to toothpick docks. My locally purchased *panga* was hidden nearby but close enough that Tomlinson noticed a new arrival among the local dugouts. It was a small Boston Whaler, *Shaman Eco Lodge* stenciled on the side. No one aboard or nearby, just some chickens and a goat. Roy, the swaybacked horse, had found his way home, too.

"Damn, the Guru's here," my pal said, disappointed but energized. "Probably already on his way to my tree house. If I don't get there soon, the guy might question the karmic imperative, say to hell with our *Ayahuasca* tea ceremony and split."

I said, "Shaman Eco Lodge." I found the name crass. "He owns the place?'

"No. Well, maybe. He lives there sometimes. There are a bunch of eco-type lodges on this coast. Mountain outposts, their own little worlds. No roads, just landing strips or water access. Five-star everything. Food, massages, ziplines, whatever the guests want. They're usually owned by big money foreigners. China is a big investor."

I knew that was true. I also knew the type of resort. They're popular in Mesoamerica. Enclaves that provide the illusion of a jungle adventure and mystic enlightenment without having to break a sweat.

"But he's not in it for the money," Tomlinson assured me. "The Guru, he volunteers, shares his herbal wisdom and only performs the ancient ceremony with—look, man, I've got to decide fast. I want to find Aléto, but this might be my last . . . you're spending the night here, so how about we do a search tomorrow?"

I faced my friend. Looked him in the eyes. "Answer a question first."

"Sure, man. You sound kinda aggro."

"You're an ordained Renzai Zen priest, right? Took you five years, a lot of time in Japan."

"Uhh, yeah. More like six."

"Your book, it's got a cult following. Hell, at Dinkin's Bay, I witnessed it. You had fans show up from all over the world."

I was referring to what some considered to be a Zen classic, *One Fathom Above Sea Level.*

Tomlinson responded, "Book's in its forty-something printing. True, true, my fans are an odd, zippity-doo-dah bunch. But they're loyal."

I stepped closer. "Then why the hell are you seeking spiritual guidance from a Minnesota thief who drives a freakin' Boston Whaler? And just happened to be in the same bar when a couple of Russians started kicking your ass?"

My friend blinked. Unintentionally, perhaps. But possibly not. "Proves we've got a spiritual link, man. An intersection like that, even unexpected, is never coincidental. But here's what sealed the deal——" he backed a step to create space "——later, it's all a little blurry, the Guru and I were discussing the Maya, the fall of civilizations. And the great meteor that will destroy this land again. An *ideological* meteor, we both agreed on that. Know what he said?"

I pressed, "And how does he know about the one-armed boy? That Mayan King business. The federales supposedly don't know, and I doubt if they care. But he does? Give me a break. Sounds more like total——"

Tomlinson, eager to convince me, interrupted. "What the Guru said was, every day we wake up, we can be sure it's not the end of the world because, you know why? Get this—*because it's already tomorrow in Australia.*"

I grimaced, couldn't help it, but maintained eye contact. "That is so . . . You actually find that profound?"

"Not until I gave it some thought. The simple clarity, man. His cut-through-the-bullshit grasp of reality. Rings like a bell to a spiritual soul like me."

Again, he blinked. Twice this time. It was a message and a secret warning. My friend was lying. Or was this just more nonsensical talk?

I knew the answer when he added, "Marion, this isn't my first trip to the coast of mosquitoes and banditos. I've got old contacts, and I've learned a lot in the last few weeks. Clowns always get the last laugh. Ever heard that one?"

I shook my head, *Nope*, because we were now communicating between the lines. Tomlinson was either babbling or he, too, had doubts about the Shaman Guru. Might even have a motive or a plan.

Hopefully not some dangerous, drug-addled plan. But this was not the time to ask.

Slowly, I said. "Okay . . . We'll play it your way."

Tomlinson's response was in the look he gave me. *Wise choice.*

"You're coming back to the tree house, right, Doc?"

I said, "First I'm going to try and find those boys. If the guy the kid shot is military, the federales will scramble the cavalry. If they don't, the camo guys are traffickers. Or narcos. Either way, I'll learn something."

Not necessarily, I was reminded. Not on a coast where crime of all types was deeply rooted and intermingled with governments local and foreign.

That was accurate, as I'd been briefed before arrival. I asked how long his psychedelic ceremony would take.

All afternoon and beyond, Tomlinson guessed. Around sunset, he would drink a concoction of boiled plants and native *Ayahuasca* vine. The Shaman would tend to him during the "spiritual journey" that followed.

"Could be five, six hours depending on how bad I get the shits," he added.

"Diarrhea? Why put yourself through something like that?"

"It's necessary. A total cleansing. You can't explore the spiritual boundary waters unless all the pipes are clean. Basic courtesy."

I said, "Stupid and dangerous, if you ask me. After that, then what?"

My concern came from experience. There's a long list of mind-altering "natural herbs" used, supposedly, by shamans but, in fact, a favorite tool of criminals. Among them was something called Devil's Breath, made from native plants similar to belladonna. Active ingredient was scopolamine which, as a microdose patch, was an approved prophylaxis for motion sickness. On the streets, though, it is known as Burundanga or the Zombie drug. It is odorless, colorless and, when slipped into a drink, or blown into the eyes as a powder, the victim, within three minutes, becomes a robotic sleepwalker and extremely suggestible. All short-term memory is erased. On a recent trip to Venezuela, an analyst had referenced twelve hundred cases targeting high-profile politicians, U.S. Embassy employees, but it was more commonly used to rob or date-rape tourists.

I knew nothing about the effects of *Ayahuasca* but there was no telling what this particular shaman would cook up.

Tomlinson replied, "The effects depend on the mind traveler. But mild compared to some of the early blotter acid from San Fran in the day. Might put me to sleep, or it could open a whole new world of consciousness. Trust me, hermano, I've ridden out ranker skank than what the Guru has to offer."

"You're sure? Let's back up here. You think he's a con man, too. I can tell."

Tomlinson can occasionally be an arrogant ass, which he proved, saying, "All saints are sinners. Only the destination matters. You're out of your field, Dr. Ford."

I grunted my disapproval. "Bullshit. Stall the guy if you need to, just promise me you won't take a sip of that crap until I get back. I'm serious. Okay?"

He made a noncommittal gesture, meaning, *I'll try.*

I fished one of the little GMRS radios out of my bag and tried to force it into his hands. "Just in case, take this. Channel nineteen or seventeen. In rainforest, it's only good for a couple of miles, but if we get to the beach there's a repeater on Roatán that—"

He interrupted, "No way, man. Electronic devices are taboo as hell at the Guru's ceremonies."

"Damn it, Tomlinson, you don't have to turn the damn thing on. Just take it in case there's an emergency."

Shaking his head, he covered his ears, an adolescent device, that caused me to say, "*Pendejo.* Gad, you're frustrating."

By rote, he responded, "*Bésame me culo,*" smiling.

The village's marina basin was shallow, a thumbnail indent in the trees. Water was murky compared to the narrow, clear water river that swirled past. I sledded my boat off the beach, stepped aboard, and used a paddle to pole toward deeper water.

"Not a sip of that ayahuasca until I get back," I warned him again. "Trying isn't good enough. Do not swallow his goddamn drug crap until I'm with you. Understood?"

Tomlinson nodded in a willful way.

I didn't hear any promises.

FIVE

When a chopper buzzed me a few miles downriver, I knew the one-armed kid had either wounded a soldier or someone with military backing. But it was not a full-on special ops scramble. The chopper wasn't a high-tech Little Bird or a modern assault platform. It was a battered Vietnam-era Huey with a fifty-cal that hung idle from the open portside door.

A flying antique was not a response worthy of a Mayan King or a feared future revolutionary.

Or was it? The Huey hammered past at tree level, tilted, banked and hovered above me. I shaded my eyes, looked up and offered a friendly, touristy wave that showed both hands empty.

In Spanish, an amplified voice ordered, "Shut off your engine. Open your hatches. Do it now."

Smiling, nodding, I complied.

"Do you have weapons? Show us your weapons."

Inside the Huey's open door, a couple of crewmen were on their feet, strapped in, one with an AK, the other with binocs. The hatches I opened contained camping supplies, food, stacks of bottled water. Fishing tackle provided an effective disguise. A fly rod, a net and a long-handled gaff were stored in plain sight. Unseen, however, beneath my baggy mosquito-proof shirt, were two holstered Sig Sauer 9 mm semis. Nor did the crewman question an orange waterproof flare kit that contained six extra mags, Gen 4 night optics, and some other esoteric devices. This included a marine VHF radio and pair of GMRS handhelds, all palm sized, light, with a crappy line-of-sight range in mountains. But useful on open water.

With a goofy grin, hands up and empty, I shrugged as if to acknowledge the stupidity of traveling unarmed on one of the most dangerous coastlines in the Americas.

The PA voice seemed disappointed. "What about the tarp? The green tarp. Open it, let us see. Are you carrying drugs of any type?"

Another submissive shrug. Another shake of the head. The tarp was a rain fly for a jungle hammock I'd packed because I sure as hell didn't want to sleep anywhere near Tomlinson.

When unfolded, the tarp covered the stern of my little boat. Nothing there to see.

The PA voice gave it a final try. "We are looking for children—children in danger. Six boys in a canoe, perhaps. Or on foot. Is very important we find them. Have you seen any children? Or one boy alone—a tiny boy with one arm?"

As the hapless gringo angler, unable to answer because of the noise, I pointed to my ears, my mouth and shook my head again. A wide-armed gesture apologized, *Nope. Sorry, can't help you.*

The Huey tilted nose-down and continued seaward along the river.

No doubt about it now. The feds or mercenaries were after Aléto, the ballsy, trigger-happy kid who, suddenly, had moved a few rungs up the ladder in my estimation. Would a person in authority send a chopper just because one of his guys had been shot in the ass? Unlikely. Not on this coast where more than a dozen people are murdered daily.

No, the feds, or someone with power, had a special interest in the boy. If they caught him, it would mean time in an adult prison—the most optimistic scenario—or worse.

I couldn't let that happen.

On the Bay Islands—Roatán included—locals paint their pangas in festive colors. Multi-toned hulls, red, yellow, blue, with matching folding Bimini tops. It was a floating celebration that flipped a communal bird at generational poverty and the daily tightrope behavior required to stay beneath the radar in a corrupt political system.

Festive colors were not my style. I'd bought the plainest craft I could find, a twenty-one-footer, its swooped bow adorned with a simple Mayan glyph of unknown meaning on a hull that was Clorox-bottle white. What had sold me was the lap-strake hull, two big storage lockers plus an overpowered 70 HP Yamaha outboard that was almost new. No console, no steering wheel. Just bench seats and a throttle. Plenty of room for coils of extra line and ground tackle in case I had to hide the skiff in haste. I'd also clamped a length of PVC to the throttle arm so I could stand up and steer. Visibility is important on an unmarked river with rocky shoals and lots of twists and turns.

Only now, watching the Huey disappear, did it cross my mind that I'd been singled out because my boat was so damn plain. It was unlike any of the hundreds of other fishing pangas used by locals on the Miskito Coast.

A lesson learned too late. On the other hand, the chopper would have reported contact with me to someone in authority somewhere. The unadorned boat containing a smiling tourist would have been deemed benign—pending a closer investigation.

I idled with the current until the chopper was out of sight, then got up to speed after checking my watch. Around the next bend, portside, was the rusty mooring post and the path that led to the lagoon. With no plot charter or GPS I had to make rough calculations in my head. How far could six boys travel in a dugout canoe that, presumably, had only one or two paddles?

It had been fifty-five minutes, give or take, since the boys had fled. The river flowed at a lazy one or two knots. So, be generous and guess they might be five or six miles farther downriver. That meant, if they hadn't already found a hiding spot along the way, the Huey would be on them within minutes.

It was a pressure situation that provided an adrenal buzz that, as only I knew, explained much of my past.

I grabbed the bowline for balance and gunned the throttle. Because of the overpowered Yamaha, the little boat jumped up on its cavitation plate and got squirrely at top speed. It danced and dolphined but that lapstrake hull made it manageable. After an estimated four miles, I negotiated a series of narrow switchbacks. The river widened. Above the tree canopy, I saw the Huey a mile or so ahead. Now in a slow hover, it plowed a classic search grid over a single, small area.

Apparently, they'd spotted the boys. Or they'd spotted something suspicious. I continued to close at speed but hugged the concave bends that usually signal deeper water in backcountry rivers. Overhanging trees and foliage provided cover.

I didn't want to be seen. Aside from that, I had no plan until I had dropped off plane, close enough to feel the chopper's wind wake. That's when I noticed a narrow, watery fissure in the jungle gloom, off to my right. It was the sort of anomaly a child might explore, but an adult would dismiss as an unimportant dead end.

At slow idle, I turned in and ducked, the passageway was so constricted. Vines, an awning of palms and dinosaur-sized hardwoods provided a pillared cavern effect. On both sides, the creek was lined by massive limestone blocks. Moss covered, lichen gray, the walls might have been a geological oddity. But I doubted it. The blocks, a ton or more each, had been masterly fitted to form a seamless conduit. Another oddity was the "creek" itself. Like an aqueduct, it cut a straight swath into an elevated incline.

The boys had taken refuge in what remained of a Mayan or Olmec village. I had seen many similar undiscovered antiquities in the region, too small, too strangled by jungle to be noticed or bothered with by archeological teams.

I killed the engine, tilted the prop clear and used a paddle. The Huey's crisscross clatter failed to drown the rainforest chorus of mating insects, frogs and territorial birds. I poled along in silence and searched for signs of recent passage. There were no telltale machete scars that cleared a path. No broken leaves or vines. I might have been the first human to navigate this cut in centuries—but for one subtle mistake a recent visitor had made.

Golden orb spiders, the size of a man's hand, are ubiquitous in the tropics. Creeks are a favorite ambush space to string their huge, silken webs. If a web is breached, the spiders are quick to spin a replacement. I've slapped my way through many such places only to return an hour later to find a whole fresh series of entrapments.

Here, though, there were no spiderwebs. Just strands of silken detritus that even a jungle-savvy traveler could not avoid leaving behind.

Now I was convinced. The one-armed boy was here, and he damn well knew what he was doing. Probably with five less wary friends, which is why the helicopter had spotted something—movement, perhaps—and had dropped in to search.

Not far ahead, the stone conduit was too narrow to spin the panga around, and full speed in reverse is a piss-poor choice if a fast exit is required. So, while there was still room to maneuver, I swung the boat outward bound, ready to fly, and hitched lines, bow and stern, to a handy branch. I gave it a few seconds and listened while bagging a few necessities.

The chopper had narrowed its grid to an indentation in an umbrella of green. A clearing, perhaps, but too small to serve as an LZ. I got a glimpse of the tail rotator . . . then the bug-eyed front windows. It hovered low and close enough, the distinctive smell—no, the distinctive *taste*—of JP-4 jet fuel wicked its way through the trees.

The boys were somewhere close. They had to be. Probably terrified, huddled in some cranny. When the helicopter settled itself and descended, I got another glimpse of activity. A crewman was being winched down to investigate on foot.

The disastrous possibilities got me moving. The kids were armed with automatic weapons. If Aléto squeezed off a few more warning rounds, that would be the end of him and his friends because the chopper's fifty-caliber would go to work. Heavy lead would prune the trees and kill every living thing beneath.

I had to intervene.

But how?

SIX

To intervene, I needed an excuse, so I invented several on the fly. Carrying a couple of props, I bushwhacked along the aqueduct toward the helicopter. Ahead and to my right, stone artifacts pierced the loam like remnants of a long-abandoned cemetery. Fractured slabs were covered with hieroglyphics. Carvings of fantasy creatures, the walking dead, severed heads in hand, jaguars and a monstrous serpent eating its own tail.

Snakes. The carving provided a better excuse to intrude.

To my left, a tree-dense mound, volcanic in shape, dominated the area. It was rimmed by debris that had once been a symmetrical wall. The wall funneled toward a tiny opening in the mound that might have been a hole dug by animals.

But it wasn't an animal den. I stopped and raised a hand in peace because seated within the opening was Aléto, the one-armed kid, tracking me with an automatic rifle.

After a tense microsecond, I pointed to the helicopter. I motioned for him to stay calm, then touched a finger to my lips. A universal signal known to children and adults: the offer of a covenant that meant, *Quiet,* and also promised secrecy.

Maybe the kid believed it. More likely, he associated me with the tall, skinny sailor he'd either saved or tried to smother. Whatever the reason, the boy lowered the rifle. But he refused to obey when I motioned for him to retreat into what might have been a cave.

Instead, he followed me at a distance, moving from tree to tree, using them as shields—also as aiming posts whenever I looked back.

I didn't look back again because the crewman was on the ground and had just unbuckled his harness. After a thumbs-up, the copter levitated to a safer altitude while the crewman unslung his AK and did a slow three-sixty.

The look on his face when he saw me—surprise, then vague recognition. Maybe he'd been the guy with the binocs. I went through the same tourist act. Dropped the props I'd brought along, smiled and held up empty hands. He approached, his rifle at low ready. Men in a dangerous profession are always, always suspicious. And, for good reason, they are secretly wary if not afraid.

When he was closer, I sensed this one was both. He was young, barely out his teens. Khakis and camo, a body armor vest, a radio mic penned there, and sleeves bloused to reveal a kaleidoscope of tats not dissimilar to Mayan glyphs. No nametag. This caused me to wonder if he was military or paramilitary. The big-time traffickers and narcos—often the same thing—employed mercenaries. Each had money enough to hire a platoon of men and own a couple of old Hueys.

We conversed in Spanish. Had to yell to be heard until the chopper was higher.

"You are the gringo, the tourist in the—"

"Yes," I said and motioned to the river. "My boat's back there. You asked about some children. Said they were in— anyway, that's not the only the reason I'm—"

The man interrupted, "Identification and passport, please."

He noticed the props I'd dropped at my feet—a folding shovel, a bucket and a stainless pole with a locking clamp at the end. A fish gaff. "What are you doing here? There is no fishing in the forest."

I said in a genial, laughing way, "You're telling me. I'm an archaeologist and a . . . well, an amateur herpetologist. But there's another reason aside from those children. You see, I wanted to warn you that—"

"A herpetologist. What is this 'herpetologist'?" He held out an open palm. "Passport please, sir."

"Of course, *Capitán*."

The man liked the sound of that.

I presented my recently issued Cayman Islands passport— one of the least known but most powerful travel documents in the world. It allowed me visa-free travel to one hundred and fifty-five countries around the world. The cover was embossed with a gold diplomatic seal.

He was impressed. "A *diplomático*?"

"*Sí*. Is nothing."

"No, it is a very important position."

He compared the photo to my face. "In the photo, you are not wearing eyeglasses, señor."

The young man had not checked many passports in his short career. Most countries didn't allow glasses. I said, "I've been trying to get used to contact lenses. Want me to take these off?"

"*Nah, nah, es no problema*. Your name is North. Marion North . . . P-h-D." The young man's nod was a salute of respect. "Ah, good day, Dr. Marion North."

North was my legal name as far as a certain agency was concerned.

He returned the passport. "Welcome to Honduras, Dr. North. You said something about the children we are looking for. Six boys. We know they are in the area. You saw them?"

"No. I mean, yes, possibly. But not here. After you contacted me from the helicopter, I saw several kids in a dugout canoe. They were paddling . . . paddling like they were in a hurry. Even when I yelled to them, they wouldn't stop. But that was a mile up the river. They're probably almost to the sea by now. I don't know how you missed them."

The man suffered a moment of distrust but that changed. "Of course. This is useful information. But—" his chin indicated the helo "—from a very low altitude, we're certain we saw at least two small boys hiding beneath the trees. Not a hundred meters from where we are now."

He watched me think for a moment before I arrived at a conclusion. "I know. When I was here yesterday, I met two men. They were very short, both of them. Indios."

The man reasoned, "From the Miskito tribe. Yes. They are often quite short. But that was yesterday."

"Late afternoon," I said. "They'd located a beehive and said they would return today to harvest the honey. I warned them for the same reason I came to warn—"

The man held up a finger for silence when his radio crackled with a request for an update. He touched his shoulder mic and shared this new information with the pilot. Oddly, his syntax became more formal—even guarded—when he informed the pilot that the gringo tourist was actually associated with the Cayman Embassy in La Ceiba.

The pilot's response was a cryptic numeric. A "ten-code" in police jargon.

The Honduran government had no reason to be wary of Cayman Islanders. This suggested I was dealing with mercenaries, not the military.

"Yes, sir. As soon as possible," the young mercenary said into his microphone. "After I get more details and finish my search."

His attention returned to me. "Apologies, Dr. North. You said something about . . . What is a herpetologist?" He began walking toward the volcanic shaped mound. "Archeology, I can be of some assistance, perhaps. There are whole Mayan cities deep in the jungle that no one, I mean no one but a few locals like myself have ever seen. An unimportant little spot like this—" his contempt was obvious "—is *nada* compared to some of the ruins I've discovered. For a small fee, I have a friend who can—"

My turn to interrupt. "Herpetology, that means I collect snakes." I picked up the stainless gaff and bucket as if they were tools of the trade. "Well, amphibians. But venomous snakes are my main interest. That's why I warned those men yesterday."

The young man stopped, one hand on his sidearm. "Snakes? What kind of snakes?"

"Exactly," I said. "When I saw them lower you from the helicopter, I came as fast as I could to warn you, too."

The man made a coughing noise. He looked toward the helicopter and asked again, "What kind? I grew up in this jungle. There's nothing I haven't seen. I don't need to be warned."

"I'm talking about the fer-de-lance," I told him. "You probably call it the 'Terciopelos'—the cutlass-head snake. Yesterday, I logged and photographed five mature specimens. Today, I've already logged three."

"Ah. The peasants know them as 'Señor Cutlass-Head,'" the man responded as if referring to a human being. "What does this mean, 'logged?'"

"That's how many snakes I counted, *Capitán*. Found them in the brush, behind rocks. In weedy areas, like this, where the brush is knee-high, you could step on one, and never even see it until it was too late. One was a monster, had to be eight feet long. All within a few hundred meters of that hill over there. Do you have any idea how rare that is? Fer-de-lance tend to be solitary—until they pair up during mating season."

The young mercenary began edging his way back through the undergrowth toward the pickup zone. "This snake, Señor

Cutlass-Head, this is not good. Years ago, I was very young, a man in our village was bitten. His face turned black. And his screams that night . . . aye-aye-aye. Sweet Mother Mary, the sounds he made, they . . . they didn't bother me, of course. But others still hear them in their dreams . . . I've been told." He looked to me for a professional opinion. "Some claim the man's testicles fell off before he died. Is that possible? What if the poor man had lived?"

I said, "The fer-de-lance is the deadliest snake in Central America. Must be something strange about this area. It attracts them. They're aggressive as hell. Extremely dangerous."

The mercenary, speaking into his coms mic, started walking faster toward his pickup spot.

"What about those children," I called after him. "I hope they're okay. What kind of danger are they in?"

Overhead, the copter pivoted and began a rapid descent. The whump-whump-whumping of rotor blades required the mercenary to raise his voice. "They need to be something . . . isolated, I think we were told. That's it. Isolated."

I followed him. "Can you repeat that? Isolated why?"

When the man turned, he kicked something in the heavy brush and nearly fell. There was a lot of swearing while he adjusted his Molle vest and leather duty belt.

I was beside him by then and saw that he'd stumbled over the rim of a narrow sinkhole. Or what might've been a well dug centuries ago—or a secret passageway. Sunlight filtered down far enough to show a jumble of rocks below.

He swore again and spoke over the noise. "They're probably all kinds of damn snakes down there. You think?"

"That's where I'd hide," I agreed.

"Goddamn, could've broken my neck. I need to mark this spot in case our guys have to come back." From his bag, he dug out some trail tape and tied a long red streamer to the nearest bush. I noted the location of the sinkhole and the clearing. It wasn't far from the backside of the pyramid mound where, I also noticed, woodsmoke lazed through the highest trees where there was no fire. Connecting the sinkhole to the mound was a game trail.

The Huey had just landed.

I asked the mercenary about the children again. Why did they need to be isolated? We had to shout back and forth before he boarded. When my question was finally answered, I waited until the copter was gone before I scanned the trees at the bottom of the mound. Aléto was where I'd left him. The rifle was no longer visible. The mercenary's explanation had been from a distance. I didn't know if the kid had heard or understood what we talked about.

It didn't seem to matter when the boy touched a finger to his lips to confirm the secrecy I had offered.

I responded in kind.

What the mercenary had told me might have been true.

"All of those children need to be isolated, sir. That's what we were told, anyway. It's because they're with this crazy, one-armed boy. Today—only a few hours ago—the little psycho stole a rifle and shot one of our guys in the butt."

Nothing too implausible about that until the man added, "Not just dangerous. He's got a disease, possibly contagious. The one-armed kid, he's a leper."

SEVEN

There's a game we play after unexpected events, from fatal collisions to a trivial missed connection. The What if? game. What if we'd turned left, not right? What if we had lingered at the airport? What if, instead of dismissing a spam call, we had not answered to hear the voice of a long-lost love?

The human mind seeks order in the random, rocket sled passage that is life. To be at the mercy of an indifferent universe is scary as hell. So we defy the existential and embrace kindlier fictions by asking, What if . . . ?

Down the road, we hope, destiny or God might at least give us a damn hint about the best choice.

I should have hurried back to the tree house to check on Tomlinson. Instead, I had spent too much time among Mayan ruins, at the mouth of what I now suspected was the entrance to a pyramid, not a cave. I'd done my best to create a bond with the one-armed boy and his small militia of friends. If Aléto had leprosy, he needed medical attention. From the looks of the others, they all did.

The meeting had not gone well at first.

Children who have been abused, abandoned, and abducted

as slave labor are not easily won over. They are jumpy, distrustful. Their every decision is based on dread. Frightened people, young or old, battle an all-consuming instinct that urges them to flee or to finally stop, turn, and bare their canine teeth.

Children are doubly sensitized. When overwhelmed by fear, preteens are either painfully timid—or very, very dangerous.

The youngsters Aléto had befriended were perilously close to the latter. The social safety net—orphanages, parents, agencies—had betrayed them all. These kids had had enough. They were done running.

This was not a snap judgment on my part.

I'd spent a patient two hours among the ruins of their lost world. So much time that I hadn't considered the consequences. A more productive approach to fate is to pose questions *in advance* of a calamity.

I should have asked myself:

What if Tomlinson drinks the hallucinogenic before I get back?

What if the Guru Shaman is not only a thief but a con man with criminal ties to foreign traffickers—Russians among them?

A more absurd possibility was that my pal, doped up like a zombie and easily manipulated, had followed his shaman guide to another beating. Or to his death?

Ridiculous? Of course. Tomlinson was a hallucinogenic warhorse. A seasoned vet, one of the founders of the movement. There was no need for me to rush away from children in need.

That's why it was hours later, in a sunset mist, I finally secured my boat to the rusted mooring. It was closer to the lagoon than the uphill hike from the village. I lugged a backpack of overnight necessities along a path that was a mild incline. It twisted and turned its way to the waterfall precipice.

Tomlinson's tree house was visible on switchbacks.

Halfway up, I dumped the backpack. I sat on the ground and enjoyed the view. The waterfall sprayed rainbow streamers. A lagoon of emerald, in filtered light, transitioned to gold, to bronze then peach. It was a pulsing process like the chromatophore transformation of octopi and certain fish. I snapped photos to impress my toddler son, Isaak, and my ex-fiancée, Capt. Hannah Smith, when I got back to Florida.

If Hannah allowed me into the house after I'd abandoned her at the altar.

Marion Ford, I thought. *You fool, you fool.*

This gave me many personal failings to ponder.

Another twenty minutes was wasted before I shouldered my load and continued upward.

The backpack could have been a hell of a lot heavier. Most of my food supplies had been donated to Aléto and his friends. This included more hungry young bellies than expected, all children near middle school age. Three girls, three boys, plus the five boys I'd seen earlier. Their faces, one by one, had sprouted from the narrow entranceway like mushrooms sprouting after a heavy rain.

Half an hour it took before all eleven kids ventured out. But only after Aléto had summoned them. And only after two of the boys, both carrying automatic rifles, had braced their one-armed leader.

Dangerous. Yes, some of those children were not just ready, they were itching to cross the line into violence.

The rest of the story, I was eager to share with my pal, Tomlinson. About presenting the kids with two dozen MREs, military Meals Ready to Eat. Entrée portions, plus desserts. A full day's supply of calories in a single vacuum-packed, rubberized bag. That plus a box of snacks, and cases of Gatorade and water.

My interaction with Aléto and his lieutenants had gotten off to a rough start. But a fire and hot food had allowed me to stay and engage in a less hostile conversation.

There was another fun nugget to share with Tomlinson: Aléto had asked about the "tall sailor with the soul of a monk."

"You spoke to him?" I'd asked the boy.

The kid's response was, "Some can look into a person's . . . his soul without words. A good man, even dead, cannot die before his time. I read this in a book."

That was all. But the remark had just enough spiritual chutzpah to bring a grin to my friend's face.

I was thinking about that—how best to set up the story— when I hopscotched rocks across the creek and crossed beneath coconut palms. In the cloud forest, darkness doesn't wait for sunset. A shadowed hegemony descends, indifferent to stars, yet brightens even the frailest of manmade light. Candles, oil lamps included.

That's what stopped me before I got to the tree house steps. The windows, the front door—which was open— communicated an uninhabited darkness. The human ear adapts to jungle. It mutes the seesaw cicada clamor. I stood, I listened. I moved beneath the house and cupped my ears.

No creak of human weight above. No movement, no voices. *Sonuvabitch*, I thought. *He's gone.*

I didn't want to accept that possibility.

More likely, my pal was asleep. Or he'd passed out after the *ayahuasca* ceremony. His spiritual guide, the so-called Guru, had probably split after yet another robbery.

I stashed the backpack, drew my weapon, and hollered Tomlinson's name several times. It startled a couple of birds from their roosting hideaways. An animal with some bulk slow-footed toward me from the brush. It was Roy, the swayback gelding. A bad harbinger. Tomlinson claimed he never ventured into the jungle without Roy.

With a tactical flashlight, I searched beneath the house. I probed the windows and the open door. The door had been knocked lopsided from its leather hinges.

This suggested a drunken exit. Or a violent intruder.

I killed the light and crept up the steps in darkness. The first floor—a fifteen-by-fifteen cubicle—was cleared without entering. The hammock hung unmolested, the sparse seating unchanged. The uppermost room, though, was a shambles of recent activity. Another broken bamboo door invited me in.

The flashlight was needed. I swept the area before slipping inside. A circle of candles had guttered themselves into a waxen mess on the Mayan altar. Chairs were overturned, a shelf of canned goods were scattered on the floor amid beer cans and fragments of a shattered kerosene lamp.

I was surprised the place hadn't caught fire.

A wooden slab served as a makeshift table. A cooking pot sat on a propane stove. An ashtray showed the men had smoked a couple of joints before getting serious about their spiritual quest.

The cooking pot contained bits of leafy twigs and an inch of caramel black liquid. I leaned, I sniffed, I winced and recoiled.

The whole damn room had the musky stink of skunks and bitter coffee.

Ayahuasca?

I exited onto the bamboo porch. Air freshened. Forest mist floated a cusp of orange moon. What Tomlinson had called his "tiki bar" was a thatched awning over a slate counter. The slate might have been scavenged from a one-room school. It was a place to sit and drink and doodle.

My pal had done some doodling with an erasable marker. Much of it was smeared by what might have been drunken inattention.

Or had it been smeared intentionally?

On the bamboo deck an empty rum bottle lay among a

sodden towel and other garbage bag litter. With a boot, I explored the mess, then focused on the counter. Still legible were sketches of architectural precision. Corner joists that interlocked with beams. A pulley system with metric numbers and notes in Tomlinson's elegant hand.

Had the rest been erased by the discarded towel?

I toggled my flashlight from white to green to infrared. The smear remained a smear until I tried ultraviolet light.

The slate fluoresced with the ghost of a recent doodle. It was a message to me, but not in elegant cursive. As if suffering an electric jolt, Tomlinson had scribbled four spidery words in haste.

Something else fluoresced that did not require ultraviolet detection. A fresh blood splatter on the counter, and a steady drip-drip trail that led to or from the stairs.

I let implications of the blood, and those four words brand themselves onto my frontal lobe.

I thought, *A harmless psychedelic herb, my ass.*

I thought, *Burundanga, Devil's Breath.*

The zombie drug—scopolamine—flashed to mind.

I wondered, *What if I'd arrived an hour earlier? How much lead time do they have? Goddamn it, Tomlinson could be dead by now.*

My reaction was physiological—an instant narrowing of focus with cold-blooded intent. It was a transformation I had experienced many times in many parts of the world.

I reread the message and mouthed the four words that Tomlinson had written.

"*Find us. Kill him.*"

I thought, *I will.*

EIGHT

The flare kit in my boat, among other things, contained a quad-lensed night optics device. NODs in tactical jargon. Night vision goggles that were panoramic binocs. The newest generation. Thermal imaging fused with infrared and standard peripheral light-gathering technology.

I've used a lot of NV optics in my time, but nothing compared to this gift from a British friend and a knighted inventor, Dr. Max Weatherby. Were it not for Mad Max, as he's known to a few, an unnamed agency would not have recruited me, nor created an alias and issued me a diplomatic passport from one of the British Overseas Protectorate Territories. In this case, the Cayman Islands.

The NODs device clipped to a headband that I didn't need right away. The moon, three days shy of full, had breached the treetops. And the nearby village was still awake when I boated upriver, hoping to stop the thieving Shaman from fleeing the area with Tomlinson aboard.

Too late. The Boston Whaler was gone.

I grounded the panga and hopped out to see cooking fires and shadow people. I questioned the closest male adult in Spanish.

Had he seen the tall gringo who had built the tree house? Had he seen the Whaler's owner leave?

Tomlinson had been right about the reticence of villagers when it came to strangers.

I got a shrug and muffled disclaimers.

"You had to have heard the boat's engine start," I insisted. "How long ago? A few minutes ago? An hour?"

"An hour," the man admitted. "Maybe more. Maybe two."

"How many men?" I asked. "One man or two? Sir, it is important that I know. I'll pay for information."

"So many questions. So many. *Two men*," the man snapped. "We don't need your money. Just go, leave us in peace."

I had offended him. It was a clumsy mistake I would not make again.

I pushed off and glided away.

How far could a small Boston Whaler travel in an hour? Two hours? If Wingo Bogdan, or whatever the Guru's name was, knew the area well, hell, he could be halfway to the sea by now. Even traveling in darkness on a rocky unmarked river, he and Tomlinson were too far ahead to take by surprise.

The place to start, I decided, was where the Guru lived. The name had been stenciled on the Whaler's hull. But where the hell was *Shaman Eco Lodge?*

My only nautical chart was under the bench seat. It was scaled for deep water, coastal mariners, Honduras to Belize. At slow idle, I folded the thing into a napkin square and dimmed my flashlight. This river, unnamed, was a miniscule line that snaked nineteen miles to the confluence of several rivers and the beach village of Rio Coco. The Bay Islands, where I'd bought my boat, was near touristy Roatán, another twenty miles across open water.

There were no icons to indicate expensive eco-resorts between me and the coast. No dot marked the village I'd just left. But I had made a few notes during my crossing and the trip upriver. I'd X-ed the wreckage of Tomlinson's sailboat. It lay scattered on a reef off the island of Utila. On the river, I'd also noted two creek entrances where there was beach enough for locals to hawk fruit and drinks to the rare passing traveler. The hawkers had to live somewhere, I reasoned. That suggested unmarked settlements of some type were nearby.

Landing strips or water access only, Tomlinson had said about private, upscale hideaways. But resorts required workers. And workers also had to live somewhere.

Two creek entrances. I locked their locations in memory and used my thumb to guesstimate the distance between them and the ten miles or so that separated the first creek from the village I'd just left. The best way to measure progress was my watch, so I twisted the bezel to the minute hand.

Twenty-one hundred hours plus ten—9:10 p.m. in civilian time on a tropic night in October.

I don't believe in luck, good or bad. This was the beginning of a process. Flashlight off, the chart stowed, I adjusted the NOD binocs over my eyes and touched the function panel. Moonlight shadows became a glowing green panorama. A cloudless cloud forest brightened with precise three-dimensional details. With the NODs, visibility was better than at high noon.

Holding the bowline for balance, I torqued the throttle wide open and rocketed downriver. A serpentine course lay ahead, a watercourse in moonlight that tracked Tomlinson's long-gone wake.

I would find him. And my face would be the last thing his captor saw before the Shaman vanished.

For a man who doesn't believe in luck, I knew I'd gotten lucky when, after following both creek entrances to dead ends, I noticed a detail I'd missed on my upriver trip in broad daylight.

It was a small wooden rectangle nailed to a tree. Tough to see. It was inland where the river looped to avoid what appeared to be a stagnant cove. The topography was familiar. I was only a mile or less from where, earlier, I'd surprised the trigger-eager one-armed boy and his band of urchins.

After swinging the boat around, I coasted in for a closer look. No wonder I'd missed the damn thing. It was a sign intended solely for locals. Intentionally made innocuous to discourage curious pests.

In Spanish, it read:

Fruit and Fish Deliveries Only.

Others Will Be Arrested!

I made an approximate X on my useless chart and idled into what I'd accurately dismissed as a stagnant backwater. But, ahead, there was an opening. A narrow gash in a barricade of trees. No PVC markers. No more signs. Why would there be? Backyard farmers and handline fishermen didn't need guidance to whatever destination that lay ahead.

I had a good feeling about this. Only isolated restaurants or hideaway resorts require food hand-delivered by neighboring peasants. And isolated restaurants never survive for long.

More evidence that an eco lodge might lie ahead.

When my propeller began to kick a sulphury stink, I tilted the engine and used a paddle. The gash in the trees widened after a switchback. I still had to duck a few branches but not many. Machetes or saws had been used to hack heavy limbs and buttress roots to keep the conduit navigable. Easy for hardened locals to deal with but not a cheery ingress when it came to monied tourists.

Somewhere ahead, I felt certain, a landing strip adjoined an exclusive eco-oasis. A fly-in destination that, encircled by jungle, was an island unto itself.

The channel ran straight and narrow for another fifty yards,

plenty deep enough to use the motor. It was not worth risking the noise, however, because ahead was a larger sign, this
one commercial grade with reflective lettering in Spanish and
English:

Employees and Deliveries Only
No Trespassing! Guard Dog on Duty!

I clenched my teeth and thought, *To hell with luck.*

I paddled a few more strokes then drifted. What if this was
the wrong eco lodge? Tomlinson had said there were several in
the area, and dozens more between here and the Yucatan. Or,
worse, what if I'd stumbled onto some kind of secret military
installation? That possibility had yet to be considered.

I didn't fear an awkward confrontation with feds. Hell,
claiming to be an American tourist was excuse enough for just
about any brand of dumbass, clueless behavior. Plus—I had
to remind myself—I carried a diplomatic passport. A British
Protectorate passport, true, yet it still guaranteed immunity
after a phone call or two.

That wasn't what bothered me. I was hesitant because, in
my long career, I'd never had to shoot or harm a guard dog. I
didn't want to start now.

The hypocrisy regarding why I'd come armed with two
semiauto nines and a knife was not lost on me. What was the
difference between an unscrupulous man and a dangerous
dog? On the Darwinian scale, a few telling qualities tilted
the balance in favor of dogs. Loyalty. Innocence. Purity of
instincts. But, hell, if fairness had any sway in the natural
world, lions would not eat vegetarians.

On the other hand, what if I'd found the Guru's hideaway?
A guard dog warning sign was a common security fiction, so
I pressed onward. First, though, I selected a sound suppressor made for me by Thompson Machine near Tallahassee and
threaded it onto a full-sized Sig Sauer P226. The suppressor's

baffle system, if I had to shoot, would dampen the report to an air rifle *thunk*.

After a few more minutes of paddling, I rounded a bend to see a commercial dock where three small boats were tied. Two Boston Whalers and a tin can garbage scow. All were branded with *Shaman Eco Lodge* logos.

Maybe there was something to be said for luck after all.

I clove-hitched the panga to a piling and did a kit check. I didn't want to bumble into a busy resort dressed like a jungle ninja. Extra clothes were stored in a hatch along with standard safety gear. To conceal the weapons I carried, a baggy shirt was required but a collared polo was more innocuous. Boots had to stay but pleated khakis and a ball cap completed my tourist pretense. The Cyborg NODs and a plastic twelve-gauge flare gun went into my Maxpedition bag before I stepped onto the dock as if I owned the place. The Whalers were moored stern first. I leaned and touched both motor cowlings. One was still warm from recent use.

Wingo Bogdan, the miscreant shaman was here. Somewhere close.

But had Tomlinson survived the trip?

NINE

I grabbed my gear and got my bearings. The dock was attached to an expansive acreage carved from the forest maze.
The grounds were landscaped, a plantation of coconut palms
and flowers. Thatched cabins overlooked a dip pool and areas
manicured for meditation and yoga. The centerpiece was a
communal lodge where, beneath a tile roof, most of the windows were dark, although a few flickered with a candle-like
glow.

I had expected music, a bonfire. Dancing silhouettes and
tiki-torch walkways and tribal laughter. It was early for vaca-
tioners. Only 10:30 on a Thursday night, the moon high and
Nordic blue. But the facility appeared to be deserted save for
a couple of people standing, smoking outside the lodge as if
awaiting a bus. Neither was tall enough to be Tomlinson. One
might have been the Shaman, but I doubted it when, from the
distance, came the baritone barking of a dog and the back-up
beep-beep-beep of a golf cart.

My guess was, the Guru wasn't the type to walk when there
was free transportation.

Several empty golf carts sat in a line nearby. Security was

lax here. I selected one, turned the key, hit the lights, and began a non-covert search.

To my left, a windsock marked a narrow corridor that was scraped clean of foliage. An airstrip. I gauged the length as I drove. More than a half mile of manicured grass as flat as asphalt. Plenty of distance for a midsized commercial prop plane to land and off-load twenty or thirty passengers.

But why?

From what I'd seen, Shaman Eco Lodge was a boutique business and business wasn't exactly booming. I circled six empty cabins that, at peak season, might house a dozen guests. In the lodge, vacant windows suggested room for half a dozen more.

Eighteen wealthy rollers on a spiritual quest wouldn't cover the upkeep for a month, let alone a profitable year. The workforce needed to keep the property trim, in good repair, and manicured would require dozens of underpaid locals.

More likely, underpaid, underage locals.

"Foreign investors," Tomlinson had said.

No doubt.

I'd done my best to stay a safe distance from the lodge, the idle smokers and any unseen staff. That became impossible when a gas-powered security cart, headlights bright, appeared from behind the lodge and sped toward me.

With a friendly smile fixed on my face, I stopped, sat calmly and waved hello. I'd been right about lax security. A bearded, sumo-sized man waved in return. He got out and approached, the leather of his gun belt creaking. The back of his jacket read *SEGURIDAD*. On his breast pocket was a small golden badge.

"Sorry about the delay. Generator problems," he said. "You must be with the transport company. Yes?"

My smile broadened.

"I thought so. We were expecting their rep earlier, much earli—" Puzzled, the man paused. "How did you get here? For two hours, we've had no electric, no landing lights. I did not hear a plane. Your plane, did it already take off?"

He spoke English with an accent. Not Chinese. More musical. Taiwanese or Filipino . . . there were many possibilities.

"Had to come by boat," I said.

"Boat?" He looked toward the dock. "Why boat? How?"

"It's a long story. There's a village upriver. No cell service, nothing. I had a hell of a time finding this place."

"By boat," he repeated, still puzzled. His handheld radio squawked. "Hang on a sec. This might be your people calling."

The security guy stepped away, but not far enough that I didn't hear snatches of conversation. Something about the generator. A broken lock. Wires cut. Vandalism and theft. A couple of guns and ammunition had been stolen.

The guard had not offered his name. He had not imposed by asking mine. A red flag. People engaged in a criminal activity do not ask personal questions.

I assessed his sidearm. A revolver, cheap plastic grips, in a holster designed for safety not a gunfight.

"Fine, fine," the man said into the radio as he returned, then spoke to me. "Honduras. The *Mara* gangs here. Criminals, all criminals and killers. Even in the middle of the jungle, they come, they rob and do bad shit. Better, I think, they are locked up and shipped—"

Mindful of what he was about to say, the guard switched tacks. "—but we are ready now. Your transport aircraft is only ten, twelve kilometers out."

I nodded as if hearing good news.

"Watch this," he said then pressed the radio's transmit key. "Make ready for arrival. ETA very soon," he told someone who had to be nearby.

There was an explosion of light. A half mile of LEDs lined the empty runway where a ground mist swirled like smoke.

"As promised. Everything on schedule. Your plane will be

in and out fast as promised." The man was beaming. He was also fishing for a big tip. "I must go now. Unlock the doors. Would you like to come along?"

I palmed a fold of hundred-dollar bills into his hand. "Sure. Why not. Mind if I ride with you? Your golf cart looks faster."

That got a smile. "It is not a golf cart. It is a four-wheel drive ATV. Even used, they're hard to find in the jungle where only peasants live. Nice, huh?"

All-terrain vehicle, I translated. "Yes, it is."

He started the engine. I slid in, passenger side. As if an afterthought, I added, "By the way, I was told to say hello to a gentleman here. A man named—if I can remember it—I think his name is Wingo Bogdan. Maybe you can point out where he stays."

"Who?"

I repeated the name.

The name didn't register. The guard had peeked at the hundred dollar bills. It wasn't an act.

I tried another route. "Maybe I got it wrong. He does the, what-do-you-call, ceremonies. Spiritualism. He's what they call a shaman."

That did register. "Ah, why didn't you say so? That is what he is called here, Shaman. Or Guru. Sometimes, Teacher, but—" the security guard reconsidered as we bounced along "—he is, well, not demanding. Let us say the man is sensitive about being treated with respect. As he deserves. He is part owner of this resort. Owner of several such places along the coast."

"You mean he's got a big ego." I said this as a test.

"Well . . . yes. But no. Not really."

"Don't blame you. The guy's your boss. Probably a rich prick. My boss is the same way. Come on, I just trusted you. Tell the truth."

When the guard laughed, his sumo wrestler belly drummed

the steering wheel. "Okay, yes. Is the way these rich men are. Even if the staff knew his name, we wouldn't risk getting fired."

"That bad, huh?"

The man's smile vanished. "Sir, you have no idea how . . . but I shouldn't say more. I was very fortunate to be hired here as the head of security. There were many qualified applicants."

"I bet there were," I said. "A lot of men would love to wear that gold badge of yours."

"You can say that twice," the man agreed. "But few could meet the requirements. It is a very important job. I don't want to lose it."

He pointed to a house that was a smaller version of the main lodge. Lights were on inside, shades drawn. "There. The Shaman lives there. See the hangar? That's his private plane."

I had to restrain myself. The temptation was to bail without an excuse, pick the back door lock, and take Bogdan by surprise. Then find Tomlinson. But the timing was all wrong. Sooner or later, I would have to disarm and duct-tape this sumo-sized guard who had an important job. Not a problem—but leaving a witness behind would be a problem.

I said, "Nice little plane. Looks like a Cessna One-eighty-two. What I don't get is, how does the guy make any money? You've got no guests here. The place is empty."

The question seemed to set off an alarm in the guard's head. "You . . . you don't know?"

I realized I'd screwed up, so I took a chance. "I'm talking about the eco lodge business. Not the other . . . his other investments."

"Ah, of course," the security guard said, then explained how the schedule worked. Twice a month, guests arrived only on Friday afternoons and departed at midday on Tuesdays. This allowed two free days bimonthly for staff time off.

"And the Shaman's other project," the guard added. He looked to confirm I understood.

"Got it. Today's Thursday," I said. "No guests. My boss, the asshole? He never tells me a damn thing."

I expected the man to smile. He didn't.

"Something wrong?" I asked.

"It's just that . . . Can I tell you something?"

"Sure. No need for our bosses to know."

He gripped the steering wheel tight. "I hate this part of my job. Shouldn't complain. What we're doing is where the real money comes from, and I've got a family to feed. But by God, twice a month I get a sick feeling. Can't sleep and I feel sick the whole next day. Got kids myself, man. Know what I mean?"

Maybe. I had suspected what I'd stumbled into. Now my certainty was about seventy-thirty. Drugs, I'd hoped. Trafficking coke or meth or fentanyl. But the odds weren't good.

I looked back at Wingo Bogdan's house. It sat in a private clearing, screened by trees. An isolated target, ideal for a quick grab and bag.

Not yet, but soon.

I was turning to refocus on buildings that lay ahead when the guard said, "Here she comes. Your plane. This is the only part I *do* like. Seeing a plane that size land."

Christ, it was an old twin prop DC-3, flying low over the trees and lit up like the *Starship Enterprise*. The aircraft was an aged vet of wars, and commerce and probably pot hauling from Miami's Rust Alley days. Its twin landing spots threw two-mile beams. They illuminated our vehicle and a cluster of structures to the right of the runway's bitter end.

"This as close as we should get for now," the security guard said. He parked the ATV next to a corrugated maintenance barn and what looked like a steel container from a cargo ship. A man in a hoodie was there, battling a big padlock, trying to get the container's double doors open. Nearby, stacked atop each other, were several plastic cages that were overfilled with squawking, complaining birds—scarlet macaws and other rarities, most likely.

"Who's your helper?" I asked.

"One of our maintenance guys. He has a slow brain and can't speak," the guard said. "Nights like this, he looks forward to acting like the boss. Me, I like to stay back and not be seen."

"Smart," I said. "A container that size, let the man enjoy his work."

The guard explained it was actually only half of a cargo container, not full sized. "That's all the Shaman says we need for now. He's owner of a couple of other lodges. Says they do an even bigger business there." He reconsidered. "At least that's what I overheard him say to someone. The shaman doesn't waste his time talking the help."

The DC-3 touched down, kicked a vapor wake, decelerated, then roared as full flaps and brakes were applied. A tidy pirouette positioned the aircraft outward bound. A boarding ladder was deployed from the doorway. It gave me time to shoot a quick video and note the partially obscured ID number on the tail.

The pilot didn't budge from his seat—unless he was one of two armed men who had donned ski masks before scrambling to the ground.

"Ándale, ándale!" one yelled in Spanish, but with a guttural, Russian accent. The other ran to the container where the doors were finally open.

This was not a drug deal. The maintenance guy snapped a ramp into place, then hustled away for a better view. The masked men took charge. They began off-loading the container's human cargo—people who, after being locked in darkness, were blinded by the sudden dazzling lights. Women in soiled maid's attire, kids in their teens or younger, mostly female, came stumbling out, weeping, pleading, a collective moan of helplessness. I'd counted most of them—eleven—before I'd seen enough.

"Goddamn it, we can't let this happen," I said to the security guard. I'd drawn my sound suppressed pistol but kept it hidden beside my leg.

He had averted his eyes from what was going on but turned with a look of surprise. "What? You should be out there supervising. That's your job. Count heads, get the money and give it to me. You *do work* for the transport company, correct?"

I said, "No one will ever know. Goddamn it, I need someone to cover my back. You said you hate this part of the job. Prove it."

The security guy pulled away. "Who . . . who the hell are you? I've got a family, kids. Just be cool, get the money. Stop screwing around."

With sly fingers he unsnapped his holster.

I brought the Sig pistol into view and didn't raise my voice. "Okay, here's how it's going to go. Put your hands on the steering wheel. Do it now or I'll shoot you in the knee."

He saw my expression and immediately complied. I unholstered the cheap revolver, emptied the cylinder, and tossed it on the ground.

I gestured with my jaw. "Get out of here. Run. Get the maintenance guy and take him with you. I swear to God, I'll shoot you both in the ass or the leg—*somewhere*. Don't make me kill you."

There was so much chaotic crying among the captives, no one noticed when I shoved the security guard and his pal toward the woods. The masked men had their backs to me, busy trying to herd their victims toward the DC-3.

I hadn't come to kill a couple of grunt employees. In the bed of the ATV was a small crowbar. They didn't hear me approach from behind. With one swing, I broke the closest guy's collarbone. He dropped to the ground. When his partner spun around, I was there with the Sig aimed at his forehead.

"Arms wide, let your weapon fall and kick it away," I ordered.

"Wait. Who in hell are you—"

I shot the man in the left foot before he could finish.

He choked back a howl and jettisoned the rifle. It was the *Ándale, ándale* Russian guy. On the back of his left hand was an ornate orthodox cross in blue.

The kidnap victims stood frozen. I started to say something calming, but the world suddenly exploded with a noise that caused me to duck low, then to dive for cover.

It took a slow moment to make sense of what was happening.

Someone nearby had opened fire on the airplane. At least two unseen shooters. It was a full-automatic assault that strafed the fuselage and punctured the cabin windows.

I rolled to my butt, weapon up and ready, but only watched because the shooters were now targeting the plane's cockpit. Three round bursts from at least two assault rifles. Twin muzzle flashes pocked the darkness not far away. It went on and on, then suddenly stopped.

The pilot panicked anyway. He got the plane rolling— another surprise that added to the chaos. The guys in ski masks got up, hands high. After a beat, they decided I wasn't going to shoot, then hobbled as fast as they could to the dangling boarding ladder. By the time they got the door closed, the DC-3 was already off the ground.

After that, an abrupt silence magnified the shock of being ambushed.

Thirteen people, teenage girls and several children, got up slowly. They were unhurt but confused. Where were their captors? Was it safe to flee? They didn't know what to do until someone in the trees hollered in Miskito patois and waved for them to follow.

I looked, I squinted. I saw who the person was.

"It's okay. Go home, find your families," I called to the recent captives. "If you need help—" I hesitated "—if you need help, your friends out there will know what to do."

As a group, they walked and walked faster, then began to run toward what I could now see was a small tribe of rescuers.

I'll be damn, I thought, and smiled.

Among them was a small boy. A one-armed boy with a rifle slung over his malformed shoulder. He also carried one of the traditional woven bags that were common in Guatemala.

"Aléto!" I yelled his name, but the kid, after a glance, ignored me.

I followed the group until my attention shifted to the roar of the Shaman's small Cessna airplane. The damn thing was taxiing in haste toward the landing strip. Pursuit was pointless, but I hopped into the guard's ATV and tried anyway.

I had just enough time to get a glimpse of Tomlinson's right-seat profile before the asshole Shaman babied the yoke back and the Cessna took off.

My luck didn't improve when I drove to the asshole's house and picked the back door lock.

The guard dog I had feared was inside, waiting.

TEN

"At least tie me up," the security guard urged. "When the Shaman gets angry, I wouldn't be the first employee he's had beaten with a whip. Or shipped off to—where do you think? As slaves, I guess. And, my God, you released all his macaws—birds that sell for four thousand apiece, so at least a half million. Señor, someone's going die for this."

The guard's name was Kazz. Chinese, he said via a Honduran father. He had surprised me on Bogdan's back porch. Could have shot me with the revolver he'd retrieved, but figured I was FBI or something, so had offered to help in exchange for leniency.

I'd told him I would do what I could. I meant it.

Kazz was a man with the remnants of a conscience. He had buddied-up with the guard dog—a nasty-looking Chow—while I'd gone from room to room collecting photo evidence. I was zipping my tactical bag as I exited which is why he feared he might be blamed for whatever I'd stolen.

"Bugs would eat you alive if I tie you up," I said. "I didn't take anything valuable, didn't move anything. Your boss won't even know I was here, so stop worrying."

But the security guard was worried. We returned to his ATV. He got in on the passenger side.

"I'd prefer mosquitos to losing my job or a beating. The Shaman will know. Like a witch, that man finds out everything."

I started the engine. "Is there a phone at the lodge?"

"In the office. When it works."

I pulled up to the front steps, and told Kazz, "Take me to the office."

We had already agreed on terms.

The lodge smelled of incense and Pine-Sol cleaner. In the office, files were locked within commercial grade steel doors. Not easily breached but I carried a pocket SouthOrd Professional lock picking tool. It included a lever bar, and a variety of foldout rakes. I opened folders, photographed more documents, relocked the drawers, then sat at the desk with a copy of the Cessna's registration, a thumb drive, some pornographic snapshots, and tabloid clippings from Tegucigalpa.

Bogdan was a scalp hunter—a sexual predator—and his fake Shaman act had paid off in a big way. The probable sources of his income could be inferred. Blackmail, I guessed. Spiritualism and psychotropic drugs had probably played a role. Bogdan had his hooks in several Honduran politicos, including one of the wealthiest men in Honduras, an old-time tycoon who, until his death a month ago, had owned a two-hundred-thousand-hectare palm oil farm, and a bunch of other food and petroleum related businesses.

I locked the name in memory: Miguel Z. Coronado.

The tabloids referred to Coronado as "the Palm Plantation Owner of Death"—the sort of lurid prose that was typical in Central America. He was accused of taking part in violent land grabs and dozens of murders of campesino activists in Honduras' Aguán Valley as he sought to expand his palm oil fortune. Diplomatic cables published by WikiLeaks showed the United

States knew of Coronado's role in cocaine trafficking but continued funding Honduras' military and police, who reportedly worked closely with Coronado's guards.

The man's death had left a political power vacuum, and the ambitious Shaman from Minnesota appeared to be eager to step in.

Sitting at Bogdan's desk, I dialed a number from memory—a direct line to a woman with a Caymanian accent. I summarized what had just happened, then gave her the tail number of the Cessna and a partial number from the DC-3.

"All noted, Dr. North. Can you send a locator pin?"

I said, "I can try. Find that Cessna, it's urgent. Tomorrow I'll make contact from somewhere near Roatán," and hung up.

Kazz trailed me out the door, down the steps to the ATV. He was having a meltdown.

"Did you steal from . . . ? Someone will notice if anything is missing from the office. And all those birds gone. I have to know. He will have someone kill me if—"

I silenced him with a warning look. Didn't speak until we were driving toward the dock where my boat was tied.

"Kazz, you need to calm down and get your story straight. Two key points about tonight: You didn't do anything wrong. And I was never here. Get that through your head."

"But, if you stole something, what if the Shaman—"

I interrupted, "Doesn't matter. Blame it all on whoever shot up the cargo plane. You, only one guy against gangbangers with automatic weapons? He can't blame you for that."

"You don't know him," Kazz insisted. "He'll fire me or punish me for not shooting back."

"That's all you're worried about?"

"No . . . but how will I explain not trying to protect the lodge?"

It was a problem easily solved.

I did a U-turn and parked the ATV in our previous spot

by the maintenance barn and the empty birdcages. I told him step-by-step what to do next.

We changed seats. He pulled his revolver, aimed at the runway and fired six rounds. I scattered his empty brass on the ground, driver's side, while he reloaded.

"Do it again, same thing," I directed.

"More?"

"As evidence," I said. "Shoot all six, dump the brass, then follow me."

When Kazz had emptied the cylinder, we walked about twenty yards away from the ATV.

"Get behind me," I told him. I had the sound suppressed Sig Sauer out, trigger finger parallel the slide.

"Wait? Why do you need a gun?"

"Because this has to be convincing," I replied.

"But you're not going to shoot—"

I took aim, saying, "No need to put your fingers in your ears," before shattering the ATV's windshield with two rounds. *Thump-thump.* Then divided a few more rounds between the driver's seat and the engine cowling.

A final flourish was to shoot out a runway LED before I thumbed the de-cock lever, popped a fresh mag, and holstered the pistol.

"Quite a weapon, huh? You just survived one hell of a gunfight, Kazz. Congratulations. No way the Shaman's going to think you ran away now."

"*Oh no,*" the man said softly. I was walking back to the ATV. He still had his fingers in his ears. He hadn't moved a step.

I turned. "What's wrong? Your boss has made a pile of money. He'll have it fixed or buy a new one."

"Oh no," Kazz said again. He stared at the ATV. "That's the only reason I got hired."

"What the hell are you talking about?"

Finally, he unplugged his ears. "When they were hiring,

those were the only requirements. To be the head security guard, you had to supply your own equipment. I already owned this badge and a pistol. But the ATV belongs to my father-in-law."

I would have said it myself, *Oh no*, if the vehicle hadn't started on the first try. And if my money belt hadn't contained a few more hundred-dollar bills.

"I don't think five hundred American dollars will cover it," the security guard complained when he dropped me at the dock.

"Look on the bright side," I told him. "When the shit hits the fan—and it will—I'm the only person who can keep your ass out of jail. You work for me now. Is that clear?"

He recognized the expression on my face.

"Yes, sir," he said.

I got in my boat and headed upriver toward the tree house, accompanied by a westwarding moon. I stopped only once. It was at the entrance to the volcano-shaped mound. I didn't expect the one-armed boy to be there, but thermal imaging showed him peeking out at my engine noise from the bushes.

He had no knowledge of high-tech NODs. I assumed he believed he was invisible. I assumed there was no way he could recognized me.

Yet, he stepped out and called in Spanish, "You shot that man. You helped us . . . helped my friends escape. Why?"

I responded, "Aléto?"

"Do not . . . stop calling me that."

The kid, with the same petulant stutter, had said something similar earlier in the day.

"If you won't tell me your name—anyway, listen. You can't hide here for much longer. They'll find you. Too many other children, they'll be seen. Can I come ashore?"

"No!" One-handed, he produced the rifle as a warning. "Answer me. Why did you shoot the . . . shoot the Russian *puta* in the leg and help us?"

The question threw me.

"How do you know this?"

"I saw you."

"No, how'd you know the man is Russian?"

"Because we . . . we know what adults don't know. Especially gringos." It was a flippant response.

I said carefully, "You, your friends, a lot of them are probably homeless. There are people who can help if—"

The boy interrupted, "Better homeless than slaves in the hotels. The restaurants, everywhere there are foreigners. Rich Hondurans. We are . . . we are *nada* to them, so they talk, talk, talk. But we *listen*. Then, as punishment—one mistake!—they sell us as—" the boy's anger forced a pause "—but you must already know."

"Kidnappers, yes. I understand. That's why I'm here," I said.

"You *don't* understand. My friends disappear, sold like birds. No matter how young, a boy or a girl, men use them as . . . use them as . . ."

"Those men should be in prison," I cut in to spare the kid saying it. "Tomorrow, I'll bring more food. Is it okay? We'll talk. I can help you."

The boy replied, "Then you do know."

"I'll tell you a secret. That's why I'm here. There's an agency—not from this country—that has the power to arrest people like that."

"Not the federales? The federales and the police are . . . you can't trust them."

"I know that. Give me a chance to prove it."

The boy took a moment to rally the pretense of being confident and in charge. "A trade . . . it is possible, I guess. More food *and* ammunition."

"We can discuss it. But trade, there's no need to give me anything."

"Let you buy us with gifts, you mean? No. You think we are helpless. But you are the one who needs help. You and the tall sailor. That will be our trade—your lives for food and ammunition." He turned to leave. "Tomorrow, I'll tie a red rag on a tree if we decide to accept."

I called to him, "Just food, but ammunition, I can't . . . Wait. What makes you think my friend's in trouble?"

The one-armed boy looked back. "*Señor*, you should have killed the Russian *puta*. And . . . and *him*, the plastic shaman, too. On the islands—" the kid used the rifle to point seaward "—there is a girl here, a maid, who heard their talk-talk-talk. The tall sailor is rich. And you, they plan to kill you and cut off your thumbs."

Interesting. The kid seemed to know what he was talking about.

"Which hotel?" I asked.

The boy shook his head.

The NODs followed his heat signature for several yards before his voice instructed, "If there is a red rag, leave food and ammunition. But don't stop. Understand? When the time is right, I will find you."

ELEVEN

Around midnight, in my bug-proof hammock, I was still awake, going over incriminating documents I'd photographed in Wingo Bogdan's office, and planning my downriver trip in search of Tomlinson. The tree house creaked in a silence that numbed the ears. A good place to sleep but I couldn't sleep.

The documents were incriminating by implication. Honduras is divided into eighteen territories, or "departments," each the domain of a governor. There are a multitude of municipalities, and governors appoint handpicked city managers to do their bidding. The power these officials wielded was such that each territory was their personal fiefdom.

Bogdan had the money and the political juice. One of the names I found in his files was familiar to me: Teoscar Brava who'd been arrested and extradited to the States for drug trafficking and sentenced to twenty-five years. DEA's multi-year investigation revealed that Brava, a former governor of Honduras, was a central figure in one of the largest and most violent cocaine-trafficking conspiracies in history. Brava had used drug-trafficking proceeds to finance his political ascent and, once elected, leveraged Honduras' law enforcement, military, and financial resources to further his drug-trafficking profits.

Now add human trafficking to the list. A dirty bunch, top to bottom.

Things Aléto had said also kept banging around my mind. *Plastic shaman.* It had a pejorative ring. And the line about cutting my thumbs off? It was precisely the sort of thing a hit man would do to avenge the disappearance of an oligarch billionaire. But how could word have traveled so fast through a network of hotel maids and street urchins?

Hard to tell what was true, what wasn't.

The boy was impressive, but he was still just a boy. Had all the symptoms of a scarred childhood—anxiety, rage, a fear of dropping the shields. All kids posture and exaggerate.

But I had to admit that not many his age were capable of leading an assault on a DC-3 and rescuing kidnap victims.

I was mulling this over when a startling possibility surfaced. If maids and street urchins were a rapid conduit of information about a hit man's threats, then a reverse flow of information about me was a probability. My presence, and the location of Tomlinson's remote tree house, might be known.

Unlikely?

Nope—not if Aléto's claims were true.

I gave up on sleep and patrolled the bamboo porch. Outside was a mountainous darkness that strobed with fireflies. I did another lap wearing the night vision NODs. No human thermal evidence, but something dog-sized—a jaguar, I hoped— was out there. Oh, and Roy the Wonder Horse had returned. The gelding was dozing by the creek.

Enough paranoia. I went inside and got busy bagging canned goods for the kids, plus a separate bag of Tomlinson's stuff. If I could talk him into returning to Florida, there'd be no need to come back here.

The man has the instincts of a squirrel, so I did a search for hidden valuables. On his sailboat, what he termed a "hidey-hole" was inside a teak bulkhead that had been hollowed and capped with a panel of matching wood. In the tree house, he'd gone to much less trouble. In a bamboo candleholder, I found a wad of Honduran cash and a beautiful little Mayan or Olmec jade amulet.

It all went into his bag.

On a shelf was the start of a library. A used travel guide, a water-scarred Tim Dorsey novel, and a hardback published in 1940: *Canek: History and Legend of a Maya Hero* by Ermilo Gómez.

Tomlinson had done some research.

I opened the book. My pal had dog-eared several pages. In pencil, he'd underlined passages and made notes.

I skimmed and summarized.

Canek, of pure Mayan blood, had despised Spaniards and Colonial rule since childhood. Although he'd studied Latin and history at a Franciscan monastery, he gained notoriety in his twenties by killing a priest with an obsidian blade, and for his fiery rhetoric. In villages throughout the region, he had condemned oppression by "a government of foreign thieves" and claimed to have magic powers that guaranteed his followers eternal life.

By age thirty, Canek was accepted by the indigenous majority as a God-sent leader, and crowned King of the Maya by local "wisemen Shamans."

Ironically, the coronation had been held in a Catholic church.

Canek's ensuing revolution, however, had been crushed by Spain's wealthy power brokers. The Mayan "King" had been strapped naked to a horse and publicly humiliated before he was sentenced to be "broken alive."

The King had died slowly. Rope tethers, pulleys, and butcher's tongs had been used as tools of dismemberment.

No wonder Tomlinson, a revolutionary to the core, was enamored with Canek the Great. So enamored that, addled by a brain injury, he had created an imaginary tie to a one-armed boy who'd supposedly raised my friend from the dead.

Or was the linkage imaginary?

When I reshelved the book, an envelope fell through the bamboo grating. It was of the manila variety, return address: *Departmento de Argueologia, Universidad de Honduras.*

The envelope had already been ripped open. I wouldn't have investigated had I known it contained a personal note.

In ink, Fidelia Martinez Brava, PhD, and the head of the department, had written in Spanish:

My Dear Tomás, I had no idea my husband had such intriguing friends. Our evening together was so fun and unexpected. I assure you, I seldom consent so quickly to . . .

I skipped ahead to the more sterile subject of archaeology.

. . . the enclosed is only an abstract of my research paper on tracking Jacinto Canek's DNA. Our department has yet to make it public. Aside from my assistants, and government oversight officials, you will be the first to read it. Do not share, please!

I stopped to clean my glasses. *Interesting.* Maybe I'd been wrong about Tomlinson—certainly not the first time. I pulled a coffee bag curtain aside, looked out the window, then took a seat and continued reading.

After months of cross referencing law enforcement and medical DNA data banks, what I told you is accurate. Jacinto Canek is, statistically, the distant ancestor of fifteen or more million people throughout the Americas. But we found only one individual with markers that are remarkably similar—an orphan child who, due to a birth anomaly (Phocomelia) was sent to a facility for impoverished children. It must have been horrible which is why we are eager to find him. As I told you, the poor boy disappeared about two years ago when—

Ouch. I stopped reading, distracted by a stabbing sensation in my eyes. I winced and removed my glasses. Got to my feet mystified—until I saw the smoky red laser beam that had been targeting my right temple.

Simultaneously, I dived away from the window just as a bullet splintered the opposite bamboo wall.

A microsecond later, the heavy report of a rifle reached the tree house.

That brief sound delay told me a lot. There was a sniper out there probably less than two hundred yards away.

I belly crawled to my gear bag and dragged it out the door. Bullets, the heavy rifle report, followed me but always high or a few feet behind.

Now I knew the sniper not only had laser sights. He had a thermal imaging scope.

No time to bother with the stairs. I kicked through the porch railing, dropped to the ground, and ducked behind the big mahogany tree. Pistol up and ready, I moved from one side to the other, searching the distance—and there it was. A muzzle flash. I elevated the Sig's green TruGlo sights and bracketed the area. Four shots rapid-fire, faster than most shooters could work a bolt.

With my back to the tree, elbows pulled in tight, I got the NODs on, then waited. Several seconds passed before another bullet cleaved tree bark. I peeked out and there he was, a thermal red cartoon 110 meters away according to the data grid.

This time I took aim and peppered the target window. Five rounds . . . then three more. The red cartoon stumbled, ducked low, then disappeared downhill. My half-empty magazine went into a pocket and I slapped a fresh mag home. I didn't want to follow the person. Not yet. Instead, I headed for the shooter's original position, moving from tree to tree.

Foliage in the area showed blood splatter. The shooter had been hit. Downhill, was another blood smear, but no evidence of a lethal gushing. The shooter was wounded, possibly in bad shape. But maybe not. I wasn't going to risk being ambushed by a heavy caliber rifle, so I hurried back to the tree house where almost everything but my jungle hammock was packed.

The bag of canned goods, coupled with the other stuff I had to carry, was a heavy load. I didn't want to make two long trips past the lagoon to my boat. What I needed was a make-shift sled or something.

No . . . what I needed was Roy the Wonder Horse, who wasn't as gun-shy as Tomlinson had claimed. After a brief retreat, the skinny gelding had returned to the succulent grass near the creek.

"Good boy, yes you are, Roy," I said. A drunken sort of euphoria is not uncommon after surviving a lethal bullet. I might have even hummed a tune as I strapped three bags to the saddle.

The horse didn't seem to mind. An hour later, in a hidden spot near the river, he even stuck around and watched me string the jungle hammock for another attempt at sleep.

I wanted to get an early start. There was a lot to do. If a red rag signaled me, Aléto's network of street urchins might become a useful source of intel. Next, when I reached the beach, I had already paid for a hotel room with Internet and a phone.

If there was no information waiting for me on where the Cessna had landed, my next best choice was to stake out the wreckage of Tomlinson's sailboat.

In a hidden compartment there, were gold coins and $100K in cash.

The "plastic shaman"—whatever that meant—wasn't wealthy, according to bank statements I'd found. Bogdan was the puppet of a criminal organization, and a greedy sociopath.

If my pal had been drugged with scopolamine, the sociopath already knew about the money—and a lot more.

TWELVE

I was a mile downriver from where I'd camped when a helicopter with government markings sailed over the trees, headed in the same direction. Behind me, coming fast, was a military-type rigid-hulled boat, two men wearing boonie hats visible.

Not good. If the guy I'd shot had survived, they were probably looking for me. I placed one semiauto pistol on the bench near my hand, the smaller Sig P365 by my left foot. Both were covered with towels. I killed the engine, and drifted along the riverbank, pretending to fish with a fly rod that was rigged and ready on the deck.

The chopper kept going. I paid no attention as if disinterested. Same thing when the tactical boat flew by. Relieved, I made a few more casts before risking a glance. The guys in boonie hats had yet to look back. Seated in the stern, though, was a young boy with Apache black hair. He recognized me and motioned with his only free arm—a dwarf arm with fingers that resembled a fin.

It was Aléto. No mystery why the trigger-eager kid had been arrested. But why the hell had he been upriver, miles from his secret camp when, presumably, they'd caught him?

It was thirty minutes after sunrise, 7:10 a.m. Mist swirled off the river. It intermingled with descending rainforest clouds to form spidery panels of fog. The fog magnified sound. It hampered visibility.

I stowed the rod and opened the throttle, slowing only for curves or when the fog thickened. A Honduran panga was no match for a military assault boat. I figured I'd lost them until I neared the creek where locals, mostly kids, hawked food from a muddy rind of beach. It was a festive place with a cooking fire and a loud boombox.

Anchored on the beach was the tactical boat. The men were seated on shore, smoking, drinking coffee, probably waiting for a breakfast of empanadas.

Fog became an ally. So did the boombox. It was loud. The music sounded like a man playing an accordion from the back of a galloping horse.

The boy noticed me but didn't stare. His good left hand was cuffed to a stern cleat.

No problem. All handcuffs in the Americas and the UK require the same universal key. There was one in my money belt. Another in my bag.

I nudged the panga beneath some overhanging limbs, tied off, holstered a pistol and slipped over the side into the water.

When Aléto saw this, he pivoted his back to me.

Smart boy.

With only my nose above water, the current carried me along, as innocuous as a drifting log. Using feet as anchors, my hands as rudders, I surfaced portside of the tactical boat's big four-stroke engine.

"Don't speak, don't turn around," I whispered.

The boy dipped his chin in acknowledgment.

I popped the cuffs, freed his arm, then ratcheted the cuffs fully closed—a mystery the guys in boonie hats might take time trying to solve.

Like an otter, the kid slid into the shallows without a splash. No need to tell him to stay low. My legs were longer. I steered him upriver to where trees crowded in and water deepened.

"Can you swim?" I said into his ear. We were in a pocket of fog, almost within reach of my boat.

He snorted as if it was a silly question. "In English, my nickname is Fin. What do *you* think?"

A smart-ass response. The alleged heir to the Mayan crown had a sense of humor.

I liked that.

When the boy was belly down in the stern, covered by a tarp, I pushed off and drifted past the festive food stop, fly rod in hand. I offered the men in boonie hats a friendly wave.

No need. There was fog. There was the music blare of an accordion on a galloping horse. The soldiers were busy eating.

Around a bend, I signaled the boy onto the seat next to me, and throttled the boat onto plane, full speed.

I raised my voice over the engine noise but not much. "What the hell were you doing so far upriver when they caught you?"

Aléto, his clothes soaked, was too excited to answer. For a few seconds, he allowed himself to be a child again. "Wow. I can't believe what just happened. So smooth, *patrón*. I figured two, three nights in jail then off to an orphanage—or prison. But, no, you show up, and . . . did the soldiers even see you?" Grinning, he looked over his shoulder. "I bet they still don't know. Like I disappeared. Poof." He turned. "You are a sly one, *patrón*. But you have to admit, I stayed cool. Very smooth myself."

Patrón was a prefix that showed respect. It meant *boss*. I got the impression the boy wanted my approval.

"You did great," I told him. "Yep, very cool and calm. And funny when I asked if you could swim."

"Cool, I was cool, wasn't I? What a trick to play on those—"

He stopped. "But how did you do it? Steal the key to their handcuffs?"

"Didn't need to. Already had one." I fished the key out of my tactical bag. "See? All handcuffs use the same key."

The grinning child retreated. I knew he was thinking, *What kind of man carries a handcuff key?* Then he noticed the NODs device that lay in my open bag. I'd needed it in the predawn darkness.

"What is that thing . . . a flashlight with eyes?"

"Night vision, it's called." I offered him the headband. "What you see now would be just as bright at midnight."

He put the binocs to his eyes. Made a child's chirp of astonishment, then, wary, handed it back. "That can't be true."

"It is."

"Even when the sun is gone?"

"Yep. Just touch a button, you don't need a flashlight."

The kid was impressed. "Like a jaguar—it sees at night. I . . . you won't believe me, but I knew this about you. And I know something else. The best way to trap a jaguar is to dig a pit and use bait the jaguar cannot resist. I fear people will do the same thing to you—and use me as the bait."

No idea what he meant, so I again asked why he'd been so far upriver when he'd been caught?

For a second, tough little Aléto had to fight back tears. My gut response was fatherly concern even though he hadn't answered my question.

"Those soldier *putas* took my . . . took my new rifle. My jacaltec, too."

"Jacal-what? What's that?"

"A long tube with darts for killing food." To demonstrate, he put circled fingers to his lips and blew. "Or kill enemies if you roast the right frogs for poison."

"A blowgun," I said. "That's the only reason you're upset? I was afraid they'd hurt you."

The boy's jaw flexed. A dwarf fist stopped the threat of tears. "Oh, they tried. They slapped my head when I refused to tell . . . tell them my name and where I'd hidden my *pipante. Bastardos.* I must go back for my canoe, and I'll make another blowgun. But not now. Now we must hide."

I steered toward the cut that led to the volcano-shaped mound. "I brought all the food I could find, but I don't see any red rag tied to a tree." With my chin, I indicated the laden garbage bag. Along with canned goods, it contained a few more MREs. "I can drop you here if you don't want me to come ashore. Up to you."

The boy motioned straight ahead, meaning *Keep going.* When we were in what I believed to be an aqueduct, he finally explained. "Sometimes, I stare into . . . stare into the fire, and I see things. I saw a jaguar—understand? A jaguar can see in darkness. I saw blood. And you . . . I saw you in a bag tied between trees. A sign. Now I know it is true."

"A sign of what? Last night, you paddled two hours upriver just to check on me?"

The boy blew a warbling signal to his friends before he spoke. "To warn you. The blood I saw. The jaguar. It was a sign from the fire that you might be murdered. Tell me—what happened? Did you shoot someone? On the front of this panga, there's a Mayan symbol that proves—"

I cut in, "You were there at the tree house that my . . . that the tall sailor built? Why would I shoot someone?"

"You are lying. Good." The kid approved. "Yes, the bamboo house in the trees. Soldiers were searching for you but they caught me instead. Did you kill an enemy? I hope it was the plastic shaman."

It was a local term for fake wisemen, the boy explained. Foreigners who pretended to know the old ways. Such people were not uncommon in Central America, apparently.

This gave him time to regain his composure. "They are

all thieves, but the plastic shaman is worse. He hurts . . . does things, dirty things, to children I know. Then sells them. Last night, instead of shooting the airplane, I wanted to shoot him."

I said, "Kid, I'm not criticizing, but you need to learn that shooting people is usually a bad idea. Not something to be proud of. You want to end up in jail?"

"So what? He's my enemy. Tell the truth, *patrón*. If the plastic shaman was your enemy, would you kill him?" The kid was staring at me. "Yes. You would. I can see it in your eyes. If you shoot him, you must promise to tell me."

My response was a careful nod before I changed the subject. "What *is* your name?"

"Don't know. Don't have one. There was a place, a workhouse for children like me." He made another fist with his three-fingered hand. "Deformed. Crippled. Lepers, we were told. They gave me a name, a *paper* name, but I hated that place. Worse than jail."

"Don't blame you, Al . . ." I stopped before using the kid's nickname.

I heard him laugh again. "Is unimportant. The tall sailor has a good heart. You will kill our enemy and lie without shame."

He puzzled over something for a moment. "Are you sure you are a gringo? In this river are snakes, there are crocodiles. A tourist would never swim here. Or get their clothes wet and trick soldiers to free a child they don't know."

"I'm getting to know you," I said. "I'm not a tourist."

The one-armed boy said, "Even if you are a gringo, I trust you, *patrón*—for now. You can call me Aléto."

THIRTEEN

Near the high, peaked mound was a firepit but no fire. It was ringed with logs and stone metates. I sat. Aléto had been joined by his rifle-carrying wingmen, the teenage maid in a soiled uniform and some of the children, boys and girls, who had been saved from boarding the DC-3.

Aléto, I noticed, was treated with deference—addressed as *Jefe*, which means Chief—even though he was among the youngest in the group.

"Where are the others?" I asked him. With all the new additions there should have been at least two dozen kids.

"Working. Making money, gathering food. Stealing if they need to," Aléto said. "Where the soldiers stopped for food, those were my friends cooking. Serving empanadas to those pigs. You didn't recognize my friends? Is no surprise. To adults, we are invisible. Especially to gringos and other foreigners. See what a fine trade you've made?"

The boy was showing his sense of humor again.

"I was busy keeping a smart-ass *Jefe* out of jail," I responded.

But Aléto was right. In my travels, poor countries particularly, the throngs of street children gradually blur into an anonymous flow.

I sat among a dozen similar kids who, for now, had been spared the indignities that awaited if they had boarded that DC-3.

Or maybe they'd been rescued too late.

I scanned their faces. Stoic dark eyes, bare arms that showed scars—fights or beatings—but emotionless. Untended hair, tattered clothes. They didn't wear the "traditional" Easter-egg-colored dresses, or scarlet bullfighter scarfs as worn by Honduran children who danced for tourists at coastal resorts.

From their appearance, it seemed unlikely these jungle castaways had been inside a restaurant or seen an expensive hotel. But I knew better now. They were part of an inconspicuous workforce, with eyes and ears, that could go anywhere unnoticed.

Aléto was still eager for approval. "Say something. Explain why I'm not a fool to bring you here."

In Spanish, I tried the predictable adult approach. Their secret hiding place was safe with me. I knew they were in danger. There were important people eager to protect them, but more information was necessary. Who were they running from? I needed the names of people they feared. I also needed *their* help—information from children who worked in resorts along the coast.

There was a language barrier. Some of the children spoke only the Miskito patois, or K'iche Mayan.

Aléto or his wingman pal translated. He was a sharp, aggressive kid with a rifle who asked me, "Yesterday, you sent the *helicópteros* away. The man they lowered on a rope, he obeyed you. Why did he obey you if you're not one of them?"

The kid had a surly attitude that would one day get him into a lot of trouble. If it hadn't already.

"His name is Balam," Aléto said, stepping close enough to whisper. "He doesn't like *chéy-lees*."

No shit, I thought, but remained calm, friendly, and shared what I'd told the crewman about snakes. "I lied about the snakes, but that doesn't mean he and the others won't come back."

Balam's smile communicated bitterness. "Hah, *ah-toys*," he said, nudging Aléto. "Is true. Many, many here." He pointed to the ground, then the trees. "Everywhere. You come back, *ah-toys*, they might kill you, too."

Ah-toy, I guessed was Miskito or Mayan for snake.

The children, most of them, nodded. It was true about lots of snakes.

Balam whispered into Aléto's ear, then demanded, "What do you want from us? You have no reason to help. We have nothing to give you. No gold. No treasure. *Chéy-lees*, when they come to the jungle, they are always after gold."

Rage. The testosterone reaction was palpable. In every gaunt face, I saw suspicion born from the communal horrors shared by all.

Understandable. Homeless children can rally after days without food, but growing up unwanted, as unloved, disposable beings, leaves scars and probably a lifelong hunger that can never be sated.

I got to my feet after saying to Aléto, "I think it's better if you explain to Balam that I'm looking for my friend, not gold. The kid scares me. Hey, you mind walking me to my boat?"

I waved and smiled goodbyes, then waited a short distance away. When the boy joined me, I was staring at the narrow entrance to what I believed to be a pyramid.

"You can't go inside," he said, a preemptory strike. "I found it. No one is allowed without my permission. Do we have a deal?"

He was talking about our trade, not the pyramid.

We started toward my boat. I asked if he'd heard of the archaeologist who'd written Tomlinson a letter about DNA and Mayan royalty. Dr. Fidelia Brava.

He knew exactly who I was referencing. It was in the nervous way he stuttered a denial.

"Have you ever spoken to her?" I asked.

"No. Never. But I've seen photographs. They say she is queen of all Honduras."

I smiled. "I thought you said you'd never heard her name before."

"Her name? Who remembers a queen's name? But I've never spoken to her or any archaeologist. I hate them. Promise you won't bring the archaeologists or anyone else here."

I said, "Even if I knew her, I wouldn't. The children call you *Jefe*. Is it because they know why the archaeologist is looking for you?"

No, the boy claimed, it was because he'd chosen to fight back rather than run away. Others had stopped running, too. For them, he'd found similar places in the jungle—ancient sites like this—where frightened children could work during the day and sleep safely at night.

"We won't always be children," he said. "I travel to these places. At night, I stare into the fire and tell them what I see."

"In Honduras, how many kids are we talking about?"

"Not just Honduras. The jungle is . . . there are no lines like on a map. Hundreds. One day maybe there will be thousands. So I have to hide from the helicopters. Treasure hunters, the archaeologists, too, because I found something they want. Something that gives me the power to . . . to do things a gringo wouldn't believe."

The story of Jacinto Canek came into my mind.

"Like what? Magic powers?"

Aléto, who wasn't tall, looked up at me. "You are an adult, but our enemies are the same. One of us must kill the plastic shaman. So wait here."

The boy wouldn't allow me to follow him to his secret place. So I stood next to my poorly chosen panga which was unadorned but for a single Mayan hieroglyphic on its hull. The glyph resembled a beaked bird with fangs.

He returned carrying his traditional woven bag and handed me a page torn from an old book. It was the photo of a jade mask, a mosaic of green, human sized, with perfect facial curvatures, eyes, nose, mouth.

He said, "This gives me the power that you don't believe."

"An old photograph?" I studied it more closely. "Beautiful. My friend, the sailor, he says you're a—" it took a moment to think of the word "—a *Curandero*. A healer. That he died when his boat wrecked but you brought him back to life." I handed the page back, smiling. "He's very lucky you found that book."

"Not a book," the one-armed boy said. "What I found is *this*—" he held up the photo for an instant "—the death mask of a Mayan king. When I sleep, I feel its power flow into my head."

I wanted to confirm what I'd just heard. "A mask of pure jade. You found it? Now you wear the mask at night?"

He looked at me as if I were an idiot. "Of course at night. I've got to sleep sometime."

"It has to be worth . . . I don't know how much. Millions. More money than you can imagine. Now I understand why you don't want Dr. Brava snooping around."

"Are you talking about the queen of Honduras?" He said this as if Fidelia might be an exception.

"Yes. Archaeologists in general."

"Archaeologists, any government foreigner, I would never sell it. Before the sun rises, I hide the mask where it can't be stolen—with a giant *ay-toy*. The largest I've ever seen. Then, later, the *ay-toy's* power flows from the mask into my head and my hand."

I was translating—*ay-toy . . . a giant snake*—as Aléto spread his dwarf fingers on his right shoulder. "It was this hand that brought your friend back to life. But the healing power comes from Kukulkan. From *Him*. The serpent God of the Old Ones."

He was pointing at the lone Mayan glyph on my boat's hull. Not a bird's head, I realized. It was the head of a snake with elongated fangs.

I said, "I'm not asking where you hide the mask. But the large snake, is it a fer-de-lance?" He didn't recognize the name, so he described it to me. The snake had a head shaped like a cutlass and black diamond scales woven over yellowish scales. Three times as long as I was tall, with a body thicker than a fat man's belly.

The kid was exaggerating. All people exaggerate when it comes to the size of fish and dangerous animals. A coded behavior that I reconfigured in my mind. The snake was huge. Maybe seven or eight feet long with a head shaped like a sword.

A fer-de-lance. Had to be.

I said, "You know this jungle a lot better than I do. But you need to be careful. That snake is venomous. You understand what that means? That means, if it bites you—well, I've read that some children have died in less than fifteen minutes. And it would hurt like hell."

"Hurts worse than hell," the boy shot back. He was pulling up his shorts to expose his thigh. "I know. I was bitten the first time I placed the death mask near the snake. See?"

Christ. On his leg were two large white divots of necrotized flesh. The fang marks there were four inches apart.

"Geezus, Aléto. Did you go to a hospital? You're lucky to be alive."

"Not lucky. *Kukulkan,* the power he gives to my hand healed me. Now the great snake knows his job is to protect the mask. And to protect me, but—" there was a smile in his voice "—I'm still careful around that big *Bastardo*."

His attention returned to the Mayan glyph on the bow of my boat.

"When I saw that, I knew we met for a reason. Our God *Kukulkan* brought you here. Tomorrow, friends and I will go to villages along the beach and talk to workers. Take baskets or bananas to sell. Perhaps even get jobs. Trust me, we will get the information you require."

"We'll go in my panga," I said.

"Better if we paddle our dugouts. Us with a gringo? By sunset, villages even in Belize, the workers would be gossiping."

I placed an envelope in his hand. "You'll need money. How will I find you?"

"We will find you," he promised again and stashed the envelope. "There's something you don't know. Yesterday, the girl in the maid's uniform? She saw the tall sailor at the tourist lodge. Said he was sick. But worse than sick. His eyes, the color of his face. Like a ghost who walks. Because she saw this, the plastic shaman had her locked up to be sold."

"My friend had been drugged, acted like a zombie," I suggested.

"That's the word, yes. Last night, in the fire—when I saw the jaguar? I knew we must find your friend, Tomlinson, very soon. I don't have the power to bring him back to life again."

"My friend told you his name? Why didn't you admit you'd spoken with him?"

The boy, being a smart-ass again, replied, "Because you had never saved me from soldiers before."

Psychic visions are fun nonsense. Even a skeptic like me wanted to believe.

I said, "You're pretty good at this. Last night, Tomlinson and the shaman escaped the tourist lodge in a small airplane. Maybe the fire told you where they went."

Aléto took me seriously. He stared into the jungle. "Perhaps.

I saw something, but it was in a dream. Dreams are . . . my dreams are sometimes nightmares. That's what I saw last night. The tall sailor, Tomlinson, running from a *dragón*. A monster. There were lots of monsters. And . . . and a tree with legs."

"A tree?"

"A fruit tree, yes. Mangoes, possibly. But it was only a dream."

Dragons, monsters, and a mango tree.

I hid my reaction, got in my boat, and started to shove off, when the kid spoke of his dream about Jaguar again. The best way to trap one was to dig a pit and use bait.

"Don't let that happen to you, *patrón*," he said. "My dream about dragons and monsters might come true."

I cleared my throat to disguise a smile. On the way downriver to my hotel and a phone, however, I remembered Tomlinson saying something about dinosaurs and a Goliath meteor that had crashed somewhere near present-day Honduras, killing more than seventy percent of all life on earth.

But dragons and a tree with legs?

The scientist in me had to laugh.

FOURTEEN

(Tomlinson Part One)

The night Wingo Bogdan landed the small plane God-knows-where, Tomlinson threw the door open, saying, "Gotta piss like a race horse," and ran for his life.

Little did he know that dinosaurs—*cripes*—life-sized predators were out there waiting in the darkness. Not that it mattered. He would have jumped and run anyway.

It had been a long, strange flight.

Or had he been telepathically transported?

All the hallucinating sailor knew for certain was that he was barefoot, the landing strip was grass, and the "Guru" had fed him a potion that made it impossible to refuse the fraud's every command.

"Do you remember your credit card info?" the fraud had asked. This was back at the eco lodge.

"Sure, Sensei. You got some paper? Jot it down."

"What about bank accounts?"

"You kidding, hell yes. I inherited a bundle from my corrupt rich family. Here—I'll make a list of the routing numbers. Got 'em memorized, man. Hand me that pen."

"What about cash in that tree house you built?"

"Chump change compared to what's hidden on my sailboat. The one I wrecked on a reef? One hundred-K in Yankee dollars plus gold coins. There's a hollowed-out teak bulkhead . . . Never mind, move over. I'll draw you a diagram."

Bogdan's eyes had lit up. "Seriously? Don't waste my time lying."

"I wish! God, how I'd love to be able to lie again."

Tomlinson didn't have the energy to deal with more of this kimchee, so he kept running to distance himself from the landing strip. Through the shadowed streets of a village, dogs barking, to a throughfare marked with one-way arrows. Hell, he couldn't even say no to road signage, so he followed the arrows, tripping his brains out in a midnight panic as confirmed by nearby church bells.

Goddamn bells. Their *clang . . . clang . . . clang* was penetrating. Worse, there were vision issues. One of his eyes was a carnivorous bug, the other a psychedelic raven. Inanimate objects—light poles, leering pumpkins, cars, a mango tree—throbbed with an aggressive heartbeat intensity. It was if they had all sprouted legs and were in violent pursuit.

The sailor hipster covered his ears and ran faster.

No use. *Shit.* Now the damn mango tree was gaining on him.

Somewhere, deep in his brain, existed a microdot of reason. "My Lifeguard Twin" as Tomlinson thought of it. When extremely drunk or stoned, the little Twin would scamper out and rescue his ass. Through Tomlinson's mouth, the Twin spoke politely to outraged husbands. The Twin was articulate and convincing with cops. No matter what degree of a slobbering wreck Tomlinson had made of himself, his Lifeguard Twin would materialize as a dependable voice of reason.

The Twin spoke now but was more pointed than usual.

Keeping running, dumbass, unless you want that tree to strangle you from behind. There's no one to blame but yourself.

Tough love, but all too true.

Tomlinson felt trapped. Trapped in a mockery of his own history. He'd been a psychotropic pioneer, for God's sake. An expert. As a lefty pitcher and baseball fan, he'd also been a vigorous opponent of what fat-cat owners termed "mandatory drug testing." No way players should be forced to comply. Drug testing shouldn't be mandatory. My god, he'd tested almost every drug there was, and some of that shit was really bad.

Bad?

Tonight, the word had been redefined. Nothing—acid to peyote buttons, ether to 'shrooms, to crank, tranq, skank, and nitrous oxide—had poleaxed his brain like the vile brew he'd gobbled down at sunset. That plus three more cups of diarrhea express because the "Guru" had commanded it.

Wingo Bogdan, he thought, *you are a lowlife child trafficking snake in the weeds.*

Tomlinson had known this from the start thanks to the one-armed boy—and other contacts he had in Honduras. So, he had played along to get more evidence, it was true, confident that a Gopher State Guru was no match for a lefty pitcher who was a true Zen Master.

Ayahuasca tea? Hah! No worries for a pro. He'd embraced the ceremony as a harmless first step to infiltrating the dude's criminal consorts, then letting the cops nail their collective asses to a jailhouse wall.

Even blitzed, Tomlinson suspected the truth. Bogdan had poisoned him with some heathen zombie drug. He was powerless to protect his bank accounts but, by God, he would run himself to death before allowing that quack to feed him more poison.

Jail hell, Tomlinson amended. True justice would be to turn the child trafficker over to his pal, Marion Ford. That would teach the sneaky son of a bitch! Doc was capable of nailing Bogdan's head to a tree, not just a wall.

This was vengeful supposition.

No, it was more than guesswork. Doc was an iceberg sort of mystery man. On the surface, he was the kindly, quiet biologist, ready to help fix a busted engine, and a good listener if confidential advice was needed.

What lay below the surface, though, few suspected or would have believed.

Tomlinson knew the truth from experience, yet, until now, he'd never stooped to conjuring his pal's darkest powers. But he'd also never been pursued by a murderous mango tree while tripping his brains out somewhere in Central America.

Ahead, moonlight reflected off the sea. A street sign pointed left to a well-lighted boulevard. Obediently, Tomlinson made a Louie and galloped barefooted down the middle of the road, indifferent to the sidewalk that edged a beach. Late-night strollers wore hellish neon horns. Helmeted specters on motorbikes blurred past leaving volcanic streamers. The air was salt laden. Rich with the taste of jasmine, diesel fumes and charcoal grilles tended by vendors.

"Hola, gringo . . . my good friend," one of the vendors called in English. "Why not stop, rest. Have something to nice to eat?"

Tomlinson stabbed a thumb over his shoulder. "You gotta be shitting me, *amigo*. Are you blind?"

Two cars, four headlights aligned, sped toward him. Christ, now he was under attack from every direction. He angled toward the sidewalk, but his big toe caught the curb, and he fell. When he looked up, another one-way sign read, *Chicxulub Astro-Crater Park.*

Chicks-uh-lube?

Tomlinson mouthed the name then leaped to his feet, turned right and ran faster. The arrow was mandate enough, but not his only motivation. "Astro-crater" actually meant something to him. He'd been seeking the exact spot where, sixty-some million years ago, a giant meteor had, at once, caused extinctions and catalyzed new life-forms on Earth.

The metaphor, when applied to his Dinkin's Bay family, might yield the secret to rebirth if he could plunge his consciousness into the bowels of the asteroid's Ground Zero.

Now, by God, maybe he'd found it. Where he and Chicks-uh-lube were located on a map, the man had no clue. And he was too wasted to parse details now.

A railed promenade jutted toward the sea. A street vendor was packing up. Foot traffic was composed of drunks and phantom stragglers . . . Gad, some with the faces of skeletons and ghouls.

Tomlinson went numb until his Lifeguard Twin chimed in.

Think, bonehead. It's October. A week before Halloween. El Dia de los Muertos, the Sombreros call it down here. Stay cool . . . breathe and keep moving.

"Sombreros? You racist cur," Tomlinson muttered.

It's your brain, your words, dumbass, his imaginary Twin countered. *Shallow-up, breathe and let the big horse run.*

Good advice. To control one's breathing was to control one's sentient emotions.

Wait . . . which wise sage had said that?

I did, Tomlinson remembered. He'd preached that maxim to every poor, besotted Zen student who'd had the misfortune of falling for his Sorcerer-on-the-Sea bullshit act.

Guilt flooded in—along with memories of too many unholy, illicit seductions to count.

Well, mortal sins no longer mattered either—not at this stage of the game. He'd been killed weeks ago in a hurricane. The clock of his karmic reprieve was clanging.

In the distance, church bells announced 1:00 a.m. Thirteen noxious peals.

Gad! This was a dangerous omen. Priests down here were on military time. A full hour he'd frittered away, yet the zombie drug still fired animated horrors in his mind.

Tomlinson checked his status astern. The predatory mango tree had been elbowed aside by a skeleton and . . . *shit*, two cops with brutal-looking billy clubs. The timing could not have been worse. During this brief hiatus, his fly had magically opened so, out of habit, he'd gone to the railing to bilge ship.

One of the cops waved his club and yelled, "Hey you, gringo . . . stop that right now!"

Tomlinson's Lifeguard Twin responded vocally and politely, "Of course, whatever you say, officer. But when nature calls . . . you know how tough it is to stop in midstream."

The Twin's fake smile vanished when several cops approached, and Tomlinson took off running again, alone on the promenade which, after fifty yards, dead-ended at a chain-link gate. Above the gate were stone columns with tiki torches and a huge sign that read: *Sendero Jurassico*

Humm . . . "Sendero" meant light. And "Jurassico" meant . . . well, it had something to do with the Jurassic period. A geologic term, no doubt, that suggested illumination might await on the other side of the fence.

Good hell, the gate was padlocked. And the cops had fanned out to surround him, billy clubs in hand.

"Señor, may I see your passport, please? It is illegal to urinate in Mexico."

This was a double-barreled surprise even to the Lifeguard Twin who responded, "*Mexico?* Officer, I thought we were in Honduras. If people aren't allowed to urinate, no wonder migrants are fleeing to . . . Never mind . . . my sincere apologies, sir. My passport, of course, you may see my passport. Do you happen to have a car and scuba gear? A small plane would be faster."

God all-mighty. Now the Lifeguard Twin's gift for brown-nosing cops had been rendered stupid because he, too, was obviously wasted.

Tomlinson panicked. After a salute of respect, he scaled the gate and hit the ground running while the cops screamed threats from behind.

A brick path provided a fast straightaway. An honor guard of mastodon tusks, dozens of them planted vertically, begat the illusion of traversing the rib cage of a gigantic animal. The path curved. It narrowed and funneled him into a primeval landscape of mangrove swamp and darkness.

Shit-oh-dear, Tomlinson thought because the darkness was alive with shadows. Towering shadows that became prehistoric silhouettes. Some were sixty feet tall on skinny reeds for necks. Others were tank-sized with multiple rhino horns and spiked tails.

The air . . . the air was different here, too. The ozone chemistry of lightning and sulphur was mixed with muck and steaming seawater. It was a fetal scent ignited by electricity. This insinuated that a meteor had crashed to earth here.

Tomlinson slowed, stooped, and selected a shard of what felt like volcanic glass. It was as long and sharp as a flint spearhead. The rock was hot to the touch, candescent with energy and magnetic weight. Some long-ago geology class at Harvard reminded him it wasn't actually glass. It was an amorphous, uncrystallized product of rapidly cooling magma.

Whatever.

The shard went into his pocket as a talisman.

He'd *found* it. Ground Zero where dinosaurs had once existed. And maybe still did judging from the encroaching shadows.

Stay cool, avoid eye contact, he counseled himself. *Pay no attention to those pterodactyls perched in the palms. Ignore that brontosaurus standing ass-deep in water. That murderous gang of sauropods, too. Hell, they're mostly harmless vegetarians.*

Geezus frogs. Everywhere he looked there were dinosaurs,

life-sized, many dozens of the brutes. No doubt they were tourist attraction ploys constructed of plaster and rubber reptilian skin.

Sure. He had stumbled into a fake dinosaur park. It was the only rational explanation.

He pressed ahead at a slow walk, aware of the background clamor of police sirens. Cops were out there assembling like wolves, so why not explore this tourist hot spot before the zombie drug fired another bout of hysteria?

In Spanish, *tranquilo* was a melodious synonym for *calm*. So he slowed his breathing and continued on, repeating as a mantra, *tranquilo . . . tranquilo . . . tranquilo*, with every step.

The effect was encouraging. He walked past the brontosaurus, no problem. One of the sauropods appeared to grin hello when he offered a friendly wave. Near the fossilized skull of a triceratops was an immature triceratops. The infant swung a playful spiked head and made bird-like chirping sounds as if it wanted to play.

As if speaking to a puppy, Tomlinson cooed, "You're a cutey-pie, yes you are . . ." Then caught himself before he reached out to pet the damn thing.

What the hell?

If the ugly little brute was made of plaster, how the hell could it chirp and swing its head? And why was that sixty-foot brontosaurus now wading toward shore?

All herbivores, yes, but this provided little solace when a giant pterodactyl buzzed him from overhead. Next, a trio of slobbering Velociraptors, teeth bared, stalked him from the distance.

Tomlinson's breathing fluttered when a volcanic tremor zapped his toes—gad, was this the killer earthquake the seismo-geeks had been predicting? The man's heartbeat spiked. The zombie drug returned in the form of batshit crazed terror. He spun and sprinted nonstop back to the entrance gate where, thank the-good-Lord, a gaggle of cops awaited.

"Arrest me," he yelled, his wrists extended to expedite matters.

"Whoa, hold on, señor!" one of them responded. "Pissing in the street is no large matter. Why are you running?"

Tomlinson didn't risk a look back. "Get those goddamn handcuffs on me or you'll find out soon enough. Hurry up!"

But the cops refused. "No . . . no, not for such an important Americano tourist. Relax. *Tranquilo . . . tranquilo*," a cop with gold stars on his collar urged.

"Huh? Important my ass. At least throw me in the back of a squad car. Or . . . geezus hell, give me those goddamn cuffs. I'll arrest myself."

"This important tourist is very drunk," someone said, and they all laughed.

The boss cop led Tomlinson through the gate saying, "This little matter of trespassing and urinating in the street is already forgotten. We value foreign tourists in Chicxulub, so I am turning you over to your influential friends."

"Friends? You gotta be shittin' me. I don't have any influential friends. And, if I did, the fools wouldn't admit it because—"

Tomlinson stopped in mid-sentence. Parked among the cop cars was a black Mercedes. Wingo Bogdan stood there holding a rear door open. With him were the Bolshevik thugs who'd recently kicked the shit out of him before demanding information about a biologist they claimed was a spy.

"Get in the car, old friend," Bogdan commanded.

Tomlinson reverted to zombie mode until his fingers accidentally touched the meteorite shard in his pocket.

Zap. A heat-lightning schematic jolted his spine.

The Zen Master shook himself. He felt a paralyzing numbness deaden the left side of his face. But he rallied enough to flash a lopsided grin and lie, "Anything you say, Guru. Nice wheels. Is it too late to call 'shotgun'?"

The thugs didn't notice Tomlinson's death stare. He was looking straight into the child trafficker's eyes.

FIFTEEN

D r. Naomi Cruz, the pickleball-playing neurologist, said to me, "What I'm afraid of is, your friend—if he actually is your friend—could have an intracranial hematoma. Blood collects, exerts pressure inside the skull, then *pop*, all sorts of bad kimchee can happen. Even a month later, permanent paralysis. He could keel over dead, or . . ."

"Kimchee?" I interrupted.

The woman, athletic, short dark hair, her dive mask on her forehead, conceded with a wry look. "You caught me. Yeah, that's one of the peculiar words Tommy uses. Guess you might be friends after all. When you pulled up in your boat, I was afraid you were a . . . that you might be in the salvage business."

"Or a thief," I said to spare her saying it. "I've known the guy for years—although it can seem a heck of a lot longer. You two must have hit it off pretty good, huh?"

She got the joke but ignored the question. "Tommy's got some quirks. Is that so bad? I find the quirky ones interesting—if they've got the brains to back it up. He was my patient for only, what?, four days before he snuck out. Which pissed me off. I tried to convince him he needed a neurosurgeon, not Doctors with Wings. We're quick fix volunteers. And I'm not a surgeon. Are you sure he's still alive?"

"As of last night," I replied.

"Thank God," the physician said, and seemed to mean it.

It had taken me a while to move the conversation this far along. I'd surprised her, me in my twenty-one-foot panga, Dr. Cruz, snorkeling alone, inside a razor rock reef where *No Más* lay aground, port side tilted to the sky. The mast was gone, hardware gone, hull ruined yet buoyant in the Popsicle-blue water like the corpse of a bleached whale.

We'd started in Spanish but had switched to English. Her accent was buffered by a chunk of time spent in some Midwestern state. Ohio, Iowa. A state with a lot of vowels. An exchange student in years past, possibly, with an ear for American slang. Profanity too. And her Honduran family had money. Just a guess. I considered the remains of what had been a forty-some-foot Morgan, my pal's floating home.

"Looks like thieves already picked her pretty clean," I said. "Dr. Cruz, I've got to ask. Your volunteer group—from what Tomlinson told me, anyway—Doctors with Wings, spends two weeks here annually. But it's been almost a month since—"

No need to complete my thought. She was one of the fast synapse varietals. Two words into a sentence, they've already projected the question, so pretend to wait patiently to respond with an answer that's already been formulated.

She said, "Are you asking if I've got a thing for your friend? Or maybe you heard about the research paper I'm working on. Valid questions. From Iowa City to Roatán *es un maldito viaje largo*. A damn long trip," she translated. "But here I am, a so-called expert on brain chemistry, scavenging my patient's boat in the middle of nowhere. How crazy is that?"

Up to her hips in water, she looked shoreward to a crescent of sand, rainforest beyond. Vines were green dreadlocks hanging from the high jungle canopy. Twenty minutes earlier, I'd seen a small airplane—a Cessna, possibly—buzz the same area before banking toward what was probably a landing strip in nearby village of Rio Coco.

"There's a third possibility, like I told you," the physician added.

Yes, there was. Tomlinson had leaked information to Wingo Bogdan about money hidden aboard *No Más*—thus my concern about small airplanes. Perhaps he'd shared even more details with this unusual, salty spoken and athletic neurologist.

I said, "I don't think so, Dr. Cruz. You don't have the look."

"Call me Naomi. Are you more comfortable speaking English?"

"For now," I said.

"Okay. What do you mean . . . what kind of look?"

"The same thing that came to your mind. That I was here to rob Tomlinson's boat."

A thief?

She found this amusing in a snarky way. "Good Christ, I didn't even know his name was Tomlinson until three weeks ago. Tommy is what he told us. Tommy John, which turned out to be bullshit when I started asking around."

I had anchored the panga and was assembling my snorkel gear. "Baseball," I said. "Like the elbow surgery. Tomlinson's a pitcher. We play on the same senior league team."

"No kidding?" She was interested but the subject could wait until later. "I figured it was because he was so out of it—a transient amnesia thing. It's rare, but none of our team thought he was faking it. Or could be he was a felon who didn't want to be extradited. Which, like you said, he didn't have . . . I just didn't get that vibe. What I knew for sure was, he told us his passport was hidden in some secret spot on his sailboat. So here I am. Find the passport or some documentation, there might be contact information."

The woman, mid-thirties, wearing a baggy shirt over Spandex dive skins, tilted her mask back tiara-like atop hair that might have been raven black when dry. She did a dismissive, theatrical thing with her eyebrows, as if she'd explained everything.

"Did you find it?" I was in the water, struggling to get my fins on over my dive boots.

"His passport? I was just getting started when you showed up." She noticed my eyes sweep the shoreline. "Nope, no boat. I had a driver shuttle me over from there." She motioned seaward to an elevated hint of green, a scattering of islands. "Cayo Faro. It's only three or four miles."

This was said as if three or four miles was an easy swim.

"The driver just took off and left you here alone—that's unusual. There's a hotel there?"

"My uncle owns a little place on the beach. Nothing fancy."

"Your uncle's surname is Cruz, the same as yours?"

I wasn't just making conversation. Spanish naming customs differ from English-speaking conventions. In most Latin American countries, each person has two surnames. Traditionally, the first surname is paternal and comes from the father. The second surname comes from the mother's side of the family. There had to be a reason the neurologist, a Honduran, had chosen only one last name.

"You ask a lot of questions."

"Well, it's not often I . . . Thing is, Doctor, you strike me as too smart to do something so risky. I mean, send your boat away out here all alone?"

The woman might have heard this as a threat. "Oh, don't worry about me. I have pepper spray, a dive knife, and so many Tae Kwon Do lessons I'm almost eager prove they weren't a waste of money. Also took shooting lessons, thanks to my uncle."

"Really?"

"Yes, *really*. Plus I have this." She unclipped a handheld VHF radio. "Press a button, and my shuttle driver . . . Iron Baby—this huge island dude. He'll be here in five minutes."

That made me chuckle. "Iron Baby? You couldn't come up with something better than that? The guy just goes off and leaves you in the middle of nowhere."

The neurologist didn't like being doubted. "I'm sure it wasn't Iron Baby's idea, and what the hell does his name matter? He drives boats, probably drunk or stoned, and maybe he had other stops to make. Fact is—well, I'll just tell you. The man scares me when he's drunk. So I paid him extra to come back in an hour. Satisfied?"

"Sure. Saves you having to explain if you'd surfaced with my friend's passport—or whatever else you might find down there."

"You expect me to apologize for wanting some privacy?"

"Just the opposite," I said. "You're serious about some research paper you're writing. That's obvious. Acquired savant syndrome is what Tomlinson told me. It's rare—even rarer than the amnesia thing, I guess."

"*Sudden* savant syndrome," she corrected. A physician researcher, careful about terminology. And still wary about being out here alone with a stranger. "So he told you about me."

"Some. Yesterday, yeah. That you're a bird-watcher and play pickleball. All very complimentary stuff."

"Humm. What I find odd is, Tommy—Tomlinson—we talked a lot. Usually at night. You know, a concussion, we had to keep him awake. Very *peligroso*. He mentioned his best friend on Sanibel, but—" she gave me a hard look "—his name wasn't Marion."

I said, "Probably because everyone calls me Doc. I'm not a real doctor. Not a physician, anyway. Marion Ford, that's my name."

Her posture, her attitude, everything changed. "You're him,

the biologist? Oh my God. He told me all about you . . . you and his *amigos locos* at some marina." She thrust out her hand. "Wow. I am so relieved. Honduras—I was born here—and you're right. It's dangerous. The Mara-gangs, pirate meth-heads, and a lot of rough asshole expat characters hang out along this coast."

She took me through some test questions to verify my identity. My laboratory was an old fishhouse. Yes, I had a toddler son, and a dog named Pete.

By then Dr. Naomi Cruz was all smiles. "In that case, I'll tell you the truth. Your buddy has reconnected with a lot of his old friends in the last few weeks. Friends of family, friends of friends. Not too hard to guess why. In Honduras, everyone knows everyone's business."

I said, "I know the business you're talking about. He's still pissed they legalized the stuff."

"Hah!" Her expression became quizzical. "You disapprove?"

"As long as they leave kids out of it, I'm all for adults doing whatever they want."

"You're a prude."

"Compared to Tomlinson, I'm—who was that Italian guy? Starts with an L," I said. "The lecherous guy, even he was a saint compared to Tomlinson."

"Lothario," she said, laughing. "Yeah, maybe I do have a thing for your buddy. Shouldn't surprise you. What woman wouldn't? He's . . . there's just something about the man. So sweet and very funny. And obviously gifted in . . . a spiritual way."

"I've heard the rumor," I said, my eyes on the water. The reef was what locals called "razor rock"—jagged limestone that dropped into a tidal swath ten feet deep where the current boiled past the sailboat's cabin. I had a couple of flashlights in my bag. We would also need a safety line and a buoy.

The woman wasn't done with the subject of her former

patient. "Doc—can I call you that? Like I told you, there's another reason I might have made this trip. And it's serious, okay?"

"Sure."

"At I-U, I had the best people I know go over his films, and we need to get Tom . . . Tomlinson back to the States and into surgery stat. He has a minor brain bleed that could get worse, they think. We're not talking days, we might be talking hours. In fact—" she stripped the dive mask off her head "—to hell with his passport. Where is he?"

"I was afraid of that," I said.

"Yeah, so, if you don't mind giving me a lift, let's move." She started wading toward my boat.

"Wait. I've got some bad—or confusing news, too."

"What's the problem? You told me he's alive."

"He is. Or was. Give me a sec, you'll understand."

Where to begin? Start with Tomlinson drugged, in a zombielike state, being kidnapped in a Cessna? Or shift to the probability that Bogdan, along with his victim, might return here soon to salvage the gold and a hundred grand in cash stashed aboard what was left of *No Más?*

The plastic shaman wasn't the macho type. He'd bring a bodyguard or two with guns.

I said, "It's complicated. But, either way, Tomlinson's going to need his passport. So we have to dive now, Naomi. Later, we can talk on the way back to wherever you're staying."

SIXTEEN

We snorkeled the wreckage together. Naomi took the lead at first. That was fine with me—easier to I.D. an approaching boat, or Bogdan and accomplices if they came through the jungle on foot.

The neurologist was an athlete. But the rip current was strong. She claimed it was spooky dark inside the cabin, and her dive skills weren't great.

It's easy to spot a novice. When they jackknife toward the bottom, their fins do a lot of pointless, noisy flailing. A failure to jettison air bobs them back to the surface. Instead of using legs for power, they employ their arms rather than use hands as subtle rudders.

Slow and smooth, that's the way it should be. Not a constant battle.

After her third attempt, the woman surfaced, snorted water, and had to lunge for the safety line to keep from being swept out to sea.

"This is embarrassing. I suck. How about we trade places?"

An athlete, yes, but also a pragmatist. No fragile ego to get in the way. I liked that.

I summoned her up-current to what remained of the sail-boat's stern. "Okay, you stand watch while I dive. But first, there are a couple of other things I haven't told you."

"About Tomlinson?" Her expression read, *Now what?*

I kept it brief. She knew about the passport, but no details about the hidden cash.

"It can't be that much money. So?"

"It's enough we could get visitors. Tomlinson might have told the wrong people about what's hidden down there."

"Now, today you mean?"

"It's possible. Underwater, don't worry, I'll hear a boat coming. But the man I have in mind, he might hike in from the village. If he does, he'll bring hired help. So keep your eyes open."

"The violent type," she said. "That explains it then."

"Explains what? I'm describing our situation. If you see anything unusual, bang on the hull three times fast." I did it. Banged on the hull with my fist. "Use the flashlight and keep banging until I surface."

She placed both hands on the stern. "Help boost me up."

The woman was perched on the tilted transom, fins dangling, while I spit in my mask, getting ready.

"Hey. What it explains is . . . Is that why you're carrying a gun?"

I turned to look at her. "What makes you think—"

She said, "I saw you slip something into your fanny pack. Sort of sneaky about it, but a gun, I'm pretty sure. What's the deal? Won't it rust? Or is that bag waterproof?"

"On the way to your hotel, we'll talk more," I said.

"Hold on there, *tigre*. Tommy, when he was really out of it, he said some very weird things about his friend, the biologist." The woman, a trained observer, keyed in on my reaction.

"Like what? Tomlinson says strange things all the time."

"Oh, just wild stuff. Foreign embassies, something about a bullet wound. Or bullet scars. And he thinks you might work for a government—well, tell you what . . . *Doc.* We'll talk about it on the trip back to where I'm staying. How's that sound?"

The smug look on Dr. Cruz's face—she'd gotten her convivial revenge.

I made a shallow descent, let the current sweep me into what was left of the helm, and then pulled my way down the companionway steps into the flooded cabin. Outside, water was gin clear. Inside, a silty detritus had collected, so I did everything in slow motion because the viz was already iffy.

No Más rested on her starboard side, angled into deep water. If I stood on the bones of the settee berth, there was an air pocket portside. Pressing my face close to the ceiling, I could snatch a quick breath if needed.

This was an unexpected perk. Opening Tomlinson's secret hidey-hole would be challenge enough without having to exit the companion way every two minutes or so for air.

I ducked under and did a gentle one-eighty. Scavengers had stripped the cabin bare of valuables. Portholes, a brass ship's bell, an antique compass and sextant and the foldout chart table on which they had once been fixtures. Galley components, fire extinguishers, PFDs, mooring lines, every useable piece of hardware, all gone.

I grabbed a few breaths and went under again. What scavengers hadn't bothered with were some of my friend's personal items because they'd been ruined by saltwater anyway. Books, a portable turntable, and stacks of the music he treasured, LP vinyl albums still in sodden dust covers. They lay in a rockslide heap along the inside starboard water line.

I fished up a few samples. I'll be damn . . . *Hot Water*, one of Buffett's first albums recorded in Key West. America's *Horse With No Name*—my pal was pals with the band, and he'd played tambourine with them onstage. Hendrix, Dylan, Bach's Fugues, Talking Heads, Danny Morgan. Acid and metal rock bands I'd never heard of.

I retrieved one more.

Shut Down Two? I laughed thorough my mask. The high IQ hip hipster was a closet Beach Boys fan. Something he'd never admitted.

Enough. I dropped the albums and watched them sashay underwater to the deck like falling leaves.

Weird, the feeling that came over me. Sentiment is not one of my normal components. I wondered if it was because, after spending so many fun, beery evenings in this cabin, I'd never paused to value the impermanence of it all.

Silly. That was emotional nonsense. The weirdest part was the closed-coffin finality of a structure that no longer had maritime value. *No Más* was just another painted name on the stern of yet another fiberglass boat, one of millions whose usefulness had run amok on a reef of one type or another.

A passage from Tomlinson's little book came to mind: *To hell with worries about the future. The future has already come and gone. We're just dealing with the fallout.*

The hidey-hole bulkhead was starboard side, forward of the V-berth. Inlaid were a trio of dead bolts, also teak, and nearly invisible. The wood had swollen. I used a Randall dive knife to punch them free. A flashlight and several air pocket breaks were required. I was prying the last Chinese-box complication open when a series of sharp raps on the hull sent me scurrying topside.

The neurologist was peering down at me when I surfaced. Her cheeks, I noticed, were flushed.

"Jesus Christ, what are you, some sort of dolphin? I timed

it—seven minutes you've been under. *More* than seven minutes. Goddamn it, I was about to come in after you."

I said, "Sorry. Almost done. Seen any boats?"

She tapped her wristwatch for emphasis. "That's not human. Hold your breath too long, you could black out. Have a seizure. *Die.* Then what the hell am I supposed to do? Steal your boat and leave your body here—that would be the smartest option. No one could blame me."

In some people, fear is vented as anger.

I said, "Thanks for your concern, Dr. Cruz," and tossed her my snorkel because I didn't need it. "Two more minutes—I hope."

"Hold on." She looked toward the jungled shoreline. "I haven't seen anything. Well, I have, but no people. You've made me paranoid. That's the problem."

I pulled myself around the stern for a better view.

"What did you see?"

Birds—parrots and macaws, mostly—the neurologist explained. They'd flushed incrementally downhill as if someone was descending beneath the trees toward the water.

I waited and watched in silence until she said, "Probably my imagination. That thing you said about thieves, some guy who knows there's money hidden here . . . I just have this creepy feeling someone's watching us. And you're . . . I suppose you know it's illegal for foreigners to carry guns. Police could arrest me and use you as an excuse."

"You were born here. You have family here," I said. "Why would they do that?"

Her response was, "Because I'm a successful woman and this is Honduras. The highest femicide rate in the Americas. Here, a dead female with a college degree is considered a good career move."

I said, "Understood. What I tell friends is, if they think something's wrong, they're almost always right. Birds don't spook from an entire hillside without a reason."

"You think someone's up there?"

"Could be. Keep your eyes open and trust your instincts. I won't be much longer."

Visibility in the cabin was soupy with silt. I pried the bulkhead open and explored a sizeable compartment with my hands. I retrieved a Pelican case—waterproof judging from its buoyancy. Soggy baggies of weed were pushed aside. The same with several ruined VHS cassettes—for the best, perhaps, considering what my pal might have filmed with the consent of his eager partners.

Lodged in a corner was a traveler's wallet, the discreet type worn around the neck. It contained my friend's passport and other documents. When retrieved, it had the heft of hidden gold coins.

I grabbed an air pocket breath and was resealing the compartment when I heard Naomi's urgent banging above.

Pushing the Pelican case ahead of me, I flew up the companionway to the surface.

"Get down, get in the water," I told her. "What did you see?"

The neurologist didn't budge. Instead, she was hollering toward shore, "Over here! Over here! It's me."

I gave her fin a shake. "What the hell's going on?"

She glanced down. "I saw him . . . I saw Tommy. He was there. Came down to the water, waved his arms, then just disappeared back into the trees."

"You're sure? Did he say anything?"

"Well . . . yes. Then he sort of hobbled off like he was scared. Or being chased. But he recognized me. I know he recognized me. We've got to go after him."

"Hobbled off? What did he say?"

She looked south to where shoreline foliage gave way to open water. "See that boat way, way out there? He pointed at it and yelled something. 'Get out of here,' I think. Or maybe it was the way he motioned with his arms. Like telling me we're in danger. But I'm pretty sure we're not."

A mile away, maybe more, a flat gray vessel with a T-top was greyhounding toward us. A military tactical rib-hull it looked like. At least one stick figure aboard.

I pushed the Pelican case and my dive bag up into her lap. "Hang on to this stuff. I'll bring my boat over. "

"Is his passport somewhere in here?"

"Don't bothering looking now. Get your fins off and keep watching for Tomlinson."

I swam freestyle up-current, got my engine started and turned the panga starboard side to the wreckage of *No Más*. "Get in and stay low. Did you see him again?"

Naomi had pivoted to watch the boat off our stern. It was coming fast. "That looks more like my ride back to the island. Iron Baby, the drugged-up giant."

I said, "Looks like there's only one person aboard. I don't want to stop unless you're sure."

"No . . . keep going. My uncle's narcissistic wife might be trying to make sure I don't come back."

"I don't know what that means," I said.

"With any luck you won't have to find out," was the woman's cryptic response. She faced forward. "That's where I last saw Tommy. He can't be far. Why the hell would he run from me?"

I followed her finger toward a patchwork of coral close to shore. Staghorns the size of elk antlers were golden flags that lined a purple tidal rip. I dodged the coral and followed the conduit of deep water. Mainland side, coconut palms leaned close enough to throw shadows on the sand. From their lazy fronds, a trio of parrots flapped skyward in protest of some disturbance.

"See those parrots?"

Naomi, the bird-watcher, replied, "Macaws. Green—they're Buffon's macaws."

"Check behind us." I already knew what she would see. The T-top boat had stopped by the wreckage of *No Más*. "If the guy's looking for you, he'll think you drowned."

"He's anchoring," she said, relieved. "Unless it's one of the gangsters you're worried about."

"Use your radio and find out," I said. "I'm going to try something. Wait here."

At dead slow idle, I beached the boat, jogged to the closest palm tree and hollered, "Tomlinson! Show yourself before I really get pissed off." I wore the traveler's wallet around my neck and placed the Pelican case in the sand. "Here . . . look. Here's your stuff."

After a long several seconds, my friend called from an uphill maze of vines, "Found my stash, huh? That's really gonna piss off the Guru, Doc. Don't want it, man. It's not safe with me."

"At least take your passport."

"No way. Bogdan intends to kill us all, you know. But I escaped and I've got a plan. So get back in your damn boat and take my stuff with you. We'll meet up later."

I indicated the distant wreckage of *No Más*. "Is that him, Bogdan?"

Tomlinson started to say, "Maybe . . . could be. The fake Shaman and maybe some giant Bolshevik—"

I cut him off. "That's between us. Come on, we're wasting time."

"Can't, Doc. Last night, I dodged a whole nightmare of ugliness—dinosaurs, all sorts of predatory shit and it changed me, man. Big-time changed me, like getting zapped by . . . well, don't get me started on meteors. About all I can tell you is, I'm gonna turn the tables on the Guru and, while I'm at it, save the life of our little buddy, the Mayan King."

I responded carefully, "Good idea. Let me help."

The man was still drug-muddled, obviously, and his sentences seemed labored. The way he slurred certain words was unlike any drunk I'd ever heard. And there was something else: I glimpsed a couple of child-sized shapes moving through the forest astride what had to be horses or mules.

The headstrong physician didn't wait in the boat. She walked past me, saying, "Tommy, it's me. Listen. You have to come with us, or—"

Tomlinson interrupted, "Whoa. Don't come any closer, lady. I bugged out before, and I'll do it again."

The neurologist repressed a grunt of frustration and halted. "Then at least take what I'm about to say seriously. You . . . your brain scans—the hematoma, it's bleeding again. You could die if we don't get you back to the States right away."

She indicated the Pelican case at my feet. "See? Thanks to your friend, you're all set. We could probably fly out tonight."

Tomlinson's response was multi-edged. "You never know who you can trust in this country . . . do you, Dr. Cruz?"

"Huh?" The woman frowned and crossed her arms. "What's that supposed to . . . ?"

I interrupted, "Hey—the guy's pulling anchor already. We've got to go."

"Hold on." She was still glaring in the direction of Tomlinson's voice. "What I told you is, don't trust anyone in Honduras you don't know well. You don't know me after our last night together? You didn't even leave a damn note, but here I am. Please listen to me."

Tomlinson limped out of the shadows. He was shirtless, haggard, and wore the same gaucho pantaloons. In his hand was the husk of a brown coconut. "Sorry, Dr. D. For some women—Doc will confirm this—sleeping with me doesn't always guarantee an introduction, let alone a note. But you're different. Where're you staying?"

The response of the pragmatic physician was mixed. "Well . . . thanks, but don't get the wrong idea. I mean, it was fun and all but, the point is, we need to get you to—"

I cut in, "Apology accepted. Now please get in the damn boat."

Behind me, Tomlinson hollered, "Heads up," and lobbed the coconut with just enough lead that I caught it without dropping the Pelican case.

"Airmail," he said, not joking, which could mean there was a note inside.

I responded by placing one of the little handheld GMRS radios on a rock and started toward the water. "Take this, leave it, that's up to you. There's a repeater on Roatán that should be in range. I've already got the frequency and tone logged in. Channel twenty-four."

From the panga, Naomi hollered to him, "I'm staying on Cayo Faro, the big house on the hill. You know the place. Want me to send a shuttle?"

I was telling her the guy had a rifle, to get down, when her handheld VHF squawked. She responded in English, which I found odd. "Is that you? Wave if that's you."

The boat with a T-top slowed, the driver—a huge male— waved from the distance.

Naomi told him, "Hang on. I'll check," then said to me, "I don't want to ride with him—not when he's drunk. My uncle's island isn't far."

"He owns an island?"

"Just a small one. Besides, I'd like to try and talk some sense into your freaked out pal."

I glanced at the T-top. "Jesus Christ, why is your shuttle guy carrying a rifle? He was aiming the damn thing at us."

"Aiming at you," the neurologist corrected. "Isn't that what bodyguards are paid to do?"

I waited until the shuttle boat had done an about-face before I dropped a stern anchor, waded ashore, and planted a bow anchor in the sand.

"You hired a bodyguard as a driver?"

Naomi said, "My uncle insists. And his bride loves giving me orders." She was out of the boat, moving toward the tree line where we'd last seen Tomlinson. "Are you coming?"

"I'll catch up," I told her.

I wanted to see what was inside the coconut husk I'd been lobbed.

SEVENTEEN

Tomlinson's note read, *"Bolsheviks are watching your hotel and the airstrip. I'll try to be on Utila tonight. White Conch Hotel at the bar. Have you figured out who she is yet?"*

Utila was a nearby island. I'd never heard of the hotel.

End of message.

I popped the Pelican case. As described, it was loaded with stacks of soiled hundred-, fifty-, and twenty-dollar bills—profit from his years of hauling pot. There was also a drawstring bag of coins minted in Russia. Gold coins from 1899, the face of Tsar Nicholas on the obverse. I slipped the travel wallet and bag inside, closed the case, and reread the note.

Aside from having to delay my response to the encrypted messages I might have received, abandoning my backstreet hotel wasn't a problem. Over the years, my travel habits have been revised and refined based on too many personal screw-ups to count. A simple rule of thumb is never leave anything in a rented room that would prevent me from catching a plane or crossing a border. That means plenty of cash in the money belt, passports waterproofed and concealed. Weaponry is occasionally problematic, but I've left more than one fine handgun disassembled and scattered across whatever country I happened to be fleeing. Cell phones are a liability. They leave a trail of breadcrumb pings, so I buy several burners and dispose of them along the way. Also disposable is clothing. I travel light: three shirts, three pairs of socks, the last clean pair to be worn on the return flight home.

A dependable pair of boots is a personal conceit. The light-weight jungle variety are best, good on and beneath the water, rugged enough to protect the feet from coral and rocks and equatorial heat.

I grabbed the Pelican case, got my boots under me and jogged to catch up with the neurologist. She'd stopped holler-ing Tomlinson's name and was followed his size 14 Birkenstocks across the sand toward an uphill forest rim. The handheld radio, I noticed, had mysteriously disappeared from the rock. One of the kids, maybe, had grabbed it.

The neurologist heard me coming but didn't look back. "Did he warn you about me?"

"What are you talking about?"

"His note. What did it say?"

I said, "He asked if I'd figured out who you are. And he'll try to stop by some bar that's on Utila. Personally, I'd rather find him sooner."

"That's all? Nothing about my *chinga* behavior, or that I'm a dangerous person to be around? Damn, he is such an irri-tating man."

"An armed bodyguard told me that much," I said. "As to behavior, Tomlinson's in no position to judge. Same with me. How does he know about your uncle's island?"

"They used to do some business together."

"Business?" I said and left the word hanging there. I had started up what looked like a path.

"Don't ask. Come on, this way's faster," she said. "When I was a kid, this was one of our favorite spots to explore. There used to be a little farm here, now the fruit trees have gone wild." She stepped on something sharp and hopped for a moment on one foot. "Damn, damn. These dive booties aren't made for hiking."

I placed the Pelican case on the sand. "Keep an eye on this. I'm going to run up and see if I can catch him. He might have been with a couple of boys on horses."

The woman said something about *Vaqueros* and *Campesinos*— that every kid in Honduras wanted to be a rich cowboy but ended up poor, working on palm oil farms. Palm oil, she said, was used in almost every food and cosmetic product worldwide.

The export had become the economic blood of Honduras.

That thought traveled with me to a dirt road atop a hill that rimmed the Caribbean Sea. Lots of hoofprints there but no Birkenstocks. Turn west, the busy port city of La Ceiba was twenty miles of risky bad road by car. Turn east, after a several miles of tin roofed housing was the village of Rio Coco where I'd paid a week in advance for a room with AC.

I looked seaward to a watercolor expanse of emerald and indigo. There was a scattering of islands, jungled peaks that jutted up hundreds of feet above the sea. The North Coast, locals call the area, or just The Coast as if no other salty border exists. It has traditionally been the most exploited area in the region, and that hasn't changed. Along with major power brokers in the Western world, there are countries on the opposite side of the Earth itching to get their hands on the mineral and petroleum bounty that has yet to be exploited.

It will happen if foreign powers continue to manipulate the region's corrupt politicos by instigating a lawless criminals-take-all society.

Trafficking is a catchall word that covers everything from smuggling rare birds to drugs to people. Few realize it's a multibillion-dollar industry that involves countries with ulterior political motives. Their intent is to destabilize the economies of Westernized nations. That's not a lunatic fringe theory as the intel agencies in some of those nations are aware. Kidnapping women and children for the sex trade is bad enough, but threatening the global economy is to declare a clandestine war.

That's exactly what occurred when well-organized factions started smuggling drugs and terrorists through a pipeline that flows north from Colombia to Mexico, Texas, and Florida. Blame the Chinese, blame the Russians, blame Islamicists worldwide—you should—but one or more covert agencies had finally decided to strike back strategically.

The diplomatic passport I'd been issued was no coincidence. For me, a small player in an international game, intercepting a Russian oligarch foolish enough to swim at night had been a good start. No telling how many other operators were out there hacking away at a global snake, killing the beast one head at a time.

I lingered at the top of the hill and stared toward the water, thinking, *The land of poor Campesinos, indeed.*

The scattering of islands where Dr. Naomi's uncle had a home drew my attention. They reminded me of the Rosarios off Cartagena, Colombia. Drug lords had purchased most of the islands and had built elaborate cocaine mansions there. Now most of them lay in ruin.

Fitting. Honduras, and much of Central America, illustrates the slow-motion cataclysms, geological and social, that make it, at once, among the most beautiful and dangerous regions on Earth. It is volcanic in form, volatile by nature and prophetic with a historic refrain that does not bode well for our species. Follow a compass in any direction and, sooner than later, you will stumble onto the ruins of several "great civilizations" that lie buried in jungle. Drug lords included.

"Business," they all referred to the trade. I might have re-gretted offering the physician a ride but for the possibility there was a connection. Poor Hondurans don't own islands, nor do their families send kids off to the States to become doctors.

Aléto came into my mind. We were in the boat putting toward open water when I brought up the subject of leprosy in Honduras.

"There used to be a leper colony near the Nicaraguan border," she said. "Hansen's disease. It's rare these days. Mostly in Asia and Africa. Why the question?"

"Tomlinson met this kid who supposedly has it. Or has symptoms, maybe."

"How old? The few cases I've heard about usually start in children under thirteen."

"That fits," I said.

"Do you have a name, or know where he is? I can send someone to check on him. Or examine him myself. Hang on a sec. You don't want this stuff rolling around the deck."

Fruit, she meant. She'd found a stalk of sugar bananas, several soursops and carambolas which she secured by stripping off her oversized shirt and making a bag of it. Then, wearing dive leggings and a white bikini top, sat to my right while I stood at the tiller.

"That's okay, you're allowed to peek," she chided and thrust her chest out. "My killer B's I call them."

"Funny," I responded. "I'll have to share that line with my fiancée when I get back to Florida."

She did the dismissive thing with her eyebrows again. "Take it easy, *Tigre*. My uncle's menopausal bride is the one your fiancée has to worry about, not me. Your buddy might be able to fill you in." She fumed about Tomlinson and her uncle's wife for a moment. "What about the boy? Do you know where he lives?"

I responded, "How'd you know the kid's a boy?" I gave it a beat. "Is the disease more common in male children?"

"Well, I just—no. Tomlinson doesn't strike me as the type to befriend little girls. That's just damn creepy. Do you want me to try and help the kid or not?"

"That's very kind of you," I said. "Hang on and tell me the names of those islands as we go past."

"Hah!" In Spanish she added, "You really are a gringo prude, aren't you?"

I opened the throttle, feeling the sun's reflection off a sandy bottom in water deep and clear enough to see copper-colored starfish fly by. If Aléto didn't want to be found, I wasn't going to blow his cover—not until I was sure of who I was dealing with. Dr. Naomi was still a blank page to me. Few admit it, but we assess and pass judgment on strangers within the first few minutes of meeting. Those judgments can be amended and updated down the line, but our instincts, which have evolved over eons, are usually dead-on.

What my instincts told me about the neurologist was that she was smart, observant, and she came from money. Possibly drug money. But her wanton woman, I'm-just-one-of-the-guys act was off-putting. It was either a shield or an excuse that created a no-entry buffer zone.

Many physicians and most cops employ a similar device, and understandably so. I no longer had a fiancée. Not officially. But loyalty in love and friendship is not just an emotional choice, it's the most rational choice if a person chooses to live comfortably inside his own head.

"What are you laughing at?" Naomi said looking at me.

"At myself. You're right," I said.

"About being a prude?"

She'd nailed it, but I said, "The kid. He's a boy maybe eleven or twelve years old. Maybe I can set something up after I drop you at your uncle's place."

"Only if you come ashore." The woman produced one of the soursops she'd foraged. It was prickly and green, the size of an avocado. "I'm going to pay for my ride by making a batch of *licuados*."

Licuados, she explained, were a Honduran favorite, sort of like a fruit slushy with rum.

"You drink, don't you?"

I said, "I'll stop for a few minutes, then I've got to go."

"But Tomlinson said he might meet you at some bar later. Why not stick around until at least sunset? Are you going to make me say it? I hate being alone with that poisonous witch, Fay."

"Who?"

"Fidelia, my uncle's wife. Fay, we call her—that's as close as she'll ever come to fidelity."

The name touched a familiar chord.

I started to ask why her uncle wasn't on the island but had to pay attention to a line of shoals ahead. We'd powered into an iceberg fleet of islands, each capped with a highland peak, most of them tiny, only a few hundred yards wide. Water was glassy slick in this protected space, a geology of coral below. I skirted the largest of them, the "pig islands"—*Cayos Cochinos*—and followed an indigo rivulet until the bottom fell away in shafts of golden sargassum light.

"There it is," the neurologist said, pointing to what might have been the setting for the old TV show, *Gilligan's Island*. It was a jungled cone encircled by palms and silver sand with an inlet where at least one boat was moored. Beyond was deep ocean.

"No lighthouse on Cayo Faro?" I asked. "Lighthouse Key" was the English translation.

"Used to be. The old foundation's on the other side." Naomi stretched her arms and yawned. "It's a ball-breaker of a climb."

"What do they do for power?"

"Used to be a big diesel generator. Noisy as hell. But the

rico suaves out here, you know, the type who can buy islands? They had the political juice to get the government to lay cable."

"Like your uncle," I said, not as a question.

"He was never that suave, but yeah. This place has some nice little touches like AC, an outdoor party bar, even a helicopter landing pad. For communication, there's a satellite phone, and we've got an outdoor shower, too. Not much privacy—as if anyone cares out here—but it's got hot and cold. Tell you what, you shower first while I tell the kitchen to get us some ice and something to snack on."

Seeing the uncle's house took me back to the cocaine mansions off Cartagena, Colombia. The builder had carved out half-ton blocks of coral and stacked them into a pair of two-story wings. In the middle was a commons area with porches and louvered teak windows all around. Decades of equatorial sun had darkened the coral to bone gray. Draped across the balcony was a new political banner in blue and red:

Vota Por la Libertad!

Vota Por la Brava!

The possibilities were coming together in my mind. The name Fidelia, which was uncommon, matched the name of the archaeologist, Dr. Fidelia Martinez Brava, who'd written Tomlinson a note about a one-armed orphan and a Mayan King who'd been butchered more than three hundred years ago.

I idled along at slow speed. "Little house on the beach, huh? Looks more like some politico's mansion," I said. "Naomi, on second thought, I'll just drop you off and get going."

The physician was speaking English into her handheld VHF, saying to a man's voice, "What do you mean you're off island? Where'd you go? I'm with a visitor who's carrying a gun." After a garbled response, she looked at me, amused. "Your buddy was right. You're a quick study. You've already figured out who my uncle is, haven't you?"

"I'm guessing he's the governor who got extradited to the

States," I replied, referring to Teoscar Brava who'd been sentenced to twenty-five years for trafficking. "Sounds like his wife has already moved on with her love life. I'm also guessing you and your uncle share at least one surname."

"Love has nothing to do with it," the woman scoffed. "Fay the sex addict—the sexual deviant, more like it. She was even worse before Uncle Teo went to jail."

"Fay as in Fidelia," I said. "She's head of the university's archaeology department, right?"

This surprised her. "*Was* head of the department. But how in the world did you . . . ?" she started to say, then backed up. "Tomlinson must have told you about Fay." The physician made a throaty sound of derision. "Did he mention she was a suspect when there was a security breach at the National Museum?"

"The museum was robbed?"

"Just the opposite. Someone broke in and left two boxes of Mayan artifacts. Crazy, huh? Some very rare stuff. Jade, a lot of carvings. A few nights later, the same thing happened."

"Another break-in? Same museum? And she was blamed for the security breach?"

"Nope, she was blamed by some wealthy collectors whose homes had been robbed. She was, you know, *terminado*, out of a job—this was two years ago—so she seduced my uncle who had her research credentials reinstated. And her salary doubled. There's a reason tabloids call her Fidelia the Fer-de-Lance. With her money and power, I'm surprised she hasn't been kidnapped. Or worse. I told you about the femicide stats."

I said, "You really don't like the woman."

She heard something in my tone. "You think I'm jealous? Well, okay, maybe I am. A little. Twenty years ago, she was crowned Ms. Honduras. Got a full ride to Stanford, then a PhD from Florida. Learned to speak perfect English, which didn't impress Hollywood, but she's acted like a movie queen ever since. Me, the plain-looking niece who's had to work her ass off for everything."

I looked toward the mooring area where I saw no boat with a T-top, no bodyguards. "Why warn them about my gun?"

She answered, "It isn't obvious? Fay is running for Uncle Teo's job, so she has a security team. Well, one dumbass guy and Iron Baby, actually. It's the way it works down here after a political coup, or some high-ranking crook goes to prison. The beautiful wife steps in and takes over his office."

From Mexico to Nicaragua, this was often true.

I said, "She wants to be governor of—what's the name of this state, or the department, I guess, that includes the Mískito Coast?"

"One of eighteen departments," she said, already bored with the subject. "You, Dr. Ford are in the *Departmento de Gracias de Dios*—don't laugh. Look it up. The largest, least populated and most dangerous department in Honduras—which has the highest femicide rate in Latin America. Impressed? If you're really hot on the subject, special election is in six weeks. Aren't you thirsty after listening to all this boring shit?"

I tried to ask about the unusual museum break-in—someone had risked arrest to return Mayan artifacts? But the neurologist cut me off, saying, "We have the whole outside terrace to ourselves, so why not have a nice cold *licuado*? If we're lucky, Fay won't make an appearance until sunset. Depending on the vibe, we might be gone by then."

I said, "You're not staying?"

She didn't answer for a moment. A big-shouldered man, shaved head, had appeared atop the marina basin's seawall. He stared at us and ducked out of view, wearing some kind of ankle cast, lots of white gauze visible.

"Who the hell's that?" she said. "He doesn't work here, never seen him before. Fay's bodyguards left the island. Hopefully, they took her with them."

"Something wrong?"

"Dunno. The way that bald dude was staring, like he recognized me. Or you, maybe. What was it you said about if something doesn't feel right, it probably isn't?"

"Want me to head back to the mainland?" I was wondering if it was the Russian I'd shot in the foot.

"Hang on. I don't want to overreact. Let's play it cool at least long enough for me to use the toilet and get my computer and stuff. You can dock there." Naomi pointed and started to get a bowline ready. "Fay hates me. Scares me a little, too. She's jealous because I'm in Uncle Teo's will."

I said, "Think that might be the real reason her bodyguard went off and left you?"

"Wouldn't be surprised," Naomi said. "The bitch is like a menopausal wasp."

After a moment of reflection, she concluded, "Nope, not surprised at all she'd like me dead. Fay could do it and get away with it, too, no problem. This is Honduras. Remember?"

EIGHTEEN

Naomi said, "I don't recommend swimming on this side of the island. Not since the scuba shops started doing cara-cara dives."

Caracara was a type of bird. It was also a local term that, in Spanish, referred to diving face-to-face with sharks.

I stood on a patio built over the water. Forty feet beneath the water's surface, coral heads resembled an acreage of wildflowers. An abrupt drop-off marked the deep-ocean rim. "Do the dive companies use chum, or do they actually feed the sharks? Either way, it's a dumb thing to do."

"That's your opinion as a biologist?" Naomi had retrieved her roller bag and returned from the kitchen with a bowl of ice and two huge margarita glasses, the rims already dusted with demerara sugar. The lady was visibly more relaxed, which made sense when she said, "Fay's not here, thank God, which explains why the maid and Iron Baby left the island. So, you know, like dingdong, the witch has fled. Temporarily."

Wearing a lavender beach pullover and Nikes, she got busy behind the bar using a battery-powered blender. On the cutting board were green coconuts, a pineapple, soursops, a mango, and some locally grown spices. Angel trumpet shrubs, their phallic orange blossoms distinctive, framed a veranda that opened into a main room I had yet to tour. Outdoor steps led down to a courtyard and a series of oversized aviaries that contained parrots and macaws. The bald guy with the bad foot had disappeared and there were no boats moored in the lagoon that I could see from this side of the island.

I said, "Chumming sharks, that's my opinion as diver. There's no research to back it up—not yet anyway—but, well . . . when shark tours were banned in Florida, some operators moved to the Bahamas. Within a year or so, two tourists—maybe three, not sure—were killed while snorkeling shallow, inshore reefs. Some of the safest areas in the world. Or used to be.

"In water this clear—" I stared down at a pier where my boat was tied "—it wasn't a case of mistaken identity. That's usually the cause. Especially in murky water. But animals, sharks included, they're smart enough to associate people with food if they're fed. Can you imagine getting out of a car where tourists feed grizzly bears? The same thing. It's just damn stupid. Tell your uncle's wife that if she gets elected."

Naomi replied, "Like she'd listen," and used the blender to mix fruit with coconut water with ice and a generous pour of Flor de Caña Rum.

"I know that rum. It's from Nicaragua," I said when the noise stopped. "I've been to the distillery. During the last revolution, it was one of the few safe places you could go in the country. Neither side wanted to blow it up."

She raised her eyes at the mention of revolution but chose not to inquire. "This rum's locally made. From the distillery in Chichigulpa."

"On the Pacific Coast?" I said. "I didn't know Flor de Caña had a factory in Honduras." As I spoke, a trio of shadows glided from deep water onto the island's crystalline rim. Hammerheads, six to eight feet long, their long dorsal fins cutlass-like.

They snaked into the shallows slowly, probably in search of stingrays. A favorite prey. I summoned Naomi with a wave. "You might be right about swimming on this side of the island."

She placed the pitcher of *licuados* on the patio table, then stood beside me, shoulder-high, her hair sun-streaked now that it was dry. "Those are nothing compared to some of the monsters that show up at night. Or used to. It's been a while since I've slept here. Have a seat. The maid must be a mind reader. The margarita glasses were already sugared when I opened the freezer. She's gone, too, so it's just you and me, Dr. Ford."

There was no bawdy inflection, which was a relief.

I said, "Doc. Just Doc is fine." My attention turned to the drink setup. As a garnish the maid, or someone, had added yellow angel trumpet blossoms to the tray. "You're not going to put those in the drinks, right? The sap can blind you I've read, which means they're probably poisonous."

"No shit, and not the first time I told her to use frangipanis instead. What are you, a botanist, too?" The woman had poured a glass for herself and was about to pour mine when I asked, "Did she know you were bringing a guest?"

"The maid? No. But she always puts margarita supplies in the freezer before she leaves the island."

I got up. "Just to be safe, let me see if I can find some plastic cups. Under the bar, maybe?"

With a napkin, she tossed the trumpet blossoms off the balcony and took a small sip. "*Umm, perfecto*, if I do say so myself. The drink won't taste the same in plastic, but you're welcome to go look. If not under the bar, there's a supply closet on the veranda. First door to your right."

When I slipped my bag from under the table, she added, "Let me guess. There's a gun in there, and you don't trust me. You're worried I'm trying to drug you, right?"

I conceded, "Or someone is. Maybe both of us."

"You're serious."

"How'd the maid know you were going to make *licuados* when you got back? I don't believe in mind readers. Two frozen glasses, not just one. And what about the angel trumpets?"

Naomi tested the demerara glaze on the rim of her glass. "Umm. Sweet. It's just sugar."

At the same instant, we both felt a vibrating rumble through the floor. It lasted for a couple of seconds, then was gone.

"A minor tremor," she said. "You get used to it. Give it a sec, and let's see if it gets any worse."

She tasted the Demerara glaze again, and continued, "Nothing wrong with this. I think you're paranoid because of what happened to Tomlinson."

"What happened to him says I'm not," I replied. "Do me a favor and don't drink any more of that stuff until I get back."

No plastic cups under the bar so I crossed beneath a trellis of scarlet blossoms onto the veranda. It was framed by a rock wall that blocked Naomi's view. "Is there a guest bathroom in here?" I called.

"Through the French doors, bottom floor," she answered. "Hurry up, I'm thirsty."

I went through the doors, down coral stairs past a guest bathroom, into a spacious main hall, high ceilinged with slow wicker ceiling fans. Ornate tile floor, retro Spanish furniture, stiff leather-backed chairs of dark wood, Mayan artwork and framed paintings on whitewashed walls of bone.

Above a fireplace, the largest painting dominated the room. A semi-nude in gilded oils of a woman, an aloof beauty, eyes of liquid amber, a raven mane that flowed over shoulders of sandlewood skin. Curls and swirls followed the upward curvature of her breasts and revealed a hint, just a hint of pink that promised one flushed areola lay beneath.

I felt an abdominal stirring. I released a slow breath. I'm not attracted to the fashion model types. Too delicate, too breakable with their predictable Hollywood angularity. But there was nothing delicate or predictable about the amber eyes that stared down at me.

A step closer I saw a toughness that bordered on the predatory which was unexpected but authentic. Women of the rarest beauty, and she was among them, are exposed to men's darkest instincts long before they exit their teens. They enter adulthood either badly scarred or fully armed to do whatever is required to protect themselves.

The woman was Fidelia Martinez Brava, PhD. Had to be. The next room, an office confirmed it. I took it all in with a glance. Framed magazine covers, photos, and diplomas. They documented Fidelia's transition from Ms. Honduras, age twenty-one, bedecked in a gown and tiara to a smiling field archaeologist in boots and khaki.

There'd been trips to Egypt, to an ancient ruin in the Ukraine, the Great Wall of China, Machu Picchu in Peru. As she'd aged, even in group photos, her beauty dominated the camera lens. Men, their expressions sheepish, seemed to wilt into a timid backdrop that made room only for her.

The photo history of her time married to Governor Teo Brava told a story. It existed only in dusty outlines where frames had once hung. The man had been banished from his own vacation hideaway.

I consulted my watch. I had a couple of minutes before she would doubt I was using the toilet, so I picked the lock on the office desk. Inside were several mini baggies of white powder—cocaine, most likely—prescription Xanax, a complicated rechargeable sex toy, more photos, and a MacBook Pro.

Fay, the archaeologist sex addict, Naomi had called the woman.

I reached into my bag, opened the computer and inserted a hacker's thumb drive. A red LED flashed green when the password had been breached. The internal microcontrollers immediately began downloading files. A mini screen told me the process would take twenty-seven minutes. Way too much time. After a moment of indecision, I returned the computer to the desk but left the thumb drive to finish its work.

It would be easy enough to contrive some excuse later and retrieve the thing.

A small, framed photo grabbed my attention. It was a picture of Fidelia taken here, in front of the fireplace. Smiling, dressed in khaki, she held a spectacular jade Mayan mask as if it were a trophy. A king's death mask. The size, the perfect contours were unmistakable. No wonder the feds and Fidelia Brava were after the one-armed orphan boy.

I managed a smile. The story about someone breaking into the National Museum and returning artifacts now made sense. Maybe. Were Aléto and his army of homeless castaways on a mission to rescue ancient treasures? If so, among the wealthy collectors the kids had robbed was the former governor and his intimidating wife. The death mask of jade, the kid had kept for himself.

I was in the office doorway, fixated on the woman's portrait, her haunting eyes, the suggestive swirls and nude contours, when Naomi's voice surprised me from the steps.

"Oh good Christ. Not again," she said with a grimace that I mistook for disgust. "Please tell me you haven't already fallen in love with that . . . that succubus. And just when I was beginning to think . . . That if I needed help, you would—" She flinched, placed a hand on her stomach and moaned again.

I walked her into the office toward the desk. "Are you sick?"

I was already blaming the licuados.

She replied, "I feel sicker now that I saw you ogling that bitch. It's not jealousy. Believe me. We've got a bigger problem. The bald guy we saw earlier? He didn't see me, but I saw him sneaking up the side steps to the patio."

"Just now?"

"What do you think? He's carrying a machete, and I'm pretty damn sure he's not here to do yardwork."

Naomi's face was pale and there were beads of sweat on her forehead. She noticed the open desk drawer. "Are you snooping or stealing? Either way, stop what you're doing, Doc, I need some . . . Oh hell. I shouldn't have drank that shit, now I've gotta make myself throw up. And water, I need lots of water."

When she stumbled closer, I caught her by the shoulders before she fell. "How much did you drink? The whole glass?"

"Goddamn it," she muttered. "Just a sip. One little sip, so the symptoms shouldn't last long. The drug, whatever it is, must've been in the ice. Or that freakin' orange flower. But why would the maid try to poison me?"

I said, "Or powder mixed with sugar on the rim of the glass. Scopolamine, you think? You said yourself it's the most common— Come on, let's get you to a bathroom. Then a hospital."

"What about the machete guy? You still have that gun? I can't puke and order him off the property at the same time."

She placed a hand on the open drawer for balance. When she saw the complicated sex toy, she made a coughing sound that was laughter. "Fay, the menopausal scalp hunter. She even came onto me one time, then told me my tits were too small. Oh—and I wasn't hot enough."

I grabbed my bag, grabbed a pillow off the couch, and hurried her into the bathroom. Tested the brass dead bolt and decided it was strong enough. "Lock the door, stay here and use the pillow if you need it." I was checking the magazine of my full-sized 9 mm while she gulped water directly from the sink spigot.

After a glance back, she asked, "Do you have another one of those? Or a knife maybe? Goddamn it, don't look at me like that. I want to be able to protect myself if he breaks in here swinging that machete."

I left her with my palm-sized Sig P365 and felt better about it when she dropped the mag and checked the chamber.

"He's probably just here looking for work," I said, going out the door.

"Yeah? What if he's not?"

"Then I'll scare him off. The last thing I want to do is shoot somebody." I paused. "And damn it, when I come back, I'll knock three times so make sure you don't shoot me."

When the door was closed and bolted, I threaded a sound suppressor onto the pistol's barrel. Then went up the steps knowing, if it was the Russian flesh trafficker, I wouldn't shoot him in the foot this time.

NINETEEN

The NFL-sized bald man was Russian. It was in his accent.
But I couldn't be sure it was the man I'd shot, despite the
medical foot booty, because he'd worn a ski mask. Now
heavy leather gloves covered what might be a telltale tattoo on
the back of his left hand. An elaborate orthodox cross in blue.

I wanted to be sure before confronting him. So, from a
screen of Easter-egg-colored trumpet blossoms, I watched and
waited, looking down on the courtyard below, all too aware
that I had to get back to Naomi fast. What if she asphyxiated?
What if the drug had caused her heart to stop?

The Russian carried a machete but Naomi was right. He
wasn't here to do yardwork. He'd come to transport an aviary
full of squawking macaws and toucans to some black-market
destination. With him were a couple of young local *Maras*—
gangbangers—judging from the spiderweb of tattoos that
covered their bodies from head to forearms. And this wasn't
their first time. They knew the courtyard's layout, and they'd
brought a wagon load of cages pulled by a small garden tractor.

No wonder Fidelia Brava and her small staff had left the
island. A woman with political aspirations couldn't risk as-
sociating with traffickers. Not out in the open. Some tourist

boaters, or a journalist with a camera, might idle past. I had no doubt, though, the profits would go to her.

With the Russian barking orders in terrible Spanish, the gangbangers got busy with what was a tedious job. Enter the aviary, catch a bird, put a towel over its head and transfer it to a cage on the wagon. These men weren't going anywhere soon, so I backtracked into the house, down the steps to the bathroom door. Inside, I could hear water running. The shower maybe.

"It's me. Don't shoot," I said after three sharp raps.

Naomi was conscious but groggy when she let me in. Haggard and pale-faced, hair dripping. She was also naked, and her balance wasn't good. I tried to help her back into the shower, but she said, "Nope. Time to puke again. What happened to the guy with the machete?"

"They're out there loading Fidelia's black-market birds."

"They?" She seemed unsurprised by my black market comment.

"Three of them, but we're okay for now. We need to get you to a hospital. Medevacked. I should be able to reach Roatán Marine Patrol. I know they monitor VHF channel nineteen. I doubt if the Russian cares if we're here or not."

The woman knelt on the cushion and leaned her head over the commode. "It's not panic time yet. I'm a doctor, remember? Go to the kitchen, bring me a box of baking soda—check the cupboards. Then come back here and hold my hair. I'm tired of washing vomit out of my hair." As I was leaving, she instructed, "Bring me a glass and a couple eggs too."

"Eggs?" I wondered if she was delirious.

"Just do it. Gargling raw eggs is safer than sticking my goddamn fingers down my throat."

I returned with the items from the kitchen, plus a big baggy robe which caused her to say, "Sweet of you, but not 'till I'm done here. I'd just have wash the robe, too." Naomi belched, wiped her nose, and made a groaning sound. "*Querido*, there's no such thing as modesty when a woman has her head in the toilet. You know how to separate egg whites?"

I did it while she gulped water and baking soda to neutralize stomach acids in her throat. Next, raw egg whites became a potent emetic when gargled, as the neurologist proved while I knelt patiently and held her hair.

"How are you feeling?" I said. She was on her feet finally, ready for the shower again.

"Are you kidding? Check the toilet. I think I might've left my anus in there somewhere."

The woman hadn't lost her sense of humor.

She accepted the robe, but hung it on a coral knob, unconcerned. "If it was scopolamine, I didn't get much of it. I'd either be unconscious by now, or in some kind of zombie trance. I've seen it—Devil's Breath. Here's a test. Tell me to do something. Like an order. It doesn't take much scopolamine to make a victim crazy suggestible."

"Okay? Put the robe on," I said.

"Is that the best you can do?" She said this in a chiding way but was relieved. "Nope. Not until I'm out of the shower. Make sure to knock when you come back."

Going up the stairs I heard a metallic crash and a fleshy bone-on-bone thud. Weapon pulled, I used the terrace wall for cover and peered out at the patio bar. The Russian lay hyperventilating on his side after tumbling backward in his chair. His empty margarita glass remained unbroken on the table. Beside it, the pitcher of licuados was nearly empty.

The Russian had been thirsty. He'd taken off his leather gloves to drink.

I gave it a sec, thinking his gangbanger crew might come to his aid. But they were still busy caging birds, oblivious to noise because of the tractor and the squawking, pissed-off macaws. I crept out. Noted the blue Orthodox cross on the man's left hand and nudged him with my foot. Slowly his head pivoted, eyeballs fluttering, his face a grotesque, twitching mask as if suffering a grand mal seizure. Violent muscle contractions signaled a brain on overload, an explosion of psychedlic electrical activity.

For a moment he became lucid. His mouth opened and he groaned something in Russian. A pleading request. Then, in English mumbled, "Help . . . I am needing."

"Yes, you are," I responded. "Roll over."

It was pathetic how desperately his body attempted to comply. A reaction to scopolamine poisoning? Maybe.

I tossed the machete off the terrace and went through his pockets. Found a wad of Honduran lempiras, cigarettes, lighter, an expensive out-the-front stiletto. In his back pocket was a thick envelope of US $100 bills in wrappers. Four thousand dollars at least. There was no gun, which I found odd.

The envelope and his cell phone went into my tactical bag. Again he whispered, "Help. Cannot . . . breathe."

With my foot I turned his head so he had a downhill view of the pier where my little boat was moored and tried Naomi's test. "Get in the water. See the water? You'll feel better after a swim."

Mightily he tried to obey, pulling himself toward the beach on his elbows, dragging his dead legs behind.

"Devil's Breath," locals called the drug because to ingest it was to give one's soul to the devil.

The Russian wasn't going anywhere fast, so I went down into the courtyard and surprised the gangbangers from behind. They threw their hands up when they saw the pistol, but with a surly reaction that was not a surrender. Nor did they move when, in Spanish, I told them to open the cages and release the birds.

The oldest Mara, all sinew and tattoo, lowered his hands.

"Who the hell are you, *cabrone*?" His eyes looked beyond me, as if expecting to see the Russian to appear.

"He's gone. I'm in charge now, so just do what I say. Open those damn cages and do it now."

When the second Mara dropped his hands, I fired a round that kicked up sand between his feet. He was just a kid, late teens at most, and it scared the hell out of him. I think it probably had more to do with the sound suppressor—an exotic piece of equipage in the minds of two peasant Hondurans.

Either way, that got them moving. But as they walked toward the wagon and the cages stacked there, I knew they were also looking for some kind of weapon to use. Attached to the back of the tractor was a tool rack. The obvious choice was an axe. There was also a small sledgehammer and a couple of machetes—always a necessity when working in the jungles of Central America.

"Don't even think about it," I warned.

Finally, they did as instructed.

The cages were made of wire mesh. A handle on the top, a wire door with a latch, several macaws or toucans crammed into each cage. Four cages had been emptied when the youngest gangbanger, not as defiant as his partner, faced me and said, "Who is going to pay us? My wife is . . . we are having a baby. She will expect me to return with money."

"How much is the Russian paying you?" I asked.

"Who?"

"The foreigner. The gringo. How much did he promise to pay?" A long pause told me the older man was trying to invent some inflated figure. He was also edging toward the tractor, so I added, "How does two thousand dollars sound? A thousand each."

"In U.S. dollars?" He didn't believe me.

The younger Mara was hopeful but dubious. "The foreigner was going to pay us in lempiras. Only about twenty dollars, American. You can't possibly have so much money."

I opened the Russian's envelope and tossed two wrapped bundles of hundreds a safe distance from the tractor's tool rack. The younger man knelt, rifled through the bills. His eyes went wide.

"Mother of God," he whispered and showed the cash to his partner. "It is true. All for us?"

I told them, "You're working for me now. That's the deal. Understood?"

Their eyes moved to the terrace, obviously afraid of the Russian.

"Don't worry about him. He's drunk. Very drunk. He'll do whatever I tell him to do. I think he's been drugged with scopolamine." In response to their blank stares, I translated, "Burundanga. Devil's Breath. Do we have a deal?"

They understood what that meant. I could tell. The younger man smiled while his partner, no longer surly, asked, "What would you have us do? One thousand dollars is a great fortune. But we have families. We can't go to jail."

"It's not a crime to set birds free," I reminded them. "I'm in a hurry. I don't want to stand here and guard you. Where's the foreigner's boat?"

They pointed to the other side of the island. A very fast boat, they said. Yes, they knew how to drive it, but didn't know the make. It had three big outboard motors and the cabin and lots of room on the deck for carrying stolen birds.

"Empty those cages and stay here until I get back. I might have some more work for you. That'll mean more money. If you try to run, I'll find you—and you have families. Remember?"

The older Mara's furtive glance at the tool rack caused me to walk to the tractor. The Russian's pistol was under the seat. A P-96 semi. The same 9mm weapon issued to their military. Ten rounds in the magazine and one in the pipe. I cleared the chamber, pocketed the mag, and tossed the weapon close their feet.

"A present from me," I said. "If the foreigner shows up, use it to scare him. But he's so drunk on Devil's Breath, I think he'll do anything you order him to do. Wouldn't that be fun?"

Their surprised expressions told me, *Yes. It would.*

On the patio, the Russian had managed to sit up. His face was still twitching, but he had regained control of his eyes.

"Don't move until I tell you to," I said. "Blink if you understand." He nodded but was confused. He stared longingly at the water, still convinced that an ocean swim would save him.

The pitcher of *licuados* or the margarita glasses had been laced with Devil's Breath. This was proof enough for me.

I hurried down to the bathroom, knocked three times. Naomi had changed into pleated fishing shorts, boating shoes and a blue collared blouse. The sort of outfit yachters wear to cocktail hour at a nice hotel. She had retrieved her computer and roller bag.

"Looks like you're feeling better," I said.

With a worried look, she shook her head. "I stopped vomiting, but I'm having some hallucinatory episodes. Goddamn it. They come out of nowhere then just sort of disappear. And I get these weird urges to take off running. You know, the first onset of a panic attack. We need to get off this island before Fidelia gets back."

When I suggested the hospital in Tegucigalpa, that we should leave now, she produced a small black satellite phone I hadn't seen before. "I'm waiting for a call from a researcher I know in Guatemala City. Called the IBM Institute. They've patented a test strip that can confirm the amount of scopolamine in my system. I'm hoping they'll overnight it to the medical clinic on Utila. The medical director there, she's a friend of mine. I've called her too. I need a drug called physostigmine, and they have it. A sort of antidote. Can you give me twenty minutes to set up an appointment?"

I said, "Sure." It would give me time to deal with the Russian.

Before I left, she held out her hand saying, "I believe this belongs to you. The less evidence we leave behind the better. Isn't that what they teach you at spy school?"

It was the tactical thumb drive I'd left in Fidelia's laptop.

She began to slur her words, saying. "Did you upload the . . . spyware? Or just steal all her files? Don't worry, I won't tell as long as you're not here . . . here to help her. If she finds out, she'll go into one of her insane rages."

"We need to leave soon as possible," I said. "I think you're getting worse not better."

"Wait. Listen. I'm talking about revenge. Fidelia is big on revenge. And she's not going to be very happy when she finds out all her black-market birds are gone. I saw what you made those workers do from the window."

I replied, "Make your calls. I'll pull the boat around to the lagoon and meet you there."

"Why not the pier where we tied up?"

The strange sci-fi pinging of the satellite phone spared me the need to invent a lie about my plans for the Russian.

She checked caller ID. "It's the White Conch Hotel, not Guatemala. Before that shit hit me, I made reservations—two rooms. Okay?"

It was the same hotel Tomlinson had mentioned in his note. There had to be a connection.

"Fine," I said, but felt certain the neurologist would spend the night at the clinic—if she didn't have to be airlifted.

TWENTY

N aomi said to me, "There's blood on your face. And your clothes, what the hell? That wasn't you I saw swimming off the pier, was it? I warned you about sharks."

"Fell in," I lied and touched the lump on my forehead. The Russian had not been as suggestible as I'd hoped.

"Well, some fool was out there in the water. A least, I imagined I saw a person floundering around. By the time I got to the terrace, though, whoever it was, they were gone."

I was in my boat, alongside the seawall. She passed me her bag and computer case and stepped aboard muttering, "Another damn hallucination, I bet. My friend at the clinic wanted to send a helicopter. But I told her we could be at the public dock in twenty, twenty-five minutes. Sound about right? She's going to have EMTs there waiting."

"Get in the boat," I told her, "before you pass out."

She did but kept talking. I sensed she feared losing consciousness. "My contact in Guatemala will overnight the test strips. There's a small airport on the island not far from the main tourist drag. Almost all the businesses and hotels are crammed along Main Street. Waterfront of course."

The island of Utila was a dinosaur shape on the horizon, eight miles or so away but the sea was flat. An easy run.

The woman, using a PFD as a cushion, settled in on the seat beside me. She held a two-liter bottle of water in one hand, the satellite phone in the other. I got the little boat up on plane, traveling at a comfortable speed over slow, greasy swells of luminous purple. The color change indicated a deep crevasse lay beneath the hull. Or a crater—perhaps from a meteorite that had forever changed the earth.

Every now and then I glanced back at Teo Brava's mansion built on a hill among coconut palms. A swarm of gulls, terns, frigates were dive-bombing an area off the deepwater pier. Depth charge explosions showered the surface from beneath. An occasional fin or scythe tail provided a boiling slick. On land or water, watch for bird activity. They are nature's most dependable trackers.

Unaware, the neurologist asked, "What happened to the guy with the machete? You scared him off?"

"Think so. I asked him a few questions, got a few answers and then he left. I'm pretty sure he won't be back for a while."

"Questions about what?"

"We'll talk about it after your doctor friend gets you checked out. It was no big deal."

Another lie.

Even drugged and suggestible the Russian had put up a fight before I'd finally bulled him off the pier. He'd caught me with a big right fist that knocked me into the water with him.

It's a Hollywood fiction that sharks, unless in a feeding frenzy, eagerly attack swimmers. But the percussion of two big men hitting the water simultaneously had scared the hell out of hammerheads. They had rocketed off, gone for good I feared. As a precaution, I'd climbed onto the Russian's back, laced his legs in mine and used a rear naked choke to put him away.

I took another look aft. The sharks had returned on this tropical late afternoon an hour before sunset. It was feeding time.

Naomi battled to stay conscious by talking. "Scaring the guy off might not have been a smart thing to do. The same with those tattooed workers. If Fidelia hired them, she'll want . . . want revenge. She'll want to know what the hell happened to her macaws and toucans."

"The Maras you're talking about?"

"The teenage gangbangers. MS-Fourteen and Barrio-Eighteen, hundreds of thousands of them in this country. They're not just tattooed for life, they're marked for life. Even six-, seven-year-old kids are forced to join. They'll do anything for money. Not shitting you, Doc. *Anything.*"

I was counting on that. I had struck a deal with the tatted pair. Gather information on Bogdan, the Guru fraud. How big was his operation? Who were the major players? Kidnap the man and hold him for me, there would be a bonus. Maybe they would honor the agreement, maybe they wouldn't. I'd given them another thousand of the Russian's money as an advance, the rest to be paid on delivery.

"I'm willing to hire five or six members of your gang," I'd told them, "if that's what it takes."

I didn't share this information with the neurologist. Tomlinson had given me the impression that he didn't trust the woman. Why would I? Not yet—even though she was probably too drugged-up to remember anyway.

The question bouncing around in my mind was, if the absent maid was unaware that Naomi was bringing a guest to the island, why were there two frozen margarita glasses drugged and ready in the freezer?

The island of Utila is about seven miles long, two miles wide, the highest elevation at the northern tip, three hundred feet above the water. Green hills and rocky bluffs. A thriving tourist industry—scuba and fishing and vacation honeymooners—had crowded in shoulder-to-shoulder along the rim of a natural deepwater anchorage on the leeward side. We were about a mile offshore when a fragrant land breeze found us, flower scented, spiced with citrus and the woodsmoke odor of cooking fires.

Naomi, sounding drunk, went on another talking jag and told me about Utila. There were only about three thousand full-time residents, and the medical clinic where her colleague worked was damn good considering the size and remoteness of the island. Interesting. But my attention had shifted to another military-looking Huey that had appeared from the mainland. It was flying low over the water, straight for my boat.

Or was it trying to intercept another aircraft?

Also angling toward us was what looked like an ultralight paraglider. It was the slow quiet variety, a two-seater, propeller cage aft, with pontoons and landing gear beneath parafoil wings that were rainbow colored. It approached from our stern, twenty feet above the surface as if on a strafing mission.

When Naomi saw it, she blinked as if trying to focus. "What the hell is . . . ? Looks like a giant butterfly. My God, so pretty. I'd love to fly in something like that one day." She waited for a sober moment. "Or am I hallucinating again? I hope to God my doctor friend has that drug I need ready."

"You're not hallucinating," I said.

"You sure?"

I pointed. "See that helicopter? Military, it looks like. Get down on the deck and cover yourself with those tarps." When she hesitated, I told her "I'm not kidding. Do it now, okay?" Either because of the drug or the tone of my voice, she yielded in a robotic way.

The two-seater ultralight descended portside within shouting distance, so low I thought it might be attempting to land.

I did the touristy thing. I smiled and waved. But then

stopped when I noticed the pilot's flowing sun-bleached shoulder-length hair. Saw his baggy gaucho pantaloons and a new wardrobe addition, a scarlet Hawaiian shirt. His surfer's two-fingered Shaka greeting left no doubt who the pilot was. With his left hand he gestured with the GMRS radio I'd provided. It had nothing to do with the cheap intercom headset he wore.

"Holy Christ, that's Tomlinson," I said aloud.

The neurologist was interested. "Tommy knows how to fly? That's . . . that's so very cool. He never mentioned that he's a pilot."

"He's not. But, when he's stoned, he believes he is because he landed my amphib a couple of times."

"Your amphib? Like a seaplane?"

"A four-seater Maule. Trust me, flying with him was a tight sphincter experience. I promised myself I'd never give him another damn lesson."

"But you *are* a pilot," she said. "A real pilot. Is that true?" Unless it was the drug talking, she meant something by that. Maybe her wealthy family had access to a plane.

"Just an amateur," I responded. "Oh . . . hold on. You see that? He's got—he's got freakin' passengers aboard. Kids. All helpless kids."

Strapped into the rear seat, which was designed for one adult, were three ragged children wearing orange PFDs. They laughed and waved while the smallest kid pointed at the chopper. *"Patrón. Patrón!"* he wailed above the noise. "The federales, they are after us, *patrón*! The tall sailor is a crazy airplane thief."

It was Aléto, his missing arm hidden by a baggy long-sleeved shirt. He, too, wore a wire headset which is why Tomlinson grinned and gave me a thumbs-up as confirmation.

Naomi was confused—or pretended to be. "You know that boy?"

I gave her a sharp look. "Stay awake, Doctor. If you don't know who he is, I'm pretty sure your uncle's wife does." I muted any response before she could protest. "We have a lot to talk about after they release you from the clinic. Don't pass out on me."

The ultralight ascended and left us behind. The military chopper was closing on us twenty times faster. If Aléto was right about thievery, I had to do something to stall the cops before they buzzed the ultralight and forced the aircraft into the water. So I killed the engine, and told Naomi, "Come out from under that tarp. Hold your stomach or something. Pretend like you're sick."

"Pretend my ass," she snapped, and called me a particularly foul name in Spanish. Very graphic. "I didn't puke enough to convince you? Why are we stopping? What I need is a nice cold drink and a bed."

I got to my feet and waved my arms in a series of back-and-forth X's. It was an international distress signal that no ethical chopper pilot could ignore.

This pilot nearly did but circled back and hovered. Over the windblast noise, an amplified voice demanded in Spanish, "We are on official business. If this is not an emergency, please try to get your engine started. Or ask someone for fuel. We have to go."

I motioned emphatically and held up my handheld VHF to indicate that we needed to talk. The co-pilot responded on the Honduran maritime frequency, channel nineteen.

"This is an emergency," I insisted. "I have a very sick woman aboard. She's a physician from an important family."

We went back and forth while I explained that she'd been drugged or poisoned. I wasn't sure. But EMTs and the director of the island medical clinic were waiting for her at the public dock.

This got a more polite response. "Señor, we are in pursuit

of a criminal. A murderer. No doubt her family is important. My captain would like to know the sick woman's name."

Murder? Tomlinson had killed someone? More likely it was Aléto and his trigger-happy pals.

I looked to the right. The butterfly-colored ultralight had just transited Utila's busy tourist peninsula where I expected them to land. Instead, the parafoil wing sailed low across the harbor toward a swampy-looking mangrove area where the aircraft abruptly disappeared. Had it landed? Or had it crashed somewhere in the uphill jungle that edged the swamp?

Either way, I had to buy the kids and my friend some time.

"Her name is Dr. Naomi Cruz," I said into the radio. "Naomi *Brava* Cruz. A physician—a native Honduran who comes from a family you know. Do you copy?"

After a few seconds of radio silence, I was asked to repeat the name. I did.

"Maybe you've heard of her uncle. Governor Teo Brava? I'm sure her Aunt Fidelia would be very grateful to you and your crew—if she wins the next election."

Naomi, even groggier than before, mumbled a protest which, because she whispered, might have been, "Please don't leave me alone. This is Honduras. Remember?"

But it was too late to withdraw my request for help. The chopper landed in a clearing near the Bando Beach Bar on Utila. By the time EMTs arrived, a giant military corpsman, his skin iron-gray, had the woman on a stretcher and was fumbling to get an IV drip in her arm.

The giant's technique did not instill confidence.

I hadn't expected a minor turf battle over who would escort the former governor's niece to the clinic. It was only a few miles away. The squabbling gave me an opportunity to approach another EMT who was waiting on the periphery. He wore rubber gloves and held a loaded syringe in his hand.

I motioned to Naomi. "Your patient, she's a physician. A

neurologist. She told me she needs a specific drug to counter-act the—"

The EMT anticipated the question. "Physostigmine, yes. We have to administer it often." He gave me a quick once-over. "You're a friend of the Brava family?"

I told him I was.

"She should be okay—if those asshole soldiers would let us to our work. Every year, it seems to get worse. A month can go by, no problem. Then a new supply of *burundanga* comes in from Colombia, and we might treat four or five cases in a day. The drug comes in little baggies of white powder the Maras sell on the street."

He looked down at his open medical bag where there were several syringes in sealed baggies. "See? I always carry Physostigmine kits ready to go. It's not a total antidote, but it can reverse the delirium. Excuse me. I have to tell those idiots that your friend needs this injection."

When the EMT entered the fray, I slipped two of the syringe kits into my pocket as backup, then tried to argue his case with the chopper pilot. But the EMT was right about asshole soldiers. The pilot prevailed and the gigantic corpsman joined Naomi inside a cargo van that served as an ambulance.

Before the sliding doors closed, the woman, frightened and still clinging to her satellite phone, gave me a bewildered look. It was as if I had betrayed her in favor of searching for my pal, Tomlinson.

Only later would I understand that it was true.

TWENTY-ONE

After sunset, I was leaning against the balcony railing of the White Conch Hotel drinking a local beer—*Barena*—over ice in a mug when, inside, the barroom went silent.

It was not the old-time saloon silence caused by the entrance of a gunfighter. It was the collective response of dumbstruck males when an elegant, self-assured woman enters a room alone, indifferent to their stares, isolated by choice and supremely at home in her own body and brain.

Next came the nervous clearing of throats. The whispered locker room asides to equally dumbstruck pals.

I turned to confirm my deduction, and there she was, a woman worthy of a painting done in gilded oils and displayed on the wall of a governor's island hideaway.

I was only mildly surprised. But I was more than mildly suspicious when Fidelia Brava, PhD, singled me out and joined me at the railing. Below, water was dark, star-streaked, animated with Van Gogh swirls from the lights of neighboring piers.

I stepped back and waited for the former Ms. Honduras to speak. It took several seconds for her to evaluate me.

"Are you going by the name on your Cayman Island passport, Dr. North? Or should I call you Marion Ford? My husband's hateful niece says you prefer just Doc. We should probably get it straight before they come to arrest you for carrying falsified documents."

Honduras is a small country. Word of my diplomatic passport had gotten around. But the information hadn't come from Naomi.

I replied, "Are you here looking for a friend of mine? Tall, skinny guy with long hair. But sometimes wears it up Rasta-like. A sailboat bum."

That evoked a private smile. "*Tomás*, you mean. He's such a fun, intelligent sort of man. It's true, I thought he might be at the bar. Is he late?"

Her years studying at Stanford and the University of Florida had rendered the archaeologist's Spanish accent into a flavoring device.

No, Tomlinson wasn't late. He'd vanished again. After hiding a stolen paraglider in a pasture, he'd led me on an uphill chase to a colony of trafficking escapees. Small wooden structures, covered with roofs of bamboo, then palm leaves as camouflage. A few terrified teens and a dozen children, mostly girls, had been hiding there for weeks. My pal and I had communicated, but only by handheld radio.

"You've got connections, Doc," Tomlinson had said when I'd found the place. "Get some jackboot agency you trust to transport them to a safe country. I'll be in touch."

"Hold on," I said, and told him what had happened to Naomi.

He acknowledged the transmission but was soon out of range.

I began to suspect this had become a sort of game with my drug-addled pal. Lead me to one criminal stronghold after another, or to some cloistered spot where kids were in trouble, then pull his phantom act by disappearing before I could catch up. The left-handed bastard—he'd lost a few miles off his fastball, but he was still evasive and quick on his feet.

"I have no idea where *Tomás* is," I told the elegant woman, which was true. "As to being arrested, dealing with the Guardia might be awkward for both of us, don't you think? Call me Doc, that's just fine. And you are . . . ?"

She touched the sizeable diamond on her left hand. "Mrs. Brava in public. Or Dr. Brava until we get to know each other well enough to—" She paused to signal the waiter for a drink then held up two fingers. Either ordering a double in this hotel where the new candidate for governor was well known. Or, less likely, ordering another beer for me.

She continued, "It's so hard to trust anyone these days. I hope it's possible. And I think it is—if we get to know each other better. *Marion* . . . Isn't that a girl's name in the States? Doesn't seem to fit a man who looks like you."

When I didn't respond, her eyes bore in. The artist who'd done her portrait was an artist, indeed. The brushwork had captured their amber lucence and a predatory darkness within that was a warning to anyone foolish enough to cross the line, any line of her own invention.

There was a storm behind those eyes waiting for a reason.

Dr. Brava's drink arrived. A double-something in a rocks glass. She took a sip while I asked, "How's Naomi doing? I haven't heard anything since they took her to the medical clinic."

The woman feigned surprise. "Not well, I would assume. You don't know?" She savored my reaction when she delivered the bad news. "The poor thing never made it to the clinic. Somehow the military—or some narcos—got involved."

"*What?* But you spoke to her. You just told me that she said—"

"On the phone," the woman cut in. "On her satellite

phone when she was in the ambulance. Our medical director, Anna-something, thinks poor Naomi might have been kidnapped. Not that it doesn't happen a lot here, but they're usually attractive women. Successful, you know? So that story's just a bit theatrical for my taste. More likely, the little *chinga* wandered off and found a new partner for the night."

I felt my face warming while the archaeologist sipped her drink, crunched a piece of ice, and gave me another look up and down. "I wouldn't call you handsome, but you're big and fit enough. And no one would mistake you for being—" she hesitated "—but your name *is* Marion. A woman can't always be sure about a man's preferences, can she? You must have said no to that dull, self-important little quack, Naomi. Don't blame you. Most men do." .

She sniffed, touched her nose, and sniffed again—a reminder of the cocaine I'd seen in her desk drawer.

That was enough for me. I stepped away from the railing and offered a polite nod. "Have a pleasant evening, Mrs. Brava."

She didn't expect that. "What . . . where are you going?"

I looked up at a sky that held no witchy moon. "I don't want to be in the crosshairs when a house falls on you. Good luck finding those ruby slippers."

She touched my arm. "Don't go. I was being catty . . . intentionally catty. It was . . . as a sort of test to see if you actually care about Naomi. The two of us don't get along. That's true. But she *is* my husband's favorite niece, and I'm worried about her. Besides, you and I have other matters to discuss."

This made her obvious lie even more unconvincing. And offensive.

I said, "You have powerful friends here, Mrs. Brava. Call your contacts and find Naomi. Until then, I don't see the point in talking."

I turned to leave.

"What about the man you murdered today? A Russian—an innocent immigrant who looks after my aviary when I'm away. Do you deny it?"

"Your *aviary*?" I smiled. "Why would I bother? I have no idea what you're talking about."

"Really? Ford—can I call you just 'Ford?' You can't live in this country without knowing who runs the gangs. There are at least two witnesses you've already bribed. That's what I was told anyway. You—a man with a diplomatic passport—has powerful contacts, too. Maybe we can help each other."

I hadn't opened all the files I'd uploaded from the woman's laptop. Too many phone calls to make and messages to read. But I'd seen enough to know that, along with her husband's political backers, she'd inherited a piece of his trafficking business. This information had already been forwarded to my embassy contact.

"Let's find a quiet table somewhere," she suggested. "Why don't you follow me out?"

I pretended to give it some thought. "After you," I said, and grabbed my tactical bag.

Until that moment, I hadn't gotten a full look at the former Ms. Honduras. Nor had I witnessed the effect she had on this busy, upscale barroom. The woman in the painting had become a living, breathing reality. Ten years older, fifteen years older. It didn't matter. There are a few rare ones who, despite their age, mark their territory with a sensual pheromone mist.

Rather than seminude, Dr. Brava had achieved the same effect by wearing a dark floral kimono blouse, unbuttoned, over a white camisole tucked into lean, loose-fitting designer jeans. A caramel handbag, a simple gold necklace, a bracelet of woven worry beads from Guatemala. Low heels of buckskin tan put a bounce in her step as she crossed the room, posture perfect, glossy dark hair and white camisole bouncing in springy counter-synch with each rhythmic stride.

It was all very casual. All articulately purposeful. The tasteful restraint of her attire only accentuated how she might look if a man were lucky enough to see her naked. Long legs, fertile symmetry of hips, breasts full and firm enough to resume their natural curvature once free of the camisole's constraints.

As she skirted barstools and tables, eyes straight ahead, her audience made a path as if reacting to an anti-ferrous force field. Even when a few bold men called to her in Spanish, *Lookin' good Governor . . . Buy you a drink, Governor?* She responded only with a quick glance and a smile.

At the open sliding doors, beneath a slow ceiling fan, the woman stopped and signaled for a waiter. Stood there, right hip canted, well aware that the eyes of every man in this crowded space were on her.

I'm not made of stone. I felt it, too. Felt her sensuality and the room's collective envy that I, not them, was the chosen one.

This absurd notion faded fast. My reasoning, I told myself, was a rational, mature awareness. At best, the woman was poisonous. At worst, she was a dangerous narcissist. The world of a narcissist is populated by only one person. Every other living thing is just stage decoration meant for entertainment. Or as an object to be debased.

Thus far in my life, I've been very, very lucky. I've never been romantically involved with one of the poisonous types, but I know men and women who have suffered that unfortunate collision. I wasn't going to start now.

There was also a more adolescent reason, I had to admit. My pal Tomlinson had already bedded the woman, and I was damn tired of following in the hipster's wake.

"You can call me Fay," she informed me after a manager had claimed there were no private tables. "Instead, he booked me into a room next to yours. It's a suite, second floor. I've already told them to send up drinks."

It gave me a chill, her coquettish tone.

I said, "What's wrong with you? The priority is finding Naomi," and took her by the elbow. "Come on—*Governor*—we can talk outside on the deck."

TWENTY-TWO

The White Conch Hotel, from the street, resembled an old-time steamboat moored over the water, affixed to a pier. It was two stories high, painted white, with a walk-around deck on both levels encased by New-Orleans-style railings.

It was a busy night at the White Conch. I'd finally found a private corner on the upper deck when the archaeologist protested, "This is just silly. My suite's just around the corner, and room service has probably already brought up our tray." She had her key out. "At least let's take a look."

I didn't follow. I had checked in an hour ago. My room—not a suite—was just around the corner, too.

The woman was pissed when she came bouncing back, a fresh drink in one hand, an open bottle of Barena in the other. "What's wrong with *me*? What's your problem, Ford? I have eyewitnesses. You murdered a man today. Maybe there was a reason. Who cares? You're a fool to refuse my help."

Naomi had mentioned the woman's "insane rages." Diplomacy was required, or there might be a scene. So I accepted when she thrust the beer into my hands. But I didn't put the bottle to my lips.

"You're talking about a trade," I said. "Okay. Tell me what

you want from me, Fay. Do it, I'll tell you the truth about the Russian—and some things I know about you."

"Oh? Like what?"

"Trust me, information that a candidate for governor doesn't want Interpol to get its hands on. After that you can decide whether or not to have me arrested."

I feared the threat would send her stomping away. Instead, those amber eyes glowed brighter and she smiled. "Forceful. I knew it. A diplomatic passport. A fake name. You're a trained operator. An assassin, I think that's what you are, Dr. Ford. Drowned a man the size of a bear. Am I right?"

I nodded once, a slow affirmation. I expected this to surprise her. It did not.

"Say it, Ford. Say I'm right."

I replied, "You're right, Dr. Brava. That doesn't bother you?"

"Are you kidding? I wish I could have been there to watch you do it. I appreciate men—a *man*—like you. No . . . In my world, archaeology—history is complex. People . . . the blue-collar types, they don't understand that certain things must—" She switched tangents to the Maya, the Aztecs. Human sacrifices, a thousand heads rolled down pyramid steps in a day. To rule, a ruler must rule. A queen needed a king.

"I'm going to be elected governor of this coast come November 29th—check the papers and then tell me we can't help each other."

As she spoke, I allowed my eyes to blur her face. The delicacy of chin, the swollen fullness of lips, her body, her scent. The genetic pool had found a separate and elevated specimen in this female. But there was a pinhole void inside those amber eyes.

I tuned in when she asked, "Which agency do you work for? You can tell me the truth. I've been to a lot of Embassy functions. I know how the world works. I appreciate the, what would you call it, the absurdity of equal laws for all in a dangerous world. When I'm governor, I think we can do some serious business together. What do you say?"

She held out her drink, offering to clink glasses. I said, "Not until I know what you want. The honest version then, yeah, maybe we can work something out."

I knew what was coming. Her queen-needs-a-king line had sinister implications. I doubted she would reveal the truth without some quid pro quo. So I nudged her along, saying, "Did you get a chance to visit Tomlinson's tree house in the jungle? I found an old book there. A book about a Mayan King named Canek. A legendary hero, three hundred years ago."

"Oh?" She seemed puzzled by the segue, but a caution light had gone off in her head. "Tomás told me he was working on some kind of hippie bamboo hut. But my God that was, what, more than a month ago?" She laughed. "Years ago, he'd done some business with my husband, so I invited him to my island. Why not? After so much time alone on that godforsaken rock, it was a vacation for both of us. Even my political interviews are done remotely. Security, they say, which is bullshit. It's more like a chastity belt sort of thing."

Her tone became playful. "I suppose Tomás shared all the lurid little details. Should I hate him if he did?"

I replied, "He never said a word. It's kind of an unspoken rule we have when it comes to women."

"Ahh . . . you're too much of a gentleman. Too bad."

"I wish. The old book, when I opened it, a personal letter dropped out. I read it anyway. It was from you, about the genetic study you did on Canek's DNA. And a kid, an orphan. What is it you want, Dr. Brava? The jade mask stolen from the National Museum? Or the legendary king's only direct descendant?"

I watched her visage change from playful to savage.

"*Both*. I want them both, and I suspect Tomás told you where to find them. Help me out, I'll help you. As if I care about some low-IQ Russian gangster. He's better off out there with the sharks."

"Probably safer, too," I said.

"You're smiling. Is that another insult?" She stepped closer, her nose near my chin. "You don't have to decide now. There's a lovely tray of snacks in my suite. If you'd like to hear all the lurid details—some men enjoy that sort of thing—we can save the boring stuff for later."

"Boring stuff has kept our species alive for generations," I responded. "And you still haven't told me your plan. If I help you find the boy, you'll have him arrested. Or use him and the DNA study to somehow promote your campaign. If I find the death mask, you'll keep it. What's in it for me?"

The archaeologist had some actress in her. "Is your opinion of me really so low you think I'd have an orphaned child put in prison? Especially that child. In Central America, the Indios—they're like superstitious sheep. They actually believe Canek the Great will return. So ridiculous. That's why I started my DNA study in the first place."

I said slowly, "I'll be damn. You skewed the data. Made it all up."

"No. I mean, I would've, but what does it matter? Rumors about the kid are already spreading. Not just Honduras, all through Mesoamerica. If I don't find him, the military or the narcos or some other candidate will, and they'll have him killed. Think about it—kings are dangerous."

"You'd let him live, I suppose?"

"Of course. I really am the best choice. I've always wanted children myself—no, I'm serious. This might surprise you, but I'd adopt the poor little cripple. An orphan kid with a birth defect? Phocomelia, it's called. Can't even wipe himself if he breaks his good arm. No one else is going to rescue a kid like that. But me, I'll give him a home. Nice clothes, an education. See? I'm not so bad after all."

I tilted my untouched beer over the railing. Watched her as I emptied the bottle into the bay and saw that I was right. The beer had been drugged.

It was in her eyes. Something else—she *knew* that I knew. The curtain dropped, the charade ended, and the predator appeared.

"You're not going to help me, are you?"

"Help you? I'm a biologist, Mrs. Brava. You need a different type of doctor."

"How dare you refuse . . . and stop calling me that. I'm no one's wife anymore. The name's Fidelia, and I know you're lying about that Interpol bullshit. Don't threaten me. Why . . . you're just a second-rate cop."

I turned my back and started walking.

That clicked her into revenge mode. "Or I could always marry the little bastard," she hollered. "Little boys grow up fast in the jungle. Train him right. After a month with me, he'll be as obedient as a dog—and just as eager. Think it over, you self-righteous ass."

I kept walking.

Before leaving the hotel, I stopped at the front desk and was told that aside from the two small rooms Naomi had booked on the upper deck, there were no other rooms available. So I strolled down Main Street and ordered dinner at Odyssey Mexican, a clean, cheery place that had internet. There I learned why the island was so busy—an international dive convention. All hotels were packed.

Shit-oh-dear, I thought. One of Tomlinson's favorite utterances.

At a seaside table, I had beef-stuffed peppers—pure protein—
a double side of salsa, and lingered. My local contact was the
Cayman Island Embassy, on Calle 11th, city of La Ceiba. I have
a long-felt fondness for embassies and consulates. They are
inviolate sovereign citadels no matter where you go in the
world. More than once I've transported myself thousands of
miles to safety by simply stepping through a welcoming security gate.

La Ceiba was just across the water, not far. I'd already
mapped it out but went over the streets again. There are oc-
casions when you must seek safe haven in a hurry.

There was some busywork to do. I used Signal, an encrypted
messaging service, that was linked to my primary contact, which
was a different embassy in a different time zone. I sent a dispatch
that included a Level Seven alert regarding my conversation
with the would-be governor, Fidelia Brava. I regarded the
candidate as unstable, a potential threat pending her election.

The next communiqué included a GPS flag marking the
refugee camp Tomlinson had discovered, and my concerns
about Naomi, a legal resident of the U.S. This was the third
encrypted brief I'd sent that documented my daily encounters,
along with my analysis when appropriate.

Something I had yet to arrange, and might soon need, was
fast transport out-country. This required a back channel note
to my unusual friend, Max Weatherby in the U.K.

I returned to the White Conch around midnight. The bar
was still rowdy, yet I went quietly up the stairs to the south-
facing deck where I tiptoed. There were no lights on inside the
suite adjacent to my room. No flickering TV screen within.

I relaxed a tad but entered my room in stealth mode. Pressed
my ear to the interior door connected to the suite. No noise,
no movement. I confirmed the security chain was in place,
then prepared for the worst as I always do when traveling. The

full-sized Sig Sauer pistol stayed with me as I moved around the room. The little P365 went under the pillow, a round chambered.

The woman who tabloids called Fay the Fer-de-lance had abandoned her mission and the hotel apparently. Good. It gave me time to clean up. Toothbrush. Shaving razor. Contact lenses were cleaned and encased before a short hot, steaming shower. I pulled the desk chair closer to the bed and got dressed again. Boots and socks beneath the bed, fireman style.

A couple of final touches. I hailed Tomlinson on the handheld GMRS, channel nineteen, and tried him again on channel 24. Negative contact. The radio, still powered up, went on the nightstand next to a Fenix flashlight and my wire-rimmed glasses. My new contact lenses were in their case nearby.

I was in the hazy netherworld of sleep when a woodpecker's tap-tap-tap almost transitioned into a dream. But then I heard the click of a metal latch. An instant later I was on my feet, gun in hand, as the interior door cracked open, stopped only by the security chain.

I stood clear of the door and approached a dusty wedge of light that angled in. Said nothing, until I heard the archaeologist speak through the little opening. "Ford. It's me. Don't be angry. I was way out of line, I admit it. And just a little drunk. Can't we at least talk?"

"It's late. Maybe breakfast," I said, which wasn't going to happen. "Take a few steps away from the door."

"What? *Why?* Take off the damn chain. What are you afraid of?"

"Want to make sure it's you," I said.

My real concern was that she wasn't alone.

The elegant lady made a husky cooing sound. The wedge of light brightened as she backed away. "You want a peek at what

I'm wearing, do you? I *like* that. Oh, and I have something else for you. An apology note. I'd like to give it to you personally."

I put an eye to the opening. The exotic beauty from the painting was alive, standing tall, legs posed beauty pageant style. This time she was seminude: Indio hair in glossy disarray, wearing a beige see-through bra and bikini panties that revealed a coifed, soft cornsilk triangle.

In her hand was a folded sheet of stationery.

"You like?"

My involuntary reaction was immediate. *My God*, I thought. *Why not?* Like the old excuse, a hotel room has no conscience.

"Go to sleep," I heard myself say. But I didn't mean it.

Her smile widened. With a single motion, she unsnapped her bra and allowed the cups to slide down her breasts, but not all the way, while she walked closer. "I was a bitch, *Cariño*. Come on, let me make it up to you. Have some fun. At least read my note. Then decide."

Cariño—a Spanish term of endearment.

The internal battle between the rational and the rationalizer began. If I didn't open the door, how could I be certain there wasn't a bodyguard inside waiting? It was a security issue. And we were both adults, after all. Narcissist or not, it would be just a onetime thing—and with one of the most visually sensual women I'd ever met.

It wasn't until I asked myself, *What would Tomlinson do?* that I realized what a sad, debasing mistake I was about to make if I followed my friend's promiscuous lead.

It was a transitional moment. "I'll read it, but that's all," I said. "Slip it under the door."

Instead, the note, rolled into a tube, was shoved through the crack and nearly poked me in the face. When I reached for it, there was a respiratory blow-dart PHEEET noise, and I stumbled backward in a haze of white powder.

What the hell? My eyes, my nostrils and lips were instantly on fire. I spun, gun raised, and damn near put a round through the door, but started to gag. Couldn't breathe.

"I warned you, *maricón*," the woman yelled, her tone suddenly cold and businesslike. "Now I'm the only one who can help you. You need a doctor. Let me in, or I'll tell Wingo to kick the door down."

Wingo? Was the Shaman in there with her?

I raised the pistol to shoot, but everything in the room was an acid blur. So I tripped blindly toward the bathroom, fell over a chair and the gun went skittering across the floor. On hands and knees I felt my way to the sink, got the water going and started to irrigate my eyes—my shooting eye first.

BOOM . . . BOOM . . . BOOM.

It was the sound of a man's heavy foot kicking the door.

Shit. There wasn't time. Squinting helped a little. I groped my way back into the room in search of the Sig P365 beneath the pillow. Found a wall for guidance but stumbled over the same goddamn chair and pulled the nightstand down atop me. My glasses and the GMRS radio landed near my head.

I reached for what I thought was the bed but found my cargo pants instead. Something hard inside the pockets—and that's when I remembered the antidote syringes I'd pilfered from the EMT.

BOOM . . . BOOM . . . BOOM. The Guru Shaman was out there, not used to kicking in doors.

Fidelia forced a moratorium, saying, "Listen to me, Ford. You'll be unconscious in a minute or two. Be reasonable. Don't cause an ugly scene with the manager—he's on my campaign team. Let us in."

With my teeth, I ripped open a baggie and used the braille method to uncap a syringe needle. At the same instant, I heard radio static and Tomlinson's garbled call of, "CQ, CQ. Doc, do you copy, amigo?"

I found the radio, pressed the transmit button, but my

paralyzed tongue managed only a few incoherent words. That's when the door crashed open, and a ceiling light brightened my blind eyes.

A voice that had to be Wingo Bogdan's ordered, "Get to your feet, you stupid oaf, or I'll shoot you in the head. We want you to answer a few questions before you pass out."

I kept the radio keyed while I stabbed the needle into my thigh and pressed the plunger. Radio off, I spun it and the syringe toward what I hoped was an area beneath the bed.

"On your feet, Mister Agent Man." Bogdan's voice again.

I did as I was told, but too late. My knees buckled. I fought the urge to vomit. Then the floor dropped me into a free-fall darkness of nauseating, neon colors.

Someone yelled for help—maybe me—before the world went black.

TWENTY-THREE

(Tomlinson Part Two)

After one brief, garbled radio contact Tomlinson hailed Ford several more times on channel nineteen but finally gave up and stowed the handheld.

"We're either out of range," he said to Pulpo, his cab driver and friend. "Or Fay the witchy woman has my pal's tongue taped to the fun meter—if you catch my drift. I don't know whether to be happy for Doc or pray for him. That reminds me, you don't have a meter on the dash. How much these wheels gonna cost me per day?"

They were in a tiny, dented Toyota, front seat. Rosary beads dangled from the mirror. Glued to the dashboard, the Virgin Mary rode point. The standard hourly fee for a cab in Honduras was around $10.

Pulpo, a White Conch from Pigeon Key—an old British *Caracol* community—had been Tomlinson's driver and guide since the pot smuggling years. They'd had many adventures, and made some money, too.

Caracols meant snails in Spanish. It's what they called the old-time White Conch fisherman down here—skin white or black, it didn't matter. Pulpo wasn't the only Islander born without pinky fingers, but his mother had been the first to register the catchy name at their church. "Pulpo" in Spanish meant "octopus," a creature with no hands but eight tentacles.

A Conch don't need ten fingers to count the difference between right and wrong, was among his favorite expressions.

"Cap'n," Pulpo said to Tomlinson, "you speaking of your radio friend we heard a few miles back? He sound drunk to me. Or maybe fell down some steps and hit his head. Meter, you say? His tongue on what kind of meter?"

Tomlinson replied, "Doc's too anal to get drunk. Too afraid of being caught with his heart exposed. Of course, he's never met someone with a meter like Fay's."

"Who?"

"I told you. Fidelia. That's her name."

"*Fidelia?* You not talkin' about Governor Brava's woman, I hope. Mawn, she be thoroughly *peligroso*. What you mean she got a—" Pulpo swerved, honked the horn, and narrowly missed a stray dog being pursued by pigs.

"*Malditos cerdos!*" he muttered, then continued, "That fine woman's got a meter on her? Never heard of such a device before."

Tomlinson lit a joint, blew smoke out the window. "A meter, oh yes, she's got a meter. Digital and manual. But back to what I was asking—here, try this." He passed the joint to his old friend, then counted out five one-hundred-dollar bills onto the console. "How's that look?"

Pulpo smiled, took another drag and held it. Sounded like Mickey Mouse when he said, "*Hermano*, that too much *plata*. Unless you partic–u–larly flush these days." He exhaled. "Wow . . . this some good *Yuyo,* man."

"*Yuyo?*"

"Yeah, *Yuyo*. It's the Indio word for some good shit. Let's go have some beers."

Tomlinson frowned. "We're just getting started. Gonna be a long night pal, and you'll earn every *centavo*. Let me ask another question. You ever break into a house and rescue someone who's been kidnapped?"

"Uhh, well yeah, sorta. But not to rescue nobody. More like a, you know, a couple of financial endeavors. You talkin' about that missing lady, ain't you."

"Point is," Tomlinson replied, "it's your expertise that counts, not the motive. What about guns? We need a couple of weapons. Machetes are cool but a gun, that's just the sort of statement we want to make to these flesh trafficking nabobs."

Pulpo glanced up at the mirror and took a deeper drag. "You crazy, Tomás. What kind nonsense you getting me involved with?"

That Mickey Mouse voice again.

"A very righteous cause, *mi socio*. Well, do you? Have a gun?"

"Cap'n, 'stead of you getting old like a normal person, you growed whacky-whacky in that young brain of yours." The man slapped the steering wheel but admitted, "Yeah, I got a gun. But it's all rusty and shit. Found it in a field, made back in Banana War times."

Tomlinson, the historian, said, "Ah yes. Late eighteen hundreds. Your brave peasants against us and our Imperialist shit kickers. My family made a lot of money off the war, as I recollect. Shameless industrialist scum, all of them." He lit another joint. "My grandmother, though, she was a real peach. Say—how far's your house. Let's stop and pick it up."

"Pick up what?"

"The gun, Pulpo, the gun. Try to stay on topic here. I need you in tip-top form tonight." He passed the fresh joint. "Another toke of *Yuyo* might help. We'll stop by your house on the way."

"No need, mawn. Gun's in the trunk. Been trying to sell the damn thing as an antique. My brother oiled her up but still looks like hell. Don't have no bullets, either. Best offer only been three bucks."

"Better yet," Tomlinson said. "Bullets are dangerous. Hell, I wouldn't know how to shoot a gun that had bullets. What about a baseball bat? Something heavy. A tool not guaranteed to kill, but with enough *oomph* to let God decide."

The hipster was pleased to hear there was also a tire iron in the trunk.

Pulpo had been piecing it together. "You know where that woman, Naomi, is don't you, Cap'n. That lil' one-armed boy figured it out. The last boy we dropped off? He's a smart one."

Tomlinson replied, "Yes, he is. And yes, I do."

They'd spent the last few hours dropping off and picking up orphaned kids—all members of Aléto's homeless guerilla army. The urchins did odd jobs for shops and hotels along the beachfront. Each had been instructed to eavesdrop, do whatever they could to gather information on Naomi Cruz. She'd been hauled off in an ambulance, but when the ambulance arrived at the medical clinic, the woman had vanished. The military corpsman who'd been tending to her was gone, too.

This new information had come from a girl who washed dishes at a taco dive the clinic staff often frequented.

It was Aléto, though, who'd cracked the case. He'd spoken to a cleaning maid who'd entered a customer's house but was ordered away by a "giant" soldier. Her words: *Giant*. Through a window, the maid had seen a woman gagged and taped to a chair.

When Aléto described the house as near a grass runway, the memory of wet grass had peeled away a blank spot in Tomlinson's brain.

Pulpo was getting nervous. "We ain't gonna kill nobody, are we?"

Tomlinson evaded, saying, "You? You're not even going inside. Leave everything to me."

"You got an address, Cap'n?"

"Don't need one, the boy told me," Tomlinson responded. "I know exactly where the place is. Slow down. Yeah . . . take a Louie on Mammy Lane. Uphill for half a mile, then another left on Iguana Road."

Pulpo remarked, "They got a lizard research station up there. Raise the dang things 'cause folks on the islands about ate 'em all, the tail's so good on the grill. Stew's even better. I could eat me some chicken-of-the-trees right now. You hungry?"

Tomlinson didn't answer. He was focused in, accessing his existential warrior, and thinking, *Wingo Bogdan, you guru fraud. If I don't kill you, the one-armed kid's army will.*

Tomlinson was getting frustrated. His right arm was numb from what he assumed was a stroke. Now an antique weapon was testing his patience. "Mother-dog . . . scum spawn! What kind of pistol you give me? Damn thing won't even open. Isn't this, what do you call it, a cylinder, supposed to at least move?"

Pulpo felt slighted. "You're holdin' there is a *Webley* pistol. That's what my brother says. Very famous during the Banana Wars. Told you it was all froze up. Why you think I was only offered three bucks? Here give me that."

The man took the pistol in both hands and tried to snap it open as if breaking a chicken bone before handing the pistol back. Even his eight strong fingers couldn't overpower the rust. "See? That's the way you supposed to do it, but it don't work. This tire iron on the other hand—" he swung the metal bar like a saber "—I don't wanna hear no complaints about this."

Tomlinson was impressed. "It's not a complaint, it's authenticity I'm after. If there's a giant goddamn soldier, whoever's in there, he sees me holding this rusty piece of shit, he'll think we robbed a junkyard. The guy I'm really after, even he'll think I'm a buffoon."

They had parked in shadows on a dirt lane near the airstrip, about a hundred yards from a plantation-type house that didn't look familiar. But there were lights on inside, a pickup truck in the drive, and a small Cessna-sized airplane moored at the end of the runway.

This gave Tomlinson confidence they had returned to what was a blank few hours in his brain.

Pulpo was taking a whiz. "Warned you, mawn. The hammer don't pull back neither. Were that not the case, that there fine antique, my brother says is worth a thousand bucks easy. Probably more."

The driver stared up at a snow-bowl of stars. A couple of satellites up there transiting while tree frogs screamed, and a distant dog barked. He zipped his pants and returned to the car. "Cap'n, it's spooky dark out here. And I'm hungry. You sure you wanna do this thing tonight, 'cause—" The Conch from Pigeon Cay was interrupted by an unexpected *click-click* noise. "What the hell was that?"

"I'll be damn, the hammer works," Tomlinson replied. He'd been toying with the old weapon. "Guess that oil your brother used did some good. Humm . . ." He put the barrel to his eye and noticed that the pistol cylinder resembled a circular wasp nest. All chambers clotted. "You sure there're no bullets in this thing?"

"Caked with mud turned rock-hard," Pulpo answered. "My brother even tried a water pick. A froze-up Banana War gun, you better off throwing the damn thing at a man's head."

"There's an idea," the left-handed pitcher said. "Or use it to fool him. But still don't think this thing's going to scare a soldier—a freakin' 'giant'—that's the way he was described. Maybe this will help."

In his pocket was the long, glass-sharp shard of obsidian he'd found at the dinosaur park. He was using it to chip away at the cylinder when a distant light distracted him. The light appeared and disappeared, as if someone with a flashlight were moving at the top of this uphill ridge where there were towering tree shadows. Several hundred yards to the northeast was a dim sprinkling of more lights, like pearls in a basket.

Pulpo, who couldn't get his mind off food, said, "Probably folks out hunting land crabs. Or iguanas. They both fine table fare, mawn. Them other lights, missionaries got a camp up there. You can hear them sometimes, singing and praising the Lord. Them Christians sure do make a joyful noise."

Tomlinson returned the volcanic shard to his pocket, saying, "I like Christians. They've got a franchise everywhere. You ready?"

This gave Pulpo an idea. "There's an all-night McDonald's franchise in San Pedro Sula. Only a four-hour drive once we get to the mainland. Maybe come back here tomorrow?"

Tomlinson ignored that. He started toward the plantation-looking house, carrying the tire iron in his left hand. The antique pistol was in the waistband of his gaucho pantaloons, pirate style.

"Stay here if you want," he said. "Any son-uva-bitch who kidnaps women and children, tonight's his last stop on the way to hell." The tall sailor, still walking, added, "After that, sure, a few beers and something to eat. But not McDonald's. Iguana sounds pretty good to me."

Pulpo locked the taxi and hurried to catch up.

Tomlinson's attention swung from a lighted house window to the airplane. He considered slashing the damn tires. Or pissing in the fuel tank. Something vicious to make the thing crash.

Trouble was, even he couldn't reach the fuel cap. And he still wasn't certain it was the plastic guru's plane.

The beat-up Silverado in the drive wasn't Wingo Bogdan's style.

That was confirmed when he went to the side of the house and looked through the window. Dr. Naomi, his assertive physician, was inside on the floor beneath a sheet. She lay motionless, eyes closed, her mouth taped, ankles bound by something. Wire or a tie-wrap.

Pulpo crept beside him and whispered, "Oh sweet Jesus, Cap'n. Don't see her chest moving. She *dead*. Let's go call the po-lice."

Instead, the Zen Master called upon his six higher powers by taking several transcendental breaths. Within Naomi, he sensed energy. He sensed a frail web of cranial sparks attempting to make contact. But the rage he felt was impenetrable.

"Bullshit, Pulpo. She's alive. Stay here. I'm gonna try to sneak in and get her. We'll carry the woman to the damn car if we need to."

He tested the window. Locked. He scurried around to the front, up the steps. Got his fingers under the lip of a larger window. It was stuck. He flexed his right hand and tried again. Really put his back into it and the damn thing slammed open so unexpectedly that he fell over the window seal, his body half in the room, half out.

Naomi's head tilted up, startled by the gunshot noise. Her face brightened when Tomlinson touched a finger to his lips and waved hello. She nodded eagerly, then gestured with her jaw toward the staircase.

Someone was up there. The *clump clump clump* of heavy footsteps was evidence. Tomlinson signaled *Give me a minute* and, in his rush to extricate himself, banged his head on the window frame. Another gunshot report.

Damn, he thought. *You clumsy gimp.*

His back against the porch wall, the hipster waited while heavy boots descended the stairs. They crossed the floor and stopped. There was the flick of a cheap lighter. Cigarette smoke drafted through the open window.

"What is your problema?" the man growled.

His voice was freakishly low. It resonated like a timpani drum when he continued to address the woman in rapid-fire Spanish.

Tomlinson struggled to translate. Something about no more noise. Did she want to continue their game-playing in the bedroom? Then a vile threat, the words *joder, desnudo, satisfecha*? all familiar to a tropical bum. And disgusting when pieced together.

He moved to take a peek but pasted himself to the wall again when thunderous boots crossed the room, and the window slammed shut only a foot from his arm. There were some muttered profanities that suggested the window's piece-of-shit lock was busted.

Tomlinson waited before risking another look. Standing over Naomi, staring down, was a shirtless giant wearing boots and army issue pants. The cigarette protruded from the bearded jaws of a cave dweller. His ears were topped by buzz-cut sidewalls, military style, arms, chest a Rorschach test of tattoos.

The bastard had to be close to seven feet tall and twice as wide as a normal male. Andre the Giant, wearing a holster and gun. The great wrestler came to mind.

Jesus Christ, Tomlinson thought. The devil had been at work here. Two or three decades ago, some poor woman had been savaged by a wildebeest. Now the devil's spawn was alive and on the loose, possibly mandated to mate with other unsuspecting human females.

On hands and knees, he crawled full speed across the porch and cursed himself again when the tire iron he carried banged the stair railing.

Oh sure, summon Satan, Tomlinson thought bitterly. *As if you're not already a number-one pick in the Grim Reaper's next draft list.*

After stumbling through some bushes he found Pulpo squatting low beneath the same side window. The driver was spooked by what he'd just seen.

"Cap'n, we gotta go, mawn. You know who that giant is in there? Trust me, we gotta go *now*."

Tomlinson whispered, "Yeah, a seriously scary wildebeest sort of hybrid. Don't even ask how I know. You recognize him?"

"No, but I *heard*. And no two people on God's Earth can look like that. Iron Baby. That's what they call him. Used to kill people for the richest man in Honduras 'til he kilt someone in the palm oil business. That's a very stupid thing to do in this country."

"Iron . . . baby?"

"Iron *Baby*. His name. Governor Brava got him off death row. Trained him as his personal servant and bodyguard, folks say. Don't know why he's dressed that way. He ain't no soldier."

Pulpo contorted his feet into duck-walking position. "Sorry about your lady friend, but there ain't nothing we can do. Not with a tire iron and a gun with no bullets. You comin'?" He started waddling toward some bushes, the Cessna-sized plane beyond.

Tomlinson lifted his eyes to the window. *Gad*. The giant had ripped the sheet off Naomi and was messing with her blouse. The woman struggled for an instant then closed her eyes and played dead.

On hands and knees, he caught up with his friend. "Wait, wait, I got a plan."

Pulpo kept duck-walking, his nerves on overload. "Iron Baby . . . wouldn't have believed it if I hadn't seen him with my own eyes. Kilt I don't know how many people, they say.

Supposedly never leaves the governor's island. Like a ghost story. But by God, he's real. Folks gonna think I was drunk. Us Conchs been after that monster for years."

Tomlinson grabbed the man's belt. "Okay, here's the plan. Hang on. *Listen.* The timing has to be just right."

Pulpo sat down hard on his butt. His head pivoted to the house, scared shitless. "A plan, you nuts?"

"Simple plan," Tomlinson whispered. "You wait for me to get to the front door, then you bang on the back door and run like hell."

The driver seemed to expect something more elaborate. "Huh? That's it?"

"Yep, nice and simple. You're fast, Pulpo. Remember those Rottweilers off Monkey River Town? Oh, and that pissed-off husband who turned out to be a cop? Dude, I've *seen* you run."

Flattered, the Conch from Pigeon Key remembered back to happier times. "Yes, Tomás, in my day, there wasn't a *federale* or a dog that I couldn't—*Wait.*" He sat straighter. "Some say Iron Baby twisted a man's head off, used it to knock some coconuts out of a tree 'cause he was thirsty. Thought that was just a rumor too, but I believe it now. And he's got a goddamn gun. I *saw* it." He thought for a moment then sighed in surrender. "Okay, okay. *Mierda.* Bang on the door, that would be just crazy. I would need that tire iron before I'd agree to something so stupid."

Tomlinson handed the bar over and said, "Old friend, that woman in there, he's gonna hurt her again really bad if we don't move fast. You know what I'm talking about."

Pulpo got to his feet because he did know. He had three unsuspecting wives, and many children scattered between Pigeon Key and the Nicaraguan border. Two of his daughters, just children, had been assaulted, one murdered. He still said the Rosary for his lost girl every night. Well . . . almost every night.

"You ready?"

Pulpo said it again, *Mierda*, and hurried to the rear of the house, sprinting occasionally to get his fast legs loose. When his old pot-hauling partner signaled, he did it. Used the tire iron, BANG-BANG-BANG, then ran like hell into the trees.

Tomlinson, on the front porch, watched the giant stop what he was doing. Watched the giant rush down a hall toward the back of the house, gun drawn.

The window banged up. He stepped in and spent a maddening two minutes freeing Naomi, then helped her to her feet. The woman was bleeding from nose and mouth, yet he averted his eyes while she got her bra and blouse adjusted.

"You'll be okay. We'll get you fixed up. Let's go."

The savvy, tough-talking neurologist, who'd seen everything, was pissed at herself because she had to fight back tears.

"That . . . that sonuvabitch." She fixated on the hall while Tomlinson got the front door open. "He's awful. A *monster*. I thought he was my . . . that he at least liked me. I know it was that poisonous witch, Fidelia who . . . who—I should kill her, next time I . . . I—"

The dam burst, tears flowed. Tomlinson thought they were safe when they reached the steps. But they weren't safe. A crashing noise and heavy boots required him to give the women a push.

"Run. *Run*," he yelled. "Across the landing strip. There's a car. Don't wait for me!"

Because there was no other option, he drew the antique pistol from his pantaloons, turned and faced the giant. The man's shoulders filled the hallway as he approached. His military holster appeared to be empty—but in his hand was a bloody tire iron. The implications were obvious. And horrifying.

Oh . . . shit.

Tomlinson hollered into the darkness. "Pulpo! Pulpo, get to

the car. The woman, Naomi, she's a doctor." Then he leveled the old Webley pistol at Iron Baby's chest. "Stop right there, you troglodyte, or I'll . . . I'll stick this up your ass."

The giant paused to consider the seriousness of the threat. He assessed the skinny sailor. Noticed the shaky hands. He grinned, gave a bellowing roar and charged, the tire iron held high like an axe.

Tomlinson backpedaled. The fingers on his numb right hand contracted—a spasmatic response to fear. Eyes closed, the room exploded with a deafening silence that fogged the air with acrid black smoke.

A wild ringing in his ears deafened the senses. Tomlinson stood dazed, not convinced the goddamn gun had actually gone off. But it had.

He stepped through a curtain of smoke into the room where the giant was hunched over, a shocked dullness in his eyes while he tried to stem a steady flow of blood. The bullet had furrowed his left thigh, now the man's Army-issue pants glistened with an expanding black stain.

Tomlinson aimed the pistol again. "I'm gonna shoot you in the nuts this time, screwhead."

The wounded man snapped his thighs together and glared at the skinny old hippie. Big wildebeest eyes sparked with a cold, cold rage, but one massive bloody hand signaled surrender.

"It's too late to crawfish out now," Tomlinson hollered. Staring down the barrel, he moved a step closer. "How about I just shoot you in the forehead? We can argue the ethics in a week or so at Hell's gate."

He would've done it, too—if the trigger hadn't frozen after the last round the weapon would ever fire. And if the giant hadn't Quasimodo-galloped out the back door.

The hipster went after him anyway, shouting, "And tell the Guru he's next!"

There was the rumble of a souped-up truck starting. A panicked spinout of gravel, and Iron Baby sped off, maybe to a hospital or somewhere to get help.

Tomlinson felt a tad dizzy. He wondered if it was caused by the zombie drug or another stroke? Didn't matter. He stumbled to the lawn and didn't stop until he was sure the truck was gone. It was.

From the shadows near the airstrip, a well-known voice called, "You got him, Cap'n, you got him. I saw it. I wanted to stab him with this, but he got away."

Pulpo appeared carrying a pitchfork he'd found somewhere, his face a bloody mess. "Come on, Tomás. Your lady friend's in the cab. Said my ear will be fine—what's left of it." The old Conch scanned the distance where he'd last seen taillights. "Iron Baby, that fool comes to Pigeon Cay we'll stick him in the damn freezer 'till we're sure he's dead."

Tomlinson knew the truth about death and the devil but said nothing. "Who's that?" he asked. A trio of small silhouettes were visible ahead.

Pulpo squinted. "*Aye-yai-yai*. There was just one of them, a little one-armed boy. Told him to skedaddle but said he wanted to speak with you. Guess there's more of his little amigos now."

Aléto, Tomlinson realized. He walked faster while his old friend continued talking. "What the hell kind of folks let their youngins run around this time of night? And what kid that age would want to? No wonder we got gang problems."

"The homeless kind," Tomlinson said, and approached the boy with arms wide but the boy recoiled from the embarrassment of a hug.

Aléto, who had a rifle and maybe a bamboo blowgun slung over his shoulder, eyed the man from Pigeon Key. "Why is he bleeding? Is he stoned from smoking *Yuyo*?"

"Uh, well, yeah. We both are," Tomlinson said. "Uhh, not that I recommended it. I don't. Smoking, smoking of any kind is . . . Anyhoo, how did you know where to find—" He didn't bother finishing because it was the kid who'd given him directions in the first place.

Aléto put a stop to the awkwardness, saying, "I don't want you with us if you're stoned."

"Along where? Where're you going?"

"To warn your friend, the *patrón*. The large man with glasses. He's in trouble because of my enemy, the plastic shaman. I know what the Shaman wants. When he gets what he wants, he'll kill the *patrón* and probably the Queen, too."

"Whoa, hold on there," Tomlinson said. "The Shaman, yeah, I get it. But the *patrón a*nd the Queen . . . ? Who the hell are you talking—" He suddenly understood. "You mean the former beauty queen and a big guy with glasses? My God. You're saying Fidelia and the Shaman have my friend, Doc? When's this going to happen?"

Aléto shrugged. "Tonight, now, I think. Tomorrow maybe. It wasn't clear in my dream. We have to go now."

Dreams. Tomlinson was totally into that. He believed every word the kid said next.

Aléto started toward his friends waiting in the bushes. "You would need a boat to help us, but you can't. Too dangerous because we have guns." He patted the rifle for emphasis. "I don't want adults who are drunk or stoned around guns."

Not happy, he glared up at Tomlinson. "I watched you. I saw what happened. You should have killed the giant. But you were shaking, too stoned and afraid to do it. If you hadn't let the giant drive away, we *would have*."

Aléto didn't say it, but Iron Baby, the giant, had been in his dream too.

TWENTY-FOUR

Even after I'd been blasted by a haze of scopolamine powder, a disciplined spot in my brain maintained a grainy recollection of events, drifting in and out, descending deeper until a brief span when I actually was unconscious.

Dead to the world. The standard phrase. That didn't happen. Not completely. For me, it might have been a conditioned response. Since childhood, I've been drawn to a rational view of the world. However, what other people felt or believed was important. I'd learned that early on. The wrong word, an uncomfortable truth, could hurt them.

It wasn't reasonable. Few people are.

I dislike inflicting pain—even when dealing with enemies. So, I've always stood back and observed from a polite distance. I'm not afraid of my feelings. I simply don't find them very interesting. Over the decades, this detachment might have numbed a cerebral region that processes emotion. If so, it has also made me less vulnerable.

Keep your guard up, the doors locked, and never ever get off the goddamn boat without a gun or a plan.

An old maxim known to a few.

A gun. I needed a gun.

Blinded by the zombie drug and already hallucinating, that became a priority while I lay dazed on the floor. I forced myself up. An alkaline paste coated my lips and tongue. I hacked and spit. Did this several times while I crawled around feeling with my hands for the full-sized Sig Sauer I'd dropped, or the bed where I'd hidden the little Sig P365. The room was a blur. My eyes burned when I opened them.

Rally. Stay awake until the antidote kicks in, I told myself. Wingo Bogdan, after breaking in, had returned to the adjoining suite for some reason. I could hear him arguing with someone.

The physostigmine syringe I'd stolen from the EMT wasn't a full-on antidote. But it was supposed to mitigate the effects of Devil's Breath.

When the hell was that going to happen?

It didn't happen soon enough.

I'd had just enough time to stash a few important items under a rug of some sort when he stumbled through the door again. I flopped on the floor and pretended to be unconscious while Fidelia Brava's voice said, "Goddamn it, don't shoot him. In fact, give me that gun. I don't trust you. You're holding it all wrong."

The archeologist did most of the talking. There was no doubt she was in charge.

"Get away, Wingo. I'll search Ford. You . . . you go through his bag. The arrogant ass always carries a gun. And his diplomatic passport. I want that too."

The Guru didn't move fast enough.

"My God, Wingo. Stop looking at him like he is something good to eat. Later, if you behave, you can help him get dressed. But that's all—unless it's something I want." There was a derisive chuckle. "Which is unlikely. You really are quite the disgusting little man. Remind me of—who was that freak? Yes, you remind me of Charles Manson with a Confucius goatee."

Instead of fighting the swirling colors in my head, I focused on the colors as a distraction. A way to remain aloof when I felt the woman's shoe nudge me a couple of times. Then she kicked me hard in the ribs. Did it twice more.

"I think he's out," she said. "How long before he wakes up? He's too big to carry, and there are people around. This man needs to walk out of here on his own."

Bogdan replied, "It varies. In fifteen, twenty minutes or so, he should be suggestible enough to talk him onto his feet. He'll still be out of it. Probably forty-five minutes before he wakes up completely. But he'll still do whatever you tell him for the next day, maybe two days. I've seen it go on for as long as four. Then he'll want to sleep around the clock."

I sensed the woman kneel beside me. She touched my face in an experimental way. I was prepared when she poked my eyelids.

I'd been through this at an Enhanced Interrogation course at Fort Sherman, Panama. Reflex physiology can't be switched off. The stimuli can't be ignored. The worst thing you can do is to pretend not to react.

I groaned, turned my head and used sleepy hands as if shooing away flies.

The woman spoke again. "Wingo . . . ? He's not out. Not completely out. Is this normal? I've only used the stuff once, and that was on my husband. With Teo, who the hell knew?— unless he was in bed."

The Guru ignored the connotations. Too dangerous to pursue. "They never are completely out. Unless they stop breathing. That's only happened once. It was at the retreat, you know our largest Eco Lodge? The one up in the Yucatan. I told the *Guardia* that I found her naked in the meditation pool. Probably a gang-rape thing. You know, blamed it on the Maras."

I felt the woman's hands on my chest. They began to explore not as a test, but in a luxurious sort of way. "Good. I don't want him completely unconscious. Hurry up and finish what you're doing. Then go."

The man made a whooping sound of discovery. "Found another gun. It was under the pillow. And some damn unusual electronics. What is he, some sort of federal cop? You said you didn't want him dead."

Still exploring with her hands, the former Ms. Honduras responded, "Can he hear me?"

"Maybe. It doesn't matter. They don't remember anything later."

Her fingers found the buttons on my khaki shirt. She began to undo them one by one. "What about you, Wingo? Are you going to remember what happened here tonight? I've never trusted you. My husband didn't either."

"Fay, your . . . the Governor and I, he had the greatest respect for what we've built together. The two of us, he'd fly in? We had talks, very private talks. I'd hate to think you don't—"

The woman interrupted, "Oh, no doubt you two have quite the . . . oral history. *But I don't want to hear it!*" She released a long breath. I felt her hands relax and her fingers moved to my belt. "Get out of here, Your Holiness. Shut the door and enjoy the snack tray like a good boy."

"Do you want me to—"

"Yes, *yes*! Put everything in his bag and take it to the boat. Take my bags, too. God, you are so irritating. What do I look like, a goddamn maid?"

"Okay, okay but which boat? His or mine? His is bigger, but mine might—"

"You decide. No . . . both boats. Just do it!"

On his way out, the Guru stumbled over a piece of shattered door. The woman slid her left hand strategically down my abdomen and waited to whisper in my ear, "So, Dr. Ford—or whatever your name is. You don't find me attractive enough, huh? *Liar.*" I winced when she gave me a painful squeeze. "Maybe there's something hiding in here you don't really need."

Another squeeze took the wind out of me.

"We will see," the archaeologist said.

Her fingers found my belt.

Was I dreaming . . . ? Among the swirling colors, it all came back so vividly . . .

At Dinkin's Bay Marina, before a hurricane destroyed our homes, the subject of dreams was a popular topic at Friday night parties.

When Mack, the owner, locked the parking lot gate at sunset, it was a sort of starting gun. Outdoor speakers played Capt. Buffett's music. There were oysters and smoked fish on the grill. We, a salty collection of liveaboards and fishing guides, would collect around a fire, bayside, near the docks.

The picnic table was only a few steps from the marina office where there is always cold beer on ice. The area was hedged by fragrant jasmine and hibiscus blossoms.

The dream instigators were Rhonda and JoAnn, a handsome middle-aged couple who lived aboard *Tiger Lilly,* a soggy old Chris-Craft yacht. The vessel's purple curtains, its Christmas lights, and potted herb garden on the stern, told you a lot about those two ladies.

They were a savvy successful pair, yet they were wistful and worrisome when it came to dreams.

One would start the conversation, saying, "I had the craziest dream last night." Then after way too many details, would ask, "What the heck do you think it means?"

Everyone has an opinion when it comes to dreams. After some wine or beer, they aren't shy about sharing.

The romantic wistful types prefer Freud, whether they know it or not. Freud claimed that dreams make it possible to act out our deepest, least understood sexual desires in a safe, consequence-free context.

Images have meaning. Any object longer than it is wide has phallic implications.

Pragmatists—I among them—accept the current theory. Dreams are a random collision of memories and thought snippets that our tidy brain does its best to copy and paste into an orderly pattern.

Images mean nothing. They are snatched out of a slovenly, synapse mess and rearranged.

Even Freud, a cigar smoker, had been quick to clarify, sometimes a cigar is just a cigar.

In my scopolamine fog, those marina parties, the adored people, came alive. I could smell the buttonwood fire, a moist heat. A mosquito tickled my ear. I brushed it away.

Jasmine-scented lips stirred. They kissed my neck and pouted, "You don't like that? Let's try something else."

A woman's voice. Rhonda or JoAnn? I wasn't sure and it didn't matter. One of them was naked, leaning over me. She placed her breasts on my chest and let their soft weight trace the length of my stomach. Fragrant lips, moist and warm slid lower.

"Maybe you'll like this," the voice said.

I tried to sit up but couldn't. I tried to protest but only managed a sleepy series of grunts. To invoke the name of . . . someone—the tall, lanky woman I loved—would have stopped everything. But her name was lost in a whirlpool and refused to surface.

It was so damn frustrating. I couldn't move, couldn't speak. Couldn't even remember the name of . . .

"Han-han-han," I babbled. Then tried to shout it, "Hannah!" which only came out as a warning growl.

"You don't like this either?" the voice chided. "Bullshit. You *love* it. Open your eyes and see for yourself how much you love it. Hurry up. Oh damn! Did you feel that? The floor's vibrating. Another earthquake. You're very close, dear. Try to hang on."

My eyelids were glued until I blinked them free. Only the bathroom light was on, the room, a Vaseline blur. But I could see well enough to know it wasn't Rhonda or JoAnn straddling me.

The name *Hannah* became another warning growl.

"Listen to you, sounding all pissed off and mad. I sort of like that," the voice said. "How mad are you? Prove it. I'm an archaeologist. We get more interesting as we age—a private joke that you would not understand." She slapped me. "Wake up and show me."

My eyes opened. The room was still a blur. But my arm, then the other arm worked. I sat and realized I could speak. "No. Won't do it," I croaked and rolled onto my side.

Minutes later, an hour later, I don't know, my ex-fiancée, Hannah Smith, returned to me in a dream. The gentleness of her face, the trueness in her eyes, and the warmth of her knowing fingers put me at ease.

It had been so, so long since I had held Hannah in my arms. We joined gently. I sometimes tried to slow her eagerness but without success.

That was enticing. Whatever Hannah wanted or did not want, pleased me as much as it pleased her.

We slept. She was gone when a man I assumed was Wingo Bogdan came stomping into the room. "Get up, get dressed while I clean up this mess. We're leaving, you oversized *Samanera fake.*"

Bogdan was a small, wild-haired man who did, indeed, resemble the psycho, Charles Manson. Crazy eyes alight, a man who wanted to be worshiped. They are not always killers, but they are a common type. You find them on the streets, sometimes in industry and at family restaurants. Narcissists desperate for adulation. And control.

I was awake but not awake. The hallucinogenic delirium

had lessened, but the hands I used to get my pants on were not my hands. Nor was the face I saw in the mirror when I tried but failed to rinse my mouth free of the taste of jasmine.

I suspected the truth then. But wasn't certain until the Guru from Minnesota complained, "What the hell did you do to Fay? Thirty minutes I leave you two alone, now she's in there mooning around all moody and quiet. Suddenly all protective of you. But me, she finds *disgusting*."

He let his anger build and launched into a stream-of-consciousness rant as if addressing me. "That's the kind of disrespect I will not tolerate. Tonight of all nights—oh, we've wanted Fay out of our business dealings for a while. Do you know what her real problem is, *Samanera*? Fay's way too attractive to be human. Uses it like a weapon to get anything she wants. As if an elevated consciousness like mine would fall for sexual extortion. Oh, beautiful women, they're all the same."

Samanera meant novice. I knew this because of Tomlinson.

He threw a few more things in a laundry bag and went into the bathroom. The toilet flushed, a spigot ran, he exited still talking. ". . . So I slipped a little something into her Maker's Mark—if the bitch drinks it. You understand what I'm saying? From now on, you only take orders from me. Not her. And always refer to me as Shaman. Respectful."

What I understood was, my erotic dream had not been a dream.

I responded robotically, "Sure. Whatever you say," not certain if I was acting or not.

The man threw my heavy money belt at my feet. "You're gonna need that. Put it on." He watched me do it as if the belt were important. "You had more than a thousand bucks in there. I took it all. Is that okay with you?"

I shrugged.

"No problem, huh? Good. I want to cash out your credit cards, too. I'll need your pin numbers. There's paper over by the phone. Go write them down."

"Sure. I guess. Whatever you say."

I did it.

"And the password to your computer."

I had to think for a moment. It wasn't an act. "It uses facial recognition. I don't know why . . . can't remember the password."

"Typical. We'll take care of that later. I hear you're some kind of diplomat. Got to be some interesting data on your laptop. That true?"

I let my eyelids sag. "No . . . no. I'm not a diplomat."

"You've got the passport. Tell the truth. You have to tell me the truth. That's the way this works. Understand?"

"Sure, yes," I said as if some terrifying weakness in my brain compelled the truth. "My job is to . . . I can't tell you."

"But you are going to tell me, goddamn it. You're going to tell me every word, and it has to be the truth. Know why? Because all you can hear is the sound of my voice. Now talk!"

I was aware of what I was saying. I was aware of how I was expected to act yet couldn't stop myself from complying. Or pretending to comply—is there really any difference in our day-to-day lives? I said, "My job is to . . . what I get paid to do is make people disappear. Important people. Kill them, usually. I'm not allowed to share that information."

"An assassin. That's your job. Like in the movies, huh? Bullshit. You're lying."

"In the movies," I said, "actors don't really die, do they? It's different when I make someone disappear."

The little man's attitude changed. Grew serious, then he laughed. "Yeah, right. Some of the crazy ideas you tripped-out tourists get when you're on . . . Anyway, what you look like to me is some junior college professor trying to get laid in a foreign country. But to Fay—" he motioned to the suite "—you're mister sweet and gentle and I'm filth. She is such a self-important *twat*. How about boats? Do you get seasick?"

I shook my head. "But I don't feel good. Like I'm going to vomit. I think someone drugged me last night."

The Guru waved that away. "Naw, you'll be fine. We're going for a boat ride. You're gonna take us to where that kid with one arm lives. Can you do that?"

Aléto and the jade mask. That's what they were after.

"Sure. Whatever you say."

Before we left, the Guru confided, "After that Maker's Mark, Fidelia should be passed out by now. If she's not, when the time's right, I want you to shoot her in the head. You know, like you're a real assassin. Will you do that for me?"

"Yes. Sure."

"Shoot her in the face, I mean. You see, I want Fay to know it's coming."

"You want her to be afraid," I said.

"Now you're catching on. That would make a lot of people in my organization happy. That's the key tonight. Make me happy. I'm ordering you to shoot her in the face. Understand?"

My response was the same.

TWENTY-FIVE

The archaeologist settled the question of which boat we were taking when she told Bogdan, "I'm riding with Dr. Ford. We'll follow you to Cayo Faro—I need to stop and grab some things. He'll lead the way from there."

We were on the dock, Caribbean stars overhead, Utila Bay a breathing mirror. The hotel bar had gone quiet, but there was still a lot of festive activity on piers and in restaurants that circled the bay's horseshoe loop.

Bogdan, in his Boston Whaler, was trying to talk some sense into the woman. He was packed and ready to go.

"Lead the way? My God, Fay, this is stupid. The guy's too screwed-up to drive and he doesn't know the area. Either come with me, or wait until morning, that's what I think. It's almost two a.m."

The woman held up a hand—*stop*—and consulted me. "How about it? It's late, always tricky at night. You're sure you know where the kid is hiding?"

I confirmed it all, saying, "I'll need my bag. There's a flashlight in there and a special something . . . a device. Yeah, a device. Military. You need a license to own it. Night vision binocs."

She brushed my elbow with her breast as if it were an accident. "I trust you a lot more than I trust His Holiness down there. Pass his bag up, Wingo. *Rapido, por favor?*"

"What he just said, there's your proof," the man insisted. "That's the kind of fantasy these people believe when they're tripping their brains out. You said yourself, you have no experience with this powder. *I do.* Tomorrow—" the man lowered his voice "—tomorrow, he's not going to remember a damn thing about the next day or two. And what about the details we discussed?" He used his eyes to flag me, the zapped-out tourist zombie. "You really want to have to deal with this problem later?"

They obviously agreed that I had to die. For some reason that didn't bother me. My numb indifference was real. The delirium seemed to ebb and flow. Yet I was alert enough to know the Guru was spiteful for several reasons. He'd expected to find the former Ms. Honduras unconscious. She wasn't. Instead, she was still dissing his authority and barking orders.

There was a third reason. Jealousy. In their bedroom suite, he'd seen her greet me with a kiss that was slightly more than friendly. And Fidelia had been making subtle body contact ever since.

Bogdan had trailed the woman like a puppy. Watched her every move with the righteous eyes of a holy man who's desperate for an invitation to sin.

The wealthy beauties are never obvious. But all the signs were apparent. In Fidelia's imagination—privately, between us—we were only a sober night or two away from actually being lovers. Never mind the circumstances or my catatonic act. A wealthy woman with her looks, her body? It made no sense—unless she was attempting to manipulate me by attaching puppeteer strings.

Or was I the one who was acting? I didn't know. I couldn't test myself by refusing a command. Or even a suggestion. I was under some kind of psychotropic influence. No doubt about that. But like hypnosis, how deeply was I under?

Fidelia had changed into attire suitable for a rough night on a boat. Slacks, long-sleeved shirt, and a hoodie for mosquitoes. She tapped a leather boat shoe on the dock, and again ordered, "Pass his bag up, Wingo. My bag, too. No more arguing."

The Guru became vindictive. "When we get to your husband's island, do you want me to wait at the dock with Iron Baby? Or come up to the house? Teo's got special privileges at Dade Correctional, so we talk on the phone a lot. Wonders why the little wife never calls. But he still loves hearing my updates."

It was a threat. Maybe the name Iron Baby was a threat, too. I'd heard it before, but the context was hazy.

On the dock, I hefted my bag and knew that at least one pistol was missing. Probably some other items, too.

That didn't matter, either.

The woman and I were alone in the quiet four-stroke Honduran panga when she scooted close enough that our knees touched. "I need to share something with you. Wingo put a drug in my Maker's Mark tonight. Or at least I suspect he did. Did you know?"

"Yes."

"Why didn't you say something?

I shrugged. Stayed busy concentrating on markers. There were red and green flashers out there, strobes on a string that led to smoother water inside the reef.

A lone finger tapped my knee and was gone. "I'm sorry we had to meet like this. Earlier, when we were together . . . I feel like a fool saying this, but it's true. You were . . . I don't know how to put it. Different. Unusually . . . kind, I guess, so gentle. *Loving . . . ?* What a stupid word. But there it is. Something

I've never had the chance to experience before. It's embarrassing . . . sad. I admit it. So very damn sad."

The actress in her was setting me up for something. I didn't react.

We skimmed along in darkness over the water for a while before she tried again. "It sounds like a lot of nonsense, I suppose. But true. All my life, I walk into a room, men looked at me like I'm a trophy they can mount on a wall. It's poisonous. Becomes more of a lifestyle than a onetime thing. So I used it to my advantage by turning them—the hunters—into targets. Which hunter had the most money, the most power? Who was worthy of undressing me? It wasn't seduction. It was a small war that didn't end until they inevitably started with their threats. The accusations, the violent jealousy. And they always did. I suppose I'm getting too personal for someone like you."

She expected a response to this heartfelt soliloquy. I ignored her.

"Silly me. Maybe I should have tried drugging men long ago. Didn't know it was so simple to make them behave like they actually cared."

She waited through a stony silence. "What, not even a smile? Tell the truth. You honestly don't remember what just happened? The way it was between us? Between us in bed? There was an earthquake, for God's sake, but you didn't even seem to notice because you were so into me. Into us. Like nothing else existed."

"Nope," I said.

"*Really*. That's very damn hard to believe. It was little more than an hour ago. You're lying, aren't you."

"Yes."

"What?"

"I'm lying. Yes."

Her laughter was the sound of relief. "Finally! That's nice to hear. But why?"

I said, "I didn't know it was you. It was a dream, that's all. My brain's misfiring. I'm not sure what's real and what's not."

She spoke as softly as she could over the noise of a boat. "Thank you. I'm not sure that makes me feel any better but at least you remember something. Devil's Breath—the powder you inhaled? I might have inhaled some, too. Not much. Maybe what they say is true. Maybe we'll both forget everything that happened tonight."

Startled when I glanced over, she added, "Relax, I'm fine. Really. Wingo did it. He drugged you. But it was my idea. There—I'm being honest for once. Do you have any idea how unusual that is for me? So now you have a reason to hate us both."

"I know."

"About being drugged? How long?"

"Not sure."

"But you know *now*. That's encouraging." She leaned to create distance and took me in with her eyes. "Dr. Ford . . . *Ford*, I am so, so damn sorry. Truly. I'm not as bad as you might think. Do you believe that?"

"No."

She smiled. "You're lying again."

"Nope."

The smile vanished and she yanked her hand free. "Stop it. The zombie drug, I know. But there's absolutely no way you were a zombie. Not when we were alone. Maybe slightly immune or something. Very big guy, not the right dose. No one could fake the sweetness. That kind of gentle . . . *intensity*. Did you? Did you fake it?"

When I only shrugged, she reached and yanked the throttle back into neutral. Ahead on the horizon, the Whaler's running lights pulled away while we plowed to a stop.

"Look at me, Ford. *Look at me*." When I did, she tapped her knuckles on my forehead as if knocking on a door. "Are you in there? I know you're in there somewhere. Tell me the truth."

I took her wrists in my hands and pressed them away. "Don't ever do that again when I'm driving. If there'd been a boat behind us, you could've gotten us both killed."

A white anchor light above the outboard motor illuminated the woman's face—an ivory cameo that was not angelic. Yet, the predator I'd met in the bar was no longer there.

She nodded her head, eager to make peace.

"You want the truth, Mrs. Brava?"

Again, eager consent while she repositioned herself on the seat.

"The truth is, I'm in and out. Feel like a zombie half the time because of that damn powder. The only reason I'm telling you is, your business partner—" I glanced at the disappearing Boston Whaler "—he ordered me to shoot you in the head tonight. No, told me to shoot you in the face. Does that surprise you?"

"I knew it," she said, as if she'd not heard the question. "I knew you weren't pretending from the way you kissed me. Especially when we were . . ." The sentence fragment vanished when my words sunk in.

"Wait! Wingo ordered you to kill me tonight? That son of a bitch. What did you tell him?"

"Told him yes. That's what he expected. He doesn't know the drug seems to be wearing off."

"You didn't *mean* it, though. You wouldn't do it."

I said, "Maybe. The drug comes and goes. But if you tell him about this conversation, I might have to."

"Oh. *Oh.*" She cleared her throat and shifted her knee away from mine. "Okay, look, am I surprised they want me out of the picture? Not at all. That's why the last few months I've lived like a prisoner on Teo's precious island. I'm spied on, always watched. They plant tracking devices—you know those little

Apple tags? In my clothes or purse. My computer bag some-times. When I make a campaign speech, it's all recorded in that prison of a house."

Both of our travel bags were at her feet. I asked, "When's the last time you checked for a tag? Never mind, open them, take a look."

She did. Claimed to find nothing, then continued, "His business partners have been plotting this ever since they an-nounced my run for governor. I figured they would at least wait until I won to get rid of me. But to actually . . . ?"

The woman gave it a moment. "In my imagination, the way I pictured it happening? They'd stage another coup then send me off somewhere. I'd be lying on a beach with a Maker's Mark in the Bahamas probably because it's closer, easier to control. I would've preferred Spain, of course. All sunny and dramatic. Safe. No strings, so not so bad. Shoot me in the face? That sa-distic little freak wants to destroy any hopes I might have for a future."

This from a beauty queen who'd once had Hollywood aspirations.

I said, "*They* announced your candidacy? Bogdan, you mean?"

"Not just him. The real power brokers—heirs to one of the richest men in Honduran history. A palm oil tycoon named Miguel Coronado. It's the way this country works because—" She reconsidered. "Wait a minute. Is that why you're really here? To arrest friends of mine, people in my family? Our organization?"

If she hadn't said this so frankly, I might have thought her admission of guilt was intentional.

"Even if I wanted to, I'm not a cop," I said and slid the throt-tle forward. "You've got about twenty minutes before we get to the island. So talk to me and hope that drug doesn't change my mind about what I was ordered to do—" Concerned about something in the distance, I slowed to idle speed.

"What's wrong?"

"Bogdan," I said. "Looks like his boat stopped. I'll check."

On this starry bright night I hadn't needed night vision until now. I opened my bag and found the night vision binoculars. It gave me an opportunity to slip the little P365 into a pocket, and to confirm I'd been robbed. My full-sized pistol was missing. Probably some other things too. I hadn't had a chance to confirm, but at least my handheld radio was still safely tucked away.

I fitted the NODs on my forehead.

"My God, very high tech. You look like a cyborg," the woman remarked. Seemed to approve. "Wingo will know the drug's worn off if he sees those."

"But it *hasn't* worn off. I'm still fighting it," I said and adjusted the focus. "Yeah. He ran aground. We'll have to help push him off. This might take a while." I stowed the NODs and got the panga on plane again. "Are you going to tell him about this conversation? He has one of my guns."

"Gun . . . *Wingo*? That's not good. He scares me as it is," she said. "How did he—never mind. It's so late, I'll put him in one of the staff cabins. That'll get him out of the way, and we can talk. Anything you want to know."

I reminded her, "I've got to go back into zombie mode. Play along or not, that's up to you."

"Wait. First, you've got to tell me the truth. What happened between us was real. I *know* it. Please don't try to convince me that I'll never—" she took a breath "—that I'm too screwed-up to feel that way again. I'd prefer not to believe it's too late for . . . oh, to hell with it."

I wasn't crazy about spending what was left of the night alone with her, a sexual narcissist, plus Bogdan the delusional mystic, and some bodyguard named Iron Baby. I was still visited by occasional streaks and pinwheel colors, so I resorted to cruelty, the woman's favorite gambit. "Look, get it through your head, Mrs. Brava. Nothing happened between us. You weren't there."

"But I was. I was there, the two of us together in bed, and we made love. And you damn well know it."

"It wasn't you," I said. "Not in my mind, anyway. I was with a woman I actually care about. A woman I can trust."

My peripheral vision had returned. We were almost to the Whaler when I noticed an oddity. The aging beauty queen was dabbing at her eyes.

TWENTY-SIX

At 3:00 a.m., alone in a guest cottage walled with coral, I was about to give myself a second injection of the antidote, physostigmine, when I heard a tapping at the heavy teak door.

I traded the syringe for a pistol and went to the window. Down the hill, not far from the dock where our boats were tied, Wingo Bogdan had been joined by a man I hadn't yet seen. He was massive, three times the size of the mystic, and he dragged one leg which suggested a deformity. Or an injury.

The process of elimination narrowed it down. The man was the bodyguard, Iron Baby, who had not greeted us upon arrival. So my early morning visitor had to be Fidelia. I'd abandoned her in the kitchen, alone with the jealous guru. Left after using a Devil's Breath drug excuse that wasn't a lie. I felt like I might pass out.

I still felt dizzy but opened the door anyway.

Fidelia rushed in, slammed the door, and bolted it behind her. "Ford, I need to stay here for a while. I'm sorry, I'm sorry. I know what I promised."

What the woman had promised was to leave me alone. The

jealous Shaman—with his relentless testing commands—was tiresome enough.

When I stepped aside, she scampered past and plopped down on the bed. "I'm afraid," she said.

"So am I. Your business partner is drunk and probably getting meaner. And he's got one of my guns. Remember?"

Outside, Bogdan and the bodyguard had found a table at the water's edge.

"It's not just that. Iron Baby, he's back. He came to my door, said he'd been shot. That he needed more pain meds and something about Naomi—disgusting things that can't be true. He sounded so crazy, I told him to go away."

Before I could speak, she interrupted, "There's something else. In the kitchen, after you left, Wingo made a pass. Tried to kiss me. He's never had the nerve to try that before. Think about it. After he orders you to shoot me in the face?"

Her thoughts shifted to what was going on outside. "Now they're both down there getting drunker. Don't you get it? If Teo wants me dead, tonight could be the night. He had to have given his permission."

I would have doubted the woman's motives, but her boating clothes were sweat soaked. Her face had paled. The same symptoms Naomi had exhibited after she'd been dosed with scopolamine. It wasn't just fear that had caused the change in her.

"How do you feel?"

"Scared as hell, of course. Teo and I didn't have a happy marriage. How could we, him a bully with someone like me? His worst fear, I think, was I'd embarrass him in public. Me, I was terrified he might have me murdered. Funny, huh? Until now. I'm just upset and shaky."

I suspected something else was going on. "Did he give you anything to eat or drink? Or did he just blow something in your face?"

"Wingo? You think he . . . ?" She hadn't considered the possibility. It surprised her. "No . . . no powder that I noticed. I'm always careful, especially around him." She thought back. "In the kitchen, though, he did do something really weird. Had this little wooden spoon, a pressure-point thing they use in meditation supposedly. Said it would relax me, but I'd have to take off my blouse. I told him to go to hell and pushed him away. That's when he did it, tried to force his tongue down my throat."

Her amber eyes floated a disturbing concern. I was thinking the same thing.

"Let me check the back of your neck," I said.

Nothing there. But when Bogdan had grabbed the woman, he'd deposited a greasy smear of gelatin on her spine just above the buttocks.

"That disgusting little son of a bitch." Fidelia was neatening her blouse. "A place I wouldn't have ever noticed, even in the mirror. Oh my God, I just realized . . ." Panic caused her facial muscles to spasm. ". . . and I might've inhaled some of that stuff earlier at the hotel. Now what? People die if the dose is too strong. It's on the news every week."

Death was a possibility.

I told her to stay calm and did my best to scrub the gelatin off her back. Next, I injected the last physostigmine syringe into her thigh. By then she was wearing a robe, ready for the steps Naomi had followed. Gulp water, vomit, then into the shower. It was a procedure done with clinical indifference. I had no idea what effect it would have on transdermal poisoning, but it couldn't hurt.

Whenever she was in the shower, I took a break and observed from the window. The guru and the bodyguard were still at the waterside table. They'd built a fire, added an ice chest and a boombox to the party. It was an eerie tableau. Heavy bass rap music vibrated through the glass while the mystic danced in a drunken munchkin sort of way. The giant, because of his leg, danced too, but used only his arms to sway back and forth in time.

I thought, *It's like they're getting primed for a human sacrifice.*

If Fidelia continued her decline, she'd soon be helpless. There was also the likelihood the men would target me, too, by first disabling my boat.

That could not happen.

I called to the open bathroom door, "I've got to go outside. You okay for ten minutes?"

As I spoke, I pulled the little Sig Sauer and did what've I've done thousands of times from habit. Confirmed there was a round in battery by thumbing the slide back a quarter inch. Even in my chemical fog, I'd done this earlier on the boat before pushing the Whaler off a coral head.

Fidelia responded, "Huh . . . ? What did you say?" It was as if she'd just awoken.

I repeated the question and did what I'd forgotten to do earlier on the boat. I released the magazine . . . then stared for a long, dull moment.

Marion Ford, I thought, *you fool.*

The magazine was empty.

There'd been a pair of full P365 mags in my bag. The Guru was too inept to clear a chambered round yet he'd been shrewd enough to steal them both.

From the bathroom came a garbled, groaning request. Fidelia needed help transitioning from the shower to the sink.

Damn it. What were my options now?

I rechecked the window. The drunks had stopped dancing. They had their heads together as if plotting something new. The bodyguard, a foot taller than Bogdan, was inspecting something in his hands. A length of lumber it looked like. Or was it a rifle case?

When I entered, Fidelia was on the shower floor, head bowed.

All the cosmetic masking tricks—mascara, eye shadow—had streamed charcoal tears down her face. Sodden dyed hair was parted by a silver furrow that no longer camouflaged the reality of her age.

She yawned a huge symptomatic yawn and flexed her jaw. Amber eyes implied there was still a spark within. "If I wasn't so damn sick, I'd be less worried about dying. Hope that shot you gave me helps. What was in it?"

The same question had been asked several times. I explained again, adding, "It's not a blanket antidote, but it helps. You'll feel better soon." I smiled down at her. "We need you healthy, on your feet before we can deal with Bogdan."

Fidelia accepted this like an obedient five-year-old.

"Yes, on my feet . . . and I *will* feel better. What I'd really like to do—after I sleep for a couple of days—is push Wingo off a cliff. That disgusting little worm." She extended her hand, and I helped her to her feet. "Don't bother with a towel, it just makes the humiliation worse. Do you want me to vomit again?"

The woman, groggy and slurring her words, seemed to slip in and out of her catatonic stupor.

I draped the towel over her shoulders and steered her to the sink. "There might be a change of plans. Does your husband have any guns in the house?"

Sick as she was, that got a quizzical response. "How many guns do you need, for God's sake?"

Rather than add to her worries, I told her to put her clothes on, we might have to leave, and I asked about weapons again.

"There used to be." She was having trouble forming sentences. "There were . . . I dunno, several pistols and rifles—shotguns, maybe. Oh, and the Army kind—an automatic something."

I asked, "A full automatic? Like an assault rifle?"

Another sleepy yawn and a shrug. "Dunno. That was before they arrested Teo and searched the house. He kept them behind a false wall . . . ? No, a hidden compartment in a wardrobe next to his bed. I never bothered to check. We've always had separate rooms."

I took a quick look outside. Yes, the bodyguard, Iron Baby, had a rifle, too. Or possibly a shotgun. The twosome had returned to the table and were smoking a joint, one tiny orange dot aglow, when they weren't pounding beers.

"His room's in the main tower?" I asked.

"The Widow's Walk, Teo called it. Any wonder I don't like going up there? But *I will* if you want me to, *Cariño.*"

"No need, Fay. Hopefully, those two will stay put. But to be safe, leave the door open and get under the bed while I'm gone."

"*Under* the bed? Even on the floor, I'll pass out." She sniffed, thought for a moment and seemed to perk up a bit. "If you're going out anyway, you know what might help get me on my feet? In my office—the desk drawer—there're these little plastic pouches that—" When the woman hesitated, I knew she was thinking about the mini packets of cocaine hidden there.

"Look at me," I said. "The combination could kill you. I'm not sure of the chemistry, but we can't take the chance. Understood?"

She attempted a bout of confusion but gave up. "And I can't risk Wingo finding me on the floor unconscious. Not while you're away. Just the idea makes me want to . . . Please, Ford. I can't imagine anything worse. Think of it as medicine— something I trust to get me on my feet. Isn't that what you want?"

I told her, "Sure it is, but hiding under the bed is safer. If they see the door open, they'll assume you're not here and come looking for me."

Except for the bathroom mirror, I switched off the lights before I left.

• • •

The former governor's bedroom smelled of cigars, and moth-balls, still furnished with waxen black wood and wall plaques as if the great man might return to the island tomorrow.

I wondered if that was possible.

The room had a rotunda view, windows all around. They allowed me to keep track of the drunks while I searched.

The wardrobe cabinet was double-doored, seven feet tall. I shoved a curtain of business suits aside and levered two wooden dowels. The secret panel swung open. Inside was a vertical rack that had once held long guns. There were also several hooks for pistols.

The *federales* had done their job. But they'd missed a few things. Wedged along the floor was a line of stray ammunition that had dropped through the cracks. Not much. Twelve gauge and .45 caliber were the former governor's weapons of preference. There was also a lethal-looking 7.62 cartridge. This suggested Fidelia had been correct about a military semi-auto.

I pocketed the brass ammo and continued my search. In a bottom drawer was a crumpled box that contained seven rounds of Blazer .380 cartridges.

They were cheap practice loads but that was okay. A .380 is a lighter, under-powered version of the 9 mm Parabellum. Anything but ideal but workable. In my little Sig, the ammo wouldn't combust enough gas to eject or cycle. I'd have to do it all manually, not unlike using an antique single shot.

That was okay, too. In an escape-and-evasion course, they'd made us substitute .380 cal as an emergency option. The cartridges would fit clonelike in my higher caliber magazine—as I confirmed by loading the seven rounds one by one. Squeeze the trigger, and ninety-five grains of lead would exit the barrel.

Probably—if moisture and age hadn't turned them all into dangerous squib duds.

I wiped my prints off the wardrobe and exited through an elaborate hand-carved door onto a patio. Elevation—at least three hundred feet above sea level—provided perspective. Cayo Faro was a rock afloat on a horizon of ocean stars. It was an ideal place to hail Tomlinson on my handheld VHF.

I tried. He didn't respond. On channel nineteen, though, a boater was in contact with the local coastal patrol. I could summon help from here if needed—but only in an emergency.

I didn't want local law enforcement around while Wingo Bogdan was still alive.

Down the stairs from the tower was a utility closet where the main breaker box was located. I foraged a few items into a bucket and lugged it through the main room past the fireplace where a familiar painting coerced attention.

The bucket waited on the floor while I stepped back to re-evaluate the haunting semi-nude in gilded oils.

Some perversity in me expected to see all the scars, the wrinkles, the toxic internal ugliness that was reality.

I did not. The aloof beauty still stared down with eyes of ancient amber. They were piercing, alive, indifferent to a future that did not exist. Where raven hair followed the upward curvature of her breasts there was no sag or stretch mark concessions. The misty hint of pink areola continued to make unobtainable promises.

The former Ms. Honduras was a rare one indeed. Whether captured on canvas twenty years ago or viewed fifteen minutes ago while vomiting into a toilet, she remained a woman of astonishing beauty.

The artistry hadn't changed. But I had. No longer did I feel a physical response to the painting. Nor to Fidelia. That was gone, had it ever existed other than in a drug-fired dream.

I didn't trust her. That was part of it. Still suspected Fidelia was trying to manipulate me into a blindsided fall. The odd thing was, I was starting to like the woman. The reversal had to do with witnessing her in the bathroom, sick, scared yet unashamed, every wrinkle and small imperfection laid bare.

There was beauty in that, too. And it was real.

TWENTY-SEVEN

I entered the guest cottage, placed my bucket of spoils on a table, and knew immediately what Fidelia had done while I was away.

The door had been closed, not open, and all lights were on. Instead of being asleep under the bed, she was pacing, alternately folding towels between visits to the window.

Fidelia was at the window now after letting me in. The frazzled hair, her frumpy indigo hoodie and flaxen slacks were blurred by the primacy of her face in silhouette.

After killing all but the bathroom light, I said, "How long have you been standing there? It's not safe. Take a step back."

She did, but reluctantly. "They're coming, Ford. I know they're coming and they're going to kill me. I've been watching. You know how dogs act before they attack? All nervous."

A compulsive fist moved to shield her nose when she sniffed. Her voice had deepened to alto, but her words flowed with a quickened rhythm as if propelled by a pounding heart.

She urged, "Come see. They've been packing, getting ready for something, so it must be true. I've joked about this, I know, I know. But I never thought Teo would actually have me murdered."

"Are they coming now? If they are, we need to get moving."

She answered, "Not yet. But they will. I know they will. My God, I've been such a fool."

There was a wastebasket near the microwave. Hidden in a balled-up wad of toilet paper were two empty mini baggies. In the toilet, I found a third. I walked closer to the window and put my hand on the woman's shoulder. The way it jolted her was confirmation.

I held up what I'd found. "How much of this did you use? What, two grams to a baggie? Please tell me you didn't sniff all six grams."

The elegant woman appeared to wilt as if I'd screamed the questions, then fell against my chest trembling.

"Please don't be angry with me, Marion. I can't handle it right now. I'm trying so hard to be . . ." She pulled away. "They're going to kill me. I had no choice. If I passed out, you'd have to carry me. That's the only reason. You *told me* to get on my feet."

Her reaction squeezed the heart as did the familiarity of hearing my first name. At the hotel bar it had been Fidelia's sharp, acerbic tool.

Gently, I pressed, "Did you put all this up your nose?"

"But it isn't much! Really. I can explain." She took a baggie between her fingers. "This? It's just a '*cremita*,' less than half a gram. Not even that. A tiny *puntita*. I'm used to it. A little pick-me-up."

She smiled to demonstrate her sobriety, then combined English with Spanish. "*De verdad*. I feel much better now. The Maya, the entheogens our royalty used, they were a hell of a lot more powerful than a few sniffs of *cocaína*."

Our royalty? Their entheogens?

Reverting to academia and her birth language were as symptomatic as the dazed eyes and rapid, shallow breathing.

The lady was dying, I feared and would soon be comatose. Why? Because, under the influence of scopolamine, she'd been so damn desperate to please me.

"Fay, you need help. We need to get you to a hospital." I got the VHF radio out, placed the bucket near the microwave, and spoke into the transceiver. "Hailing any vessel, any station. Pan-pan-pan, this is an emergency. Q-S-L please."

"Marion . . . what are you doing?" She was standing by the damn window again.

"Calling for a medevac. Get away from there—they'll see you." I pressed the transmit button and repeated the emergency call and added our location.

In a room of solid coral, a static response was not unexpected.

She said, "But you can't do that. Only the military and narcos have helicopters. And they still follow Teo's orders. Don't you see what's happening? They'll kill me anyway."

After another long look outside, she turned and allowed the window to frame the back of her skull.

"They're there, coming, coming toward the house. Iron Baby is carrying something, a rifle, looks like. But I don't think he would hurt . . ."

I lunged two steps and swung the woman clear. A beat later, the window exploded—a three-shot burst that showered the floor with glass.

Are you okay? Are you okay? We went back and forth like that, until I told her, "Grab your cell phone. Just the few things you actually need and stay on your knees. We're leaving. I'll try to slow them down first."

Not easily done with a pocket pistol that contained only one reliable cartridge and seven possible duds. I nudged the teak door open, crawled out, and peeked over a coral railing into the Caribbean darkness.

Distance added to an iffy equation. The giant bodyguard was fifty-some yards away, limping up steps that led uphill from the beach. He'd slung the rifle over his shoulder. Behind him, Bogdan trotted back and forth, terrier-like—a moving target that intentionally used the big man as a shield.

The deceptive little fraud hadn't told Iron Baby their adversary was armed.

If I'd had a full magazine, I would've made the plastic guru pay for it right there. One flesh trafficker down, an unknown number to go.

That wasn't an option. I've never been a gifted pistol shot, so I braced both arms on the coral ledge, and found the big man's center mass with the front sight's tritium glow. Held it there, allowed Iron Baby's silhouette to blur, and squeezed off my only dependable round.

There was a high-pitched yelp. The pistol cycled a .380 cartridge into the chamber before I realized that I'd missed and hit Bogdan.

"*Son-uva*—I've been shot, I've been shot," the little man wailed. He zigzagged off holding what appeared to be his ear. The bodyguard stumbled after him.

It gave me a chance to take aim again. I skewered the man's bulk with a green dot, held my breath and fired. But instead of a satisfying nine-millimeter KAH-WHACK, the pistol belched a feeble *pop* that hissed.

A squib round.

Damn it.

I'd experienced this malfunction only twice in years of shooting. It had little to do with mismatched ammo. Occasionally, rarely, you get a bad load even if you buy the expensive stuff. The primer ignites but there's not enough propellant, so the bullet lodges inside the barrel. Chamber another round, pull the trigger, and the weapon will explode.

I didn't have the time or tools to clear the barrel, so I crawled toward the guest cottage, thinking, *We've got to get the hell out of here fast.*

But how? Anyone on the pier would be an easy target for a man with an automatic rifle.

The same if we were lucky enough to make it to my boat.

Thinking about the boat, I remembered the plastic twelve-gauge flare gun in the safety kit. A very poor choice as a defensive weapon. But it was there if needed.

Fidelia had disappeared into the bathroom. Rather than relieved that I'd returned, she instructed through the door, "Do yourself a favor and leave without me. I can't go anywhere. Not now. Got . . . terrible stomach cramps. I'll just slow you down."

Diarrhea, I translated, caused by the cocaine.

We had abandoned modesty an hour ago. I went to my tactical bag, tapped out two tiny tablets of Lomotil—"Slammers," my operator friends called them—and stepped into the bathroom with a bottle of water. "Drink, stay hydrated, and take these pills. They're fast. Those guys aren't used to being shot at, so we're okay for now. It'll be a while before they try again."

"Then what? Marion, we can't stay here, not if Teo gave them orders, and I can't . . ." Hunched over on the stool, she seemed to relax a bit. "Okay, I get it—because you have a gun. You scared them off, so we're safe. Think maybe they got in Wingo's boat and left?"

"Could be," I lied, and allowed the woman her privacy.

It was pointless to admit my pistol was useless, so I got busy preparing the cottage for the inevitable visitors. The mismatched ammo I'd found went into the microwave. The same with the rusted ball of steel wool. I set the timer to fifteen minutes but left the oven door open—for now.

The bottle of propane was a more calculated touch. I placed it on the counter next to an old gooseneck reading lamp. A sharp rap with a butter knife cracked the bulb and left the electrical filaments exposed. The filaments glowed orange when I pulled the chain.

The propane valve remained closed, but not for the same reason I'd left the microwave door open.

A more subtle touch.

I returned to the shattered window, glass crunching beneath my feet. No sign of the wounded Guru, but the bodyguard had returned. The careful way he slunk from tree to tree said that he was wary of being shot.

"Get your clothes on, it's time to leave," I said to the bathroom door. "Those tablets I gave you are working by now. The cramps are going away, right?"

This subliminal suggestion was another lie. But it worked. Fidelia came out fully dressed; had even raked a comb through her hair.

"You know . . . I do feel a little better. Between those pills and the shot you gave me, maybe I can manage to get to the pier. When do you want to leave?"

"Now, and we need to move fast," was my response.

The bodyguard had worked his way to some bushes near the steps.

I crossed the room, gathered my tactical bag and found an extra pair of leather gloves. Rather than toss them, I placed the gloves in her hand. "In the lagoon, is there a small boat or something? Anything that floats big enough to hold us both?"

"Oh my God, they're down there again, aren't they?" After a glance at my expression, she rushed to list our options. There was a diesel-powered sort of barge, bouyant lounge pads for suntanning and several paddleboards.

"Too loud or too small," I said. "We need something that'll get us around the island without being seen."

"There's a canoe. No one uses it, but I'm sure there are paddles somewhere. Would that work?"

Good enough.

I sent her alone toward the patio. Told her to stay in the shadows, exit through the front of the house, and find a place to hide. I'd be there soon.

It didn't take long to close the microwave door and engage the fifteen-minute timer. Or to power on the lamp with the broken bulb.

The propane tank was left untouched on the counter. When the men entered and saw an obvious booby trap, their reaction would be to turn the valve the wrong way and save themselves.

TWENTY-EIGHT

We were in the canoe when the men—one of them, anyway—found the breaker switch I'd flipped before leaving the former governor's mansion.

"The power's on again." Fidelia was on the deck facing me, a towel over her legs and a bucket nearby.

I paddled while she watched the house.

"See . . . ? Lights on in Teo's bedroom, now they're downstairs. It's still hard to believe my own husband—even as much as we hated each other—wants me shot in the face. *My face.* That's not murder, that's . . . it's more like desecrating who I am. Can you imagine what a bullet would do to my face?"

The woman had hypered herself into a monologue of dark unfiltered fears. Sounded out of it but her mind came and went. I could relate. I remembered Bogdan, at the hotel, saying his victims remained brain numb for a day or two, then slept around the clock.

Sleep. The craving had finally hit me. It arrived as a narcotic fog while I paddled. Tried to lull me into unconsciousness if I blinked my eyes closed for more than a few seconds.

Fidelia was still talking. "The Maya weren't any kinder. Used needles to scramble a victim's brains, then decorated the skull like a trophy. What they believed is, there's no higher form of sacrifice than a human head. Think he'll do that? Put my skull on the mantel under my painting? I used to love that painting, but not the way I look these days. Over the fireplace, that's where my skull belongs after all the terrible shit I've done in my life."

There was a pensive silence. "Know something? I want to adopt that boy. I do—not just because of who he might be. Or because the kid robbed me and the museum. It doesn't do my vanity any good to say this, but I'm older than I look, Marion . . . ? *Marion*, are you listening?"

A grunt sufficed while I concentrated on paddling. Two strong J-strokes starboard side . . . glide. Three rudder strokes portside.

She continued talking.

"I should've realized what I'd miss, not having a child. No one wants to die without—I mean, just vanish from the planet? But now—because of the menopause thing?—it's too damn late. You never said. Did you actually see the jade death mask?"

I replied, "Just a photograph," and consulted my Bathys dive watch. Phosphorus numerals said it was 4:16 on another calm Honduras morning. This was motivation enough to stay awake.

"Drink some more water," I told her. "Hopefully those two will stay busy until we're sure the the motor on my *panga* starts."

Nine minutes from now—if I'd timed it right—the men would be inside the cottage when the microwave exploded—a harmless distraction. In movies, throw live ammo into a fire, bullets whiz around as if shot from a gun. That's not what happens. There's no chamber to provide resistance so, when the powder detonates, lead and brass separate without much destructive force.

It might make one hell of a boom, though.

The one-pound propane tank was a less predictable ruse.

As Tomlinson might say, the mini fireball—if it happened—was up to God, and the stupidity of the men determined to kill the archaeologist. *Kill me, too, after what they would soon experience.*

We lost sight of the house after rounding the island's rocky eastern ridge. Far out to sea were the navigation lights of Maritime's eighteen-wheelers. Cargo ships, diesel enclaves a quarter mile long, eerily underpopulated like ghost ships. Their illuminated decks were stacked with containers that, after sunrise, would resemble a payload of Rubik cubes.

Farther out on the seaward cusp was a cutter-sized vessel. Military possibly, set apart by its towering navigation lights. Honduran navy? Could be.

I thought Fidelia had dozed off, but she was alert enough to ask, "Out there, is that a helicopter?" She sat up. "Yeah, a helicopter. Damn it—you promised you wouldn't call."

A tidal rip required me to rudder closer to shore. Close enough that heat radiated off the rocks, and the tang of mangrove swamp flooded over a distance from the barrier reefs of Belize.

"Freighters headed for the Panama Canal," I explained. "You're looking in the wrong direction."

"No, no, I'm not." She focused on the mainland. "Just a minute ago, it was there. Flashing lights, not like those."

A pair of cargo ships miles out to sea is what she probably meant. So I scanned the coastline but saw only the humpbacked contours of Cayo Faro and islands that formed an archipelago.

"Relax. I didn't call in a medevac."

"But you did. I was there."

Paranoia, but she was right. "Okay, I called but no one heard me."

"How do you know they didn't hear you? Maybe you couldn't hear *them.* Flashing lights, red and green, a long way away. I didn't imagine them, I'm . . ." She lowered her face into her hands. ". . . or maybe I did. How long do these damn hallucinations last?"

More worrisome was the mix of coke and scopolamine. It seemed to be paralyzing her respiratory system.

I said, "Turn around—see where we are? We're almost there, so try to lay back and take long, slow breaths."

Ahead to the left, the house of coral sat above the pier where two small boats were moored, the panga indistinguishable from the Boston Whaler. The compound was alight with windows. Lights were on in the guest cottage, too.

I rechecked the time—almost four-thirty in the morn.

"Two minutes," I said to myself. We were only a few strong strokes from the dock.

Fidelia heard me. "What are you talking about? Two minutes until what?"

I motioned to the guest cottage, but no explanation was necessary. As we glided, a silent explosion fired the windows like a giant flashbulb. A mini sec later, a muted boom reached us.

"What the . . . My God, did that . . . Are you trying to burn down my house?"

"Not likely, but you'll need a new microwave," I said, and swung the canoe abeam the panga. After a long minute, it happened again. A fireball blasted the cottage door wide and illuminated the waxy undersides of nearby palm trees.

It also disgorged two stumbling profiles. Wingo Bogdan exited first. He threw himself on the patio deck, rolled, got up, and sprinted a crazy circle because one pant leg was on fire. From what was left of the flames, the bodyguard emerged either in shock or too pissed off to care. He moved purposefully, head swiveling as if searching for a target to blame.

"Get in the panga. Hurry," I whispered. "The fire should burn itself out in a minute or two."

I followed her aboard, shoved the canoe adrift, and started the engine.

"He sees us, Marion." Fidelia had poked her head up. "Let me try and talk to him. Iron Baby likes me. He's probably just drunk."

Christ. The woman was delirious.

Before I could power onto plane, she was on the casting deck, waving and yelling while the bodyguard looked, looked again, then leveled the automatic rifle.

I lunged, pulled her beside me, and spun the boat full speed along the shore where mangroves failed to shield us. A triad of sledgehammer blows hammered the hull. When I raised my head, the bumblebee *buzz* of a bullet snapped past my ear.

The former Ms. Honduras sounded furious, not befuddled, when she got to her knees and shrieked, "It's me, you idiot. Stop! Stop shooting!"

The shooting stopped.

We had rounded the island's rocky point before the archaeologist spoke again.

"You think Iron Baby heard me? I must've snapped, something in my brain. Iron Baby, it was stupid to think he'd listen. We got lucky."

Her spacey slur had returned now that we were out of view.

A strategic act? Or was she right about good luck?

I had my doubts until a test question was provided by the lights of an aircraft sledding toward us from open sea.

"A helicopter's coming," I said. "You weren't imagining things. But think about it—why send the military to kill a woman who's already been drugged? More likely, someone heard my distress call and it's a medevac."

I slowed and used a flashlight to inspect the panga for damage. A trio of 7.62 rounds had punched holes through the fiberglass a few inches above the waterline.

"Damn it."

"What's wrong?"

"Boat's leaking, but we'll be okay—if we don't have to stop."
I reached into the transom well and twisted the plug out of
the main scupper. Water boiled in until I got the boat on the
plane. When the prop's vortex had suctioned the deck dry, I
plugged the scupper again.

"What do you want to do?" I pressed. "The clinic's five
miles of open water, on the other side of the bay. We can't out-
run them, and you need help."

"Not their kind of help, no. I warned you. The clinic's no
good either. If Teo gave orders, they'll find me there, or anywhere else if I go for help. Marion, we've got to hide somewhere
until it's safe for both of us. Are you sure we're not sinking?"

The chopper—probably the same narco-era Huey—tilted
nose-down and hovered above the coral mansion a half mile
away. A searchlight blazed on, a dazzling wedge of white. The
copter pivoted and dissolved the darkness that separated us. If
the door gunner opened up with his fifty-cal, he'd prune the
mangroves and we'd soon be dead.

I increased speed as the Huey descended behind the tree
line.

"That's where the landing pad is," Fidelia said. She had to
speak louder now. "The pilot must know we've already left.
Think they'll come after us?"

If the pilot was in contact with Bogdan, I reasoned, yes,
they would.

She seemed to accept that. "Tell me something. If you didn't
have to worry about me, what would you do?"

I would've cached my gear ashore, set the boat adrift with
an anchor dragging, and planned a surprise attack. But I didn't
say it.

"Doesn't matter," I told her. "What I'm afraid of is, your
respiratory system might be shutting down. Or a stroke. If we
don't get you to a doctor soon, you could . . ."

"Die, I know. What I can't get out of my mind is how I'd look if they shoot me in the face." She touched her jaw as if picturing her shattered skull beneath the painting done in gilded oils. "I couldn't stand that. I *won't*. Isn't there a safe place we can hide until morning? In the jungle somewhere where you're sure we won't be found? I think you know the place I'm talking about."

It was obvious what the archeologist was suggesting. What seemed to be manipulation, however, became dubious honesty when she admitted, "I hope I'm not dying but, if I am, I'd like to wear the jade mask my ancestors wore. History's important to me."

We had departed the archipelago's shoals into unprotected water where slow cobalt rollers mimicked the rhythm of off-shore waves. Five miles across the bay, a necklace of lights traced the coastline.

The woman, curled up on the deck at my feet, pulled a tarp over her. "I'm too tired to argue, but what I told you earlier, about how I felt? It's true. You decide, Marion. Wake me up when we get to wherever we're going."

To the west was La Ceiba, population of more than a hundred thousand. A hospital and the Cayman Embassy were there—our safest, most logical choices.

To the southeast, a void marked the entrance to a river that snaked into jungle where the one-armed boy had lived without interference for months.

I glanced back at our bioluminescent wake. The Huey was airborne again, searchlight on. When the aircraft sledded west toward La Ceiba, I did what I probably would have done anyway.

If I was being manipulated, it would be obvious soon enough.

It was.

• • •

We were several miles upriver, not far from the one-armed boy's camp, when the Huey reappeared, but not from seaward as anticipated. It hugged the jungled contours to cloak engine noise, then pivoted free over the water. Visibility was already obscured by fog in the first warm rays of morning.

I heard the chopper only seconds before I saw it. Just enough time to hop out and drag the boat into a group of overhanging limbs.

"Wake up," I told the woman. When she refused to stir, I shook her shoulder. "Wake up."

No response, and every shallow breath seemed a struggle.

Fog amplifies sound. A quarter mile away, the chopper hovered as if to confirm its target was near, then accelerated. Through an awning of branches, I watched the aircraft soar by, skids low over the river, a helmeted man inside the cabin strapped to the dangling fifty-cal automatic.

Rotor blades spun a whirlpool of mist when the chopper ascended and turned for another pass.

They have thermal imaging, I guessed. Or Fidelia was carrying a tracking device. Willingly or not, it didn't matter for now.

I shook the woman's shoulder again and shouted, "Wake up. You hear me?"

Her lips, gray not gilded, exhaled a crackling sound that might have been her last breath. I checked for a pulse—felt nothing in my haste—and tried to do a lot of things at once while administering CPR.

An orange box beneath the seat contained a standard Coast Guard safety kit. Between chest compressions, I loaded a plastic twelve-gauge flare gun and placed it at my knees next to the VHF handheld.

Thirty compressions, then ventilate mouth-to-mouth after two deep breaths. The woman's lips tasted of lip balm and salt. I counted aloud above the copter's WHOP-A-WHOP roar as it slowed downriver, and the door gunner fired a brief experimental burst.

Many yards closer, he fired again—bracketing rounds that suggested the pilot was unsure of our exact location.

That meant they weren't using thermal imaging. Fidelia had to be carrying a tracking device.

I dumped the contents of her purse on the deck. Nothing unusual there. So I rummaged through her roller bag with the same mystifying results, which is when a tornadic downdraft hammered the trees and signaled that we were out of time.

The twelve-gauge flare kit came with three additional rounds in a plastic magazine. After another cycle of CPR, I shoved the mag into my pocket and followed the stink of jet fuel to the river's edge. The Huey was there, suspended life-sized above the water, aft cabin door open wide amid a torrent of displaced spray.

The door gunner saw me. His head tilted in surprise when I raised the flare gun, and he dived for cover before I fired. An orange streamer banged off the interior wall and dropped to the deck still blazing.

I reloaded and pulled the trigger again before the crewman could secure his weapon and slam the starboard door closed.

Maybe the Huey had a fire suppression system. It would explain why the pilot angled the copter skyward and departed at high speed. Get help and call in another gunship. That would be his plan.

Kneeling over the woman, I continued CPR and watched the helicopter exhaust a smoky contrail until it disappeared west above the jungle canopy.

Honduras' largest palm oil plantation lay a few miles to the west, the boy had told me. A major trafficking outpost with its own small army—as my state department sources had confirmed via yesterday's emails.

This was not a place to linger, and I would have given up

on the woman if I hadn't felt a faint thump . . . thump . . . thump when I touched her neck for what I assumed would be the last time.

On the VHF, I hailed Tomlinson.

No response.

I hailed any station, any station.

Same thing.

On the river, I jumped the boat onto plane and steered the last quarter mile or so toward Aléto's jungle hideaway. When I was sure Fidelia was breathing, I tried the radio again. This time, my hipster pal came back saying, "Hey Doc, I read you loud and—"

That's all I heard before I glanced aft and saw a Boston Whaler round the distant bend. Two men aboard—Wingo Bogdan and the giant bodyguard, both oblivious to my boat several hundred yards upriver.

At planing speed, I skidded into the limestone aquifer, killed the engine and began assembling items I might need—the flare gun. A hundred feet of braided anchor line, the come-along winch, a plastic rain poncho, surgical gloves and a screwdriver to try and clear the barrel of my jammed Sig Sauer.

Not as an afterthought, I strapped on my Randall dive knife, aware of the Whaler's approach.

The former Ms. Honduras lay in a fetal position on the deck beneath the tarp. She had to know we were being followed.

I said to her, "This isn't going the way you planned is it, Fidelia?"

I didn't expect her to hear or understand. But she did.

Her eyes opened. "They're after me, Marion. You're just an inconvenience. I wish you would've believed me while you still had the chance."

I asked, "Where did you hide the tracking device?"

She was too sick to deny it. Bogdan had zipped it into my money belt.

TWENTY-NINE

(Tomlinson Part Three)

Tomlinson spoke into the mic of his wire headset and told Pulpo, "Quit saying we're lost. It's impossible to get lost over the ocean. Too many directions to choose from to be lost. I'm cruising, looking for a sign. It's the way my brain works. I'll know when I see it."

They were in the stolen ultralight somewhere near the islands of Utila and Roatán, a few hundred feet above the water. Hard to be certain because of dense fog that had yet to be burned away by the rising sun.

Pulpo, strapped into the aft seat, responded, "I should be driving. That's what I do, Cap'n, drive tourists around. Tell them all about our beautiful country and never get lost. Let's trade places. There ain't no signs up here in the sky."

A moment later, he swore and said something in Spanish about his missing ear. The bleeding had stopped but, mawn, the *puta* had hurt like hell for a while.

"Maybe it's because I've never been in an airplane before," the islander theorized. "I read that, up in space? The astronauts, they say they heal faster. On the other hand, could be

I'm better 'cause of that fine Dr. Naomi. I'm gonna take her some flowers when we get back to the medical clinic."

In the cupholder near the joystick was a warm *Presidente* beer and the GMRS radio. The radio garbled a familiar voice, and Tomlinson said, "Been expecting this—the sign I mentioned. Doc can give us directions."

By trial and error, it had taken the bluewater sailor only minutes to learn that his left hand controlled the throttle cable. His right hand controlled the plane's ups and downs, and its turns via the joystick. What he had yet to learn was never, ever let go of the stick or the aircraft would dive like a wounded duck.

That's what happened when he grabbed the radio, already saying, "Hey, Doc, I read you loud and . . ." which caused the plane to plummet nose-down through a plateau of fog.

"Whoa, whoa . . . *shit-the-bed.*"

His bottle of beer banged off the overhead wing scaffolding. The radio tumbled weightlessly for an instant, and Tomlinson nearly went out the door with it when he lunged for the damn thing.

A hundred feet or less above water, they broke clear of the fog where the sailor finally got control of the stick. He leaned back and leveled off in an aquamarine world of muted sunlight but perfect visibility.

Pulpo said through the com system, "*Aye-yai-yai* . . . this is much better. Now that I can see, I know where we are. But why are we flying toward Roatán? My missing ear isn't bleeding . . . or are you hungry?"

Tomlinson was also trying to get control of his breathing. "*Thank sweet Baby Jesus,*" he whispered, then adjusted the wire microphone. "Yep, basic meteorology one-oh-one. Fog pancakes in layers over water this time of year. You know me. If everything else fails, give science a try."

"See there, Cap'n? You always were smart. But next time

mi socio, warn me before you do that again. I almost vomited out my nose."

The bottle of beer had landed in Tomlinson's lap. He chugged what was left, used his beard as a napkin and looked to the north. "Roatán, huh? Perfect. Gives us a solid landmark for triangulation. Now all we have to do is find my pal, Doc. I'm pretty sure he's shit-up-a creek."

Pulpo was unfamiliar with a village by that name. "Unless you'd like to see where I live?" he said. "The Pigeon Cays, they a park now. Government moved us Caracol folk west to Conch Cay, but locales call it Cayo Hueso 'cause of the graveyard."

Cayo Hueso.

The name registered subliminally in Tomlinson's head while he got his bearings by checking the sun. It was a huge, boiling half-star afloat somewhere over Cuba.

"At least we know which way is east," he reasoned. "Which means we gotta make a Randolph to get to the mainland. After that, easy-peezy. Just fly the coastline until we see the entrance to the river. The kid—the kid with one arm you met? Find the river, we're almost there."

Pulpo hadn't given up on a quick stop on Roatán. "There's a bar on Conch Key—*Found Me A Home Cantina*, it's called. It ain't far. It's right there. See where I'm pointing? Captain Billy—he's a Bayou-White Conch—he serves a fine breakfast—snapper with mangoes and fish gravy. Right on the water, we could land near my pole house if you gotta pee."

Tomlinson had a lot on his mind—primarily, the fear of crashing this damn toy plane before someone ambushed Doc, as Aléto had prophesized. He started to rebuke his old taxi driver pal but stopped and turned up the volume on the wire headset.

"Conch Key? Didn't you just say locals call it Cayo . . . Cayo something?"

"Yeah, Gov'ment folks says it Cayo Caracol—caracol meaning

'snails' in Spanish. But same as Conch which is the only sort of snails anybody eats around here. You'll like that fish gravy."

Intrigued, Tomlinson continued toward the eastern tip of Roatán, close enough already to see a scattering of houses built over the water on pilings. Each house was painted in bright competitive colors, blue, red, pink, beneath roofs of thatch or rusty tin. On the sunrise side of the bay was a Singapore style mansion with palms, a helo landing pad and circular drive.

He tilted the Ray-Ban aviator shades he'd commandeered along with the ultralight. "Nope, you called the village something else. A name sort of familiar, but I lost the . . . possibly because I might be tripping again. But no worries—I'm used to functioning with my brain on the fritz."

Pulpo snapped his fingers. "*Cayo Hueso?* Yeah, but only to the locals 'cause of the graveyard. That name goes way, way back to pirate times. What was that, the seventeen hundreds? Look—we're almost over the village now."

Cayo Hueso.

A light went on in the sailor's head. "My god. On old Spanish maps, that's what they called Key West. Bone Key. Same name." He was getting excited. "Don't you get it? Universal Mind has led me here. We'll do a quick flyby, but that's all. You heard what the kid said—we've gotta find my amigo."

Pulpo was torn. It was sort of like old times having the pot-hauling hipster around. But he'd forgotten how *peligroso* the crazy gringo could be.

"Or you could just drop me off," the man suggested. "Don't have to land—there's deep water near my dock. Go slow enough, I could jump."

Tomlinson thought, *Good old Pulpo. It's true, those old-time Conchs take care of their own.* He was already smiling at what he saw below.

What the government called Snail Key was separated from Roatán by a deepwater inlet that was fringed by a fishing village. Terraced hills to the north, red tiled roofs among palms and gumbo limbo trees. The little graveyard fronted a narrow main street where locals on bicycles did their shopping and dogs slept in the shade.

Something else caught his eye. Moored in the middle of the bay, alone as if abandoned, was a vintage sailboat, twin masts with a cabin built of wood. In the dawn light, the vessel glowed with a golden resonance that squeezed the bluewater sailor's heart.

He said into the microphone, "That boat, the old one, ketch rigged. Forty, forty-five-footer. Is she for sale? The rich suit who owns that mansion probably owns the damn boat, too, huh?"

"Oh, that's Cap'n Billy's boat, and she is fine, fine indeed. Before him, that vessel was used to smuggle guns to Cuba— built by turtle fishermen down on the Caymans. Native lumber, so it be plenty solid. But Billy, he wouldn't sell her—unless you bought his bar, too. He's been trying to sell that place for years."

Tomlinson sighed and thought, *I'm in love.*

His eyes took in the qualities of a fishing village that was idyllic and alluring, and he said, "A time vortex, man. Know what we're looking at? That's Key West more than a hundred years ago. Or . . . Dinkin's Bay but with more funk."

Now he was thinking, *Mack, Jeth, all of them would love to have an honest reason to claim they were actually Conchs.*

Pulpo replied, "Key West? Naw, mawn, Key West, that in Florida. Even I know that. There's my pole house. See those nets strung off the dock? Used to be turtle kraals, but now we just raise conchs for market. Next door's the Fisherman's Co-Op. Got a big ol' walk-in freezer—and we all know how handy that can be at beer-thirty. Wanna take a look?"

Tomlinson remained focused on the ketch-rigged sailboat and the fishing village. "Later maybe, when we have more time," he said. "Not sure if the vibe's right but I definitely want to check out that bar. Pulpo—you didn't lose that machete, did you? I'm pretty sure we'll need it."

Again, the man from Pigeon Key pointed but was more animated. "My house, my house—it's right there, Cap'n. I don't mind jumping. *Really*."

"I forgot how much I missed the old days," Tomlinson mused. "You're right. We've got some serious scores to settle, but there's no need to jump. Not yet anyway. Later, I'll buy you all the beer and fried iguana you want. What about that machete?"

In Caracol creole, "cutlass" is what old-timers still called a machete, but Pulpo had recent history on his mind. "Got it here in a towel, Cap'n. But that tire iron didn't work out so good for me, so you be carryin' this machete if there's someone you want kilt this time."

The machete hadn't been packed with killing in mind. It was more of a safety precaution in case they went down in the jungle and had to cut their way out. The same with the flour sack containing a pint of tequila, two flashlights, several candles, a couple of Sativa pre-rolled blunts, and other necessities required for a predawn takeoff on a beach that had no runway or lights.

Pulpo had already opened the tequila.

Tomlinson said, "You know, now the sun's up, I'm really getting into this flying thing. Reminds me of my Harley Hog days—except for the landing part. Don't worry, second time's a charm."

He babied the ultralight into a slow bank southward, found a hole in the fog, and climbed until he had a view of the village of Rio Coco just two miles or so across the bay. The empty coastline angled seaward. A patch of beach and a couple of fishing pangas marked the entrance to a river that carved its way inland, volcanic peaks poking through clouds beyond.

Tomlinson motioned. "See those boats? That's where we're headed. Tough part—aside from finding a place to land, of course—is gonna be finding my friend and the one-armed kid. Goddamn, everything sure looks different from up here. Hang tight, I gotta take us lower."

Pulpo was watching something else. "Hey, Cap'n, what the hell's that? Looks like that *avión's* about to crash."

"*Avión?* What the hell are you talking about?"

The man from Pigeon Key used his hands to swivel Tomlinson's head toward a spot in the highlands a few miles upriver. "*That* avión. Looks like it blew a cylinder head, or someone shot the damn thing with a rocket."

Tomlinson almost released the joystick again to shake a victorious fist because of what he saw. It wasn't an airplane. It was a helicopter belching smoke as it escaped above the tree line and turned west where there was probably a military base or a narco stronghold of some type.

"A sign," the hipster said. "Didn't I tell you I'd get some sort of sign?" He pampered the joystick into a low pass over the fishing boats and turned upriver before explaining, "In the middle of Fumbuck nowhere, if someone shoots a helicopter with a rocket, I guaran-damn-tee you Marion Ford is somewhere nearby."

"Who?"

Tomlinson tilted his Ray-Bans again, reached and yanked the half-empty pint of tequila out of his friend's hand.

"Not sharing is the ugliest form of alcohol abuse, *compadre*. Pay attention," he said. "I'm talking about the guy we're looking for—Doc Ford."

A contrail of fog followed the river inland where treetops pierced the mist. To a novice pilot, they resembled outstretched claws eager to snare the ultralight and drag it down.

Earlier, landing had been only a vague concern. Now the reality of the situation was kicking in.

"If you had to guess, how wide you think this river is?" Tomlinson asked for the umpteenth time. "Fifty, sixty feet? I'm guessing the wings on this thing aren't even half that. No *problema*, right?"

Pulpo readjusted the headset over his missing ear. "Stop sounding nervous, Cap'n. Mawn, you makin' me nervous just some of the shit you say. Maybe you should've worried about knocking the wings off earlier."

"Hell, I'm surprised we made it this far," Tomlinson countered. "There's gotta be a landing strip around here somewhere. All the ganja and coke flown out of this country over the last twenty years? What we need is a view of the whole layout."

He opened the throttle and ascended several hundred feet above a topography of rolling hills and jungle. A few miles to the west was a plateau of palm trees, tens of thousands of palms planted in orderly rows clear to the horizon. A geometric pattern of dirt roads sectioned the trees into grids. Another road—this one paved—led to an area that was fenced where a pluming smokestack marked the location of a factory of some type.

"Aye-aye-aye, you don't wanna go near there," Pulpo warned. "That whole section is owned by the richest man in Honduras—or was until he died. In these parts, Cap'n, you don't fly over Mr. Coronado's palm oil plantation unless you wanna be shot. Or worse."

Tomlinson thought, *Crapola. A perfect place to land.*

"I don't know, man. Lots of flat land out there. I can think of worse things than being shot down by some fat cat industrialist tycoon."

Patiently, the taxi driver explained that being forced to work on the plantation was a lot worse than crashing in the river where there were crocs and snakes and piranha. When he didn't receive an immediate response, he tapped the crazy gringo on the head as a misdirect and pointed. "Over there—that hill sorta looks like a pyramid? That's the area we last saw the *avión*."

"The helicopter that got rocketed?"

"Or blew a head gasket," Pulpo corrected. "This was the direction it was headed. Probably came from Mr.Coronado's factory. A man that rich, he's got his own army—or did before he died and the devil took his mean ass to hell."

Tomlinson already had his suspicions regarding who actually ran this beautiful but screwed-up country. By now, his cop-savvy pal, Doc, probably did, too. Even so, the bluewater sailor felt all discombobulated. A disturbing case of landlocked vertigo until he refocused on a pyramid-shaped peak visible through a strand of fog that marked the river.

"By God, Pulpo. Your sense of direction is even better than Roy's. I know exactly where we are now."

"Thank you. Who's Roy?" the taxi driver asked but was disappointed by the hippie's response.

"My horse. You'll meet Roy if we live through this shit and piranhas don't eat us."

Tomlinson banked the ultralight toward the pyramid, but then decided it was better to arrive unseen and unannounced. "I'm going to swing downriver and land against the current. You cool with that?"

"Don't matter, does it?" Pulpo had retrieved the fifth of tequila and drained what little bit was left. "You're gonna do it anyway."

"That's the spirit, *compadre*. Something we got going for us you probably don't realize is, this little engine's not much louder than all those damn tree frogs and insects. Listen—I can hear the little bastards from here."

Tomlinson was still chuckling when he began their final approach, the river amber-stained red below. In synch, he butterflied the joystick, got his feet on the float pedals, then killed the engine when they were low enough to glide the last hundred yards. Steering twin fiberglass skis was like steering a hay wagon on ice, and he'd damn near nailed the landing when two unexpected things happened at once. Ahead, for the first time, he noticed the Guru's Boston Whaler which was empty and adrift. This moment of inattention caused one of the skis to hit a rock, which swung them into overhanging trees. But not hard.

Tomlinson touched a finger to his lips and got out, carrying the machete. "Wait right here," he whispered to his old friend. "Back in a minute."

It was an optimistic guess. It took several minutes to slide through mangroves into ancient hardwood trees where the loam was spiked with the stone remnants of a long-gone civilization.

He paused to take a whiz and allowed his sensory gifts to explore the area.

Above the cicada scream of insects, there was a sound . . . a ratcheting sound like a sailboat's coffee grinder-winch. Then the voices of men. Two men, at least, one of them arguing—or pleading. The other man rational, cold, detached.

Both voices were familiar.

Tomlinson zeroed in and took several quiet strides closer. In a theater of Mayan stonework, beneath a giant cocobolo tree, was his friend, Doc Ford, and Wingo Bogdan. The Guru, with his wild hair and Confucius goatee, was unchanged but for his charred pant leg—and a sawed-off shotgun that he held at waist level.

Oh hell. I've got to do something . . . At least yell to distract the bastard, the hipster thought.

But he didn't. He couldn't move because Doc . . . Doc had changed. It wasn't just the rain poncho and surgical gloves he wore, nor the coil of rope at his feet. It was the way he moved, the way he spoke. Curiously devoid of emotion.

The biologist showed zero emotion now when he slapped the shotgun to the ground, ducked beneath a flailing punch, and used both arms to cradle the Guru's head from behind. Then whispered something into the dying man's ear after snapping Bogdan's neck with the abruptness of a hangman's trapdoor.

My God . . . that horrific sound—like cartilage cleaved by an axe.

Tomlinson backed a few steps. This was not the Marion Ford he knew. It was someone else—the clandestine neighbor who, three or four times a year, disappeared from the marina for weeks at a time, then fronted vague excuses upon his return. Doc was a favorite topic of supposition among the liveaboards. But the reality of this man—this stranger—existed only in the darkest suspicions of those who believed they actually knew the biologist.

For Tomlinson, it was a peek behind the curtain, and he stood transfixed while another drama unfolded that was private, even intimate. A secret not to be witnessed or shared. Ever. Even among the two of them.

Ford hefted the corpse and used the rain poncho as a body bag. He paused to check the Guru's neck for a pulse. Dutifully, he lowered the weight of his knee onto the man's jugular and consulted his watch while he waited. A few minutes later—it seemed much longer—Wingo Bogdan's body had been trussed like something sold by the pound in a market, then winched into the high limbs of the cocobolo tree.

A wind burial, the Zen master rationalized. *There's at least a sort of redemption in that.*

Ford was an expert when it came to complicated knots. He did a bullwhip sort of thing with the rope, and the working length fell free, yet the Guru's body remained aloft, hidden in the forest canopy.

Tomlinson stepped behind a tree when the biologist made a radar-like three-sixty. He coiled the rope, put the boat ratchet in his bag, and was conversing on a handheld VHF as he walked away carrying the Guru's shotgun in the crook of his arm.

The hipster heard a British voice speak muffled words punctuated by radio static, and acronyms that had a military ring.

Even when dissected phonetically, the words were jarring. And meaningless—HUM-INT. I-MINT. KOM-PRO-MAT.

The last decipherable thing the biologist said was, "When you send the cavalry, I'm invisible as far as they're concerned. And anyone who's with me. Understood?"

Ford halted long enough to do yet another strange thing. He removed the leather money belt he was never without, unzipped it, and extracted something hidden within. A coin, it looked like. Or a GPS tag. Something silver. He inspected the object, then hurried off in the direction of a clearing.

Tomlinson gave it a few seconds before bulling his way through vines toward where he'd left Pulpo and the ultralight.

I'll never mention this to Doc or anyone else, he promised himself. *For his sake. Not mine.*

The last part was a lie, and he knew it. The truth was, he was staggered by the brutality he'd just observed. Chastened, in fact, by his inability to process such inhuman behavior.

On a spiritual level, the deficit was humbling. And inexplicable. Although a self-proclaimed pacifist, Tomlinson had spent much of his life interacting with drug-fueled crazies—sellers and buyers—in a world where the barometrics of violence could shift, in a nanosecond, from sunshine and lollypops to "Whose dead grandmother just crawled into my bed and stabbed me?"

Oh, he'd met some truly twisted psychos in his travels. Not the least adventurous being a Frisco loony ward where he'd spent a year receiving electroshock therapy and hand jobs from a nurse who had the fingers of a Bavarian milkmaid.

The Zen Master was no dilettante when it came to savage madness, that much was true. Yet never in all his years had he encountered a man capable of killing so coldly, with such clinical dispassion. It was as if there wasn't a gnat's hair difference between squashing a bug and snapping the neck of a flesh merchant like Wingo Bogdan.

Tomlinson had always admired Marion Ford—in an amused bipolar way. But the homicide he'd just witnessed demanded a moral gut check. This begat an internal debate that continued to the river's edge where he finally came to a decision regarding his murderous pal.

The reality was, Tomlinson was impressed to the core by Doc's coldhearted virtuosity. No remorse, no anger, no clinging to petty social conventions—even the Buddha would've been impressed. Granted, certain images and sounds—like the crunch of a human head being twisted off its axis—were sure to trigger midnight bouts of the screaming meemies later. But when it came to Doc, so what? The man was a field biologist, for God's sake—a demographic that ranked with coroners on the sensitivity scale. It was about time someone had the balls to tell guilt to fuck off by taking a murderous and righteous action.

The hipster felt better after that—until he stepped into the water and saw that the ultralight was empty.

"Pulpo . . . Pulpo!" he hissed.

Fog had silenced frogs and screaming insects. Water dripped from massive rainforest leaves.

"Pulpo, damn it. Can you hear me?"

Mid-river, something big broke the surface. Mist parted in the morning sunlight, and what appeared to be a fallen tree was nosing toward him. But the tree had a pointed serpent's head. It had a jagged tail, and jaws serrated with stalagmite choppers.

A crocodile, the brackish riverine variety. The thing had to weigh close to five hundred pounds.

Tomlinson snatched the bag full of supplies from the ultralight, retreated to the safety of the woods, and did a quick inventory.

Well hell . . . One of his Sativa blunts was missing and the fifth of tequila was empty. So Pulpo had wandered off stoned and drunk, or the croc had snatched the man while he'd been enjoying some prime kush.

"Pulpo? Goddamn it."

Tomlinson knew better than to yell, so he was startled when the fog echoed a response that was not an echo.

Gunshots. Three heavy-metal reports caused him to duck low. They seemed to originate from the pyramid-shaped mound where Aléto and the homeless kids were hiding out.

By now, Doc was there, too.

Tomlinson grabbed the machete and started to move, but Pulpo's voice called from the river's mist, "Cap'n, is that you? Keep talking. Mawn, I'm all turned around. Don't know which way to swim."

Yelling, "I'm here. I'm here, this way," the hipster stumbled down the bank to the water's edge where he had a better view. The taxi driver's head drifted seaward while his arms flailed in a pointless circle. The saltwater crocodile was a few dozen yards downstream, its torpedo-like mass on a collision course.

"Keep swimming, Pulpo! You can make it."

The man from Pigeon Cay began taking long sloppy strokes toward shore. But too late.

Tomlinson panicked. The world went silent and in an instant of mindless clarity, he dived in headfirst. When he surfaced, the croc was on him, its yellow eyes snakelike with sinister black slits that were pupils.

He swung the machete—and missed.

The river exploded in a whirlpool frenzy. Pulpo vanished beneath the surface.

THIRTY

The one-armed boy said to me in Spanish, "*Patrón*, did you hear that? Just now. Like something big fell out of the sky and landed in the river. It wasn't an earthquake. That makes a different sound."

I said, "In a fog like this, our ears can play tricks on us. But those gunshots were definitely real."

Three shots rapid-fire we'd heard, military weapon caliber. Aléto had been seated on a stone bench near a fire until I'd returned from the rainforest after dealing with Wingo Bogdan. Just him, no other children around that I'd seen since our arrival. A lot had happened during my thirty-minute absence.

I'd left Fidelia, who was breathing normally and alert, in a hammock strung between trees. She had disappeared, too.

The boy tilted his head for a few seconds, expecting to hear another splash. "It wasn't my imagination. Do you think someone is coming after us?"

I told him, "I doubt it, not yet." The reason I believed this had yet to be confirmed, so I continued, "I could be wrong so you need to hide. Where's Mrs. Brava?"

The kid made a point of not looking at the pyramid-mound

behind him. The entrance I'd seen earlier had been camouflaged with branches. The boy's wingmen, both armed, were probably in there with Fidelia. Maybe some of the other children, too.

He said, "I don't understand who's shooting. You said the giant and the plastic shaman left in their boat."

The bodyguard, Iron Baby, was the only one who could be described as a giant, and I had no idea where he had disappeared to.

I explained, "What I said was, the Shaman's gone. That's all. Didn't mention anything about their boat or the guy he was with."

"What do you mean gone?" the boy insisted. "Why won't you tell me? You wouldn't have come back so soon if you had killed him. Or did you? Did you kill our enemy?" He searched the sky to the west, alert to the possibility another helicopter might return. "If you didn't, he will send soldiers from the plantation. Every day they look for me. But they always search far away. Seldom close."

We were standing, him with a full auto AR stolen from the bird poachers. Me armed with just a knife, Bogdan's cheap 12-gauge, and a pistol that required a gunsmith before it would work. I walked past him toward what I believed was the entrance to a Mayan ruin buried beneath a thousand years of volcanic ash and jungle.

The boy raced ahead and faced me. "You can't go in there. Balam and Kimee will shoot you. That's what I ordered them to do. Shoot anyone who enters without my permission."

Balam was the angry, aggressive kid I'd already met. Kimee was the boy's other loyal pal, I guessed.

Aléto stared up at me, ragged black hair trimmed with a knife, his face a ledger of abuse. So many scars for such a young child.

"*Patrón*, you swam in the river to help me. I don't want to, but I will. I'll shoot you. What if the woman dies? If a foreigner is there when it happens, the Old Ones will not allow the beautiful *Reina Madre* to return to this life. Do you understand?"

No, I didn't, but I understood his Spanish. He'd referred to Fidelia as the beautiful "Queen Mother." It was starting to make sense. He'd recognized the woman from a photograph he had mentioned earlier. A photo that had impressed this twelve-year-old orphan enough to cloud his judgment.

I said, "Before I left, she seemed a lot better. If something changed, we need to get her to a hospital."

"No! No hospital. The Queen stays here with me." It was the reaction of an adolescent protecting the mother he'd never had.

"Listen to me. She's an archaeologist, not a queen. Not a real queen," I said. "If Mrs. Brava told you that, she's . . . she's misleading you. Maybe even tricking you because you're right. Soldiers are coming. If not today, soon."

The boy shook his head. "Wait, I'll prove she is a Queen."

He fetched his woven bag from near the fire and smoothed out a twenty-year-old magazine cover. It was not the goddess from the painting. The pose was standard maidenly fare—a young woman in a gown, hair sprayed like a confectionery, wearing a tiara and a ribbon. Yet through some trick of lighting or osmosis, Fidelia's sensuality had breached the camera's cold lens.

"Queen of all Honduras," Aléto said. "I knew she would come here. For two years I've known—even tried to give her reasons. But it had to be her choice. Now it is."

I sighed, resigned. "*Nino*, we're all fools. I'd tell you we grow out of this sort of *mierda*, but that's just more *mierda*. Bullshit in English. You understand?"

"No. *No entiendo*."

"Never mind. It's the same in any language, which I don't understand either," I told him. "You have to get your friends packed and ready to leave. You're probably right about the soldiers. But I have people coming, too. Some in a helicopter. Maybe by boat. They're going to help you and the other kids."

"Federales?"

"No. Well, in a way. But from a different country. Not Honduras. These people, you can trust."

The boy, confused, wondered if *I* was trying to trick him. *"Patrón*, no matter what you say, you can't go inside—it's a sacred burial place for royalty. I'll shoot you if I have to."

From the kid's expression, I didn't doubt it.

I nodded. "Fine. You stay here and look after the Queen, but I need your rifle."

"What? You have that."

The sawed-off 12-gauge, he meant. It lay open on the bench where he'd been sitting.

"We'll make a trade. Temporarily. A shotgun is exactly what you need. A defensive weapon. See? It's got a leather sling. You can carry it over your shoulder."

The boy wasn't impressed but continued to listen.

"I want you to stay in there—" I indicated the camouflaged opening "—and don't come out until I'm back. I'll cover the entrance again when you're inside. Okay?"

He wrestled with that for a moment. "Tell me the truth. The Shaman, did you kill him?"

"It's possible someone did," I conceded. "Your rifle, Aléto. I need it."

"If he's dead, where's his body. It can't be far—you didn't have time to dig a hole. If the federales come they'll find him and blame me."

When I reached for the rifle, there was an electric moment before he surrendered it. I checked the chamber then the magazine, saying, "Here's a trick I hope you never need. When people look for . . . let's say a missing person. They search the ground, they check cars, abandoned buildings, and they search the water." The rifle's magazine locked into place. "But they never look up at the sky."

Aléto liked what he was hearing, and liked me better for sharing a confidence, but didn't understand.

"You put the Shaman in an airplane? I would've heard a helicopter."

I waited until he was inside the tunnel entrance, a distant flickering candle visible within, before saying, "In the trees, niño. No one ever searches the trees for a missing person—and they won't unless you tell them. We got a deal?"

Reluctantly, the boy touched a finger to his lips. A pact we both understood.

I did a better job of camouflaging the entranceway, then started toward a clearing that was no longer marked with a red ribbon. I knew because I'd pocketed the ribbon after tossing Bogdan's tracking tag into the deepest shadows of the sinkhole.

If Iron Baby still had Bogdan's cell phone, that's where I would find him—or so I believed, until Aléto came running after me, calling, "She's gone, patrón, the woman is gone. Balam and Kimee, they're gone, too."

He fell in beside me as I jogged toward the mound. "How's that possible? I told you to stay out here and keep watch."

"I did. Sat by the fire the whole time you were gone." The shotgun was slung over his left shoulder. He banged the stock with a fist. "I should've checked on them. But the woman— the Queen—she seemed so weak. And my friends, they have rifles. Believe me, Balam is not afraid to shoot."

He thought for a moment. "Maybe those were the shots we heard. Balam or Kimee trying to protect her. But when we heard them, the shots seemed far away."

Another ugly possibility stopped him at the entranceway.

"The giant," he said. "We should have killed him last night. But . . . how could he have known she was here?"

I had no idea what that meant but it would have to wait. "How many entrances are there?" I asked. The boy's reticence was obvious. "Look, you either trust me or you don't. That's up to you, but I'm going in there and have a look around."

My careful camouflage job had been trashed. The kid didn't protest when I found a flashlight, got down on hands and knees, and crawled into an earthen tunnel reinforced with hand-hewn beams. Gradually, head clearance improved, and the tunnel transitioned into a narrow passageway constructed of volcanic slabs. The candle I'd imagined earlier wasn't a candle. A propane lantern led me into a cathedral-sized room, the walls a matrix of carvings and hieroglyphics.

The boy was behind me, still carrying the shotgun, when I got to my feet. "No foreigner has ever been in this sacred temple before," he said. "It's wrong, the worst sort of luck. You won't tell anyone, will you?"

I said, "I'm afraid they're going to find this place soon enough. You should be proud you lasted this long. Really. You're a gifted young man, Aléto."

He and his friends had made this ancient ruin livable with sleeping mats spaced to create the illusion of individual rooms. Pallets of bottled water, a plastic privacy curtain and a Coleman stove were anachronistic necessities. There was a main table for eating, and several smaller tables where boxes of food and books were stacked.

"Show me the other entrance," I said.

I followed him into an anteroom where there was an adobe chiminea and fire pit for cooking. When he stopped to light another gas lantern, I spun a couple of the books open. One was an expensive hardback: *Ancient Maya Politics* by Simon Martin. The other book was familiar: *Canek: History and Legend of a Maya Hero* by Ermilo Gómez.

Both belonged to the Honduran Museum of Natural History according to the embossed bookplates.

Aléto observed my reaction and started walking again, the lantern held high. "I only steal from thieves," he said.

I responded, "It's not stealing if you return it to the rightful owners. When we have time, I want to hear how you and your pals pulled off robbing the National Museum. You're the one who should run for governor."

Upset as he was, the kid couldn't hide an involuntary smile. "A lot of adults would like to hear that story, *patrón*. But I made a promise to the janitors who paid us to do their work. I wouldn't want them to go to jail." He started to say something else, something about who should be governor— "Her, not me"—then stopped, looked at the ground and asked, "Did you feel that?"

Yes, I'd felt the shock wave tremor, too. "Like the floor was vibrating," I said, "but it's gone now. An earthquake. We shouldn't be in here."

The kid motioned for me to stay quiet. It was several seconds before he spoke again. "We're safe. It happens a lot. *Cabrakan*— the God of thunder and volcanoes. Cabrakan jokes. He jokes a lot to remind us who is in charge. Come on."

Through what had once been a door was the most ornate wing I'd seen so far. Bracketed by columns were two open stone sarcophagi on a funerary table that might have represented a raft.

I asked, "Were those empty when you found them?"

"No," the boy responded in a way that meant the subject was not to be pursued. "Those aren't for foreigners to see. Come on."

We came to the backside of the chamber where a portion of wall had collapsed. Rock slabs, debris, and white chalky dust everywhere. Visible in the dust was a slurry of footprints. It was as if several people had come through dragging their feet.

"Have you seen those tracks before?"

The boy shook his head. "When I realized my friends and the woman weren't here, I ran to find you. I should've checked the portal—" he raised the lantern "—but I knew that Balam and Kimee would never try to leave this way."

I switched on my little LED flashlight. "A portal? I don't see any openings."

"Clap your hands, *patrón*."

"What?"

"Your hands. Clap your hands and listen for an echo. I would show you," he said with a wry inflection, "but it's the one thing I can't do on my own."

I did as directed. Clapped my hands twice and was surprised to hear a *Chirp-Chirp* echo.

Aléto said, "It's the voice of the quetzal bird."

I tried it again, three times—Chirp-Chirp-Chirp—and thought about the Mayan ruins at *Chichen Itza* where I'd witnessed a similar phenomenon.

"It's the way the Old Ones found hidden places in pyramids," the boy explained. "The stone mountains built by those who came before them. The Olmec, our books say. Stay here for a second. You can't come any closer until I say it's safe."

He shifted the shotgun to his right shoulder, grabbed the lantern and scrambled over the rocks, then down an incline where he disappeared as if an unseen wall existed. I could hear him speaking Quiché Mayan to someone or something while I used my light to inspect the footprints.

The prints were confusing—until I got on my knees and toggled the light to ultraviolet. The UV spectrum reveals details that many animals can see but humans cannot. A series of fluorescent blue-green specks showed where a scorpion had recently crossed through the white dust. There was also the waffled tread of what might've been a small boating shoe.

Fidelia had been wearing boating shoes, I remembered.

Other details, though, had been blotted by a cookie cutter imprint that was twice the size of a normal human foot. I figured it was an anomaly caused by a fallen rock—until the dust began to move like iron filings influenced by a magnet. Fascinated, I watched as the cookie cutter imprint was transformed. It took me a moment to realize that a seismic event, not a magnet, had defined what was the unmistakable imprint of a gigantic boot.

Damn, I whispered. Then said it again aloud and jumped to my feet. "Another earthquake," I hollered. "Aléto. You hear me? We've gotta get out of here."

Compared to earlier, this was a more serious shock wave. Dust spouted from joist lines in the walls, and I heard the chalkboard screech of stone grinding against stone.

"Aléto! Come on." I called his name several times, then gave up and braved the quaking rocks to where lantern light steered me into what remained of a limestone portico.

The boy stood near a narrow opening in the wall, his back to me. In his good left hand, he clutched what looked like a ship's hawser—very thick rope. He seemed indifferent to the ice floe-shifting of the floor beneath our feet.

"Kid, we've gotta get out of here. Now."

When he turned to face me, I saw that I'd mistaken a hawser cable for a caramel patchwork of reptilian scales that was a snake—the guardian fer-de-lance he'd told me about. The reptile had to be ten feet long—longer if its head hadn't been crushed.

What had happened here was obvious, but difficult to process. Fidelia or Iron Baby—maybe both—had stolen the jade death mask. But our brain prioritizes when its lifelong anchor—the planet Earth—threatens to swallow us up or cast us into space.

I yelled, "Leave the snake here, we have to go. Come on before the ceiling collapses."

The kid remained focused, seemingly indifferent to what was happening around us. He stared into the opening, a low passageway already littered with dust and volcanic shards. For the first time, I understood why Aléto had gone silent.

A few meters inside on the passageway floor was a child's decapitated head. It had been placed there strategically as a totem to forbid entrance.

My own revulsion was so intense I spoke to him as if calming a wounded animal. "You're going to be okay, Aléto. I promise no one is going to hurt you. The best thing you can do for your friend now is to get out of here alive. What do you say?"

The boy refused to look at me. "The giant killed Kimee. Maybe Balam, too. I have to find him before he kills the *Queen Mother*."

I tightrope-walked closer. "He's Mrs. Brava's bodyguard. I'm pretty sure I know where he is. Do you hear me? If we hurry, maybe we can catch him."

Aléto placed the snake at his feet near the shotgun and whispered the name, *Kukulkan*, and something else in Quiché I didn't understand. When he sensed me reaching for his arm, he recoiled and came up holding the 12-gauge. Not pointed at me but close enough.

At the same instant a slab of passageway roof collapsed. An explosion of dust startled me as much as the noise. By the time I'd waved the cloud away, the boy—and the shotgun—had disappeared into an opening that had shrunk to the size of my thigh.

I hollered. I shouted his name and muscled blocks of sandstone aside in a panic. My head wouldn't fit into the opening, never mind my shoulders. My flashlight showed that the inside of the passageway was sealed off, yet I kept working until the floor of the portico imploded and nearly sucked me down with it.

Enough.

I ran from that ancient funerary—there's no other way to describe my escape. Told myself I wasn't abandoning the child to a slow death by suffocation. The smart thing to do, I rationalized, was to rush to the clearing and try to effect a rescue from the other end of the passageway. On the way, I would radio the cavalry and demand a team with digging tools instead of guns.

There were no other options.

The pragmatist in me agreed. But the father in me despised the truth, and the truth was I would probably never see the boy alive again.

A more bitter reality pursued me through the trees to the clearing: If I hadn't used the tracking tag as bait, Iron Baby wouldn't have found the passageway. He wouldn't have beheaded an innocent child.

THIRTY-ONE

(Tomlinson Part Four)

Pulpo was explaining to Tomlinson that the next time he was attacked by a crocodile he preferred the company of a Pigeon Islander, not a gringo who didn't know how to swing a machete.

"Us Conchs take care of our own," he reminded the hipster for about the thousandth time in the last two decades.

They had plodded, clothes soaked, from the river through the jungle toward the pyramid-shaped mound. The sun was higher, fog had thinned, and the taxi driver was still jazzed by adrenaline and the blunt he'd smoked. He couldn't stop talking.

Tomlinson listened until he got tired of listening.

"Take care of your own, my ass," he said. "Bring a baseball bat if you want to compare swings. What threw me off was your drowning act. Admit it. You took a dive so that goddamn dinosaur would miss you and eat me."

Something downriver attracted his attention. "Hey . . . what's that boat doing there? It should be halfway to the bay by now."

The Boston Whaler, he meant. Instead of floating free and

adrift, someone with a lot of muscle had pulled it halfway up onto the bank.

Pulpo was intrigued. He preferred to return home in a boat, not a toy airplane. "If it's abandoned, I claim salvage rights. That's law of the sea, Cap'n. Whoever says it first owns it."

Tomlinson was more concerned about Doc and the one-armed boy. Where the hell were they? But Maritime Law was one of his specialties. "Dude, it's not like calling shotgun."

He was expounding on the subject when Pulpo interrupted, "*Madre de Dios*, that damn crocodile's back—see it? Laying there off the stern of my new boat. Here—take the machete and try to hit it again. Maybe you'll do better this time."

Tomlinson saw the riverine croc, but he noticed something else, too. A wildebeest-sized shape was lying in the weeds next to the Whaler. The object was fleshy, not moving. It might explain why the croc was on its four legs, edging closer to the boat as if in ambush. The Zen Master's powers didn't require him to sniff the air and make a face of disgust. There was no odor, but he did it anyway.

"Keep that machete handy and watch my back," he instructed. "I've got a real bad feeling about this, you know? It's in the air. Like a speck of acid at the base of my spine."

Pulpo voiced the first fiction that flowed into his head. "That happens to pot haulers sometimes just before they get shot. Or if there's a *torremotto*—you know, an earthquake. Or some really bad *mierda's* about to go down. Hurry, take this. It's better if you scare the animal away first so I can inspect my boat."

Tomlinson accepted the machete. He slid it into the belt of his pantaloons and walked close enough to the Whaler to recognize what was lying next to it. Without taking his eyes off the crocodile, he called, "Have a look—it's Iron Baby. I think he's dead. Come here, I'm gonna need some help. The croc thinks he's dead, too."

The man from Pigeon Cay spun around and started walking in the other direction. "How you know he's dead? Folks say to kill Iron Baby, you gotta cut his head off and hide it. Or freeze him like a fish."

"Freeze a dead body. You shittin' me?"

"Like a zombie, man. Everyone knows that. Tell me what happens when I get back."

Tomlinson was losing patience. He didn't want to get in a tug-of-war with a five-hundred-pound croc that was only slightly bigger than the legendary psycho who lay spread eagle on his back in the weeds.

"Get over here, damn it. Grab some rocks or something, anything to scare that brute away."

Pulpo hurled a tree limb, then a couple of whelk shells. The crocodile opened its jaws and hissed. Tomlinson waited a few seconds, summoned his friend and they both crept near enough to stare down at the giant man's body. Tomlinson took a step closer, he knelt, then jumped to his feet.

"Geezus hell, maybe he is alive. Shit, yeah. The bastard's still breathing."

Pulpo taunted, "Warned you, mawn. You got the machete, you know what to do—but don't miss this time."

"I'm not chopping his goddamn head off," Tomlinson said without looking at the islander. "Wait. Maybe it was my imagination. If he's not dead, he will be soon."

Slowly, again he knelt.

"Yeah . . . blood everywhere. What happened to his face? And his hands—they're all swollen up, too, like some kind of allergic reaction. Maybe he was poisoned."

Inwardly, the sailor was disappointed. Doc was more of a hands-on type of guy when it came to killing.

Pulpo made the sign of the cross and turned away. "Or shot by a very fine shot," he said, referring to two grape-sized holes symmetrically spaced beneath the man's eyes. "But that don't mean Iron Baby's dead."

Tomlinson sort of agreed until he factored in the necrotized flesh around the facial wounds. The wounds hadn't congealed although the giant had been lying here long enough to attract insects as well as that damn croc.

"Naw, he wasn't shot. I think something bit him in the face. Something with really big fangs, and jaws that had to be, what?—" Tomlinson used his mathematical eye "—at least four inches wide. Do you have monitor lizards in Honduras? Komodo dragons are venomous as hell they say."

"Just iguanas, and I already told you about those," Pulpo said. He dropped a couple of whelk shells on the ground. "Throw these if you need to. I'm going to get in my new boat and see what else I've salvaged. It's bad luck hanging around dying folk. Even someone famous as Iron Baby."

"Or one hellish big snake," Tomlinson muttered. He was considering the size of the puncture wounds when a strange, rumbling sound interceded, and the ground began to shake.

Another earthquake, he thought.

"A *torremotto*," Pulpo agreed. "I warned you about *mierda* hitting the fan." The little man had one leg over the Whaler's bow, but suddenly dived aboard yelling, "That animal's hungry, Cap'n. Run . . . get away."

Tomlinson looked up at quaking trees, still not concerned until he saw the crocodile snaking full speed toward him.

Greedy swine, he thought, and backpedaled away from Iron Baby's body. He raised the machete like a sword and said aloud, "You want him so bad, he's all yours. Hope you're immune to—" he didn't know what had bitten the hybrid human, so finished lamely "—You two carnivores are like a snake eating its own tail."

The symbolism was lost on the croc, but it was hungry. The creature chomped down on Iron Baby's leg—yep, the man was still alive. He yelped, barely conscious, and struggled until the animal tossed its head back to get a better grip, then dragged the giant into the river. There were bubbles. Unsavory gaseous noises of a higher pitch than the seismic rumble that had gotten louder.

"Get away from them trees, Cap'n. They fall on you mawn, you dead." The man from Pigeon Cay had abandoned the Whaler and was escaping toward a clearing near the back of the mound.

Tomlinson didn't budge. It wasn't because he enjoyed watching the crocodile's death roll, or Iron Baby's horrific splashing before bubbles percolated up through the water's surface.

No. It was because on the Whaler's casting deck was a large woven bag that Iron Baby had left behind—and Pulpo had overlooked.

The bag was open, its sea-green contents alluring—but improbable. He'd seen a lot of Mayan artifacts, photographs of many more, but there was only one such treasure the size of the object that summoned him to the deck of the Whaler.

Tomlinson took his time—a nod to superstition—and expected to be disappointed when he opened the bag. Instead, he backed away in awe of the relic the bag contained.

You have no right to even touch something so beautiful, his conscience scolded. This was true. But the quaking earth and the gunshot sounds of trees falling to his left, to his right, reminded him this was no time to quibble with destiny.

Destiny. Yes. There were no coincidences in the sailor's spiritual world. Even though he was unworthy, he had been chosen to guard this treasure by the pure process of elimination: He hadn't run away. His body wasn't in the river putrefying for some reptile's late-night snack.

Destiny's standards weren't high, true, but the results couldn't be argued. Fate had dealt him cards that he had no choice but to play.

Tomlinson took the artifact between his palms, holding it like a piece of Ming Dynasty china. He marveled at the size and weight—ten inches tall, eight inches wide. The thing was hypnotic—the masterful inlaid stonework, the onyx eyes that stared back with indifference, if not contempt.

The bluewater boat bum then did something naïve. The

mosaic's perfect contours charmed him into holding the ancient relic to his face. For an instant, he felt history's cold weight against his skin. An instant later, an electrical shock nearly knocked him to the ground.

It's a freakin' miracle I didn't drop this goddamn thing, he thought.

Nope, he realized. Not a miracle. It was a celestial warning. And the very last warning he would get if he didn't honor karma and a plan that had joined him with the sacred Mayan death mask.

The woven bag was the expensive type with a shoulder strap. Before stowing the artifact, he hefted the bag and felt an unexpected weight.

Sinister, what fell out when he dumped the contacts on the Whaler's casting deck. Christ, the bag contained a bloody military knife, a child-sized pinky ring, and what looked like a lock of Apache black hair.

A child's hair? My God, had Satan's spawn murdered Aléto, or a member of the kid's street urchin army? That's what the vibe was telling him.

Iron Baby, he thought. *Tomorrow, I might be at the gates of Hell. But you'll still be just a reptilian turd.*

Tomlinson draped the bag over his shoulder, a casual touch that might deflect unwelcome questions. Pulpo was a minor concern, but still a concern. His old partner, although trusted and true, clearly had an ugly greedy side—but who didn't after years of profiting from the drug trade? It could be argued that, because the jade death mask had been found aboard the Boston Whaler, the mask belonged to the first person who had claimed salvage rights.

Take it easy, the Zen Master counseled himself. *You're being too hard on a dear old friend.*

Or was he? White Conchs were a devious lot. Everyone knew it was true. Their willingness to do murder—albeit quietly—was the stuff of legends. Why, of course—the degenerate little pothead wouldn't hesitate to claim the artifact at a Maritime Law tribunal in Tegucigalpa.

This could not be allowed to happen. No, Destiny had entrusted this relic—a jade mask worth millions—to a gringo with loftier ideals.

Me, the gringo, Tomlinson acknowledged.

On his way up the hill toward the pyramid mound, he touched the bag and vowed, *No one's touching this but the hereditary King of the Mayan people.*

Another electrical shock zapped the hipster's fingers, and caused him to eagerly amend:

Or the rightful Mayan Queen.

The helicopter that thundered past overhead wasn't a beat-up old clunker like those used by narcos and flesh trafficking mercenaries.

Even Pulpo recognized the difference. They had taken shelter beneath a Madera tree where he said to Tomlinson, "You see that? Thing was all black and shiny, no numbers or letters. Looked like a spaceship. Think it could be? A spaceship?"

Tomlinson saw the chopper all right. He was busy wondering, *Is Doc intentionally trying to piss me off by calling in the CIA?*

Who else could afford that kind of high-tech Star Wars shit?

It was a matter of unspoken trust. There was no doubt the biologist occasionally had to rub elbows with unsavory government types. Fine. Between friends, it was one of those don't-ask-don't-tell deals—sort of like not discussing hemorrhoids. Certain topics in any relationship deserved a free pass—cold-blooded murder, for instance.

But to openly consort with the CIA—instigators of much of the world's evil?

Pulpo remarked, "Wonder why the helicopter's doing that? Kinda weird. Out there circling around over the jungle where—" He stopped, wide-eyed. "Oh damn, that fool's over the palm oil plantation. Remember what I said? Richest man in Honduras, he's got his own army—well, before Mr. Coronado went to hell he had his own army. I bet they shoot that spaceship down."

Tomlinson grumbled, "Never bet against the Christians In Action. They'll waterboard your ass."

"Who? Hey mawn, thought you said you like Christians. I *am* a Christian, already been water dunked—baptized we call it." Pulpo's attention shifted. "Where'd you get that bag? What's in it?"

Tomlinson tucked the bag under his arm and turned away, secure in his old friend's short attention span.

He was right.

"Oooh, looky there . . . That *avión* is sure enough asking for trouble."

Fog had lifted to treetop level, reconfigured as a misty plateau that alternately cloaked and revealed what was happening two miles away. The high-tech copter spun on its axis, tilted nose- down and vanished. An instant later, twin shafts of blue light pierced the lower regions of the mist in a series of microsecond bursts.

The men waited through a long silence, thinking it was gunfire. They expected to hear the Gatling rattle of ammunition. But there were no ancillary sounds.

"Jesus Christ," Tomlinson whispered. "Lasers. They're shooting laser beams. I don't know, man . . . Or some kind of sonic weapons crap. How many paisanos work on that plantation?"

"Thousands, mawn. No flashing lights gonna hurt them caballeros, though. I'm surprised that spaceship ain't been shot out of the sky yet. Whoa—cool. Now they're doing fireworks."

Star-bright sparklers were jettisoned from the upper layers of the mist and drifted slowly, still sparkling, toward the ground. After several seconds, when the men expected to hear nothing, a series of thunderous booms rolled through the jungle canopy. Birds, tribes of howler monkeys, responded with wild screams. A final petroleum *BOOM* ignited a fire-ball that narrowed into a tentacle of black smoke.

"Diesel fire, Cap'n. Diesel and rubber. The only things make that kind of smoke. That *avión* ain't killing workers. It's blowing up Mr. Coronado's machinery. Airplanes and such."

The man from Pigeon Key liked what he was seeing. *"Tu mi culo,"* he added as an invocation, then studied the tree limbs. "Amigo, you feel that? The earthquake, it stopped. That was a pretty big one so maybe the worst part ain't done."

Tomlinson was preoccupied. His pal, Doc, had materialized as if he'd crawled out of a hole in the clearing a few hundred yards away. The man was on the radio apparently speaking to the high-tech chopper that was angling downriver toward the bay, as if in search of another target.

"What do you mean the worst part? Hold on—" he looked at Pulpo and pointed "—that's my friend, the biologist. We need to tell him what happened to that—"

The little man had shifted into survival mode. "No time, no time, Cap'n. After a bad *terremoto*, gotta worry about mud-slides and that river flooding. You best take care of your little airplane. Me, I gotta secure my new boat."

Pulpo, with his fast legs, had almost made it to the Boston Whaler when a terrible rumbling noise thundered down the valley. He stopped and gave Tomlinson a helpless look because they both saw it coming, a torrent of brown that snaked the river's path through the jungle, pushing trees and boulders as it descended from mountain peaks in the distance.

Pulpo mouthed the word, "Run!"

Tomlinson hollered, "Get in the boat!" and loped toward his friend Doc, who watched from higher ground a football field away.

Only once did he look back. Good ol' Pulpo was on his knees aboard the Whaler, sledding downriver at a lethal speed on an avalanche that could not be escaped.

Rivulets of brown water had branched off like lava, and were bulldozing toward Tomlinson now. He clutched the death mask to his chest and waited . . . waited until he felt the inevitable crushing weight of impact. Then thrust the relic out like a shield as he rolled and tumbled and pitchpoled among boulders and dying birds. He couldn't breathe. When he opened his mouth to shout for help, mud choked him.

The Zen Master's brain retreated into a safer, quieter space. Once again, he was aboard his sailboat, *No Más*, caught in a hurricane that hadn't changed anything. Not really. Seas were running thirty, thirty-five—Christ, he could feel the chaos crushing his ribs.

That was okay. This had happened before in how many lives? *You've got to ride the big horse until the ride ends.*

That old maxim from his LSD days came back to him.

Good horse, yes you are, Roy, he assured the stallion who had a GPS in his brain.

In Tomlinson's imagination, Roy bucked, but in a knowing way. It launched him headfirst into a familiar bulkhead. In this incarnation, the results were different. Instead of being cast into a white void that was death, he was awake and alive after the water had swept him into an earthen tunnel. The tunnel exited into a chamber adorned with carvings and a matrix of hieroglyphics.

Alive? he wondered. *Another near death experience? How long is this bullshit going to go on?*

Nope, he had to be dream-walking. Nothing new about that. In Tomlinson's hands, the jade death mask sparked with the resonance of a divining rod.

This form of communication was new in his experience.

You've got to ride the horse, he reminded himself and allowed the relic to lead him into a chamber bracketed by ornate columns. In the middle of the room, two stone coffins lay on a funerary table carved into the shape of a raft.

Sarcophaguses, the Zen Master amended. Both of them covered by stone lids.

Something he had never done—not intentionally anyway—was impose on the dead. But he was being led by a force, an irresistible amperage that gave him the strength to heft one heavy lid a few inches aside, then the other heavy lid.

Tomlinson stepped back and nearly wept when he recognized the mummified face of Aléto, the hereditary King of the Maya. Next to him was the former Ms. Honduras. Fidelia was still achingly beautiful in death.

Into his mind floated the image of a third coffin, a hallucination—had to be—for the coffin was made of brass, not stone, and it contained the corporeal remains of Mack, the much-loved owner of Dinkin's Bay Marina.

An instant later, Mack's coffin dissolved. It was replaced by a Japanese funeral urn favored by Buddhists.

"Screw it. I'm not ready to die," Tomlinson moaned. "I'm dreaming this crap, damn it. I've had another . . . ?"

Another what? Another stroke or another concussion?

He touched a hand to his head, then yanked it away when he felt a trickle of blood. The sacred jade relic was real—no doubt about that. It could not be defiled by a foreigner's blood spore, so he took a breath, hesitated between the two stone coffins and waited for a sign. Seconds later, maybe hours later, his hands completed the ceremony by positioning the jade mask on a face that had not been his to choose.

Overhead, the slab ceiling creaked and exhaled stringers of dust. The floor buckled and Tomlinson stumbled back to the earthen tunnel's exit where he collapsed for what seemed a short time. When he awoke, he crawled on hands and knees outside where the air was fresh, but the sun had traveled into the Western sky. There was a helicopter—no, two helicopters. One had just taken off and the other was closing to land in a clearing where Doc Ford stood giving orders to men who wore generic blue coveralls.

Was this actually happening? Or was he still suffering a residual nightmare because of that mind-blowing zombie drug?

Tomlinson had walked this tightrope too many times to surrender to insanity and catheter privileges at some yuppie nuthouse. He had to get reality—and his story—straight, even if it meant crawling back into the funeral chamber.

That's what he did an hour later, with the biologist at his side as the mediator of reality. Somehow Pulpo had survived the avalanche. He was there, too.

Doc said to Tomlinson, "Don't worry about hallucinations. It can take days for that scopolamine crap to wear off. Aléto told me the same story—well, a similar story after we dug him and the woman out of the rocks. That the only reason Fay—Fidelia—is alive is because she was wearing a jade mask. Thing is, she didn't have the mask when we loaded her onto the chopper. Crazy, huh? I'm guessing Iron Baby, the bodyguard, stole it."

Tomlinson suspected Mayan sorcery, not craziness. He was finally convinced, however, that the boy and the former Ms. Honduras had not been mummified—the first of several revelations. This came as less of a surprise because, after braving the Earthen tunnel again, he'd seen for himself that the stone coffins were empty. And it was true: the death mask he'd placed on the face of a beautiful Queen was gone—along with Fidelia's nonexistent corpse.

To put Pulpo at ease, the biologist added, "Those men out there from the helicopters? They're not cops. No one is going to ask questions about . . . well, about certain people who've gone missing—or what you might have seen this afternoon."

He let that sink in before referencing a laser attack on a palm plantation that had never happened.

"You didn't see or hear anything. Understand? Keep that in mind and you don't have to worry about a piddly little thing like a stolen Boston Whaler. You've both got a crime free pass today."

Pulpo had cuts and scrapes, and a broken nose. He liked

the sound of that. "Mawn, I never see nothing that can get me in trouble. Think maybe those men can help me pull my new boat out of the mangroves?"

Doc replied, "I'll have them use one of the choppers. Then we're leaving, and no one is going to say a damn word about this for at least a month. Understood?"

The man from Pigeon Cay grinned. His missing ear and his nose had been bandaged by a medic who, like the others in blue coveralls, wore a black face stocking. The bandages added a covert flare when he answered, "Me, I like eating better than I like talking, Cap'n. But why a whole month?"

Later, Tomlinson asked Ford same question when the two of them were alone in the twenty-one-foot panga, headed for Gálvez International Airport on Roatán.

This time the biologist provided a confidential answer. "Because a guerrilla war started today, and the special election is in just a few weeks. We don't want to be around for either one. If the traffickers didn't kill us, government mercenaries would—depending on who gets elected."

Tomlinson sat in the panga's bow thinking about two women, both lovers, with ties to Teoscar Brava, the corrupt former governor. And a remote island where there was a beautiful ketch-rigged sailboat, and a place called *Found Me A Home Cantina*.

All of these elements were, to him, alluring sirens on a rock straight out of Ulysses. They required investigation.

He said, "I'm not leaving, Doc. Not yet. I know I imagined a lot of what happened today. But I didn't imagine all of it. Want proof? Mack . . . Mack's dead, isn't he?"

Ford wasn't surprised. His friend had a gift for deducing fact from a string of subtleties that less perceptive people didn't notice. "A heart attack three weeks ago," the biologist admitted. "The funeral was good, but Mack's wake was one for the history books. People asked about you. If you don't come back, what should I tell them? That you're down here alone, an easy target? Pal, if the traffickers can't find me, they'll come looking for you—no matter what happens in the next election."

The next election. There it was again, but politics was something the two men seldom discussed.

The Maya Key ferry dock was only a few hundred yards from the airport terminal. Tomlinson waited until he'd heard a lot of unnecessary instructions about the panga's quirks before saying, "Tell them the next wake isn't going to be mine, but I'll be there."

Ford actually showed some emotion. "I was hoping you'd come around. Means you're going to see a doctor, I hope."

The fun-loving neurologist, Naomi, would be among Tomlinson's first stops, but he said, "Tell you what, how about I find a decent rental house on the beach, and you fly down with some of the regulars in a month or so. Dinkin's Bay in exile. You know, an early Christmas party. How's that sound?"

"In a month," Doc said, and handed Tomlinson a sealed envelope. "Don't worry, it's just the title to the boat, and a note about Aléto. I figured you'd pull something like this. Take a look when you get time."

"What about the kid? Want me to read it now?"

The biologist shook his head, hefted his bag, but stopped after only a few steps. "Uhh, do me a favor. Don't tell the locals you're planning a party. No matter how the election goes, I'll still have a few enemies here in a month. That means you have enemies. Understand? I'm not sure if our marina could handle another funeral right now."

Tomlinson, who'd traveled the world, believed he understood the vagaries of Third World politics as well as anyone, including his pal, Doc.

He was wrong.

THIRTY-TWO

On a Sunday in the second week of December, I flew solo first class from Regional Southwest, made connections in Tegucigalpa, and landed at San Pedro Sula International, Honduras.

I was a day early for Tomlinson's party on Roatán, but nine minutes late for my meeting at the British Consulate which is on 10th Calle, only a few blocks from a McDonald's franchise that Tomlinson's pal, Pulpo, had highly recommended.

Tardiness, however, is frowned upon in state department circles.

My contact at the consulate said, "A quick ring would've been nice, Dr. North. But now that you're here, let's plow through this folder, shall we?"

The woman, starched blouse, pleated slacks, hair combed back to accommodate humidity, was not employed by the consulate but had top clearance and senior connections.

I'd already reminded myself not to react to the pseudonym on my diplomatic passport.

She sat at a temporary desk in a soundproof cubicle, adjusted her reading specs, and looked at her laptop with disapproval.

"Certain people—not just in Honduras—are concerned

about a relationship between the recently elected governor of the *Departmento Gracias de Dios* and a friend of yours—" the woman squinted at the screen "—a Mister . . . Sighurdhr Tomlinson. Did I pronounce his first name correctly?"

I shrugged and said, "Tomlinson and Dr. Fidelia Brava. Yes, I'm aware they're friends. To what degree, I don't know but—"

"*Governor* Fidelia Brava," the woman corrected.

"Yes, ma'am, sorry. Tomlinson and I, we've only spoken a couple of times in the last month."

The woman, a senior officer, knew better. "That's all?"

"No . . . well, we made contact almost nightly, but it's by shortwave radio. Morse code, ma'am. So the nuances of a conversation—" I risked a smile that didn't go over well "—it's not an effective way to discuss personal matters."

These days people—especially well-educated fast-trackers—are intimidated if Morse code is mentioned. Quantum theory, at least, they can discuss without sounding like provincial boobs.

She spun the computer around. "Much more than a friendship, I daresay. Have you seen these photographs of Mr. Tomlinson? They appeared in various Honduran media. Some people find them quite troubling, indeed. Any insights, Dr. North?"

I scooted my chair closer while she swiped through a series of images. Tomlinson at an inauguration ball . . . a ribbon-cutting . . . exiting a government jet . . . a costume celebration that required traditional Quiché Mayan dress.

Fidelia and my pal were in every shot, as was Aléto. The boy, unlike Tomlinson, was visibly uncomfortable. He'd had a stylish haircut and wasn't used to expensive clothes. A contributing factor might have been his new prosthetic arm and hand, the fake hand always buried in the boy's right blazer pocket.

I sat back and said, "For one thing, I'm surprised Tomlinson was issued a security clearance. Didn't realize he was that charming."

The paperwork had taken some back-channel manipulation,

the woman admitted. Then added a dose of guilt by adding, "All done strictly on your behalf. Anything else?"

"Well, I've never seen him in a tuxedo before, but he cleans up pretty good. The Mayan headdress though—all those feathers—that was a bad choice."

"A terrible choice," the woman agreed as if I'd proved her point. "It's offensive not just to the indigenous people of Honduras, but to indigenous people worldwide. Which leads us to the next matter. The child in these photographs, do you know him?"

It wasn't a question. It was a test. Senior officers don't ask questions unless they already know the answer.

I said, "Yep, certainly do. His name's Aléto. An orphan, in the early stages of Hansen's disease. But treatable. A very gifted kid. What about him?"

"His name is not . . ." Her face had colored. "That cannot be his name—not if we want World Aid conduits to continue funding this project. Are you familiar with the Spanish word, 'Aleta'?"

I replied, "It means 'Fin' in English. Aléto is the masculine form. A nickname because of the way he was born—his right arm. So what?"

"It's insulting, that's what. The name ridicules the boy's birth dee—his irregularities. It's like naming a hydrocephalic child . . . well, I can't even bring myself to say the word. We've already had to quash nasty op-ed pieces in the *Times*— London and New York. We can't allow Governor Brava to be labeled as insensitive—world media would burn her at the proverbial stake. You must have some influence with this man . . . *Tomlinson*. He clearly has influence with the new governor."

"I can try," I told her.

"No, Dr. North. You will address this incendiary matter, and you will succeed. Is that understood?"

I'm not good at cowering. What this senior officer from

some no-name agency needed was a tranquilizer and some real-life field experience.

My temporary obedience would have to do.

"Aye-aye, ma'am," I said.

"Here's another thing. In an interview, your friend referred to the Governor as 'Queen Fidelia.' And the tabloids are already calling the child the 'hereditary King of the Maya.' I'll be frank." She slammed the laptop closed, and gave me the elevator summary, which I re-summarized point by point.

Fidelia wouldn't have been elected were it not for the boy—and the jade death mask which she'd incorporated into her campaign. The voting demographic here was eighty percent indigenous, either Miskito or Mayan. The department's state capital, Puerto Lempira, had no paved roads—that's how backward the area was. Yet, the woman's popularity had boomed throughout Mesoamerica—Nicaragua to Mexico—when she'd filed to adopt the orphan who had leprosy but could not be named Aléto.

"Now that damn mask has become a sort of cult symbol of revolution," the woman continued. "We're trying to create a democracy here, Dr. North. Not a monarchy. What certain people fear is, if we don't keep Governor Brava on a tight leash, she'll be the next President of Honduras. Or the Queen if she so chooses. You know what has to happen in that case."

I thought, *I'll be damn. Aléto and his clairvoyant dreams.*

The kid had it nailed from the start.

The senior officer glared before inserting a threat. "In a note you gave Tomlinson a month ago, you inferred the only practical solution. That's right, we've read it. Your exact words were—"

I interrupted, "I know what I said. I was concerned about the kid's well-being. If Fidelia had abused him in some way, yeah. 'She needs to be out of the picture.' I think that's the way I put it. Are you saying that you want me to—"

"To have her . . . To have the woman, uh . . . post-dated?
No, Dr. North. We already have someone lined up if . . . some
kind of intervention is necessary."

"Who?"

"Someone familiar with the situation. Governor Brava has
a rather dark track history, I'm afraid. Racketeering, sexual extortion, cocaine use . . . well, that's all I can tell you. Sooner
than later, the woman needs to go."

I said, "I'm paid to evaluate and assess situations like this,
and in my opinion, that would be a mistake. Fidelia has been
taking pretty good care of the kid from what I've heard. In
fact, I read she's offered to turn her island into a safe haven for
kids in trouble. That doesn't sound like a politician who needs
to be post-dated."

I slid my chair back and stood. "You're pissed off about
something else. Explain, or I've got things to do. My work
product can't be the issue. How many trafficker pipelines were
shut down since my last visit?"

The answer was already known to me. The local Maras,
the Russians, and one Chinese syndicate had all suffered
significant setbacks. The best news—which I couldn't discuss—
was that more than three hundred children had been rescued
from traffickers, most of them imprisoned at tourist retreats
along the coastline. This included most of Alèto's urchin army—
except for two, one who'd been beheaded, the other boy who
was still missing.

The senior officer knew all of this. She backed off, but not
much.

"Okay . . . here it is. There are certain agencies calling for
your scalp because of the Christmas party you have planned."

I said, "*What?* You're kidding."

"Please don't try to deny it. Why would you agree to such
a thing? As a clandestine asset, you are aware of the meaning
of the word 'clandestine' are you not?"

I took my seat. "Just a few friends from Florida. I don't see the harm. That's why I flew down separately."

"A few friends. That's what you were told?" She opened her laptop and readjusted her reading specs.

A sense of doom came over me when I saw that. "Yes, ma'am. That's what I was told. Look . . . this is entirely my fault—I'm not an expert at Morse code. You see, I have a computer program that translates—"

"A group called the Key West Parrot-somethings have reserved a charter bus for tomorrow," she interrupted, reading from the screen. "Luminaries from a Hollywood Zendo and several professional baseball players are also due to land on Roatán in the morning, including a particularly sketchy left-handed pitcher named—"

"*Hollywood?*" I said. Now I was pissed off and also mystified.

The senior officer peered at me over her reading glasses. "You seem upset. Good. You've caused a security nightmare for this country, and you're going to help us put a stop to it."

"You want me to call off the party? Great," I said. "I'm on it."

"Not so fast," she said. "Immigration isn't going to let the people I mentioned into the country. What we have to stop is a killer hired by Teoscar Brava to assassinate his wife, the current governor. Oh yes, and to steal the ceremonial mask. He's offered to pay an extra quarter million dollars if it's recovered."

Again, she swung the computer screen around. "Do you recognize this man?"

It was a blurry head shot of someone in the shadows. "Maybe. But the guy I'm thinking about is dead. Killed by a crocodile supposedly. When was that picture taken?"

"This morning at a place called Pigeon Cay off Roatán. As a precaution, Fidelia Brava and the boy are in protective custody."

I said, "If someone got close enough to snap a picture, why didn't they take care of the problem?"

"Because the person who took the photo was murdered—

almost decapitated—minutes after he uploaded this file," she replied. "Local authorities are looking for the killer, of course. But, as a courtesy, we thought you ought to have a chance to clean up this mess yourself."

"What about my friend, Tomlinson? Does he know what's going on?"

The senior officer replied, "Certain people think he's too talkative to risk with classified information. Same with your friends from some place—a marina, I think it is—on the west coast of Florida. It was too late for authorities to turn them around."

The Dinkin's Bay light tackle guides, Jeth, Neville, and Big Alex had arrived three days ago to get in some fishing before the festivities. With them were the elegant ladies from *Tiger Lilly*, Rhonda and JoAnn.

"Damn." I got up in a rush, already in tracking mode, but unprepared. The only weapon I'd checked was my full-sized Sig with one extra magazine—all that was allowed under my diplomatic passport. That's why I'd been a few minutes late to an appointment that could've been taken care of with one encoded phone call.

Now I was furious.

At the door, the senior officer said, "Assuming you do find Mr. Tomlinson, please stress the importance of the business we discussed."

"What business. Oh, geezus, you don't mean—If he's still alive, you mean?"

"Yes—about the importance of changing the boy's name to something more acceptable. The world has become far more empathetic, Dr. North. Your Wild West days are over—we hope."

I knew I was putting this job on the line when I turned and said, "Wish that were true, lady. But it's not—thanks to certain people like you."

THIRTY-THREE

At sunset, I idled into the harbor on the backside of what locals called Conch Cay, tied off, and found Tomlinson's friend, Pulpo, drinking rum inside a thatched-roof bar that had a view of a golden-hued sailing ketch anchored nearby.

In isolated jungle outposts, fringe acquaintances behave like long-lost family when reunited. Pulpo, who appeared to be wobbly, threw his arms wide. "Cap'n Ford. I told Tomás you'd find his panga at the airport. Welcome to Cayo Hueso. Let me show you around."

"*His* panga?"

"Sure, yeah, mawn. Tomás has the title. He showed me. I'd be jealous if my clever brother hadn't fixed the holes in my new Boston Whaler. Come, follow me."

I liked the little guy. He'd handled himself like a pro after nearly dying in the earthquake. On this Sunday evening in December, though, the man was a few minutes past drunk-thirty. No surprise he went on a talking bender about the body parts he was missing. An ear, two fingers, and his nose had been smashed so flat that he couldn't see it without a mirror.

Except for the missing fingers, he blamed Tomlinson.

"Yet, as a good Christian, I've forgiven that crazy hippie

who is a terrible shot. It's the way us White Conchs are. Know why? 'Cause a man don't need ten fingers to count the difference between right and wrong."

Whatever the hell that meant.

I was getting short on patience. "Where's Tomlinson and the others? They knew I was coming."

"In the big house over there." The man motioned vaguely toward Jamaica, then directed my attention to the ketch-rigged sailboat anchored in the last rays of sunset.

"Old wooden turtle boats, they beautiful, huh? Tomás bought that ketch-rig. Didn't think she was for sale, but the man wouldn't take no for an answer."

This was news to me. "He's fixing it up?"

"Yah, sir. Paid cash which is why I've forgiven that dangerous hippie. What we're gonna do is, sail along the coast and rescue youngins—orphans, got no homes. Make them babies safe before they end up slaves in some country where they got nothing but sand dunes and camels. Russia, maybe. Know what else he gonna buy, Cap'n?"

We had returned from the seawall and were approaching the thatch-roofed bar where a weathered sign over the door read, *Found Me A Home Cantina*.

"He's buying this place and the docks for your fishing guide buddies. You fellas and them ladies, too, gonna have a place to live. How's that sound?"

"Sounds like you were both stoned when you came up with the idea," I said. "I need to ask you something. A month ago you told me Fidelia Brava's bodyguard—Iron Baby? You said he was dead. You're sure about that?"

The question made the Islander nervous for some reason. "Not even sure I know the gentleman you're speakin' of."

"Huh? The big guy," I said. "The freak who tried to kill a lady friend of mine and knocked your ear off with a tire iron. Tomlinson told me the whole story." I paused to reassess just how drunk the little guy was. "Why the hell are you pretending you don't remember?"

"Oh . . . *the giant.* That's who you're talking about."

"Geezus," I said. "The same one who killed Kimee, that boy we found after the earthquake."

Pulpo, who was a piss-poor actor, feigned surprise. "Why didn't you say so? I didn't say the giant was dead. Said a crocodile ate him. Iron Baby, he ain't human, that's what folks around always claimed. Don't see why you're so interested in a man who's dead enough as it is, far as I'm concerned."

"Here's the thing," I began and told him about the blurry photo and hinted that Tomlinson was in danger even though Fidelia and the one-armed boy weren't here.

This time the Islander seemed genuinely confused. "What you mean the one-armed kid ain't—? Mawn, I best walk over to that big house and check on what you say."

"Where is it?" I said. "I'll go with you."

"Naw, they all asleep the last I checked. Stay here, be back in twenty minutes."

Before Pulpo hurried off, he summoned the bartender. "Hey Billy, a beer for *mi amigo.* He's a . . . how you say, a famous . . . uhh, bio-test in the States."

"A biologist," I said, "and I'm not famous."

I slid onto a stool and ordered a *Barena* over ice until the bartender treated me to a Hatuey, a pretty good beer that seems better because it's from Cuba.

"That one's on Tomlinson," Billy told me. "And dinner's on your fishing guide pals from Florida. Good guys, classy. Same with the ladies, JoAnn and Rhonda. How does fried snapper and fish gravy sound?" The man had a Bayou accent and knowing blue eyes that saw beyond the obvious.

I did a discreet survey of this airy tropical bar, seeing rafters adorned with dollar bill mementos, yacht club pennants, ceiling fans, and a waterside patio where locals were hunched over a table, slapping down domino tiles that cracked like gunshots.

"Pulpo—he seems a tad confused today," I said.

The bartender was smiling. "The locals from Pigeon Cay— White Conchs they call themselves, no matter the color. They're a tight bunch. Take care of their own, and they're never as confused as they seem."

I explained that I meant no offense. "Thing is, he wouldn't say where my friends are staying. I've got the address, but don't know the streets."

The bartender was still smiling. "Sure, I can help you there. But I'm afraid your friends got ambushed by Mr. Jose Cuervo after lunch. They've been fishing three days straight, and you know how that goes. Said they'd be back around sunset, so stick around. I can put your order in later. Ford, is it?" We shook hands. "I'm Bill. Back in a sec."

Good bartenders have a gift. They adapt to their job by acquiring what some call "bartender ears." They hear everything and tailor the conversation—and how much they participate—to fit their clientele. Bill read me correctly and did most of the talking when he wasn't busy.

He said, "When you came through the channel in your skiff, did you notice the big house, the two-story job on the point? That's where they're staying—the Plantation House. You, too, I guess. But there's no need to go rushing over there. Enjoy your beer."

I wondered if the name was coincidental. "As in palm oil plantation?"

"The new governor set it up," the bartender replied—an evasion, perhaps. "She landed about three hours ago in a chopper. Governor Brava, you ever see that woman in person? Never thought I'd say this about a *politico*, but by god, she's drop dead gorgeous."

I got to my feet. "You sure? I was told she couldn't make it."

"Oh, she's here all right. No mistaking the new governor. Her and a younger woman—not nearly as . . . Well, I'm not gonna say. But fit-looking, you know? They got off with one bag each, just them, no one there to greet them."

"Not even Tomlinson?" Another alarm bell went off in my head.

"Yup. I wouldn't worry about it. They're fine. Siesta Sunday, you know. They just need some quiet time for a while," he said. An odd remark for a bartender.

A fit-looking woman. I was wondering if it was Naomi while Billy motioned with his chin. "The house, the landing pad, it's just over there. Swing around and take a look." He returned to the prep sink to make a pitcher of margaritas.

Plantation House stood on its own grounds just down the shoreline. It was a blue layer cake structure with walk-around porches and a gently pitched tin roof of white. The second floor was visible above an island of coconut palms. On the harbor side of the property, there was a boathouse and what might have been a pickleball court. A windsock near the water marked the heliport.

From the railing, I watched Pulpo. I expected the little man to stagger toward the Plantation House. Instead, he walked an S-pattern a few doors down and disappeared into the Fisherman's Co-Op building where there was a hydraulic hoist and commercial boats moored stern-to. A stenciled sign outside wall promised, *Pescado, Camarones, Langosta.*

The Co-Op sold them all, fresh and quick-frozen.

Streetlights blinked on. Chickens and white seabirds gathered to roost in the waning afterglow of nautical dusk.

Billy returned with a fresh glass of ice for my beer. "Best seat on the harbor right there where you're sitting. That's what I do every day since I bought this place. Watch the boats come and go, and the occasional rich corporate types land in helicopters."

I took a chance. "Who runs the palm oil plantation now that the old guy is dead? What was his name. Coronado something?"

The bartender demurred by using his bar towel, so I mentioned that I'd heard the bar might be for sale.

"Always," he said. "Since I sobered up, which was twelve years ago and one month after I took title. Yeah, Tomlinson made an offer. A fair offer, and I accepted. But he'll back out, I expect. They always do when they realize the dream of living as an expat is just that. A bullshit fairy tale. Locals, though, the Conchs gave Tomlinson their approval, at least. That's rare. He's only the second one they approved of in twelve years."

"Why didn't the first buyer take it?"

"I did," Billy said, and took pleasure in the punch line. "The fact I was born here before my folks moved to Pascagoula might have had something to do with it."

My eyes came to rest on the pretty forty-some-foot ketch classic moored off the beach. "Do they have to approve selling your sailboat, too? I heard that's a done deal."

The bartender wasn't finished with the subject of Americans living overseas. "The same with your marina buddies. Two days ago, they were hot to move down here. Raved about the fishing. And the food and the women—and the open markets, of course. Best fruit in the world. But this afternoon, I could see the charm is already wearing thin. They'll be ready to go home after your Christmas party. That sailboat, though, yeah, she's a keeper. I made your buddy a good deal."

"Classic lines," I agreed.

"Yep. She carried me all over the Caribbean until we finally dead-ended here. Did you happen to notice her name?"

"Later, I'll take a look. Selling a boat that nice, isn't that sort of like burning a bridge?"

I got the same evasive smile while he noticed my glass.

"Beer over ice. We used to do that in Southeast Asia, Colombia, Panama. Places without refrigeration. The preppy types looked at me like I had three heads."

He walked away, served a couple of drinks, and came back. "You ever been to the Balboa Yacht Club?"

He was talking about Panama. This was subtext. A test of some type. "Yeah, the Canal Zone. Great sunsets, and some guy would usually play taps. Friend of mine stole a barstool from there once."

Billy liked that. "Sounds like we have some of the same crazy friends. What about Fort Sherman? I heard the survival training school there is pretty tough."

There it was. The connection.

"Used to be pretty tough," I said, "before the Chinese took over the Canal Zone and they closed the school down. Hey, uhh, Bill, is there a reason you and Pulpo don't want me to go knocking at the door of the Plantation House?"

"Not now, there isn't," the bartender, who'd been an operator somewhere, said. "I figured it was you the moment you walked in . . . Commander Ford, isn't it?"

I left cash on the bar and gathered my tactical bag. "We've got things to talk about. I'll be back before the kitchen closes."

"You won't be sorry. But hey—instead of going to the house—you'll just wake your friends up, most likely—what I suggest is, walk across the street to the Fisherman's Co-Op. There's a kid there, a boy with one arm. He was asking Tomlinson about you this morning. You know who I'm talking about?"

I stopped and looked at him. "You didn't say anything about a boy getting off the helicopter."

"Because he didn't," Billy said. "The governor doesn't even know he's here. That's what I was told. The kid I'm talking about is considered a . . . well, he's become a big deal on this coast. The locals don't want anything to happen to him."

I placed my bag on the barstool. "Is he in trouble? Where is he?"

"The kid? He broke into the Co-Op a couple of hours ago, I heard, and won't come out. Which is no big deal. Usually. The federales give the locals a lot of space when it comes to taking care of their own. Tradition, I guess. The Conchs know the rules—if they do something bad enough to make the tabloids, the evidence can't leave this island."

I said carefully, "You mean the boy can't leave if he did something—"

Billy interrupted, "The *evidence* can't leave. Someone needs to talk some sense into the kid. Pulpo and Tomlinson have been taking turns. Couldn't hurt for you to give it a try."

I asked the obvious questions. Was the kid armed? Had he hurt someone?

The Conch from Pascagoula refused to elaborate. Then sealed the topic by changing the subject to his Cayman-Islands-built sailboat which had recently been purchased by my pal.

"I'm not what you'd call super creative, so I tend to name things after songs," Billy said. He pointed to the weathered cantina sign as an example. "I named my boat the same way. You'll be able to see it from the Co-Op docks. The places you've been, Skipper, you'll be one of the few who figures it out."

Outside, I walked to the water near where the sailboat was moored—the name, INCOMMUNICADO, in crimson script on the stern,

Another one of Aléto's predictions popped into my mind. Nothing to do with the beautiful ketch rigged classic.

The prediction had something to do with him being used as bait to lure me into a trap.

THIRTY-FOUR

*T*he *best way to trap a jaguar is to dig a pit and use bait,* Aléto had told me.

The boy's prophecy came back word-by-word as I approached the Fisherman's Co-Op, a building of concrete block where a single window showed a light on inside.

I'm used to ignoring paranormal nonsense, but had to admit the kid had some unusual gifts. He'd correctly intuited the impact a Mayan death mask and rumors of royalty would have on the local population.

The possibility of an ambush took on added credibility.

Even on a Sunday night, an hour after sunset, this remote village should not have been asleep. Not in December. Yet, in small houses along the waterfront, curtains were pulled and, aside from stray dogs and one wakeful goat, the street was deserted among a sprinkling of early Christmas lights.

The locals *knew.* They knew something was going on at the Fish Co-Op. Something bad enough to be worthy of *federales* and tabloid headlines, perhaps. My suspicion was, they didn't want to risk being called as witnesses against the hereditary king of their own ancient people.

What the hell had Aléto done this time? I could picture the

kid, pissed off, or worried about something, paddling up in his dugout canoe, armed with a rifle. Or a spear. Or a blowgun.

The kid was a trigger-happy traditionalist. He'd already shot at least two men.

But it was the hired killer the senior officer had mentioned, not the kid, I was worried about.

On this road of packed shell, goosenecked streetlights created luminous atolls along the corridor. I avoided them and drew my pistol before slipping into the shadows behind the Co-Op where there were garbage cans, and a refrigeration unit elevated off the ground. I was about to move to the front of the building when a man's silhouette approached from what might've been the Plantation House. He carried a flashlight, not at all concerned about being seen.

I stepped back until he was closer then stepped out because it was Jeth, one of the Dinkin's Bay fishing guides.

"Doc? Hey, man! We've been waiting for you up at the rental place. Why are you carrying a—"

I holstered the Sig Sauer and walked him into the shadows. Jeth is the tall muscular one with a cleft chin, so he resembles the hillbilly strong man in the old TV show, *Beverly Hillbillies*. His once severe stutter had all but disappeared over the years—a good thing because Mack, in his will, had left the marina to him and the business-savvy liveaboard ladies, Rhonda and JoAnn. This included the obligation of answering phones and speaking to the occasionally tight-sphinctered members of the Sanibel Planning Commission.

"Go back to the Plantation House," I told him. "Tomlinson and I will be up there in a little bit—if I can find him."

"*Find him?* Come on, we figured that you two . . . what the hell's going on, man? This whole day has been so freaky, I don't know if I'm dreaming or not."

"What's the—? Are you still drunk?"

"Me? No." He pulled away. "Feel like I've been drugged,

Doc. All we did was drink half a bottle of tequila at lunch. And a couple of beers."

"Calm down. Not so loud," I said. "Drugged? What makes you think . . . are you hallucinating?"

"Halluci—what? If you mean am I seeing crazy stuff when I close my eyes, no. I'm just sleepy as hell. Same with the others." His head pivoted. "Where is Tomlinson? The governor lady—Governor Fidelia? She was totally out of it 'till about ten minutes ago, and she sent me to—" Jeth had to think "—she sent me to fetch him and something else." He snapped his fingers. "Oh yeah. Some kind of important . . . a life-sized dee-decayed mask. Said the thing was stolen from her bedroom."

"Decayed mask? You mean jade mask?"

"Uhh . . . maybe. Said it might be hidden somewhere in there." He indicated the Co-Op building.

"Where'd she get that idea?"

"Got me. That woman tells you to do something, you just do it. You know? Tomlinson's the same way. Did you know he bought a tu-tu-tuxedo?"

I said, "She has that effect on men."

"Oh yeah. The governor has the hots for him, too, and said she looks forward to meeting you when you get here."

Meeting me? As if we hadn't spent time together? The potion didn't exist that could block out that memory.

Rather than press the point, I stayed on track. It took a patient minute for Jeth to get his story straight. It sounded like they'd all been drugged with some kind of sedative—except for Naomi, the neurologist who was an expert on brain chemistry. She'd disappeared an hour ago after making a pitcher of *licuados* for the group from Dinkin's Bay.

I was glad the bartender was off the suspect list. But Naomi? I'd seen it coming but had stupidly let her drop off my radar because she'd been dosed with scopolamine. No doubt about that—and she wouldn't have put her own life at risk.

Again, I told Jeth to go back to the rental house, and this time instructed him to stand guard over Fidelia.

"What's the problem, Doc? Is it because she's an important governor?"

"Politics is a dangerous biz," I said. "Tell Neville and Alex. Don't take your eyes off her for a second."

Some gentle convincing was required. Jeth would take two or three steps away then return to unload what had become borderline paranoia. His primary concern was endearing.

He said, "Doc, promise me you're coming back to Dinkin's Bay. We're gonna rebuild the marina, right? We've all got to live there again. Life won't be the same if we don't."

The man had not only been fed a Xanax or two, he was stil drunk.

"Sure, darn right we will," I said. "Get going. We'll talk later."

"Hold on. What I'm worried about is, now that Mack's dead, you think I'll do a piss-poor . . . a bah-bad job. That you and Tomlinson are gonna move down here because you think I'll screw things up. Honduras is nice and all but, man, this ain't home. Rhonda and JoAnn think the same. We all do."

I told him, "With you in charge, the marina will be better than ever." I gave the man a reassuring pat on the back. "Go on now. Tell the others we'll be there soon as I find Tomlinson. And tell them to close the curtains and stay in the damn house—especially the governor."

When he was gone, I slid along the wall and put an eye to the window.

One look, and I knew that this trap—if it was a trap—had been set up by a boy who actually believed he was the hereditary King of the Maya.

• • •

The Co-Op's fish market was closed on this Sunday evening. The refrigerated display case had been cleaned, tubs of ice emptied. Above the counter and a cash register was a chalkboard where yesterday's prices had been erased. From this angle, I could see only what was behind the counter. To the right was a bank-vault-sized door that was a walk-in freezer. The stainless door handle had been locked with a shear pin attached to a wire.

It was the sort of rig used to secure boat propellers. This didn't seem odd on an island where Islanders had to be innovative—until I noticed another anomaly. Angled against the freezer door was a handcrafted spear, intricately carved, with a black obsidian blade. The blade was curved like a tile cutter, and the handle was speckled with something that might've been tree sap.

Or was it blood . . . ?

I removed a small LED light from my pocket and rapped a knuckle against the windowpane. Did it again before a bizarre blue face sprouted above the opposite side of the service counter. It was joined by a second face, this one red, both decorated with Mayan symbols in white and black paint.

They were the faces of children, not masks. The shorter of the two was Aléto. No shirt, just baggy shorts and no prosthetic right arm. Not surprisingly, he stood with his rifle already aimed at the window. The other kid had to be his pal, Balam. He held a bamboo blowgun to his lips, also aimed and ready to fire.

At least one of Aléto's wingmen had not been decapitated by the killer, Iron Baby. *Good.*

I held my hands up, shined the light briefly and stepped in front of the glass. When Aléto recognized me, he lowered his weapon and ordered Balam to do the same. Between the two of us, we got the window cracked a few inches.

He said, "*Patrón!* I've been waiting on you. Only you I can trust because of what has happened. We need someone bigger . . . with more muscle."

I looked past him and saw that Balam still had his blowgun ready. "Where's Tomlinson? He and another guy—a friend, are supposed to be here. And there's a woman missing from the house, too. Dr. Naomi—you know, from Doctors with Wings. Remember her?"

When the boy's attention darted from the front door to the walk-in cooler, I noticed a smear of blood on the floor and thought, *Oh hell* . . .

"What happened, Aléto? Tell me the truth. Where's Dr. Naomi?"

Behind him, Balam, his face macaw-red and streaked with skeletal symbols, said something in guttural Quiché—a warning, it sounded like.

Aléto shushed the boy and used his short-barreled rifle to indicate the front entrance to the store. "The tall sailor and the Islander with the missing ear are out there. They wanted in, but I won't let them. So they're sitting by the water smoking *Yuyo* and drinking beer. Send them away, *patrón*. I don't trust adults who are drunk and stoned. We need your help, but they can't be around to see."

"Aléto," I said gently, "where's the woman, Dr. Naomi? If you hurt her, even killed her, you can tell me. I'll do my best to get you away from here."

Balam said something in Quiché Mayan and had to be shushed again before Aléto looked at me with eyes that were volcanic black because of the blue and white face paint. He shook his head. "We didn't kill her, but I would've. She tried to steal the jade mask."

"Where is she?"

"She hates the governor. It was something I had to do."

I said, "They hate each other. Just tell me where she is."

"*Listen*. Without the mask, the Queen Mother will die. That bad doctor woman, I told her the same thing—" he nodded toward the walk-in freezer "—that I hid the mask in there. So she came to steal it. If the woman is dead, it was the God *Kukulkan* who let her kill herself."

I had to take a breath and focus. "What do you mean, *if* she's dead? You trapped her in the freezer and used the mask as bait? How long has she been inside that damn thing?"

The boy, who had no wristwatch or cell phone said, "How long does it take for a fish to freeze? Twenty, maybe thirty minutes? That's what we don't know. *Patrón*—" the kid moved to the window's opening and spoke confidentially "—Balam says it would be smarter to kill all of you than to be arrested for murder."

When I replied, "He's right, that's the smart thing to do," the boy was startled. When he took a step back, I levered the window up and crawled inside while Balam yelled threats. The commotion must have alerted Tomlinson at the front of the building, because someone began banging a shoulder against the front door.

Balam turned toward the noise, the blowgun to his lips. I brushed past Aléto, removed the shear pen, and stepped into the darkness of the walk-in freezer, a vault so cold my breath fogged.

A dry coughing sound required me to use the LED. I shined the light around and was shocked by what I saw.

"Jesus Christ," I said to the boy, who stood looking in. "You didn't mention stabbing someone with that damn spear."

Aléto replied with the chilliness of a king who didn't mind lopping off a few heads, "It was the only way to be sure. It was in the book about Canek. To kill a priest, he used an obsidian blade. The tall sailor gave it to me."

"What? Gave you the spear?"

"The glass blade. It's from a meteor. The night he found it, he was attacked by dinosaurs."

There was no time to respond to this craziness. I rushed in, pushing boxes of frozen fish aside and checked Naomi for a pulse. "Help me get her out of here. She's still alive." I rolled her over before adding. "And here's the mask. She was lying on it."

The mosaic of jade had a surprising density. The stone tiles were cold enough to burn the fingers which Aléto seemed not to notice when he took it eagerly into his hands.

Behind me, the front door of the Co-Op store burst open, and two drunken figures came stumbling through. I wrestled the woman over my shoulder and heard one of them say, "*Ouch. A damn wasp or something just buzzed past my ear.*"

I lugged her out of the freezer, yanked the blowgun away before Balam could shoot a second dart, and forced both boys to hide behind the counter with a whispered threat:

"Stay there, don't say a damn word until I get back, or you'll both go to jail."

Naomi was conscious and her teeth were chattering. Tomlinson recognized me. He had pulled a bamboo splinter out of the drywall behind his head. Didn't seem to notice the sparse feathers or the serrated tip. "Doc, hey man! Whoa . . . who the hell put Naomi in the freezer? Is she bleeding?"

"No. Get out of my way. We need blankets and you two need to get her into some warm water."

Pulpo held the door open while my pal continued to eye the blood smear on the floor. "Where'd those boys go? The little delinquents wouldn't let me in."

I motioned to the open window and went down the steps. "They left in a hurry because that's what I told them to do. Naomi just had some bad luck, that's all. She must have gone into the freezer and the door locked behind her. The kids had a hell of a time getting the thing open."

Outside the air was salt heavy, temperature in the high 70s. Stars glittered through an umbrella of palm fronds. A gooseneck lamp on the docks showed the hydraulic hoist and the stern of the ketch-rigged sailboat moored nearby.

I passed Naomi to Tomlinson who cradled her in his arms, while I said, "I assume the electronics on your new sailboat work. What's the water temp?"

By then, the neurologist was trying to wrestle herself free, mumbling, "Put me down, goddamn it. I can walk. Someone . . . Could someone please build a fire?"

She was drowsy, and her speech was slurred, but she was coming around.

"Water's low eighties," he replied. "And I've got a full medical kit aboard. Floor heater too. Hypothermia, you're supposed to warm them up gradually. That's what they taught us at Outward Bound in Maine. Hey—" Naomi was scratching at his arms "—stop that. How about we take a nice warm swim?"

She swung a wild hand and slapped him hard across the face. "You've been screwing that bitch, Fay. Get your hands off me. The mask—" she tilted her head up "—where's my goddamn jade mask?"

Pulpo, stoned as he was, had the good sense to say, "What I'm thinking is, Cap'n, it's probably not smart to have those two women in the same house. Why not swim the crazy lady out to your boat? A beer and some snacks would be nice."

Tomlinson made eye contact. He looked from me to the Co-Op building where the front door, instead of open, was now closed.

The question he wanted to ask, but didn't, was, *Where is the jade mask?*

He had other questions, too. I dodged them all by saying, "Why don't you run your new boat a couple miles offshore, we'll talk later. I've got stuff to do here."

"Stuff," he said. "Like what?"

I said softly, "Like getting rid of another body."

Pulpo put his hands over his ears, and walked fast toward the water, saying, "I didn't hear nothin,' mawn. We goin' swimming or not?"

There was no need for me to explain that Iron Baby lay inside the store, frozen solid, his eyes wide after having his throat slit with an obsidian blade.

ACKNOWLEDGMENTS

Before thanking those who contributed their expertise, time, and good humor during the writing of *Tomlinson's Wake*, I want to make clear that all errors, exaggerations, or misstatements of fact are entirely my fault. This applies to the savvy, jungle-tested friends who accompanied me or helped facilitate my many trips to Cuba and Central and South America, particularly the Miskito Coast of Honduras. Ostensibly, our trips had to do with fishing or giving away baseball gear to kids (at least, that's what we told border guards), while I focused on testing regional pepper sauces—long a passion of mine—and making copious notes on the politics of that volatile region.

These stalwarts include Gary Terwilliger, Jeff Carter, Giorgio Araújo of Cartagena, Colombia, my Panamaniac colleagues from the Canal Zone, Capt. Bob and Mindy Dollar, Jay Sieleman, Tom Pattison, and other associates at the now defunct Fort Sherman Jungle Survival Training School near Colón. My gifted editors at *Outside* magazine, John Rasmus, Mark Bryant, Terry McDonell, and Alex Heard, also played key roles.

Insights, ideas, and medical advice were provided by Dr. Brian Hummel, Dr. Richard Salisbury, and my nephew, Justin White, PhD.

Pals, advisors, and/or teammates are always a help because they know firsthand that writing and writers are a pain in the ass. Thanks go to Stu Johnson, Dan Cugini, Eric Rasmussen, Rich Gale, Ron Iossi, Jerry Rehfuss, Victor Candelaria, Gene Lamont, Nick Swartz, Kerry Griner, Mike Shevlin, Jon Warden, Davey Johnson, Barry Rubel, Mike Westhoff, and behavioral guru Don Carman.

Bill Lee and his orbiting star, Diana, as always, have guided the author safely into the strange but fun and enlightened world of our mutual friend, the Rev. Sighurdhr M. Tomlinson. Equal thanks go to Donna Terwilliger, Wendy Webb, Rachael Ketterman, and Capt. Olivia Chase.

Finally, thanks to my amazing sons, Lee and Rogan, for helping me to finish the last two lines of another book.

Randy Wayne White
Sanibel, Florida